# The King's Scrolls

# The King's Scrolls

Ilyon Chronicles – Book Two

Jaye L. Knight

Living Sword Publishing
www.livingswordpublishing.com

**The King's Scrolls**
Ilyon Chronicles – Book 2

www.ilyonchronicles.com

Published by Living Sword Publishing

Proofread by Kim Huther
www.wordsmithproofreading.com



ISBN 13: 978-0-9837740-5-1
ISBN 10: 0983774056

To my King whose ways are higher than my ways and thoughts are higher than my thoughts and who always has a plan and a purpose even in life's most difficult moments.

ILYON
N
W
E
S
SAMARA
AMBERIN
STONEHELM
SINNAI MTS.
ARCACIA
SIDIAN
OCEAN
GRAYLIN VALLEY
DUNLOW
VALCRE
KINNIM
LANDALE
ARDALUIN BAY
FORT RIVOR
MERNIN
KEATON
FALSPAR
TROAS
ARDA

Graer Mts.
Arvael
Trayse River
Bel-gard
Andros Ford
Dorland
Wildmor
Krell Mts.

# PROLOGUE

THE MESSENGER SLUMPED to his knees with a gargled choke. Richard bent closer and gripped the man's shoulder in a crushing grasp. "You should never have returned with so little information. I warned you once about wasting my time just so you could have a few more pennies to spend in the taverns."

The man opened his mouth as if to protest, but only a wheezing breath slipped out, and he toppled to the dungeon floor. Richard scowled at his still form. A pathetic waste of an informant. Competent men weren't easy to find these days. If only he hadn't lost Holden. He had been one of Richard's best . . . before he'd turned traitor and joined the rebels. Oh, he'd tried to hide his face during the ambush in Landale, but Richard had recognized him, and someday he would pay for his betrayal.

Richard reached down to wipe his dagger on the dead man's shirt before fumbling as he slipped it into its sheath. With a curse, he raised his hand and opened and closed his fist. His scowl deepened at the numbness in his fingers that threaded up through his wrist and forearm. One of these days, he would find out exactly who had shot the arrow into his shoulder during the ambush, and they, too, would pay for his continual discomfort. But right now, he had more pressing matters than his growing list of those deserving of his personal revenge.

He left the body in the dungeon for the guards to dispose of, and made his way up into the palace. The halls lay dark and empty at this late hour, but light leaked from under the emperor's office door. Richard let himself in without knocking. Having grown up in Auréa Palace, he shared a familiarity with the emperor that few had the privilege to claim. They were brothers, almost, thanks to his mother's fortunate connection with the royal family. If it were not for her efforts to gain him a place as the previous king's ward, he may never have even reached knighthood—not with his father squandering away his inheritance while Richard was not yet four years old and getting himself killed shortly after.

The creak of the door drew Daican's attention. He looked up from his desk and leaned back in his chair as Richard approached.

"One of my informants returned from up north."

Daican's dark brows rose. "And?"

"He's hiding out somewhere in the Graylin Valley."

Now the emperor frowned. "There are almost a hundred villages scattered across that region. He could be in any one of them. He didn't give you specifics?"

"No," Richard said in a cold tone.

Daican pushed up from his chair to pace, not as one might in agitation, but more in contemplation. Richard did not move, but his eyes followed the emperor. Finally, he stopped and faced Richard again.

"What about the Scrolls?"

"No word on them."

Daican glared at some spot across the room, ire now rising to his eyes. "We must find him and the Scrolls. Should either of them fall into the rebels' hands, it will only empower them. We need to stamp out this rebellion before it grows out of our control."

"I have other informants still searching. One of them will turn up something." Richard may have lost Holden, but he still had a few left who possessed the ruthlessness and cunning to get the job done.

Daican returned to his chair, running his fingers along the edge of his desk. "What about the situation in Landale? Has Captain Goler come any closer to discovering the whereabouts of the Altairs and their friends?"

"Not according to my latest reports."

The captain was about as incompetent as they came. He'd had four months to do his job, and yet hadn't managed to bring in even *one* of the rebels. Richard almost scoffed at the memory of the buffoon's request to be made baron of Landale if the current one proved to be a secret traitor. At this rate, he'd likely find himself thrown out of the army for miserably failing his duties.

Daican's face matched his sentiments on the subject. "I'm beginning to wonder if Goler is the right man for the job. If he can't find a group of outlaws hiding out in the woods, I'll have to send in someone who can."

Richard flexed his fingers once more. The last thing he desired was to visit that uncivilized plot of land again, except, perhaps, to seek revenge. "Once the hatchlings are ready, it will aid in the search."

This seemed to put the emperor in a slightly better mood. "What's their progress?"

"The drake blood has accelerated their growth. We should have a large force ready by the middle of next year."

Daican shook his head, his eyes going hard. "I want the rebels found before then. Every day, word of their exploits reaches farther across the country and emboldens our enemies. I'll not have anyone delaying my plans."

"Of course," Richard replied. "I'll have our resources shifted there." Perhaps he should replace the whole garrison—with Goler the first to go, of course.

"No," Daican stopped him. "Find the scholar and the Scrolls first. Then we'll focus on the rebels."

KYRIN TUGGED THE collar of her coat closer to her neck as an icy breeze rattled the stiff branches above her. A shiver crept down her back, but she held her focus on the road below. She swept her gaze up and down the path, scanning the gray forest in between for the slightest movement. The men had found good hiding places, even without the aid of thick summer foliage. Twenty yards downhill, she could just make out the dark brown sleeve of Trask's jacket, but only because she'd watched him hide there. Anyone else, except perhaps Jace, would have missed it.

She rubbed her thumb lightly over the nock of her arrow, already fitted to the bowstring. Something nudged her elbow, and she looked over at Jace, who nodded to the right. Her gaze shifted back to the road, and her pulse quickened. A group of horses appeared through the bare trees. She cast a glance to her left. Kaden's alert stance signaled he had spotted them too.

Everyone remained perfectly still as the company of eight riders maintained a steady walk toward them. When they came almost parallel to Kyrin's position, she spotted the captives trudging along on foot between the horses—a man and wife with their young son and daughter—one of the farming families from Landale Village who followed Elôm. Their shoulders were hunched against the breeze. None of them appeared properly clothed for the elements. Goler must have forced them from their home without time to prepare for the long march to the barracks.

Kyrin squeezed her cold-pricked fingers around her bow and held her breath. Any moment now . . .

Trask and Warin broke from the trees with swords drawn and stood side by side on the road. "Halt!"

At the head of the group, Captain Goler reined his horse to a stop. His hand shot straight to the hilt of his sword, his expression one of pure loathing. "You'll not have these prisoners this time."

"Oh, I think I will." Trask motioned to the forest. Rayad, Holden, Mick, and a few of the other men left cover on either side of the road. "Release them."

Goler leaned forward and rested his gloved hands on the pommel of his saddle. "They're enemies of the emperor."

Kyrin narrowed her eyes. He should be erupting with threats by now. "He's stalling."

Her heart rate picked up once more in warning that something wasn't right. Jace nudged her again and drew her attention to stealthy movement in the trees. About halfway down the hill, between them and the other men, soldiers snuck through the brush on foot. She counted as each one appeared. Five total. No doubt the same number hid on the opposite side of the road. Counting the men with Goler, they outnumbered Trask's group two to one.

"I won't stand out here in the cold all day," Trask said impatiently, his focus still fixed on Goler. "Release them now."

"No." Following his refusal, Goler's men burst from the trees to surround them. His lips curved in a vicious grin. "Surprise. Now, drop your weapons; I'm taking you in." He leaned forward to leer down at Trask. "And this time, you die."

He slipped his sword halfway out of the scabbard, but Trask stopped him. "I wouldn't do that."

Suspicion bloomed on Goler's face. Neither Trask nor his men reacted in concern over the ambush. "Why not?"

Trask shrugged, his voice deceptively light, as if speaking to an old friend. "I really wouldn't want one of my men to have to shoot you. That would just make things messy. It's too cold to stick around and make sure you don't bleed to death."

Goler eyed him, and then shifted to look around at each of the men with Trask—none of whom had bows.

"Oh, I'm not talking about the men you can see."

The captain's gaze swung back to Trask then jumped to one of his men who'd been part of the ambush. "Did you see anyone?"

"No, sir."

"You're sure?"

"Yes, sir."

Goler's confidence returned. He smirked at Trask. "You're bluffing."

Again, Trask shrugged and cast the briefest glance to his right.

The signal. In a smooth, practiced motion, Kyrin drew back her bowstring. In her periphery, Jace did the same. She focused on Goler. He made an easy target, sitting in all his self-importance atop that huge battle horse of his. But she shifted her aim a little, down and to the left. The string slipped off her fingertips.

A split-second later, the arrow struck the ground just in front of Goler's horse, sending up a little spray of dirt. Jace's followed. The horse snorted and tossed its head, stepping backward and almost bumping into one of the other horses. Cursing, Goler jerked the reins to get it back under control.

"No one move!" Trask shouted as the soldiers looked nervously into the trees. "The next shots won't be in the ground."

Kyrin and Jace had two more arrows nocked and ready in case they needed them, though she prayed they wouldn't. She'd only ever shot attacking ryriks before. Still, she'd protect Trask and the others if she had to, and wouldn't hesitate to keep them out of Goler's clutches. The disturbingly clear memories of her own time in the captain's barracks left a sensation of cold in her stomach that matched the wintery air.

Goler gave Trask a scathing look before his eyes flicked downward. His jaw went hard. Jace's arrow was easily recognizable as matching the one he'd had removed from his shoulder just a few months ago. He sent a murderous glance in their direction.

Trask took a step closer to Goler. "Drop your weapons and dismount. One wrong move and you'll get shot."

"You won't kill us," Goler sneered. "You're too soft, all of you, otherwise you would've just killed me and been done with it a long time ago."

"We're not murderers. We don't want to kill you, but we'll do what we must to protect the innocent. Now, drop your sword and get off that horse before I order my men to give you another arrow wound to recover from."

His veins bulging in his neck, Goler refused to move, and sarcasm laced Trask's next words.

"Come now, Captain, getting yourself injured or killed will only spoil your plans to become baron."

Goler's face flushed deep red. Rising stiffly, he swung his leg over the saddle while Trask ordered the other men to disarm. Following their captain's surrender, they handed their weapons over. Trask walked up to Goler and confiscated the captain's sword and dagger. Goler leaned in close, and Kyrin tightened her grip on her bow as the man uttered words she could not make out.

"But not today," Trask responded to the obvious threat, and he turned to his men. "Tie them up."

Warin and the others moved to do so as Trask walked over to the prisoners and freed them.

The man took Trask's hand. "I don't know how we'll ever thank you, my lord."

"It's my pleasure, Roland." He smiled at the man's wife and children. "You'll be safe now with us."

"Only until I hunt you down," Goler growled. "You can't hide forever."

Trask waved him off and led the family away from the road as the others finished binding the soldiers. When they were secured, he walked back to Goler.

"As soon as you work yourselves loose, you'll find your horses and weapons about a mile up the road . . . just like last time."

He smirked at this last bit as he turned away, and the captain spat, "I promise you, one of these days you and I will have it out."

"Looking forward to it," Trask threw over his shoulder.

Guiding Roland and his family, he and the other men disappeared into the forest. Kyrin, Jace, and Kaden remained in position for another couple of minutes to make sure Goler and his men didn't work themselves free too soon. When they'd given the others a head start, they rose from their hiding place and hurried to their horses.

The entire group met up again a couple of miles from the ambush sight.

Trask scanned the faces. "Everyone accounted for?"

After a quick headcount, they rode together toward the northern area of the forest surrounding Landale, following a winding route deep into the trees, with the riders behind taking care to cover their trail.

Camp provided a welcome sight as heavy, gray clouds gathered overhead. Kyrin smiled upon arriving. It had expanded in the months since she'd first come here from Valcré after escaping execution for her faith. Ten completed cabins sat nestled in the trees, with smoke rising from every chimney. Trask, upon everyone's insistence, was given his own cabin to share with the senior members of camp, while those they'd rescued from the emperor's persecution occupied the others. Tents and temporary winter shelters were scattered about for the rest of the men. It wasn't what many would think to call home, but it was the best Kyrin had known since early childhood; a place of security after the danger and hardship she'd faced—the memories of which, even now, disrupted her sleep some nights.

At the corral, the group dismounted to unsaddle the horses. Trask led Roland and his family toward the cabins to warm up, but he paused near Kyrin.

"Good work today. You were right."

She shrugged. The important thing was they all had made it back in one piece and weren't dead or on their way to the barracks right now. Every time they faced Goler, they ran that risk. "I knew he'd eventually realize he could set a trap for us with the way we keep intercepting him."

"It saved our lives."

"Glad I could do my part." Kyrin smiled at Roland's family as they passed by, but grew serious. They would have to be more careful next time. "He won't fall for it twice, though."

Trask nodded. "Hopefully, he'll call it quits for the winter. He won't want to be riding around much once snow falls."

Kyrin agreed, and Trask walked on.

Once she finished unsaddling her mare, Kyrin joined Kaden and Jace. "Come on, let's get warmed up. Lenae will have hot cider waiting."

Kaden blew on his hands and grinned, his cheeks red with the cold. "Sounds good; especially if there are some of those sweet rolls left from breakfast."

Kyrin sent Jace a look of amusement. Did her brother ever not think about food?

"What?" Kaden demanded.

She chuckled. "Nothing."

He squinted suspiciously at her, but their attention shifted as they left the corral.

"That was a good shot today, Kyrin. You sure startled Goler."

She looked over at Lenae's son, Jeremy.

The young man gave her a wide smile, apparently forgetting that Jace had been in on the shot too. "You're probably about the best archer in camp."

Kyrin laughed a little. Jace could surely outshoot her, at least when it came to moving targets. "I don't know about that, but thanks."

They walked on, though Kaden sent a look over his shoulder. "You know he's trying his hardest to win you over?"

A smile played on Kyrin's lips. He'd been trying since she'd first set foot in camp over the summer. What had started out as shy, awkward compliments had grown some in confidence. He was a sweet boy, like his mother, and she was careful not to hurt his feelings. "I know." She smiled up at her brother. He didn't share her amusement. She bumped his arm. "Seems like you don't ever want me to get married."

Jeremy was one of only two young men who had ever shown her persistent interest, and Kaden hadn't been particularly enthusiastic about either of them, though he did actually like Jeremy. That was a step up from his view of Collin, the charming, but overly-flirtatious young man who'd been with them in Tarvin Hall and then promoted to Auréa Palace at the same time as Kyrin.

Kaden frowned. "I didn't say that. It's just that whoever it is will have to meet with my approval first."

Kyrin gave a low chuckle. "Good luck to any man who tries."

She glanced over at Jace. He, too, stared back at Jeremy, a somewhat brooding wrinkle in his brow. When he turned around, he met Kyrin's gaze, his vivid blue eyes serious. He was every bit as protective of her as her brother.

"You don't like him either," she said.

"I don't mind him."

Still amused, but thankful for their concern and protection, she put their minds at ease. "Well, I'm not interested anyway, so you two don't have to fret."

Satisfied, they dropped the subject. Halfway to the cabin, Tyra trotted across camp to meet them. The black wolf went straight to Jace, who paused to pet her. When he walked on, she fell into stride between him and Kyrin.

A cold, blustery wind gusted through the trees. Kyrin shivered and looked up through the bare limbs. "I wonder if it will snow."

Jace glanced up. "It might. It'll rain at least."

Kyrin was willing to bet he was right. He always sensed things like that.

A flood of warm air hit them as they opened the door and stepped into Lenae and Kyrin's cabin. The older woman was just setting a fresh loaf of bread on the table, and she looked up.

"How did it go? Are they safe?"

Kyrin nodded. "Everything went as planned. Goler did have an ambush set, but he gave up when he realized we were prepared for it."

A pleased smile softened Lenae's face. "Good to know everyone's safe. I've been praying since you left. Now, why don't you sit down and have some cider? Looks like you could do with some warming up."

Kyrin, Jace, and Kaden shrugged off their coats and hung them by the door before sitting at the table. Lenae poured them each a mug of cider and set a plate of sweet rolls between them. Kyrin gave her brother a grin and wrapped her fingers around her warm, steaming mug with a contented sigh. Despite the emperor's constant desire to hurt them, life was good.

A NIGHT OF thunder and driving rain gave way to brilliant sunshine and warmer temperatures the next morning, offering one last taste of fall before winter set in. Everyone took advantage of this opportunity to finish final preparations for the long, cold months ahead. At one edge of camp, opposite the cabins, Kyrin carried a bucket of water to the shelter shared by Kaden, Jace, Holden, and Trev. The men were up to their elbows in mud as they finished filling in any cracks that would let cold air into the shelter.

"Here you go." She set the bucket near Jace. She knew better than to get too close to Kaden. He'd already spattered the hem of her dress with mud. She gave him a warning look, just to make sure he didn't come any closer before she backed away.

The men thanked her and gathered around to wash up.

When she turned toward the cabin, movement drew her attention to the far side of camp where a lone, dark-skinned rider rode in.

"Tane," she said in surprise.

The others looked up. Shaking off their dripping hands, they followed Kyrin across camp to meet the talcrin. Nearly a month had passed since they'd received any word from Valcré. While no news was usually good, Kyrin was pleased to see him.

After all, he'd been the one to help her escape the city after her near-execution. She would always be thankful for the risk he took in doing so, and for how he'd helped her transition into a completely different life than she'd always known.

They met up with Trask, Rayad, and Warin along the way and gathered around their visitor.

"Good to have you back," Trask told Tane as he dismounted. "It's been a while."

"It has." He turned to face them, his silvery eyes twinkling with a smile for each of them.

"Anything significant happening in Valcré?"

"Actually, there is; but first, I've brought a couple visitors. I hope you don't mind."

Trask glanced past him. So far, only Tane and his horse had shown up in camp. "Not at all. Where are they?"

A grin lit up the talcrin's dark face. "They'll be here momentarily."

His gaze shifted upward. Trask frowned, reflecting the confusion of the rest of the group. Kyrin looked over at Kaden, who shrugged, but then a gust of wind blew overhead. It came in a steady rhythm that rose in volume and rattled the branches above. A huge, dark shape dropped from the sky. Kyrin gasped and turned her head as gusts of air buffeted and whipped her hair into her face. She brushed it away and set her wide eyes on the creature that landed several yards from the group. Three more followed and landed directly behind it.

Kyrin's heart pattered. Four magnificent dragons stood right at the edge of camp. With a faint rustle, they folded their wings at their sides. Her mouth hung open for a moment. She'd seen airborne dragons from far off only twice in her life, but never up close. The stunning creatures had lean bodies, agile limbs, and long necks to support their smallish, egg-shaped heads. Two smooth horns, each a foot long, swept back from the tops of their skulls, and all four had wide, ice-blue eyes with a slice of black for a pupil. Three of the dragons sported shining black scales that covered their backs and seeped down into dark green scales, almost like a paint horse. The fourth dragon, a female, was similar, but with slate blue and cream scales, and a slightly more petite build.

Mesmerized, Kyrin nearly overlooked the dismounting dragon riders, but the foremost rider caught her eye and fascinated her almost as much as his dragon. He was a little shorter than average, but that did not detract from his commanding appearance. The way he stood with his shoulders back and feet braced gave him the air of a man not intimidated by anyone. Even Kaden, with all his bravado, couldn't quite claim such bearing.

Though it must be chilly riding dragons this time of year, the man wore a sleeveless leather jerkin that left his well-toned brown arms bare, except for a pair of dark leather bracers over his forearms. His black hair fell long in front of his chest—some strands interwoven with leather strips and glass beads, the blue hues of which caught the light as he moved.

With a gentle pat to his dragon's shoulder, he turned to the group, sweeping each of them with eyes that shone like sapphires and were a bit larger than normal. The other three riders resembled him in appearance—short, yet strong, with long dark hair, brown skin, and large, vivid eyes. They, too, were dressed predominately in leather.

"They're cretes," Kyrin murmured, breathless. How many people ever saw the elusive race anymore? Certainly not many, since they had all left Arcacia long before she was born. But here they stood in camp, and she had to remind herself not to stare. The last thing she wanted was to give a rude first impression.

The head crete approached them, carrying himself with all confidence. Kyrin sensed a certain air of pride from the rest of the group as well. Tane met the man, bringing into stark contrast the great difference in their height, but the shorter man seemed to take no notice of it.

"Captain, let me introduce you to Lord Trask, son of Baron Grey and leader of this camp." Tane motioned to Trask, who stepped forward. "Trask, this is Captain Verus Darq of the Hawk Clan."

The two shook hands.

"Welcome," Trask told him. "It's an honor to have you and your companions here. What can we do for you?"

"Thank you." Captain Darq's voice was strong and clear. He glanced at Tane. "We've come to seek your aid at the recommendation of both Endathlorsam and Imhonriltane. The matter is complicated, but I believe it to be of concern to both our peoples. It's also very time-sensitive and must be acted upon quickly."

"Of course." Trask turned, motioning. "You're welcome to come with me to my cabin to discuss it. And, if you do not object, I'd like to include two of my senior men."

"I don't object," Darq said with a shake of his head. "I, too, shall bring my lieutenant."

Trask faced the curious group around him. "Warin, Rayad, will you join me in the cabin?"

They both nodded, and Trask looked back at Darq. "Are you and your men hungry, Captain? We have plenty of food and coffee to offer."

"That would be much appreciated. Thank you."

On the way to the cabin, Trask asked Lenae if she would bring food and coffee for the captain and the other riders. With her nod, the group moved on, passing by Kyrin and Kaden. Kyrin tried not to get caught staring, though she couldn't take her eyes from the crete captain. He was, perhaps, only an inch taller than her five foot seven, but definitely not lacking in any capacity. Kaden would insist otherwise, but Kyrin wasn't even sure he could have beaten the crete in a fight. The man looked too agile and well-trained for that. She took note of his weapons—two short swords strapped to his back, with a bow and quiver, and a set of daggers on either side of his belt. Yes, he was prepared for any foe.

Kyrin's eyes shifted to his lieutenant as he passed by. The man was slightly shorter, but just as strong and well-armed. He appeared to be a few years younger than Captain Darq and had deep green eyes instead of blue. A jagged scar marked one of his cheekbones and piqued Kyrin's curiosity. Though still impressive looking, he didn't share the captain's commanding presence and seemed more than content to follow his lead.

Kyrin glanced up at Kaden to see if he shared her interest in the riders, but she found his gaze still attached to the dragons. She smiled at the admiring look on his face. He'd always had a deep fascination for dragons. How many times had he dreamed of flying out of Tarvin Hall on one when they were little?

"Kyrin, want to help me with the food and coffee?"

Her attention shifted to Lenae, and she followed the older woman to their cabin. At the door, Kyrin had to take one last quick look back at their visitors before joining Lenae to prepare meals for them.

"I wonder what they could need Trask's help with?" Kyrin said, her voice a little hushed with the mysteriousness of it. Obviously, Sam and Tane knew them well, but she had no answer as to how.

"So do I." Lenae shook her head, sharing the curiosity. "I've never seen a crete before."

"Neither have I."

"They're quite impressive, aren't they?" Lenae set plates and a fresh loaf of bread on the table.

"Very," Kyrin agreed as they gathered the coffee cups.

In a few minutes, they had four plates laid out with hearty

venison sandwiches, fried potatoes left from lunch, and apple tarts. Lenae brought two trays from the cabinet and placed two plates on each, with the coffee.

"Kyrin, why don't you take a tray to the other riders while I take one to Trask's cabin?"

Outside, a little shiver raced through Kyrin as she approached their guests. She'd be awfully close to the dragons. They might be stunning, but she had a healthy respect for how dangerous they could be. They could kill her in a second with their sharp, curved claws alone, never mind their teeth and ability to breathe fire. At least the cretes seemed to have them well-trained. In fact, they looked rather docile as they sat and peered around curiously.

When Kyrin drew near, Kaden joined her, no doubt to get as close as possible to the dragons. She didn't think he had stopped watching them since they'd arrived. Jace commanded Tyra to stay, and followed along, too, but kept more distance.

Kyrin smiled when she came to the first crete and offered him a plate and coffee. He accepted it with a bland "thank you," and rested back against his dragon to eat, his expression closed off to conversation. However, the second crete, the youngest of the group, met her smile with his own when he thanked her.

She stepped back with the empty tray, unsure of what more to say or if she should even hang around. Supposedly, cretes were an aloof race and didn't trust outsiders. The first crete she served certainly fit this description.

The younger crete took a swig of his coffee and set his eyes past her. She peeked over her shoulder at Kaden who, of course, stared at the dragon. The female creature gazed back in mutual interest.

"Go ahead," the crete said suddenly. "You can touch her. She loves attention, and she'll only attack if I tell her to." A sly glint sparkled in his spring-green eyes.

Besides Jace, Kyrin had never seen anyone with such bright and colorful eyes as these cretes.

Kaden looked at him in awe. "You can do that?"

The crete nodded. "Dragons are highly intelligent. You can teach them almost any command. Storm, here, is young, but she learns fast."

Kyrin smiled at the delight in her brother's eyes as he stepped closer to the dragon and ran his hand over her grayish-blue neck scales. A grin split his face.

"She's so smooth. Kyrin, come and feel it."

Kyrin stepped to his side and laid her hand on the dragon. The scales were, indeed, very smooth, reminding her of the polished marble stair-railings in Auréa Palace, but they weren't cold. Warmth radiated through them and into her fingers. The dragon, still watching them, let out a little rumble, almost like a giant cat's purr.

"I told you she liked attention," the crete said, grinning.

Kyrin chuckled and glanced at Jace. She motioned for him to come closer, but he shook his head. This certainly had more to do with the crete than the dragon. He was very fond of any type of animal. She hated for him to miss out on such a rare opportunity, but she wouldn't prod him to join in. She faced the crete again.

"So they can breathe fire?"

"For short bursts, but that's usually all it takes to deter any threat."

"That's incredible," Kaden breathed.

While he continued admiring Storm, Kyrin observed the dragon's rider. He appeared to be in his early to mid-twenties—about ten years younger than Captain Darq—though his exact age was impossible to guess. Cretes were said to mature faster than humans, so he could be anywhere from seventeen to twenty-five. He, too, wore a sleeveless jerkin. Brown tattoos, a little darker than his skin, marked both his shoulders. Darq and the other cretes had them as well, but Kyrin hadn't taken a good look at them until now. This man's were a complicated pattern of spirals and dots, but the shape of a fox stood out in the center of his right shoulder.

Though she tried to be discreet, he must have caught her studying him and suddenly extended his hand to her. "I'm Talas, by the way. Talas Folkan of the Fox Clan."

Kyrin took his firm but gentle grip. "I'm Kyrin Altair."

Kaden turned to offer his hand. "Kaden Altair."

"The Altair twins," Talas said with an upbeat tone of interest. "We've heard about you."

Kyrin lifted her brows. "Really?"

"Yes. We have connections in Valcré, just as you do. News travels surprisingly fast between here and the forests of Dorland."

"With dragons, I can imagine," Kaden said with another envious look at Storm.

Talas smiled at his enthusiasm for the animal.

Kyrin glanced at the other crete. A frown creased his forehead. Apparently, he didn't think much of Talas's show of friendliness. He watched them out of the corner of his eye, with his chin tipped at a slight angle, but didn't say a word.

"How do you train a dragon?" Kaden asked.

"You have to start when they're young," Talas explained, "before they begin to fly. You teach them basic commands, and then, once they're able to bear your weight, you take them flying."

Kaden looked fascinated, but Kyrin's mind filled with all the many things that could go wrong. "Isn't that dangerous? What if they don't follow your commands or you fall off?"

Talas flashed a wide grin. "Oh, it's dangerous, but danger has never stopped a crete. We thrive on that sort of thing. With dragons, you form a bond of trust that grows stronger with time. The early stages of training young dragons are full of uncertainties.

Many riders have died in the process, but a well-trained dragon is a lifelong companion, and they're the lifeblood of the cretes." He patted Storm fondly, and the dragon let out another rumbling purr.

Kaden stared at the animal, his expression setting in determination. Kyrin could have said just what he was thinking before he spoke.

"So . . . what would it take for someone like me to get one?"

Talas let out a short, but friendly, chuckle. "Well, that would depend on your connections and relationship with the crete people."

Kaden's shoulders slumped. He didn't have either.

Talas quirked an eyebrow. "We'll see what happens. I'll keep you in mind."

Kaden's eyes brightened considerably at this. "Thanks."

A door shut on one of the cabins. Kyrin looked back as Trask and the others approached.

"We'll discuss it and make our selections," Trask said to Darq as they drew near.

The captain faced Trask once they reached the dragons. "You can expect the others tomorrow. Thank you for your willingness to aid us."

"I'm glad you sought us out. We're more than willing to help. As you said, it's important to us as well."

The two of them shook hands, and Darq mounted his dragon. The other cretes followed suit. Talas grinned down at Kyrin and Kaden from Storm's back.

"It was nice to meet you. Perhaps we shall meet again soon."

"I hope so," Kaden replied.

He and Kyrin stepped back and, at the command of the captain, all four cretes and their dragons took to the air. Kyrin and Kaden watched until they were out of sight, and then Kaden shook his head and looked at her.

"Someday, I'm going to get one."

Kyrin chuckled softly. "I believe it."

Once all signs of their surprise visitors had gone, Kyrin's curiosity kicked in again. She and the rest of camp gathered around their leaders, their eyes filled with questions.

"Captain Darq was sent here by one of the elders of their city," Trask explained. "Years ago, his eldest son, Josan Silvar, felt called to leave Dorland and study the words of Elôm written in the King's Scrolls. His father was against it, and they parted on unfriendly terms. To complicate matters, Josan's younger brother, Torin, followed him. Their father has since realized his error and wishes to see his sons, since he is advanced in years and isn't sure how much time he has left. Contact was never maintained between them so, for the past months, the cretes have been attempting to locate the sons."

Kyrin shared a look with Jace, who quietly appeared at her side. It seemed an odd thing for the cretes to involve them, but she didn't let her thoughts wander too far from Trask's explanation.

"The cretes have discovered that the two men are somewhere in the Graylin Valley, though they don't know where exactly. For years, Josan has been teaching people there about Elôm through letters that circulate from town to town. He also began making copies of the King's Scrolls and is in possession of what may be Arcacia's last complete collection of the Scrolls, since the last few kings have slowly destroyed them."

Kyrin remembered Sam mentioning this tragedy to her and Kaden back at Tarvin Hall when he'd taught them verses from memory. At the time, he wasn't sure if any copies survived.

"I'm sure I don't have to tell you how important it is that the Scrolls remain out of the emperor's hands," Trask continued. "The problem is that Daican knows just about as much as we do. He's sent men to the Valley to search for Josan and the Scrolls. Fortunately, like us, they don't know Josan's exact whereabouts.

"That's where we come in. The cretes aren't able to visit the villages without drawing suspicion. Captain Darq has asked me to put together a team to join them in the search. The goal is to find Josan and Torin and the Scrolls before Daican does. This is of utmost importance. As Arcacia slowly falls to the worship of idols, we must protect those with great knowledge of Elôm so that they may pass that knowledge on. The emperor will do everything he can to suppress it, but we must never let it die."

Murmurs of assent were whispered through the group.

"Our one advantage is that the emperor is searching for a man named Taan. That's the name Josan uses to sign his letters. It's the crete word for hawk, his clan. Now, it may not be long before Daican realizes this, but for now, it buys us a little time.

"I'll continue discussing this with Warin, Rayad, and Tane, and decide who will be part of the team. As soon as we make our decision, we'll let you know. In the meantime, I ask you all to pray. Not only will it be a dangerous mission, but time is against us. The emperor's men will soon arrive in the Valley. We must find Josan before they do."

A FEW SILVER and copper coins clinked into Timothy's callused hand—a little more than half of what he usually earned for a day's work. He frowned and raised questioning eyes to his employer, who almost towered over him. Harold shifted, balking, before he said gruffly, "You're too small to do everything that needs doing around here."

The words stung Timothy's dignity. Sure, he was a bit shorter than the average man, but he was just as strong and hardworking. He'd slaved for Harold for years. With an effort to swallow down any trace of bitterness, he responded quietly and evenly, "Sir, I do everything you ask of me."

Harold mumbled under his breath before coming out with something intelligible. "Well, it isn't enough."

Timothy held the large man's hard, immoveable gaze. This had nothing to do with his abilities or work ethic. This was something else—something he had no power to change.

Harold's eyes narrowed. "You're just gonna have to accept the pay or . . . look for work elsewhere."

Timothy closed his fingers around the coins. How easy it would be to walk out and not return—to leave the stress and grueling days that were enough to break a man's will. Temptation called him to do just that, but he knew better. He turned for the door.

"I'll be in tomorrow," he said over his shoulder.

A heavy sigh rose from his chest as he sensed the smug look that followed him. Grabbing his bag, he walked out of the mining supply warehouse and faced the bleak view of the dingy buildings and crowded streets of Dunlow—one of Graylin Valley's hundreds of mining towns. And, like most, it was dirty and gray—all rock and not a speck of green in sight. Timothy had never set eyes on a full-grown tree. Any that might have taken root had been felled long ago for mine shoring.

Just across the street from the warehouse, the gathering of homes and shops looked as though they'd slid down from the mountain slopes, settling in cramped, haphazard rows along the narrow valley floor. A perpetual cloud of smoke from the constant burning of the ore smelters shadowed the town and coated everything, from the buildings to the inhabitants' lungs, in thick grime. Timothy longed for the cool, pristine air higher in the mountains.

He turned south, away from the smokiest, busiest northern area of town, and quickened his pace. The sun had already descended behind the mountain peaks, as late afternoon gave way to evening. It didn't leave him much time. He took familiar shortcuts through the alleys, having to turn sideways to navigate most. Even then, stone or rough wood siding scraped at his clothes.

Timothy glanced up at the mountains towering high over the town on both the east and the west, like silent, imposing guardians. When he dropped his eyes, he caught a glimpse of one of Dunlow's seven working mines—the four largest belonging to Gary Tolman and Terrance Riggs. Their mines faced each other on opposite slopes like two opposing forces ready to clash, with the town as their battlefield. Indeed, the two bitter rivals had town loyalties almost split in two. Timothy shook his head to rid his mind of mine politics. He heard of little else at work.

At the far end of town, he took a rocky, but worn, path up a slope. He winced as pain burned along the strained muscles in his legs and lower back. Rising well before dawn and working all day always left him dead tired, but that was just the way of life these last seven years. Few in the Graylin Valley could claim better. One just had to accept it if he wanted to make the best of it. It wasn't as if he had any other choice.

In a few moments, he reached a small plateau. Here, by some miracle, a scattering of grass grew in stubborn clumps, and the air was not quite so thick. He breathed deeply. A stiff, cold breeze swept across the valley, blowing his dark hair into his eyes. He brushed it away and shivered. Soon, snow would fall and make it too cold to come here. He would have to start searching for a new meeting place; perhaps one of the livery stables, like last winter. At least the animals would provide warmth.

With only a few minutes to himself, he sat down on a large rock and propped his elbows on his knees. Clasping his hands, he bowed his head and rested his forehead against them. He did not speak, but his heart opened in prayers to Elôm. As always, he began with prayers of gratitude, expressing his thankfulness for his job despite its unpleasantness, for Elôm's promises to guide and provide for the needs of His children, and for His blessings. He asked for strength and alertness, as well as for wisdom in the next couple of hours.

These prayers continued, encompassing many areas of his life and the people in it, until the crunch and scraping of feet on rock drew his attention. He raised his head. A ragtag line of people made their way up to the plateau toward him—eight children between the ages of six and twelve, along with five women. Their clothes were all patched and worn, not unlike his own, but they wore smiles on their faces. A young boy with unruly copper hair and a face full of freckles rushed up the remaining distance when he spotted Timothy.

"Mister Carliss!"

Timothy felt far too young for the title of Mister—he was only twenty—but the children's mothers expected them to use good manners, so he did not discourage them.

"Hello, Danny," he greeted the exuberant nine-year-old.

"I studied by myself last night," the boy puffed out his chest, "just like you told me."

"Excellent. Soon you'll be able to read anything you want. Then you can help your sisters learn."

Danny's nose wrinkled. "I s'pose so."

Timothy just smiled and moved on to greet the rest of his students, trading kind words with the women, most of whom weren't much shorter than him. This was one of the larger groups he'd had the privilege to teach over the years. Some in town resented him for it, believing he considered himself above them, but he merely loved knowledge. He certainly wasn't anyone of any consequence, and hardly a real teacher, but it seemed only right to share what he learned with those who thirsted for it. His brother always said he should have been born to a talcrin family. He used to dream of attending one of their grand universities, but daydreams weren't a luxury many could afford in the Valley. He'd had to let them go, lest they lead to discontentment.

In comfortable familiarity, the women and children arranged themselves on the ground in front of him. He loved their eagerness despite the fact that most of them worked as long and hard as he did. With little time to spare, he got right to work, dictating a simple sentence for them to copy. Their heads bent studiously, some using broken slates they'd managed to scrounge up, while most just traced their words into the dirt.

A few moments later, Danny's head shot up. "Mister Carliss, did I spell 'em all right?"

Timothy pushed away from his rock and knelt next to Danny to study the boy's work.

"Yes, you did. Very good."

The little boy beamed, and Timothy gave him a grin as he moved on to check the rest of his students. They progressed rapidly, even the youngest ones. At every session, Timothy prayed this knowledge would someday help them attain better lives than they knew now. More than half of the town's inhabitants never received such learning.

For the next half hour, he helped them work through more sentences and reading. It was most important to him that they read well. Through reading, they could learn any number of other subjects. A whole world of knowledge opened up to them this way.

While helping one of the girls with a tricky set of words, Danny called Timothy's name again. He looked up to gently remind the boy to wait his turn, but Danny pointed toward town. Timothy's gaze shifted. Someone ran up the path to the plateau. He rose for a better look and recognized a teenage boy who sometimes made it to class when he wasn't too busy working.

When the youth reached them, he stumbled to a halt, panting.

"There's . . . been . . . a cave-in," he gasped out, bracing his hands on his knees.

A chill gripped Timothy. The town always waited in dread for the next inevitable disaster at the mines. Each one left behind widows and fatherless children—something he knew firsthand. Behind him, the women gasped and murmured in fear, reminding him he wasn't the only one present.

"Which mine?" he asked and held his breath.

"Tolman's north mine."

It was as if someone punched the air right out of Timothy's lungs. His gaze flew to the farthest mine. *Not that one.* The urge to run as fast as he could to the mine almost overwhelmed him, but he halted the spiral of his fear-driven emotions. He wasn't the only one with a loved one there. Two of the women he taught had husbands who worked for Tolman, and one had a son.

He formed his expression to project calm and confidence, and turned to meet their fearful eyes. After dismissing the other students, Timothy joined the two remaining women in gathering up their children. With the youngest in his arms, Timothy led the way down the slope. His heart hammered a deep, painful rhythm into his breastbone as terrible *what ifs* lurked in his mind. What would they find at the mine? The little girl he held clung to his neck. Would she ever get to do the same to her father again? The ache of uncertainty throbbed in his chest, and he turned to the only thing that could help.

"Elôm, we pray right now on behalf of the men at the mine, that there are no casualties and that all are safe. If anyone is trapped, I pray for rescue, and for any injured, healing. I also ask for strength for the families." He paused to swallow hard. "If there's any loss, give comfort and guidance to those of us who are left behind to mourn."

He glanced at the women. Tears pooled in their eyes, and their lips moved in their own pleas to Elôm.

Rushing through the twisted streets, they finally arrived near the mine. Hundreds of women and other family members had already gathered. They pushed on as far as they could, but were unable to see through the crowd. After straining for any glimpse of activity, Timothy turned to the women.

"I'll try to get closer and find out what's going on."

"Please, find our husbands," one of them begged, her lips trembling.

"And my son," the other added as Timothy handed her daughter over.

"I'll try."

With a prayer that he could fulfill the promise, Timothy worked his way through the crowd. Progress was slow, but eventually he made it to the barricades the mine officials had erected around the mouth of the mine. Men rushed about, many plastered in gray dust. Some had blood glaring through the grime. Timothy's eyes darted from man to man. *Please, Elôm.* He gripped the barricade, digging his fingernails into the wood as the sights and sounds brought memories rushing back.

"Help me accept Your will, Lord," he whispered as he fought the despair that always descended when this happened.

The words had barely left his mouth when his gaze locked onto a man just emerging from the dark mine. Thick, gray dust coated him from head to toe, but Timothy recognized him instantly. His heart leapt. He moved along the barricade. "Aaron!"

After his fourth call, the other man turned and spotted him in the crowd. He hurried across the distance.

"Tim," he rasped, and then doubled over, coughing.

Timothy ducked under the barricade and gripped his older brother's shoulder. "Are you all right?"

Aaron nodded and cleared his throat. "Yeah."

"What happened?"

His voice still rough, Aaron answered, "Most of the lower south section came down." He shook his head, sending a rain of dust from his short hair, his eyes pained and intense. "I was just heading down there. I don't know how many made it out."

Timothy worked his throat. "Jim Reddin, and Mark and Willie Barnell, were they down there?"

Aaron let out a long breath. "I think so."

Timothy closed his eyes. "Please, Lord, let them have made it out."

"Carliss!" a voice boomed.

Aaron turned as the mine foreman strode toward them, barking orders.

"Get back inside and climb down that rubble. See if you can find anyone else down there."

"Yes, sir." Aaron turned back to Timothy for a moment. "I've got to go."

Timothy moved with him. "I can help." He was as good a climber as his brother, if not better.

But Aaron held him back. "No, it's too dangerous. The rest of that section could come down at any time."

Timothy was about to argue that he might need an extra hand if he found someone trapped, but Aaron cut him off. "Listen, Tim, I really don't think I'm going to find anyone down there. Right now, it's the wounded who need help, and the families. You're good at that."

Timothy grimaced. Aaron shouldn't have to go alone, and what if the rest of the section did collapse? He bit down hard and nodded. "All right."

Aaron clapped him on the shoulder and turned back to the mine.

"Be careful," Timothy called after him.

"Always," Aaron threw back over his shoulder.

Timothy watched until he disappeared into the mine and sent prayers after him. Only Elôm knew if he would come back out. The weight of it pressed down on Timothy, and he struggled with the intense pull to follow his brother.

"Get back behind the barricade!"

Timothy flinched, and his attention snapped to the angry foreman. "Sir, I can help with the wounded."

The man narrowed his eyes. "Are you a physician?"

"No, but I can clean wounds and assist in any way needed."

The foreman glowered, but jerked his thumb over his shoulder. "All right; they're being treated over there."

Timothy gave a quick nod and hurried on before the man could change his mind.

Though he had witnessed mine injuries before, Timothy's stomach recoiled when he approached the triage area. Men lay moaning on the ground or on wooden planks used as makeshift stretchers. After a preliminary glance around, he found all four of Dunlow's physicians. He drew a fortifying breath and made his way toward one he knew well and considered a friend. Along the way, he scanned the men, but didn't recognize anyone.

"Whit," he said as he came near.

The aging physician squinted up at him through a pair of old, slightly bent spectacles. "Timothy."

Timothy knelt next to the miner he was working on. The man's face was set in a tight grimace and his chest rose and fell in an uneven rhythm.

"Is there anything I can do to help?"

Whit nodded with relief and gratitude showing through his grim expression. "This one has some busted ribs. You can help me get him tended and comfortable so we can move on to the next."

Despite the cold, Timothy pulled off his coat and rolled up his sleeves to get to work under Whit's instruction. They worked as quickly as they could to get to the next patients. Over sixty men needed attention, and many were far worse off than the man with the broken ribs, as Timothy soon discovered. Broken and crushed limbs needed to be set, and large wounds stitched. He spent most of the time holding men down while Whit tended their injuries. Though he had a strong stomach, he ached for them, especially the seriously wounded who were more likely to die from subsequent infections than to survive. At each man, he silently prayed for Elôm's healing hand on him.

Timothy had just finished helping Whit bandage a man with a long gash in his leg when a low rumbling vibrated through the ground, up into Timothy's knees. Men shouted. His head snapped up, and his eyes flew to the mine. Dust billowed from the mouth, and falling rock echoed deep inside. His heart stopped, and he scrambled to his feet, rushing toward the mine. Halfway there, a mine official grabbed his arm to stop him. He tried to pull away, but another man joined in to hold him back.

"My brother's in there," he said desperately.

Unable to break their hold, he could only watch and plead with Elôm for Aaron's life. Heart-pounding seconds stretched into agonizing minutes. *He's not coming out*, the realistic part of his mind tried to prepare him, though Timothy clung to hope. *He has to.* But, with each minute, the hope diminished and morbid thoughts crowded in. If Aaron was gone, would he even have a body to bury?

Grief settled, compressing his lungs and cutting deeply into his chest. His throat ached with tears that rose up to blur his eyes. He'd feared this day for all of his life.

Yet, through his watery vision, he picked out movement. With a blink, he brought a shape into focus and gasped as Aaron stumbled into view. Commotion swept through the crowd, and the men released Timothy. He rushed to his brother's side as Aaron fell to his knees. Hunched over, Aaron coughed and gasped, spitting out dirt. When he finally caught his breath, he traded a wide-eyed look with Timothy that revealed how narrowly he had escaped death. His hands shaking, Timothy helped him to his feet and embraced him tightly. *Thank You, Elôm!*

They only had a moment before the foreman rushed up with questions.

"What happened down there?"

Still breathing heavily, Aaron shook his head. "The rest of the section came down." He winced, his voice hoarse. "We're not going to find anyone alive down there. It's all solid rock."

KYRIN STIRRED THE large pot of simmering beans and meat as Lenae added the spices. Her gaze drifted once again to Trask's cabin. So far, he and the others had not yet emerged. Curiosity led her to making speculations as to who would be chosen to join Captain Darq and the cretes. There were many men qualified for such a mission. She swept her gaze across camp. Men milled about or talked in groups. She wasn't the only curious one. On the other side of the fire, Kaden and Trev discussed the cretes and, of course, the dragons.

The sound of a door closing drew all eyes to Trask's cabin. Conversation fell silent as Tane and Rayad approached the fire while Warin walked toward another group. Tane's focus rested on Kyrin, but Rayad looked around camp. When the two men reached the fire, the talcrin announced, "Kyrin, Kaden, Trev—Trask would like to speak to you."

Kyrin exchanged a look with her brother. She and Kaden seemed unlikely candidates for the mission, if that's what this was about. She handed her spoon to Lenae and turned toward the cabin. Before she went far, Rayad touched her arm to stop her for a moment.

"Have you seen Jace?"

She shook her head. "Not since the cretes left."

Rayad gave a small nod, and she hurried to catch up with the others. At the cabin door, they met Warin, who had brought along Holden and Mick. They all traded curious glances as they stepped inside. Trask waited for them at the table, which was much too large for the small space, but perfect for meetings.

He welcomed them with a smile. "Please, have a seat."

Kyrin, being the smallest, squeezed back into the corner with the men on either side of her. Trask did not sit, but stood facing them, his hands resting on the back of an empty chair. Kyrin took a quick glance at the maps spread out on the table before her eyes rose to focus on their leader.

"I know how curious you must be, so I won't keep you waiting," he said. "After our discussion, we've decided that you are five of the people we'd like to have on this mission."

Kyrin's eyes widened. She had never thought she'd have an active part in it. A glimpse at Kaden confirmed that his expression matched hers. They were two of the youngest members in camp, besides a couple of the village children.

"Are you sure we're all . . ." She looked again at Kaden. She didn't doubt his ability as a warrior, but neither one had the experience of age. This mission was of utmost importance, after all. Her eyes slid back to Trask. ". . . qualified? I haven't really been a part of something like this, and I know my fighting skills wouldn't match anyone at this table."

But Trask gave her a kind smile and an affirming nod. "Yes, I am. We've selected each of you based on what we believe you can bring to the team. You, Kyrin, have proven to be a valuable asset in complicated situations, and you never know when your people-reading skills will come in handy. We need more than just fighting power."

His eyes now switched to her brother. "And Kaden—you, Trev, and Holden have had the professional training most men in camp haven't. We pray it doesn't come to that, but I think the cretes will appreciate a certain degree of professionalism if we find ourselves facing the emperor's men."

He then came to the last man in line. "You, Mick, have also had training, and not only that, you're from the Graylin Valley, correct?"

Mick nodded. "Lived there twenty-three years of my life."

"Then you know the area better than any of us. Each of you will have an important role in this. However, the choice is up to you. These aren't orders. You can choose not to go. This mission does present risk. It's a race against the emperor's men."

Kyrin faced Kaden in consideration. He'd go in a heartbeat.

Trev was the first to offer a nod. "Count me in."

Kaden was right behind him, followed immediately by Holden and Mick. Trask nodded to each of them and then focused on Kyrin. If he thought she could add to the group, then she wasn't going to argue. "I'll go."

He smiled. "Good. We'll be leaving in a couple of days. Speed is crucial, and we have a lot of ground to cover in a short time, so Captain Darq is sending us dragons and a couple of cretes to teach us the basics of flying. We—"

"Dragons?" the question burst out of Kaden. "We get dragons?"

Trask's eyes twinkled. "Yes, we'll each be given a dragon. It's the cretes' way of demonstrating their friendship and gratitude for our help. They hope to establish a close link between our group and their people, which would be very valuable to all of us."

Kaden's wide-eyed half grin said he didn't hear anything beyond 'yes'. He and Trev exchanged a quick glance, looking like two little boys who'd just received the most extravagant birthday gift.

Kyrin stifled a chuckle, not wanting to disrupt the conversation, but Trask didn't get a chance to speak further before the door opened. Rayad entered first, followed by Jace. As the door closed, Jace scanned all the faces with a look of confusion and, perhaps, slight apprehension.

"Come sit down," Trask invited.

Jace moved to the table and silently took a seat. He didn't look entirely comfortable being the center of attention, and Kyrin sent him a quick smile to ease his nerves before Trask spoke.

"I've just finished explaining to everyone that, after our discussion, we've chosen them to be part of the team to join the cretes on their mission. You're the final member who would complete the team. We could certainly use your skills, but it's your choice whether to go or stay."

Kyrin studied Jace as he took this in and thought it over, though his expression never changed. She didn't think he had made up his mind yet when he asked, "Who's going?"

"Everyone here has chosen to go, except for Tane, who must return to Valcré, and Warin, who will watch over camp in my absence."

Jace's eyes shifted across the table and lingered a moment on Kyrin before he nodded. "I'll join you."

His decision brought another smile to her lips. It was for her he had chosen to go along—to keep her safe.

Gloomy dusk had fallen at the mine by the time all the anxious family members had carried away their wounded men. Long, painful nights lay ahead for most of them. Timothy cast his tired eyes around the nearly-empty area, and the weight of exhaustion and sorrow almost dragged him straight to his knees. Eerie quiet had begun to settle. His gaze fell on those still waiting behind the barricades, clinging to a rapidly dying hope.

His heart sank when his eyes rested on one of the women he had come here with, Susie Barnell, and her children. Her fourteen-year-old son, Willie, had joined her, suffering only minor injuries in the cave-in, but her husband was nowhere to be found. Timothy could only assume that the man lay under the tons of fallen rock inside the mine. Their eyes met, and her desperate plea for good news tore at his heart. He looked around helplessly, but knew he needed to be the one to tell her. No one else would be as sympathetic to her pain. His throat clogging, he sent a desperate prayer heavenward and walked toward the family. He bent under the barricade and straightened in front of them.

Timothy opened his mouth to speak, but tears already pooled in her eyes, and he had to swallow before his voice would work. "I'm sorry, Susie . . . Mark didn't make it out."

Shock held her frozen for a moment, but then a sob broke free. Tears coursed down her anguished face as she clutched her youngest daughter to her heaving chest while the others clung to her skirt, their young faces drawn in confusion and grief. Two tears tracked down Timothy's face as he looked over at Willie, who stood dumbly. Then, realization and responsibility landed squarely on the boy's shoulders. Despite his grief, he stood up a little taller and put his arms around his sobbing mother and siblings. Timothy watched, heartbroken, as the boy became a man right before his eyes.

His voice caught as he murmured, "I'm so sorry. If there's anything . . . anything I can do . . ."

He wasn't sure if they even heard him in their daze, and what could he truly do to bring relief beyond praying for them? Nothing would dull the pain for a long while. But Willie gave him a quick, pained glance of acknowledgement before the family turned to leave the mine.

The very last ounce of Timothy's strength seemed to drain away, and he stood cold and paralyzed as, one by one, the others faced the awful truth about their own missing men and departed. His breath was shallow and difficult, his heart crying with them. Memories flickered through his mind of standing next to Aaron on another cold night just like this one.

An uproar of voices tore him from his daze. He straightened his hunched shoulders and recognized Aaron's angry voice rising above the rest.

"What do you mean we won't be paid in full?"

Timothy brushed his sleeves across his damp cheeks and turned. A group of miners stood around the wages booth, where they usually received their day's pay. Bearing torches, they resembled a mob, but the mine owner stood his ground and glared down from atop a wagon. Timothy worked his way closer.

"You didn't work a full day so you won't receive a full day's wages," Tolman announced.

A loud grumble swept through the men but, again, Aaron spoke for the group. He'd always had good standing and respect among the other miners who knew how fiercely he fought for their rights.

"We've been here since dawn. We worked tirelessly to find any survivors in that deathtrap of a mine. We all risked our lives here. We deserve full pay. That's what most of us need to survive each day."

Tolman puffed out his chest, which only succeeded in magnifying his ample girth, and shook his head. "I pay for a full day's *work* and productive labor. Either take what you're offered, or take nothing. If you keep up this demonstration, I'll have you arrested, and you can look for work elsewhere."

Outrage swept through the group, and Timothy was afraid they would turn into a mob. It wouldn't be the first time. Three years ago, ten miners and four of Tolman's hired guards had been killed in such a fight. But after a few shouted insults and threats, the outcry died—once more on account of Aaron's influence.

Timothy breathed in relief. They'd seen enough death and tragedy for one day. Grudgingly, each man accepted his cut wages and the crowd dispersed, though many still grumbled.

Timothy waited until he spotted his brother leave the wage booth with his meager share of coins and hurried to his side. Aaron's face was grim and too deeply lined for his age. Anger still lit his eyes at the cruel injustice he and the others had to bear. He stopped to face Timothy, and a little of the ire melted into concern.

"Are you all right?"

Timothy gave a hesitant nod, not sure how to respond. He cleared his throat, which still ached with emotion. "I had to tell Susie about Mark."

Aaron winced. "We lost a lot of good men today." He reached out and squeezed Timothy's shoulder. When he spoke again, contempt sharpened his voice. "And, on top of it, we have to suffer Tolman's greed."

He shook his head with a glance back at the disgruntled and defeated miners. His shoulders sagged, and his weary eyes shifted back to Timothy. They were both about ready to collapse on the spot. The thought of having to walk all the way across town was almost too much.

"Let's go home," Aaron murmured as they turned their backs on the mine. "Josan must be worried sick."

This thought alone was enough to propel Timothy forward and keep them both moving at a good pace.

They walked in silence most of the way, consumed with their thoughts. Now that both had suffered pay cuts, they had very little to show for today. They would certainly feel the impact, especially since Timothy's was permanent. He glanced at his brother, reluctant to give him the news. With a deep breath and prayer for provision, he said, "Harold cut my pay again."

Aaron stopped abruptly and spun to face him. "What?" Even

in the darkness of the alley, his scowl was evident. "What excuse did he give this time?"

"He said I'm too small to do the work he needs me to do."

Aaron snorted in disgust. "You do three times the work of that good-for-nothing son of his."

"It's just his way of saying he doesn't like that I'm half crete. He's doing it because he can. He knows I won't quit."

"Maybe you should," Aaron muttered, his blue eyes flashing in the moonlight with a vividness more indicative of their mixed blood than Timothy's brown ones.

He shook his head. "No one else would hire me . . . except for the mines."

"No." Aaron gave a firm, decided shake of his head. "I promised Father I'd protect you. I won't have you working anywhere near the mines."

He moved on, his stride determined.

Timothy released a heavy sigh and caught up with him. "We may not have a choice."

"I'll make sure we do," Aaron replied in a stubborn tone.

Timothy didn't know if that was possible anymore. It wasn't as if his brother could pick up many more shifts at the mine. To do so would require him to devote his every waking hour to work. But he let the matter go. Only Elôm knew what the future would bring. Besides, his brother had fought to take care of them since their father died. He wasn't about to make that job any more difficult by arguing.

At last, they reached the far edge of town. Nestled on a bare, rocky piece of ground sat a rundown cottage. The wood siding was dried out and cracked, and the front shutters hung precariously from their rotting leather hinges. But warm light poured through the small, smudged windows and the open door, silhouetting a figure waiting for them.

Their feet starting to drag, Timothy and Aaron trudged the

remaining few yards home. The man at the door, propped up on one leg and a pair of old crutches, welcomed them with a relieved smile.

"I heard about the cave-in. I've been standing here praying ever since, waiting to see you two walk up."

His voice mingled with sorrow and exhaustion, Aaron responded, "Well, we made it, but at least thirty others didn't, unfortunately."

Josan's lips set in a thin line. "Their poor families."

He stepped back to let Timothy and Aaron inside.

On the way in, Timothy touched the crete man's shoulder and looked into his dazzling blue eyes. "I'm sorry I kept you waiting all this time for news."

A sad smile creased Josan's brown, careworn face. "I'm sure there were others who needed you more than I did."

Timothy gave a slow nod and closed the door against the nighttime cold. He hung up his bag and coat and turned as Josan worked his way around to the fireplace, barely squeezing between the table and a cabinet with his crutches. If only the cottage was a bit bigger so he could navigate through better, but they couldn't even afford to repair it, much less add on. However, they had a solid roof over their heads. Timothy thanked Elôm for that. At least they didn't have to resort to living in a tent, as some miners did. Not yet, anyway.

Josan stirred the contents of a small pot. "I've kept supper warm."

"I think I'd better get cleaned up first," Aaron said, with a glance at his clothes. Everything, including his skin, was all one color—a dirty gray.

He headed out the back door. Timothy followed, his arms covered in blood and grime from the wounded miners. Outside, a washstand leaned against the cottage. They stripped off their dirty shirts, and Aaron tossed Timothy a rag. He dunked it into the basin and started scrubbing his body, gasping as the icy water bit his skin. It reminded him again of the coming winter—the most difficult season to survive in the Valley. Far too many people died of exposure, illness, and starvation every year. He usually did not fear such a fate for himself, Aaron, or Josan, but this winter would surely be their hardest yet. Still, even as he thought this, memorized words entered his mind to comfort and reassure him. *The young lions do lack and suffer hunger; But they who seek the Lord shall not be in want of any good thing.*

Once clean, they entered their small, shared bedroom and pulled on fresh clothes. Neither said much. If Aaron was still thinking about how they would afford the provisions they needed, he didn't mention it.

Back in the main room, Josan waited for them at the head of the table. Timothy sat down at the crete's left hand, while Aaron occupied the seat opposite him. With a soft sigh, Josan eased into his own chair. Timothy reached out to help him prop his crutches against the cabinet. The years had not been kind to the crete. Yet, he wasn't even that old. Despite his missing leg, he still displayed signs of youthful strength, and his long hair was far more brown than gray, but his lined face told a different story—much like Aaron's.

If only they could somehow make his life easier after all he'd done for them. Josan had looked after the two of them ever since the mine collapse that had killed their father and cost Josan his leg. Through all the many ups and downs of the past several years, he had been the one to hold them together and remain a positive example of contentment and steadfast trust in Elôm. He was always the first to make any necessary sacrifices.

This manifested itself when, immediately following a heartfelt prayer, Josan divided their lean supper, pouring less of the thin soup into his bowl than into Timothy's and Aaron's. When he came to the last small spoonful, he moved to divide it between the two of them, but Timothy stopped him.

"Give it to Aaron."

His brother looked up to protest, but Timothy didn't give him the chance. "You work even harder than I do and need it more." Sure, Harold worked him hard, but at least he didn't have to swing a pickaxe and move rock all day. He didn't know how his brother did it sometimes. It just proved that being shorter had nothing to do with how they could work.

As stubborn as he could be, Aaron was too tired to argue over it tonight, and silently accepted the extra portion.

Timothy brought a bite of the soup to his mouth, the weak broth settling on his tongue. He swallowed slowly and took small bites in hopes of tricking his stomach into thinking there was more than there actually was.

"I'll be off in another day," Aaron broke the silence that had settled. "I'll go hunting. We'll need anything extra we can bring in this winter."

"I'll go with you," Timothy told him. Thank Elôm their one day off a week was the same; otherwise they would barely see each other. Timothy wasn't sure what he would do if Aaron decided he needed to work seven days a week just to keep them fed.

Aaron nodded with a bit of a smile—a good thing to see after today. Though Timothy wouldn't be able to help much in the way of hunting, since any innate archery skills that came with crete blood had somehow skipped him, at least he could carry back game. It would be good for the two of them to get out of town and into the mountains for a while.

For the last few minutes of their meal, they filled Josan in on everything that had transpired at the mine, and about their pay cuts. When they finished, they cleared the table of supper dishes, and Josan turned to Timothy.

"I finished making copies of the letter. You can look them over if you'd like."

"I'll do that before I study." Timothy knelt down in the corner of the cottage near the fireplace and pried up a loose floorboard. Reaching down into the hole beneath, he fished out a worn leather satchel containing the most valuable possessions they owned. He set it on the table and pulled out the Scrolls. Each one contained copies of the words of Elôm, written by God-inspired men through the ages. To Timothy, they were more precious than all the gold in the Valley.

Across the table, Aaron reached for a scroll, and Josan joined them. This had been their nightly routine for many years—to sit after supper and study together. It always brought Timothy back to the days of studying with his father. They'd spent hours poring over the Scrolls together. Even as a young boy, Timothy had soaked it all in with an insatiable hunger. His father had always told him he was special, and that Elôm must have great things planned for him. Timothy suspected this was only the praise of a proud father, but he kept himself open to any opportunity Elôm presented.

Before taking his own scroll to study, Timothy skimmed through the stack of parchments Josan had passed to him. Each one contained a letter, sharing a portion of the Scripture from the Scrolls, as well as words of explanation, comfort, hope, and exhortation. He checked for errors, making sure each was identical, right down to the one word signature—*Taan.*

Nodding, he laid them near Josan. "They all look good. I'll deliver them tomorrow night."

He normally would have delivered them right after supper—heaven knew the faithful believers of Dunlow needed the encouragement after the mine accident and the growing threat to their faith—but Timothy didn't think his body would take him more than a hundred yards from the house. Already he struggled to stay awake.

Quiet came again as Timothy rolled open the scroll before him. The words were like a soothing, warm bath to his battered soul, and he drank them in with as much ardor as when he was a child. Through them, he could hear Elôm speak—something that was difficult in all the day to day hardship—and it restored him.

He kept no track of the time, but read until the words blurred in front of him and forced him to stop. With a sigh, he rubbed his gritty eyes and looked across the table. Aaron sat, his chin propped in his hand and his eyes closed. It was a wonder he hadn't collapsed even before their study.

Timothy shook his head. How could his brother ever do more to take care of them? He would work himself to death. He had done so even when their father had been alive just so Timothy would have even a little extra time to study with the man.

Timothy would never find a truly adequate way to express his gratitude for his brother's unselfish care. He could only keep thanking Elôm for a brother so dedicated to his family. Things could be much different. After all, quite an age gap existed between them—a full twelve years. Timothy had been a surprise child, and with his birth claiming their mother's life, Aaron could have grown up bitter about the loss. Instead, he'd spent the last twenty years doing everything in his power to protect his little brother. If only Timothy could find some way to lighten the load.

He pushed to his feet with straining muscles. Josan looked up from his scroll, and Timothy gave him a half smile as he walked around to Aaron. He shook his brother's shoulder to bring him to consciousness. Aaron looked up, blinking his tired eyes.

“Let’s go to bed,” Timothy said.

Aaron rose without speaking and followed him into their bedroom, where he practically fell into the bottom bunk. Timothy crawled up into his, pulling the coarse covers up to his chin, and managed a few silent words to Elôm before sleep claimed him.

THE FIRST TELLTALE swish of approaching dragon wings rustled the trees shortly after lunch. Excitement rippled through camp as everyone so eager for their arrival gathered to watch the sky.

In moments, the first dragon dove down through the trees, scattering dead leaves as she came to a graceful landing. Kyrin smiled in recognition of the rider—Talas. She'd hoped Darq would send him to teach them to fly. A second female dragon landed next to him, this one bearing a female rider. Nine more dragons followed behind them—six males and three females.

All around Kyrin, the people from camp murmured in awe, especially the children who launched into begging their parents for a dragon of their own. Kyrin grinned and looked up at Kaden. He'd talked of little else for the past twenty-four hours, and was just itching to go flying.

She looked around for Jace. When she spotted him lingering at the back of the group, her smile faded. He'd been unusually withdrawn since their meeting the day before. He took pains to hide whatever bothered him, but he couldn't hide it from her completely. The vibrant sea-blue of his eyes had a way of deepening when he was in turmoil.

Putting it aside for now, she turned back as the two riders dismounted from their dragons. She had never felt particularly tall, especially next to her brothers, but she did now. Though near to Kyrin in age, the crete girl who'd accompanied Talas barely reached five feet tall. Like the crete men, her clothing was mostly of leather, but in a more femininely constructed vest that she wore over a sturdy lavender-colored shirt, along with a short wrap skirt over a pair of dark leggings and knee-high boots. Did she also have any similar tattoos under her sleeves?

"Welcome back," Trask told Talas as he stepped up to meet them. "We've been eagerly awaiting your arrival."

Talas smiled widely, taking in the sight of the gathering. "I see. And which of you are to join us in our mission?"

Trask motioned them forward. As Kyrin and Kaden approached, Talas grinned at them and said to Kaden, "Looks like your wish came true."

Jace was the last to join them, and claimed a spot next to Kyrin. She offered him a gentle smile, hoping to reassure him. He looked very reluctant about the whole thing, as if he would rather watch from the shadows somewhere.

With a nod of apparent approval, Talas said, "A couple of you know me already, but for those of you who don't, I'm Talas Folkan of the Fox Clan. And this," he motioned to the crete girl, "is my cousin, Leetra Almere of the Hawk Clan."

Kyrin's eyes shifted again to the female crete. Despite her small stature, she made full use of every inch of her height, standing tall and proud, her hands planted on her hips. Black hair fell to her waist and sported an array of beads, leather, and hawk feathers. Her flashing lavender eyes tangled with Kyrin's momentarily. Kyrin wasn't sure she liked the imperious vibe she sensed, but tried not pass judgment too hastily.

"Leetra's one of our finest dragon riders," Talas told them.

The crete girl's face remained stoic at his praise. Humility, like friendliness, didn't appear to be a crete's strong suit.

Following his introduction, Talas stepped forward to meet

each individual in the group. Leetra remained where she was, apparently content to gather their names from there. Talas worked his way down the line, shaking hands and greeting everyone with an enthusiastic smile. His grin was especially wide when he came to Kyrin and Kaden.

"I'm very pleased to see that you two will be part of the team. I enjoyed our talk yesterday, and look forward to getting to know you."

Jace was last in line. He said his name with a slight tremor of hesitation and looked away in embarrassment when he had no family name to give. After all, the cretes were, at the very least, meticulous about their lineage. Kyrin's heart reached out to him. If only she could encourage him, but she was grateful that Talas, in his accommodating way, greeted Jace no differently than he had everyone else. He did give Jace a keen look, no doubt guessing his mixed blood, but it didn't seem to give him pause.

Talas then turned back to Trask and the business at hand. "We plan to meet up with Captain Darq the day after tomorrow in the Sinnai Mountains. I know that's not a lot of time, but it'll give you the rest of the day and tomorrow to train with your dragons." He added good-naturedly, "Don't worry; there's nothing to it."

He motioned for them to follow. "First, you'll have to choose your dragons. There's one for each of you."

All eyes turned to Trask for the order of their selection, and a smile grew on his face. "Go ahead, Kaden, you choose first."

Kaden's eyes went wide. "Really?"

With Trask's nod of confirmation, Kaden just stood staring at the creatures for a moment before Trev clapped him on the back with a teasing grin. "Hurry up; I want my turn."

Kaden eyed each of the waiting dragons. Finally, he nodded to a sleek male dragon, who peered at him with just as much interest. "I want him."

Talas nodded his approval. "That's Exsis. You two will get along splendidly. Now, who's next?"

Trask looked over the group. "Kyrin, why don't you choose next?"

She smiled, her heart already set on a particular dragon. One of the females had scales of a slightly bluer hue than the others, and reminded her of the necklace her father wore. "I'd like the female one next to Exsis."

"That's Ivoris, but we always call her Ivy," Talas said. "She's from the same hatch as Exsis."

Kyrin traded a grin with Kaden. "Twins. Perfect."

The rest of the men talked amongst themselves and made their selections. The final pick came down to Jace and Holden, with one male and one female dragon left.

Holden turned kindly to Jace, so differently from the hostility he'd once shown him. "Which one do you want?"

Jace shrugged. "Doesn't matter. You choose."

"I guess I'll take the male then."

"That's Brayle," Talas told him. "And Jace, you've got Shalmar. Now, let's introduce you."

The group moved forward again, closer to the dragons, but Kyrin slowed when Jace hung back. His attention had snagged on the ninth, unclaimed dragon that had arrived with the cretes. She lay off by herself, her head on the ground and her eyes half closed with disinterest—the opposite of the other vibrant and curious dragons.

"What's wrong with her?" Jace asked.

Talas looked over his shoulder, first at Jace and then at the dragon. "Gem? Her rider died in a training accident with another dragon." The crete's voice dropped regretfully. "She's been this way ever since. She barely eats or shows interest in anything. We brought her along in hopes of distracting her, but it isn't working. Dragons can go some time without food but, at this rate, she probably won't survive long."

Jace's gaze lingered on the dragon, and Kyrin sensed his sympathy for the creature. Tyra was proof of his soft spot for injured or sickly animals. Finally, he joined the group, though he seemed distracted.

"We need to introduce each of you to your dragons to let them know you're friends; otherwise, they won't let you ride them." Talas motioned for Kaden. Stopping in front of his dragon, he said, "Exsis, *ámi*."

The dragon let out a little rumble and lowered his head to sniff Kaden, who smiled and laid his hand on Exsis's head. Kyrin would never forget the joy in his eyes.

"It won't take long for the two of you to form a bond." Talas turned to encompass the others. "They're young dragons—about two and a half years old. The older they get, the stronger they'll bond with you."

Now he gestured to Kyrin and introduced her to Ivoris. The female dragon lowered her head and rested her scaly chin in Kyrin's outstretched hands before emitting a deep dragon purr. Kyrin chuckled and stared into her sparkling eyes, her breath taken that this magnificent creature now belonged to her. Others would have paid fortunes just to get their hands on a dragon.

One by one, Talas introduced each member of the group to their dragons. No one said much, but words didn't seem adequate at this point. Kyrin forgot all about Leetra, until the crete's clear voice rang out behind them and startled her.

"Now that you've met your dragons, it's time to begin our lesson."

Almost as one, they turned to face her. She stood with her hands still on her hips and an impatient gleam in her eyes. Kyrin shifted. If only Darq had sent just Talas to teach them.

"As you can see, each dragon is already saddled. We'll show you how to tighten the saddles and remove them after flying. Tomorrow, we'll teach you to put them back on."

Kyrin's brows inched up at the girl's drill-sergeant manner of instructing. There'd been enough of that sort at Tarvin Hall. She glanced at Jace. He didn't appear impressed at all.

"The saddle will be your primary tool for controlling your dragon; at least in the beginning." Kyrin's attention snapped back to Leetra. "There are two bars on the saddle. One, which will be in front of you, is like a saddle horn. If you have to hang on, grab that."

Kyrin breathed out a short, quiet laugh. *If* they had to hang on? Why would they not, especially when taking off and landing? Apparently, cretes didn't think like that.

"The bar in front of it is the one you'll use for control. When you shift it left or right, straps put pressure on the dragon's neck, just like neck-reining a horse. The same goes for pushing the bar forward or back. Push it forward to dive lower, and pull back to climb. Does everyone understand?"

Down the line, they nodded. If they didn't understand, no one would admit it. Leetra certainly didn't invite ques-tions or anything she might deem incompetence. Kyrin glanced at Talas. His expression displayed a cross between amusement and exasperation.

"Dragons can also be commanded by voice," Leetra moved right along. "*Ámi* means friend. If you want your dragon to wait somewhere for you, stay is *tolla*. To tell them to follow you, the command is *réma*. For flying, *unai* is up, *taro* is down, *eidi* is right, and *fen* is left . . ."

Kyrin didn't know how the others would remember all this. She would have to refresh them all later when Leetra wasn't around.

". . . and if you happen to be attacked, the command for fire is *roven.*"

Kyrin cast a wary glance at Ivoris, and then at the other dragons. The men did the same.

Leetra arched her brow at them. "They're smart enough to understand when it's given as a command or merely spoken. These are the basic commands, but there are many more that can be learned. Dragons are always trained in the crete language. They're incredibly intelligent creatures. More intelligent than any dog."

She said this peering straight at Tyra, who sat near Jace, but kept a respectful distance from the dragons.

Kyrin stiffened. She looked at Jace. His jaw muscles bunched, and a cool light glinted in his eyes. Kyrin shot Leetra a hard look, but the crete girl gave no notice as she went on speaking.

"Talas and I will help you with your saddles, and then we'll have our first lesson in flight." She made it sound more like a chore than something she had any desire to do.

"Now?"

Kyrin darted a look at Jace again, not quite believing he'd been the one to speak. He fidgeted, as if he couldn't believe it either.

Leetra's gaze bored into him. "Yes, now. What did you expect?"

Jace hesitated. "Aren't we going to get to know the dragons first?" The usual strength in his deep voice gave way to the slightest tremor only Kyrin would have noticed.

She stared at him. It was so unlike him to speak up, especially to someone like Leetra. That's when it registered—the flicker in his eyes she had only seen on, perhaps, one other occasion. Fear. Now things started to piece together in her mind, and her heart squeezed.

"You'll get to know them while flying," Leetra responded flatly. She tilted her head. "Why? Are you afraid?"

Jace went rigid, and his throat worked as he swallowed.

Indignation zinged through Kyrin, setting her protective instincts on fire. She stepped forward to eliminate a little of the distance between her and Leetra, bringing the crete's eyes to her.

"I am," she declared. Leetra gave her a suspicious look, and Kyrin raised her hands to her hips, mirroring the crete's stance. This time she was the one who took full advantage of her height—a good seven inches on Leetra. "We haven't grown up around dragons. Some of us hadn't even seen one before yesterday. You can't expect us to be comfortable enough to just climb onto one we don't even know yet and entrust our lives to it."

Leetra's chin rose a fraction, but something slight changed in her expression. It wasn't understanding, but perhaps a grudging surrender.

"Fine," she huffed. "Just be ready to fly out after tomorrow."

Kyrin gave a curt nod, and Leetra faced the rest of the group. "So who *will* go up today?"

"I will," Kaden volunteered.

Kyrin had to smile. No one would have been able to keep him from flying at his first possible chance.

In the end, everyone chose to brave the skies except for Rayad, who was with Kyrin and Jace on wanting to get to know his dragon first.

Kyrin joined Kaden as Talas showed him how to tighten Exsis's saddle. At least she could learn that. Once properly secured, he crawled up and adjusted the cupped stirrups affixed to the side straps.

She gave him a pointed look. "Be careful." While Talas made it out to be easy, she wasn't about to lose her brother to some freak accident his first time out on a dragon.

"I will," Kaden replied, already breathless at being only moments away from fulfilling his longtime dream.

Kyrin stepped away as the others mounted. From Storm's back, Talas said, "Whenever you're ready, just give the command." He then commanded his dragon, "*unai,*" and took off. The other five riders followed, with Leetra and her dragon bringing up the rear. Kyrin had to turn her face away as the gusts of air stirred up dust and leaves. When she looked up again, the dragons were just disappearing over the trees heading north. Ivoris watched her brother go and then turned questioning eyes to Kyrin.

"Tomorrow," Kyrin told her, not sure if she would understand.

But it seemed to be enough when Ivoris settled in to wait. Kyrin gave her the command to stay just to be sure, and then walked over to Jace, who still stood at Shalmar's side.

He sent her a guilt-ridden glance, but didn't meet her eyes. "You could've gone with Kaden." Despite the power behind his voice, he always spoke softly. She'd only ever heard him raise it once, when he was in such distress the day after ryriks had attacked them.

She shook her head. "He's the daring one, not me. I much prefer to get to know Ivoris with my feet on the ground."

Jace stood silent, his brows bent and his jaw tense. Kyrin leaned in a little to see his face better and spoke gently. "Will you be all right?"

He winced and admitted, "I don't like heights." He turned his face away.

Kyrin touched his arm. "Many people don't like heights. That's nothing to be ashamed of."

"It is if it will prevent me from going on the mission." His tortured eyes locked with hers.

She held them, losing her voice for a moment. He was truly scared. She squeezed his arm and tried to project understanding and encouragement into her words. "You'll be all right. You have all afternoon to prepare. I'm sure, once you spend some time with Shalmar, you'll feel more confident about it. And I'll be here the whole time to help you in any way I can."

Jace's uncertain gaze rose to the dragon.

"Just spend time with her and see how you feel," Kyrin urged him.

He gave a slow nod. With a bright smile, Kyrin turned back to Ivoris, but out of the corner of her eye, she noticed Jace's gaze switch from Shalmar to Gem.

*COWARD*. JACE CLENCHED his fists with the agony of the emotions warring inside him. How could he let something as trivial as a fear of heights prevent him from joining the others? He'd faced fear all his life, and had moved forward in spite of it. But this was different—something gut-gripping and paralyzing that had lurked inside him ever since he was a child whenever he faced the danger of falling more than a few feet.

He had to overcome it. Somehow. He would never live it down if he remained behind out of fear. And what if he did stay behind and something happened to Kyrin that he could have prevented? How much more frightening was that prospect than flying?

The chill this brought to his bones jumpstarted his courage and, most of all, his determination. He stepped closer to Shalmar, though he didn't actually believe getting to know the dragon would make an ounce of difference when it came time to fly. He'd only needed to buy more time to get a hold of himself.

He laid his hand on the dragon's neck and let his fingers trail over her warm scales. He couldn't deny the pull the creature had on him, stirring the deep, innate love he had for animals. If only it involved nothing more than riding her like a horse, or having her as a pet like Tyra. He glanced over at his wolf. She maintained her distance with a watchful eye and stared at him as if asking what he would do.

Jace dropped his hand to his side with a heavy sigh and had no answer. Shalmar turned her regal head to watch him. It didn't seem right to form a bond with her when he held such uncertainties. Would he ever truly ride her? He just couldn't see himself flying.

His shoulders sagging, he turned away from her, and his eyes landed on Gem. Her sad state triggered the same compelling urge to help her as when he'd first found Tyra as a wounded pup. It drew him toward her. The dragon's blue eyes followed his movements. A couple of feet away, he paused. "*Ámi.*"

The dragon blinked, but otherwise didn't respond. Jace walked closer to stand at her shoulder. He reached out to touch her, and a tremor passed through her scales. Slowly, he ran his hand down her shoulder, considering what he could do for her. What did he know about dragons? Judging by the way she laid there, wings drooping into the dirt, she was probably starting to weaken from lack of food.

He glanced at Shalmar again, torn. If he pursued this, it would use up any time he had to get to know the other dragon. But, in the end, it just wouldn't make one bit of difference to his fear. He motioned to Tyra and walked away from Gem. On the way to their shelter, they passed Kyrin and Ivoris.

"I'll be back in a little while," he told her.

"Where are you going?"

"Hunting," Jace said over his shoulder. He wasn't sure how to explain his decision, nor did he feel up to trying. He simply had to do it.

At the shelter, he collected his bow and quiver, and strode out of camp. On the edge, he looked down at Tyra.

"Deer," he commanded, pointing deeper into the trees, and the wolf trotted off in search of a scent.

Two hours passed—longer than he had hoped—but Jace returned to camp with a small doe slung across his shoulders. A few sets of eyes regarded him curiously, but he set his mind on his task.

None of the riders had returned yet. Ivoris, Shalmar, and Rayad's dragon rested together to enjoy the warm rays of afternoon sun, while Kyrin and Rayad must have gone to the cabins. Gem hadn't moved at all since he left. He walked up to her and let the still-warm deer slide down. Although he knew better than to expect anything, disappointment still stung when she didn't react to the meal. Did the cretes have a command for 'eat'?

"Come on, girl," he murmured, but she didn't even look at him. He sighed, drawing his brows together, but he wouldn't give up just yet.

Walking the length of her neck, he sat down near her foreleg. He'd had to coax Tyra to eat at first too. He looked at his wolf, but she still wouldn't come within ten feet of the dragons.

"It's all right." He motioned to her. "Come here."

She took a hesitant step and then stopped, refusing to take another. Jace moved to meet her halfway. "Come on."

She moved slowly until she came within his reach. He put his arm around her and drew her closer. "It's all right."

He looked back at the dragon. "Gem, *ámi.*"

For the first time, she offered a true response to him. Very slowly, she dragged her chin across the dead leaves to peer at the wolf. Tyra squirmed in Jace's grasp, but he held her still.

"*Ámi,*" he repeated.

The dragon's nostrils twitched as she took in Tyra's scent. Then, just as slowly, she slid her head back to its original resting place and let out a long breath. Jace scooted backward to sit at her side, drawing Tyra with him. The wolf stood rigidly under his arm for several minutes. She'd bolt if he released her, but he stroked her fur and spoke to her softly. Finally, she relaxed and lay down beside him. Jace leaned against Gem, and soon the warmth from the dragon's scales radiated comfortably into his back. It soothed the tension in his muscles.

A few minutes later, leaves crunched, and Kyrin walked into view.

"There you are." She glanced at the deer. "Any luck?"

Jace shook his head. "She doesn't have any interest in it. Maybe, if she trusts me, I can eventually get her to eat it." It was a long shot, but what else could he do besides just let her die?

Kyrin glanced over at the other dragons, her eyes lingering on Shalmar. If she questioned his decision, she didn't voice it. Instead, she smiled. "I hope you can get her to eat. It would be a shame for her to die."

"I wish I knew more about dragons, if there is anything else I could do for her."

She gave the dragon a sad look, but encouraged him, "I think you're doing everything you can."

For the next couple of hours, Jace stayed near Gem—talking to her, rubbing her neck, anything to gain her trust. His eyes strayed to Shalmar several times. Deep inside he knew he was stalling and avoiding his biggest challenge, but he wasn't ready to face it yet.

Near sundown, he lifted his eyes to the sound of the other dragons returning. He rose as they appeared and landed nearby, admittedly relieved to see that everyone had returned safely. Anything could have gone wrong. The men dismounted in an exchange of laughter and back and forth chatter, their voices raised with the thrill of adrenaline. A pang of longing for such camaraderie stabbed Jace's chest. These men were his friends, yet the ease between them still did not come naturally to him, especially tonight when his fear had kept him from joining in their moment.

He hung back so as not to interrupt it. Maybe they wouldn't even notice him, but Leetra and Talas shifted their attention in his direction. The crete girl's bright eyes landed on the deer, and then jumped to him. "That won't work. We've already tried."

Heat prickled up Jace's neck and along his scalp, while a little flame of indignation kindled in his heart. He was only trying to help.

Talas stepped in, relieving a small particle of his discomfort. "It's kind of you to try. You never know. She might have eaten it. At this point, any attempt is welcome. We've exhausted all our efforts."

Jace gave a stiff nod, avoiding eye contact with the crete's cousin. Had he known the true measure of turmoil this mission would bring, he might have talked to Kyrin about the two of them staying behind. But it was too late for such gutless action now.

By this time, the others had gathered. Kyrin hurried to meet her brother, whose face was red and windblown, but lit up with a huge grin.

"That was incredible!" he told her in a rush. "Just wait 'til you try it. You'll love it. You'll never want to come back down."

Kyrin laughed. "I look forward to it."

A painful loneliness rose inside Jace, seeing her enthusiasm. If only he could share it, but just listening to them elevated the rhythm of his heart. No matter how he tried, he just couldn't imagine himself in the air—on a dragon or otherwise. He didn't want to spoil her excitement, but without her standing with him, he felt even more the outsider.

Talk of the flight dominated their supper conversation. Everyone wanted to hear about it, and the new dragon riders were eager to share. Jace took a seat off to the side next to Rayad and tried to shut out all the voices while he ate his supper in silence. So much talk of flying turned his fear into a clawing panic in his stomach. He had to get a grip but, so far, he was losing the battle. Distracted, he nearly missed Rayad's quieter voice in the commotion. His attention snapped to him.

"Are you doing all right?" Rayad looked on him with the compassion and understanding Jace had grown so used to in the last couple of years. Besides Kyrin, no one knew him better.

He shrugged. He'd told Rayad many things since the man had rescued him from a cruel life of slavery, but his fear of heights had remained secretly locked inside him.

"You know," Rayad said, leaning closer to keep the conversation between them. "I'm not real keen on this either. Riding dragons isn't the sort of thing you try for the first time at my age." He offered Jace a smile. "But we'll get the hang of it."

Jace swallowed, though it stuck in his throat, and he managed a brief nod. Only time would tell if that were true and, right now, time slipped away faster than he wanted it to.

The nighttime temperature dropped and warned of frost by morning. Jace buttoned his coat and moved in closer to the fire with the others. Thankfully, their talk of flight had subsided and, without hearing about it every other minute, he was able to relax a little for the time being. Most of camp had gone off to bed, but those selected for the cretes' mission remained outside with their guests, where Talas delighted them with a selection of beautiful melodies from a small wooden flute. Some of the tunes were slow and haunting, while others were much more lively and cheerful. Jace had never heard anything quite like it.

When Talas finished some time later and tucked the flute back into his jerkin pocket, they all gave him a round of quiet applause. He accepted it with a grin of appreciation.

Across the fire, Trask stretched and said, "It's getting late. Talas, if you're tired, we have a place for you in our cabin, and Kyrin and Lenae have made a place for Leetra in theirs."

"Actually, it's not so late for us. We only sleep a couple of hours before dawn. We also never sleep on the ground if there is a choice," Talas replied. "We always come prepared with sleeping hammocks to hang in the trees. But thank you for your hospitality."

Trask looked a little surprised. "Will you be warm enough out here?"

Talas nodded, showing no sign of chill in his sleeveless jerkin. "We're used to harsh weather. Only in the dead of winter do we really begin to notice it." He smiled at their curious expressions.

Jace could tolerate most harsh weather, but certainly not to the extent the cretes could. Even tonight he wouldn't have been comfortable without a coat.

Leetra rose from her place beside Talas. "I'm going to go put my hammock up." She walked off without a glance at the others.

Jace relaxed a little. The girl seemed especially short on patience this evening, particularly when Talas had decided to play for them. Her presence didn't help the nerves he battled.

When she was well out of earshot, a wry little smile came to Talas's lips. "You'll have to excuse her. I'm sure much of her behavior would be what you consider rude."

Jace breathed a short breath and caught Kyrin's eye. She raised both her brows, telling him how she felt.

"The thing is, we cretes are very blunt," Talas explained. "We state things exactly as they are. This is normal between cretes, but I'm afraid it doesn't come across well with others. It also takes a long time to earn a crete's trust and respect, so we hold ourselves at a distance. My generation isn't used to dealing with other races, outside of the giants. I apologize for any discomfort this causes."

Though Jace would rather avoid Leetra's company, Trask gave an understanding nod.
"We're all learning how to interact with each other. It'll come."

Talas agreed.

"So what makes you so different?" Kyrin asked. "You don't seem to have any difficulty interacting with us."

Talas chuckled, linking his hands behind his head as he leaned back against the log behind him. "I'm an odd crete. Just ask my family. I get it from my grandfather, apparently. They say the two of us and my youngest sister are entirely too friendly and charming for cretes." The grin he flashed proved this. He shrugged. "It's why Captain Darq invited me along, I guess. To smooth any ruffled feathers. It's either a gift or a weakness, depending on who you ask."

Laughter rippled around the fire.

Across camp, something scraped against the bark of a tree. Jace looked over his shoulder just as Leetra hoisted herself up on a branch and then climbed higher into the tree with the ease and quickness of a squirrel, all the while with a bundle on her back. His eyes widened.

A good twenty feet off the ground, she stopped and tested a branch above her head. Then, perched on the one below and without even hanging on, she pulled off the bundle and unrolled her hammock to hang from the branch. Once it was secure, she crawled in, nestling into the material as it swayed in the air.

Jace looked away, his mouth dry. He swallowed several times before the moisture returned enough for him to ask Talas, "Aren't you afraid of falling out during the night?" He wouldn't get a moment's rest if he had to sleep that way.

Talas glanced at his cousin and shook his head. "We've been around heights since infancy. Our cities in Dorland are built a couple hundred feet off the ground in trees that can reach four hundred feet sometimes. The only way to get from place to place is by dragon or bridge. It's the crete way of life."

Jace's heart sputtered, and his palms grew damp. He gasped a silent prayer never to have a reason to visit a crete city. He'd be paralyzed from the moment he arrived.

"Well," Talas said, pushing to his feet, "it may not be late for me, but it is for you. Tomorrow will be a busy day, so I'll let you get some sleep. Again, thank you for your hospitality."

With echoing goodnights, he walked away and everyone rose to stretch their legs and head off to their sleeping quarters. On her way, Kyrin smiled at Jace.

"Good night," she told him. Her voice lowered. "Sleep well. Everything will be all right."

He wished he could believe her as he murmured "good night". With a sigh, he watched her walk away and disappear into her cabin. Then he looked toward his own shelter and winced. He would never sleep tonight. Not even caring to try, he walked over to the dragons to check on Gem. Tyra followed, no longer hesitant. When they reached her, the dragon and deer were exactly where he'd left them. Another wave of disappointment doused his dwindling hope. He was failing at everything today.

At the sound of footsteps, he looked over his shoulder. Talas was on his way past, with his hammock tucked under his arm. He paused, his green eyes glittering in the starlight.

"If you do get her to eat that, I'll be impressed." He smiled and walked on.

Jace turned back to Gem and knelt down near her head. He ran his hand along the back of her long neck.

"How am I going to get you to eat?" he whispered, shaking his head. He'd run out of ideas.

He stayed at her side a few minutes more, until a frosty gust of wind creaked in the trees and sent a chill through his body.

Pulling his coat close, he rose and turned toward the shelter. He might not sleep, but at least he would be warm. That's when Gem raised her head for the first time all day. It wasn't much, but her wide eyes opened fully, glinting like her namesake as she peered up at him. He'd been around animals enough to understand that look—a pleading look. She didn't want him to go.

Jace glanced at the shelter, then back down at her. "All right, I'll stay a while longer."

He moved down to sit near her foreleg again, where her scales would offer some warmth against the cold and shield him from the breeze. He'd only just settled in when Gem shifted, rustling the leaves and dried grass as she lifted her wing just enough to create a small, tent-like space next to her body. Jace looked at it and then caught her staring at him. His brows dipped, and she continued to stare. He glanced at her wing again. Did she want him to crawl under it?

Her incessant stare finally prompted him to move. What did he have to lose? Crawling past her foreleg, he ducked under her wing. Putting his hand out to steady himself, he found her belly scales as warm as rocks that had sat near a fire. He sat down, his back against them, and the heat quickly seeped through his clothing and warmed him all over. He motioned to Tyra, who crawled in with him, and Gem nestled her wing around them like a warm cocoon. Resting his head on Gem, a little smile came to Jace's face. Maybe things weren't so hopeless with the dragon after all.

DARKNESS CLOAKED THE room, but for the slices of warm light peeking through the cracks in the door. Timothy hurried to tug on his shirt and block the cold their thin walls couldn't completely ward off. He then slipped out of the bedroom, letting in as little light as possible. In the main room, his eyes landed first on Josan's empty bed and then found the crete in a chair near the fire.

"Good morning," Josan's low voice greeted.

Timothy echoed him and stepped to the table, where two small candles illuminated the satchel of scrolls. He reached for one and set a chair at the fireplace opposite Josan.

"Is Aaron still asleep?"

Timothy nodded as he took his seat. "I know he wants an early start, but this is the only day he can sleep in a little. I'll wake him in a while." Aaron had returned home from work last night especially exhausted after spending the whole day helping the other miners try to clear the rubble from the cave-in. He'd barely managed to eat his supper before heading straight to bed.

"It's the only day you have to sleep in too."

Timothy shrugged and held up the scroll. "I'd rather read." A couple of hours of extra sleep wouldn't make much difference anyway. Not like reading the Scrolls would.

Josan gave him a warm smile that reminded Timothy of his father and left a comforting affirmation in his heart. One of the things he missed most was the encouragement his father was always so quick to give. He rolled open the scroll in his lap and found where he'd left off reading the night before. After a while, he came to a familiar passage that he turned to often.

*Do you not know? Have you not heard? The Everlasting God, the Lord, the Creator of the ends of the earth does not become weary or tired. His understanding is inscrutable. He gives strength to the weary, and to him who lacks might He increases power. Though youths grow weary and tired, and vigorous young men stumble badly, yet those who wait for the Lord will gain new strength; they will mount up with wings like eagles, they will run and not get tired, they will walk and not become weary.*

He sighed as the words filtered through his mind. They had been a rock to him in the last years, with exhaustion dogging every waking moment. It was as if the very town itself was built on weariness that only seemed to grow stronger. He saw it in the faces of their neighbors—especially those who secretly shared his faith. Something dark and sinister was sweeping across their land, adding to the heaviness of their burdens. People were scared. Timothy had witnessed this firsthand while delivering the letters the night before. Two families, who normally accepted them with gladness, had turned him away and refused to take any more. He couldn't blame them, but it hurt to see their faith shaken by fear. *Give us all renewed strength, Lord.*

"Is there something you want to talk about?"

Snapping from his wandering thoughts, Timothy blinked and settled his eyes on Josan. "I was just thinking about last night. With all the news of arrests and executions in Valcré, I'm afraid that, soon, no one will accept the letters. I want to encourage them not to give in to their fear, but it's difficult when I know as well as they do that we could all be killed for it."

The conflict constantly warred inside of him. He desired to live his faith boldly and empower others to do so as well but, at the same time, he struggled against his repulsion at the thought of lost lives. While he wouldn't hesitate to die for his faith, the prospect of others perishing ripped at his soul.

Josan's face softened in compassion. "Unfortunately, we live in a time where we may be forced to choose between denying our faith or dying for it. Elôm knows I've spent my entire life praying it wouldn't come to this, but it has. We can't change that. But we can continue to encourage those around us, and use every opportunity to point to Him. It may come to a time where only one or two will listen, but you know Elôm wants us to press on, even with just those one or two."

Latching on to these words, Timothy felt not only a renewed sense of purpose, but also the renewed strength he sought. He smiled at Josan as he thanked Elôm for the blessing of a wise mentor.

Door hinges creaked, and Timothy looked over his shoulder. Aaron stepped into the room, shoving his arms into his jerkin.

"What're you trying to do, make me lazy?" he asked as he adjusted the collar and worked on the buckles.

Timothy and Josan traded a quick smile.

"I wasn't going to leave you for too long," he assured his brother as he rose to put the scroll away and return his chair to the table.

Josan reached for his crutches and pushed himself up. "I have breakfast and lunch made for you." He nodded to two small wrapped bundles and a cloth-covered plate.

Aaron lifted the cloth to uncover two pale biscuits and small wedges of cheese. "Thanks, Josan." He looked across at Timothy. "We'll have breakfast on the way. We need to get to the high country if we're going to see anything, and that'll take a couple of hours."

Timothy went to the door, where he pulled on his coat and boots. Aaron strapped on his bow and a full quiver of arrows. After packing their lunches into their bags and filling their waterskins, they each picked up a biscuit and cheese wedge.

"We'll probably be late," Aaron told Josan at the door. "Don't wait on us for supper."

Josan nodded, and Aaron pulled the door open. Timothy shivered at the icy dawn breeze as they stepped out. He glanced at the clear sky. It was no longer the black of night, but a deep blue. Lights already twinkled across town as the inhabitants set about another grueling day. He and Aaron turned and set out to the south, the scraping of rocks underfoot ringing out in the frozen air.

"I'll be praying for a successful day," Josan called after them.

Timothy raised his hand in a wave of thanks.

Josan watched them from the door until they were well on their way down the valley. He breathed out a sigh that lingered as a white cloud in the air. He wished for all the world that he could give them better than this. Often times, he thought of taking them to Dorland, to his people. They would be safe there, and comfortable. But those forests lay a long, long way from this valley. With barely enough money to live on, and his handicap . . . He shook his head.

Yet, that wasn't what kept them here. Not really. He would have moved them out in a heartbeat if he truly believed it was Elôm's will for them. After years of pleading prayers, he had not yet received 'yes' for an answer. For some reason beyond his understanding, Elôm wanted them here, and though only Aaron knew of this, he believed it was because of Timothy. Elôm had a plan for him—he was sure of it. So, for better or for worse, they remained and waited. Like Aaron, he was willing to sacrifice anything—his comfort, his other leg, even his own life—to help Timothy succeed.

The two young men finally faded from his sight, and his eyes drifted to the dreary sight of town. Of all the places and ways Timothy could have grown up. He could have lived in a city and received formal teaching. His father could have had a safer, less demanding job that wouldn't have cut short his life. He had been such a wonderful father, guiding young Timothy in his ever-growing faith. Even living among the cretes, who normally didn't have time for books, would have presented Timothy with more opportunities. But he was here, in this mean, dirty town, where he was constantly strained to his limits just to help bring food to the table and still have time to spend in Elôm's Word—something he craved even more than his body craved rest and nourishment. *Why is this, Lord?*

But Josan knew better than most that Elôm operated in ways no soul of Ilyon could hope to understand, and he trusted his Lord's promise that it would come to good in the end.

Jace was warm. Too warm, actually, and wedged in between two immovable objects. How had he gotten into such a predicament? Sleep still clouded his mind, but then it all cleared. His eyes blinked open. Pale sunlight shone through the underside of Gem's wing. He raised his head. The dragon had wrapped her own head around under her wing and cradled both him and Tyra between her neck and body. He didn't even remember her doing it. How deeply had he slept? He hadn't expected any sleep last night, considering his turmoil.

When he shifted to relieve his cramped muscles, Gem's eyes popped open. Lifting her head, she looked at him a moment, then pulled her neck away and lifted her wing to let him out. Tyra rose and trotted out first. Jace pushed to his feet and ducked out after her. Chilly and invigorating morning air washed over him as he stretched the kinks out of his back and shoulders.

Beside him, Gem arched her back and stretched out her wings. She peered at him, her eyes alert and vibrant. Then something caught her attention. She stepped forward and sunk her claws into the deer that still lay there. Lowering her head, she tore a massive bite off its hindquarters and gulped it down. Jace's mouth dropped open. One corner lifted in a smile as she devoured the deer piece by piece. Joy like he'd rarely known filled his heart and a whispered, "Thank You," passed his lips. It wasn't often he felt that a prayer of his had been answered.

"Well, I *am* impressed."

Jace spun around.

Talas stood behind him, wearing a look of true admiration that grew into a grin. "You have a gift."

Jace shrugged. He'd only shown Gem concern. It wasn't as if he'd actually done anything. He glanced past Talas and caught sight of Leetra. Her expression lifted in what he believed to be surprise. However, she quickly erased all hint of it. He didn't need her approval, anyway.

Gem finished the deer and brought her nose around to whiffle the hair at the back of his head with her hot breath. He looked back and rubbed her chin. After a little purr, she began making other cat-like noises that seemed much too dainty and sweet for such a large, fearsome creature.

"There's no doubt about it," Talas said with a chuckle. "Whether you like it or not, Gem has adopted you as her new rider. You'd have to kill her to get rid of her."

Jace shook his head. "I'd never want to do that."

As if showing her appreciation, Gem rested her chin heavily on his shoulder, which nearly tipped him off balance.

Talas laughed again. "I'm sure you'll enjoy her. She was always an affectionate one."

Jace reached up to pat Gem's cheek. The dragon then lifted her head to gaze curiously toward the cabins. Jace turned to find Kyrin walking toward them.

She smiled brightly. "Looks like you and Tyra have a new best friend."

"I guess so," he responded. As she drew closer, he said, "Gem, *ámi.*"

The dragon chirped and lowered her head to examine Kyrin, who rubbed her chin, eliciting a purr. Kyrin giggled. "She's a sweetie."

"This is why we tried so hard with her," Talas told them. "We knew what a shame it would be to lose her." He looked over his shoulder at the other dragons. "I guess this means we'll have to find a new rider for Shalmar. I'll have to discuss it with Trask."

Good thing Jace hadn't tried to bond with her. He certainly didn't need two dragons to care for. Though he didn't know exactly what that care would entail yet, the way Gem had gulped down a whole deer in less than five minutes had him imagining hunting trips devoted solely to feeding the creatures.

Kyrin nodded to Talas, saying, "You can talk to him over breakfast. I came to let you know Lenae has it just about ready."

Talas rubbed his stomach. "I look forward to it after the meal last night."

"She's an amazing cook," Kyrin agreed.

Drawn by the promise of good food, Talas headed down toward the fire. Kyrin lingered behind with Jace. Stroking Gem's neck, she looked up at him. "Are you going to have breakfast?"

He hadn't given it much consideration yet this morning, but thoughts of flying rushed into his mind, and his stomach promptly tied in a knot. "I don't think so."

"Me neither," Kyrin said sympathetically. "My stomach's been doing somersaults all morning."

He stared into her eyes, trying to read the thoughts behind them and decipher whether or not she said it only for his benefit, but he lacked her acute observation skills. She appeared entirely serious.

"I still don't know if I can do it," he confessed.

A little frown crinkled her forehead. "Have you always been afraid of heights?"

Jace nodded and dropped his eyes. Where was his courage? How could it have so completely abandoned him?

"Is there a reason?"

Jace winced, and a chill rippled through his body at the vague, yet gripping, memories stored deep inside him. "I don't remember it exactly. I was only five, at the most. I fell in a pit—an old well, maybe. I can't remember how, or who got me out, or if I was hurt. I only remember falling." Even now, the memory of it turned his mouth to cotton and made his palms damp.

"I see," Kyrin murmured. "It's hard to overcome things like that, especially when it happens as children." She smiled sympathetically. "There's a cave near my house back home. My brothers used to play there all the time, but once they scared me so badly that I still don't like caves."

The understanding and kindness in her expression couldn't help but relieve some of his fear. It forced him to remember that he wouldn't be around to protect her on the mission if he didn't go through with this. In the end, that fear had to trump his fear of heights. He focused for a moment on Gem before his eyes rested back on Kyrin.

"Your brothers were mean to you."

A lovely little chuckle bubbled from Kyrin. "They're brothers. That's what they do. But they always make up for it." Resting her hand on his arm, she nodded to where the others had gathered for breakfast. "Come on. We don't have to eat, but I'm curious who will get Shalmar."

The time had come. Either he had to face his fear or admit defeat in front of the whole group. Jace's insides squeezed as if his stomach were going to cave in on itself as everyone, including Warin, who now owned Shalmar, gathered at the dragons. He focused on calming himself and controlling his pulse. Though he maintained an appearance of attentiveness while Talas instructed him on how to saddle Gem, the words didn't quite penetrate. His own admonishments and misgivings warred too loudly in his head. While every nerve in his body screamed for surrender, his sense of duty and need to protect Kyrin kept him from fleeing.

Still, he had to fight to make his tense limbs work when it came time to mount. Gem crouched down, and he gripped the saddle to drag himself up onto her back. She straightened as he settled in, and he momentarily squeezed his eyes shut. The dragon wasn't too much taller than a horse, but it still dizzied him. And though he trusted Gem, some irrational fear scrambled through his mind that she might take off with him before he was ready.

*Get a hold of yourself.* He shook his head. Never in all his life had he been such a coward. Fearing he had no soul, fearing he would hurt someone or would see someone he cared about hurt—those were rational fears he struggled with—but this? This was childish. He gritted his teeth. Why couldn't he just let it go?

He glanced at the others who were either mounted or in the process of mounting. What he wouldn't give for even a small amount of the confident anticipation that radiated from Kaden's expression. Even Rayad looked ready to get this over with. A groan rose in Jace's throat, and he looked around for a distraction while he battled his nerves. His eyes caught on Kyrin. She stood with Talas, who listened closely to something she said. When the crete nodded, she gave him a quick smile and then mounted Ivoris.

Talas turned to face his cousin. "Lee, you can work with everyone who has been up already. I'll instruct the others."

The girl's eyes narrowed. "Why can't we all work together?"

"Because. Now go on. We'll be right behind you."

Leetra's brows shot up at his firm tone, and she cast a glance at Jace. His neck and cheeks burned. Some part of him had hoped his fear wasn't quite so apparent, but he'd been fooling himself.

"Fine," she sighed. She set her gaze on the others. "Let's go."

In a flurry of wings, most of the riders took to the sky. Jace grabbed the saddle bar when Gem flinched in anticipation, but she stayed where she was. Even so, his heart battered his ribcage. He wasn't ready for this. Panic-fueled impulses to escape assaulted him with every heartbeat.

Once the dragons flew out of sight, Talas walked over to Gem. Jace shifted, struggling with humiliation, but Talas spoke kindly.

"I just wanted to let you know you're in good hands. Gem has four years of flight experience with a rider. Dragons are trained never to let their riders fall so, if anything happens, which is highly unlikely, she'll catch you. You can trust her."

Jace sucked in a deep breath and gave a brief nod. Right then, Gem looked back, as if asking him to trust her.

Talas walked back to Storm, and Jace watched him mount the dragon without a saddle, since Warin was using his on Shalmar. How the crete could fly without it baffled him.

"Ready?" Talas asked.

Jace glanced around. Everyone watched him, waiting. The pressure of their gazes settled inside his chest. Tremors passed through his hands as he gripped the saddle bar, and he bit his bottom lip, almost too hard. *Come on.* He had to do this. Sweat trickled down the center of his back. How many foes had he conquered before this? And now he couldn't even move.

"Just get her up, and she can follow Storm until you're ready to fly on your own."

Jace breathed quickly in and out. *Just get her up.*

"Gem . . ." He worked his throat to try to loosen the next word. Finally, scraping together every fleeing scrap of courage, he commanded, "*Unai.*"

The seconds that followed sent terror streaking straight through him. He locked his jaw shut to keep from taking back the command as Gem spread her wings. A moment later, she launched into the air, and it was as though both Jace's stomach and his heart were left behind. He gripped the saddle bar so fiercely his fingers hurt, and he squeezed his eyes shut.

"Elôm," he gasped, but the speed sucked the plea right out of his mouth.

Somewhere amidst the rushing of blood and wind in his ears, Talas's voice came through.

"Gem, *réma.*"

After a few mind-numbing seconds, they stopped climbing and evened out. But Jace couldn't open his eyes. Not yet. First, he had to focus on breathing. The thought of the ground rushing by, far below, paralyzed him. Yet, he couldn't just sit there and wait it out. He'd overcome one hurdle—now he had to face the next.

Still barely breathing, he forced his eyes open. The sight stole any air he'd managed to take into his lungs. Many miles of the forest stretched out around them, bringing a dizzying mix of awe and terror. His eyes watered in the cold wind. He closed them for a moment more and, once again, summoned his courage.

When he opened them, he focused on Gem's head to ignore the heights for the time being. Right now, he had to get his lungs to expand and his heart to cooperate. He wasn't altogether sure it was even beating. All he could feel was a dull ache in his chest that worked its way through the clenched muscles of his arms and jaw.

Several minutes passed in a blur until, finally, some intelligent thoughts seeped through the pulsing panic. One of the first things to come to his attention was how secure the saddle actually felt. It really would be hard to fall off, unless Gem tilted too sharply. It also became clear how much the dragon loved flying. The act came as naturally to her as walking did to him. These small revelations helped free up his lung, and, though his grip on the saddle bar didn't loosen, some of his muscles began to relax.

Eventually, he risked a look around. Kyrin, Rayad, and Warin flew nearby. When he looked ahead, past Talas and Storm, he spotted the others in the distance, who appeared to be trying out more skillful maneuvers. Jace shook his head. As long as he could take off, fly to a certain destination, and land again, it would be enough for him. He had no desire to attempt anything more. He'd leave that to someone like Kaden.

The last thing Jace paid any attention to was the path of the sun, but a good while later, Talas pulled back to come alongside him.

"Ready to try it on your own?" he shouted over the wind.

Jace swallowed the panic clawing his throat and tingling across his nerves. "I don't know."

"When you are, just use the guide bar or commands, and she'll go wherever you want her to go."

Talas put more distance between them again, and Jace contemplated. Really, what had he to lose? It wasn't like he and Gem would crash to the ground if he made a mistake. He couldn't rely solely on Talas to lead them all the way to the

Graylin Valley. He only had one short day to master this. Still firmly grasping the saddle bar with his left hand, he reached for the guide bar. Gem's head perked up at the connection between them.

With a heart-whispered prayer, Jace nudged the bar to the right. In a smooth motion, Gem moved out to the right of Storm. Talas glanced back and gave Jace a grin. In that moment, relief showered Jace. He hated heights and the terror of falling—he always would—but he'd faced it. He'd conquered the fear. Now he could join the mission and wouldn't have to face the embarrassment and shame of cowardice.

The sun was well past its peak when the entire group landed back at the edge of camp. When Jace slid down from Gem, his legs almost gave out. He stood, gripping the saddle until his bones solidified again, and relished the firm ground under his feet. If he could, he'd never go up again, but at least that dreaded first flight was behind him. The uncertainty had been the worst.

Patting Gem's shoulder, he murmured, "Good girl."

He stepped away from her and pulled in deep breaths. This was the first time his heart rate had a chance to normalize in the last several hours. He hadn't been so emotionally and physically drained in a long time. Already, his body ached from the prolonged tension. His thoughts drifted toward his cot. It would feel good to sleep tonight.

A moment later, Kyrin came from Ivoris with a huge grin on her face. "You did it!"

She threw her arms around his neck. He stumbled back a step as his legs wobbled, but then regained his balance. Kyrin didn't seem to notice. Releasing him, she looked up, her eyes alight. "I am *so* proud of you."

Warmth spread through Jace's chest, momentarily erasing the aches and making all the fear he'd faced worth it. It made no difference what anyone else thought. He'd succeeded, and she was proud of him.

The height of the mountains released something inside Timothy. It was as if he could breathe more easily and think more clearly. Perched at the very edge of a cliff, he stared out at the surrounding mountain peaks, lit up in brilliant shades of orange and pink from the sinking sun, and praised Elôm for displaying such glory. If only Josan could see it. Sometimes Timothy didn't know how the crete survived in their little cottage when he should have lived in the trees. But everyone had to adapt to their circumstances.

Pebbles scattered as Aaron slid down the descent behind him, and he turned away from the cliff's edge.

"We made good time," his brother said as he shifted his pack.

Timothy agreed. In another hour they'd be home, both loaded down with fresh meat from two mountain goats. Elôm had answered Josan's prayers in abundance. At least they would have food on the table long enough to figure out how best to deal with Timothy's pay cut.

Aaron took the lead, and Timothy followed him along a narrow ledge no sane person would normally consider passable. But they were both as surefooted as the goats they carried. That aspect of their crete blood had not skipped over Timothy—their ease at great heights. He would have loved to build a cabin up here in the cliffs, far above the grime and smoke of the valley. Perhaps someday, if life ever changed. And maybe he'd even have a family of his own. But he'd want to be able to provide for them far better than he could now. He didn't see things changing drastically enough in the near future.

They picked their way along at a good pace, and caught their first glimpse of Dunlow shortly after sunset. Lanterns bobbed in a line in the distance as the miners headed home for the evening. According to Aaron, they'd still been disgruntled about their pay cuts. Hopefully they hadn't stirred up any trouble without Aaron there to be the voice of reason.

Timothy's thoughts snapped away from the miners, and he slid to an abrupt halt when Aaron reached out to stop him. In the growing dimness, about a hundred feet below them, six soldiers marched along the road toward town—their stark uniforms standing out against the deep blues and grays of twilight. Timothy's arms prickled under his sleeves as a chill swept through him. Neither he nor Aaron said a word until the men were well past.

"What do you think they're up to?" Timothy asked in a low voice.

Soldiers in Dunlow were rare. He hadn't seen any since the emperor's decree concerning the worship of any gods besides Aertus and Vilai. Was that what had brought them here? His thoughts jumped to Josan, and his heart gave a heavy thud.

Aaron shook his head. "Maybe they're here about taxes. You know how tight-fisted Tolman is."

His tone held hope that it didn't mean anything more than that, but doubt wormed and twisted in Timothy's gut, warning him of something more sinister. He tried to dismiss it. He was probably just on edge because of his conversation with Josan. But one glance at Aaron told him his brother was just as edgy.

"Come on," Aaron said finally.

At the cottage, they shrugged off their heavy packs and groaned as they stretched their sore backs. Pulling out their bundles of meat, they placed them in a sturdy, locked box. This much food would be a strong temptation for both wild animals and people, even those who normally wouldn't be considered criminals.

Blowing on his chilled fingers, Timothy followed Aaron to the door, ready to rest, eat, and get warmed up. Josan smiled and stoked the fire as they walked in. "You're pretty early. I hope that means the hunting was good."

"We got two nice goats," Aaron told him, but there was a noticeable lack of enthusiasm in his tone.

Josan frowned and straightened to face them. "What happened?"

Timothy and Aaron hung their coats and equipment by the door as Aaron answered, "We just saw six soldiers on their way into town."

Timothy watched Josan's reaction carefully to gauge his concern. The lines in Josan's forehead deepened, but then he said, "If there were only six of them, it can't be cause for too much concern."

Aaron shrugged. "I hope you're right."

LUCKILY, ENOUGH OF Talas's instructions from the day before stuck in Jace's mind, and dragon saddles weren't too much more complicated than a horse's. With a couple of glances at the others to be sure he was doing it right, he successfully saddled Gem without the need to ask for assistance—a great relief. His fear of heights was enough of an embarrassment for a while. After fastening all his belongings securely at the back of the saddle, he took a mental inventory one last time. Cold-weather gear would be essential, with winter ready to set in. Satisfied, he pulled on a pair of wool-lined leather gloves.

Sunlight glowed orange low in the trees. He turned to scan the rest of the group. Most of camp still slept at this early hour, though Warin and Lenae stood nearby. Lady Anne and her father, Sir John, had arrived a short time ago to see them off. While the others exchanged their farewells, Jace knelt in front of Tyra and rubbed her neck. He had never left her alone for more than a day before. He glanced around camp. No one seemed to mind her now, but leaving her alone unsettled him.

"I'll be back soon," he murmured. If only she could truly understand him. He looked into her trusting eyes. It would be hard to leave her comforting presence. She had always been one of the few constants in his life, and offered a sense of security he hadn't fully realized until now.

The approach of footsteps drew Jace's attention. Lenae bent down beside him to pet Tyra's head.

"Warin and I will look after her," the woman promised with a smile. "She's welcome in my cabin whenever she likes."

Comforted, Jace nodded. He may not trust everyone in camp, but he did trust her and Warin. "Thank you." He rose to his feet again and gently commanded Tyra, "Stay."

The wolf tipped her head, but obeyed.

Final goodbyes echoed around Jace, and everyone moved toward their dragons. Mounting Gem, he looked once more at Tyra, and then focused on the day ahead. His heart rate picked up, anticipating the flight. He blew out a slow breath and glanced over at Kyrin, who offered him an encouraging smile. Recalling the pride in her eyes the day before steadied him.

"Our prayers go with you," Warin told them.

Trask thanked him, and then nodded at Talas and Leetra. "Lead the way."

The two cretes and their dragons took to the air. Wings flapped all around. With momentary hesitation to gather his courage, Jace commanded Gem to follow. Again, the climb snatched his breath away, but this time he managed to keep his eyes open. The trees rushed by in a dim blur. A wave of fear threatened to take hold but, once they leveled out, he forced it down and relaxed in the saddle.

Their first glimpse of the Sinnai Mountains came into view a couple of hours before sundown. Jace looked on them with interest and a good measure of awe. It had been years since he'd seen any mountains. The jagged peaks were silhouetted against a gold-tinted sky and, below them, rocky brown terrain and clumps of trees cast long shadows in the evening light.

He looked south. Though it was not quite visible from this distance, Valcré wasn't far away. He grimaced at the thought of it; not only because of the emperor, but also because of his past memories. He couldn't think of Valcré without Jasper's harsh voice echoing in his ears, or remembering the cold rejection of eyes peering at him as if he were something altogether inhuman.

Fixing his gaze back on the mountains, he shook off the recollections. The number of miles they had covered was incredible. On horseback, the journey would have taken two full days to reach this point, but the dragons had made it in less than a day, with only two short stops along the way. Though he would always prefer horses as his mode of travel, Jace couldn't deny the practicality of flying.

The large shape of another dragon soared into the sky when they neared the mountain cliffs. Ahead of the group, Talas waved a greeting. Jace recognized the new dragon rider as Captain Darq, and they followed him deeper into the mountains. Gliding between the steep peaks, they came to a narrow plateau of rock and scrub bushes, and set down there. It was barely wide enough to accommodate all the dragons, and Jace had to stop himself from glancing over his shoulder, where there would certainly be a steep drop. With confident maneuvering, Darq turned his dragon around to face Talas and Trask.

"I'm glad you made it in good time." His eyes made a quick sweep of the group, and he nodded in what appeared to be satisfaction.

"Any news?" Talas asked.

"I've been keeping an eye on Keth." Darq gestured over his shoulder. Jace looked past him, but whatever town he referred to wasn't in sight. "A company of soldiers arrived two days ago. Yesterday, they sent a small party north, I assume, to Dunlow.

Then, this morning, the rest of the company followed."

"I guess they didn't find anything in Keth then."

Darq shook his head. "It would seem not." His gaze shifted to Trask. "I don't like that they're ahead of us. We must try to overtake them, but we can't pass over Keth just because they did. I know you've traveled far today, but would you and your people be willing to make a quick search of the village this evening?"

"Of course," Trask said without hesitation.

"Good. It's only a small settlement, so it shouldn't take long. Once we know Josan isn't there, we'll head to Dunlow. I've sent the others ahead to set up camp and keep an eye on things. If you can avoid the soldiers and make a quick search of Dunlow tomorrow morning, we can move on before they're finished and keep ahead of them."

Trask nodded. "We'll do everything we can to make that happen."

"We appreciate it. I'll show you where you can leave your dragons out of sight and get down to the village."

With a command, they all took to the air again and continued to the west. A couple of minutes later, they landed in a deep ravine and dismounted. Darq motioned to them as he climbed the sharp rise at one side, and they followed him up to the edge. When Jace discovered the sheer, two-hundred-foot drop on the other side, he sucked in his breath and shrank back involuntarily. Heat flushed his neck. He glanced at the others, but no one seemed to notice.

Once he'd come to grips with the height, he set his focus out past the drop. Down in the rocky valley rested a small mining village, comprised of around one hundred fifty rough buildings and tiny shacks scattered across the outskirts. It looked almost dead. If not for a couple of people moving off in the distance, he would have thought the village abandoned.

After taking a moment to assess it, Trask said, "Since the soldiers have moved on, it's probably safe to split into pairs. We'll cover the area faster that way." He shifted to look at them. "Kaden, Trev, you two take the northwest corner. Kyrin and Jace can take the northeast. Rayad and I will cover the southwest, and Mick and Holden the southeast. We'll meet in the middle."

Each of them nodded and descended the rise to return to the dragons, where they collected their weapons.

"Ask around for Josan Silvar," Darq told them, "but don't mention he's a crete. We don't want that name getting back to the emperor in association with the cretes and have him piece things together."

With these instructions, Trask took the lead along the narrow, washed-out ditch that led out of the ravine and worked its way down to the valley floor. At least it didn't involve any sheer cliffs. At a steep section near the bottom, Jace half-stepped, half-slid down the loose gravel and then turned back to offer Kyrin a hand. She smiled her appreciation, and he helped her down. The ground evened out a bit after this, and they came to the edge of the village. Here, the group split in half, heading to either end. When Jace, Kyrin, Kaden, and Trev reached the northern end, they paused before splitting again.

"Be careful," Kyrin told her brother.

"You too." Kaden sent a purposeful glance at Jace.

Gripping his sword, Jace gave a slight nod to assure him that he'd take on the whole village and die before letting any harm befall Kyrin. Satisfied, Kaden and Trev went on. Kyrin watched them for a moment, and then looked up at Jace.

"Ready?"

Jace peered at the streets ahead of them, but didn't find anything of immediate concern. He nodded, and they walked into the village. They passed the first buildings, on the lookout for any people or shops where they could gather information, but quietness surrounded them. The place seemed nearly as dead as it had from above. It sent a cool prickle along Jace's skin, and he scanned every corner and alley carefully.

"I sure wouldn't want to live here," Kyrin said in a low murmur. "It's so . . . gloomy."

Jace agreed. There wasn't a tree in sight. That alone bothered him. The only place to seek cover would be up, into the mountains.

They went a little farther, and he self-consciously tugged his sleeves down past his wrists to conceal the dark hair along his arms that was a little too telling of his ryrik blood, and made sure his hair covered his pointed ears. If they ever did come across anyone to question, the last thing they needed was for someone to suspect him of being a ryrik. The only things he couldn't hide were his eyes. Maybe he hadn't been a good choice for this mission. The cretes had come to Trask for help so they wouldn't raise suspicion, and here he risked just that. He cleared his throat, loathing himself as he said to Kyrin, "I think you should do the talking. Someone might notice I'm different and get suspicious."

She said nothing, but nodded and pulled her shoulders back with a determined expression.

Jace sighed. He hated putting the burden on her. She would have been better off with Kaden instead. But he could at least protect her. He set his focus back on the roads ahead. They could hardly be called such—only hard-packed, crooked paths between the buildings. It appeared that the founders had built the town in a hurry—however long ago that was. He and Kyrin stuck to the largest, most well-traveled paths. Jace was just beginning to wonder if they would find anyone when, at last, they came upon a wrinkled, hunched-over old man. Thick dirt and grime coated him as if it had been there for years.

Kyrin took a breath and walked up to him. "Excuse me, sir?"

The old man squinted up at them, his weather-beaten face full of deep lines. "Aye?"

"Do you know a man named Josan Silvar?"

The man's eyes closed further as he mumbled the name back to himself and tugged at his long, scraggly beard. Finally, he shook his head. "Never heard of 'im."

Kyrin gave him a kind smile. "Thank you for your time."

The man grunted and hobbled on.

"He looks like he's lived here for a quite a while." Kyrin turned to Jace. "Surely he'd know Josan if he were here."

Jace agreed. Though they continued the search, everyone they met had the same answer. No one knew Josan Silvar. However, Jace did get the sense that the villagers were nervous. Many hesitated and darted shadowed glances at him before answering Kyrin's questions. It could have been him, but he suspected something else had them spooked.

Not quite an hour later, they arrived at what appeared to be the center of the village. All the major paths converged here, so they stopped. They didn't have long to wait for the others. Kaden and Trev approached a few minutes later, quickly followed by the rest of the group. Everyone had had the same experience.

"All the villagers we talked to said they didn't know him, and no one appeared to be lying," Kyrin told Trask. "I don't think Josan has ever been here."

"Well, you had better luck than we did," he replied. "Most people we met only shook their heads and walked away."

"Maybe I seemed like less of a threat," Kyrin suggested. "I think they're all on edge from the soldiers. We probably weren't the first ones to question them."

"All the more reason to get ahead of the emperor's men." Trask looked up at the mountains. "Let's get back to Darq and move on to Dunlow."

Dusk had overtaken the land when Jace first noticed the thick gray smudge on the horizon ahead. He frowned. At first, he thought it only a cloud but, after drawing closer, he concluded that it was smoke. Before he had a chance to discover its source, Darq veered off deeper into the mountains. Jace scanned the peaks and spotted a small pinprick of light. It quickly took the shape of a campfire, and they all landed on a plateau, thankfully wider than the last.

He dismounted and sighed when his feet touched the ground. He'd forgotten how taxing travel and new situations could be. He joined the group gathering in front of the dragons, where the two cretes from the campfire met them. One was Darq's lieutenant, who Jace had heard Talas call Glynn. The second crete was a stranger. Captain Darq took over introductions. It was a quick formality, with no great show of friendliness, particularly not from the new crete. He didn't say a word beyond giving his name—Falcor Tarn. Jace wasn't sure how it was possible for someone so much shorter to look down on him, but that's exactly what the crete did. Arms folded, he peered at them through hard blue eyes and never once came close to breaking a smile. Jace sensed no welcome from him at all, when at least the others, like Darq and Talas, displayed gratitude for their help.

Dismissing the crete's cold reception, Jace turned his focus to unsaddling Gem, who nuzzled his shoulder as he worked. Despite his weariness, he smiled and patted her neck. After a full day of flying with her, he did trust that she wouldn't let him fall.

Leetra crossed his field of vision on her way to her dragon. Jace couldn't help but notice how Falcor followed her and helped her with the saddle. It was the first time either of them smiled, though it did nothing to soften Falcor's rock-hard features. Jace dropped his eyes back to his work so he wouldn't be caught watching. He had a feeling neither one would take kindly to it.

Once the dragons were settled for the night, the group moved to the fire, where Glynn prepared supper. Jace joined Kyrin and Kaden in a small group off to the side, away from their disagreeable crete companions. For a long moment, they said nothing, but when Jace looked at Kyrin, he found a frown on her face as she stared ahead. He followed her gaze to Falcor and Leetra. The two sat at the opposite side of the fire, so close that their shoulders touched.

He turned to Kyrin again. "What's wrong?"

"I was just watching Falcor." She shrugged.

Kaden gave a small snort. "And I thought Leetra was unfriendly."

Kyrin glanced at her brother, but remained focused on the crete couple. "Falcor certainly is that." She shook her head, her brows still wrinkled as if she were trying to solve a puzzle. "The other cretes have only been wary of us, but with him, it's more. He doesn't like us."

Jace narrowed his eyes as his gaze settled on the crete, who talked quietly with Leetra. The hardness in his expression hinted of cruelty, which Jace had experienced too much of in his past.

Talas joined them a moment later, and the tense mood abated.

Kaden nodded to Falcor and Leetra. "They seem close."

Talas's brow quirked wryly. "They're betrothed. No doubt they'll be married as soon as we get back to Dorland."

"They're good for each other."

Jace fought a smile as Kyrin whispered her brother's name sharply, frowning at him.

Kaden shrugged, but was a little contrite when he looked at Talas. "Sorry."

But Jace had to agree with Kaden. They were a perfect match.

Talas just looked amused by it. "Don't be. You're starting to sound like a crete, just stating the facts." He chuckled, then lowered his voice a little. "Don't mind Falcor. He doesn't like me either. He's as crete as they come. That's why Leetra likes him."

"*Likes?*" Kyrin questioned. "Don't they love each other?"

Talas tipped his head in consideration. "They're a good match. They both know it and like it. Cretes are very practical. Love isn't always what first brings us together. Many times, it follows. I think they love each other . . . in a way."

Kyrin just shook her head. "I could never marry someone I didn't truly love."

Jace contemplated this. Though he didn't know a thing about love, he agreed with Kyrin. If he were ever to marry, it would have to be based on something far more than being a good match. But the thought of marrying was so foreign to him that he'd never given it any consideration before—maybe because he always knew, even without thinking it, that it would never happen. How could it? What kind of husband would he be? And what woman would ever marry him?

"So, what about Lieutenant Glynn?"

Kyrin's question snapped Jace from his wild thoughts. How had his mind worked its way down such a strange, unfamiliar path anyway? He shook off his strange curiosity with the subject and glanced over at the crete in question. Darq's lieutenant hadn't spoken more than a quiet greeting when they'd met. Yet, he didn't exhibit the same coldness as Falcor.

"Glynn is a man of few words," Talas responded with a smile, but it faded. "His mother died when he was young, and his father, well, let's just say alcohol is his constant companion. Glynn's brothers are quite a bit older than him and not much better. No one really knew what was going on with them until Darq happened to come by during one of Glynn's father's drunken rages several years back. He'd beaten Glynn up pretty badly, and not for the first time, apparently. Darq stepped in and invited Glynn to come stay with his family. They've been like brothers ever since. Glynn might not say a lot, but he's a good man, regardless of the situation he came from."

Jace looked at Glynn again with a stirring of kinship. While his own abuse hadn't come from family, he did understand it. He didn't know much about the cretes, but it seemed every race had their issues and individuals who resorted to violence and cruelty. With a glance at Kyrin, he found the look of sympathy and compassion in her eyes that had helped pull him out of his darkest pit. The rare people like her were the ones who made up for the cruelty he'd always found much more common.

TIMOTHY DRAGGED A length of chain off a supply wagon parked outside the warehouse. His shoulders burned as it slid down and they took the full one-hundred-pound weight. Gritting his teeth, he carried it into the warehouse and dropped it on the ground with the five others he'd already unloaded. He braced his hand against the wall and wiped his dripping forehead. His drenched shirt clung uncomfortably to his skin.

Complaints crowded in with his fatigue, but he combatted them by thanking Elôm it wasn't mid-summer with the sun beating down on top of him. And at least he still had his job, despite the way Harold snapped and grumbled at every opportunity. If he could just hold onto it until spring arrived. Food wouldn't be quite so scarce then. It would take practice, but at least he could spend the days hunting. He just had to convince Harold of the benefit of keeping him through the winter.

He filled his lungs with the welcome cool air and straightened, stretching his back before heading to the wagon for the other four lengths of chain still waiting. When he stepped out of the warehouse, sudden ice encased his body and froze him in place. Harold stood outside the main shop, watching as five soldiers approached the warehouse, straight toward Timothy. He broke himself loose, but his heart beat sluggishly. He had only enough time to send up a desperate prayer and attempt to gather his wits before the first soldier reached him. A quick glance at the man's uniform told Timothy he was an officer. His stomach caved inward. None of these men had been in the group he and Aaron had witnessed. They were new, and they certainly weren't in town due to taxes as Aaron had hoped. Such business would have taken them to the mines.

The officer was quite young for a man of his position—maybe only a couple of years older than Timothy. His brown eyes suggested friendliness, but this offered only a fleeting comfort.

"I'm Captain Marcus Altair," the young man said, introducing himself. He did not speak harshly, yet his voice was crisp with professionalism as he scanned the warehouse behind Timothy, before returning his full attention to him. "According to your employer, you're half crete."

He waited expectantly.

Timothy looked toward the shop where Harold stood with his hands on his hips and his thick brows sunken. Had the man even considered looking out for Timothy's best interest, or had he blurted out his mixed race the moment the soldiers entered the shop? Dragging his eyes back to the captain, Timothy nodded in confirmation.

"What's your name?" Marcus asked.

"Timothy." He stood straight and tall to disguise his unease, and looked at the captain straight on. "Timothy Carliss."

"Timothy, we're looking for a crete man named Taan. We have a few questions for him. Do you know him?"

A phantom fist drove straight into Timothy's gut. He knew it. They were here about the letters . . . about the faith he had in Elôm. His skin went cold again. If these men gained the information they sought . . . He steadied himself and shook his head. After all, the name didn't actually belong to anyone. It was only a signature on the letters—a clan name.

"No."

The captain's gaze probed his for truthfulness, and Timothy held it without wavering. If he let his uncertainty slip now, they'd see right through him.

Finally, Marcus moved on to his next question. "We also heard you live with a crete man. What's his name?"

Timothy's heart hit his ribs with a solid thump. Instinct urged him to guard Josan's name at all costs, but if he refused to answer, it would mark him as guilty. They'd arrest him and find Josan anyway. Josan would never want that. Timothy could almost hear his adamant insistence that he answer the soldiers.

"Josan Silvar." Having to say it left his mouth bitter, as if he were condemning Josan with every word. He added quietly, "He's a friend."

The captain gave a short nod, keeping up his professional manner. "Where do you live?"

Timothy's throat squeezed around the words to block them, but he forced the answer. "In a cottage, on the far side of town." He gestured with a tip of his head, and heaviness pressed down on him. They would surely go there next.

"And is Mister Silvar there?"

"Yes." *I'm sorry, Josan.*

"Thank you for your cooperation. We appreciate it." Marcus turned and motioned to his men to follow.

Most of the soldiers moved immediately, but Timothy caught one of them watching him. He had the same brown eyes and hair as the captain, though he stood a couple of inches taller. Timothy couldn't read his expression. It was almost as if he were trying to figure something out but, in a moment, he fell in behind the other soldiers.

Timothy remained rooted to the spot until the men disappeared down the street. Then his breath gusted out of his lungs as the weight of the situation crashed in. He ran toward the shop.

Harold had gone inside, and looked squint-eyed at him when he burst through the door. With their questioning, the soldiers had now branded Timothy with suspicion, which would not be easy to live down in front of his employer. He snatched up his bag. "I need a couple of hours. I'll be back as soon as I can. I can work late to finish—"

"No." Harold's gruff voice cut in. "You can't just run off whenever you feel like it."

Timothy spun around to face him, and a spark of fight flared inside his chest. The man barely let him rest long enough to gulp down his lunch every day; surely he could spare him for an hour or two just this once. He forced himself to speak calmly. "I just want to be with Josan if the soldiers question him." If Harold hadn't tipped them off in the first place, he wouldn't need to go. "I won't be long."

Harold shook his head stubbornly. "You'll stay and work or you'll not come back at all."

The choice smacked Timothy like a physical blow, and he stood in crushing indecision. If the soldiers only questioned Josan as they had him and left without trouble, then he would throw his job away for nothing. They'd have to live only on Aaron's wages. It would never work.

He grimaced and almost dropped his bag, but some gut feeling stopped him. Even if the soldiers didn't cause trouble now, they could question others who might reveal that Timothy delivered the letters. That would lead them straight back to both him and Josan, and they would all certainly be arrested. The icy sensation churning inside him warned of this more sinister outcome. With a desperate prayer that he'd made the right choice, he looked at Harold. "I'm sorry."

He then turned and walked out the door. A moment of uncertainty gripped him, but outside, his focus centered on Josan and how little time he had. He glanced toward Tolman's mine. He could never find Aaron before the soldiers reached their home, so he dashed into the street. He had to get to Josan first—whether just to warn him or more, he wasn't sure yet, but he prayed for guidance.

Using all the most familiar shortcuts, Timothy raced through Dunlow. When he caught a flash of gold and black, he slowed and peered around the corner. Marcus and his men stood in the street, talking to a couple of the townspeople. Though Timothy couldn't hear their words, the men were nodding, and one gestured toward the edge of town. Doom settled around Timothy. Even if they knew nothing of the letters, if the men worked for Terrance Riggs, they might say anything just because Aaron worked for Tolman.

Timothy ducked into an alley and pressed on, not slowing even when his leg muscles felt like they might rip from strain and fatigue. He and Josan would need every second he could buy them to figure out what to do. *Please, Elôm, give us time.* He repeated the prayer in his mind. Right now, they were the only words he could formulate.

At last, panting, he scrambled up to the cottage and shoved open the door. "Josan!"

The crete fumbled for his crutches, using one and the edge of the table to push himself up. "What is it?"

Timothy could barely breathe and put his hand to the cramp in his side, but he forced out the words. "Soldiers are on their way here. They questioned me about the name Taan. They must know about the letters. They're coming to question you."

Josan's already-large eyes widened. "Do they suspect me of writing them?"

"I don't know." Timothy braced himself against the table and dragged a deep breath into his burning lungs. "They seem suspicious of anyone with crete blood. I saw them questioning people on the way here. What if someone saw me delivering the letters? If they learn anything about that, they'll arrest us."

He was always careful when he went out to deliver the letters, but all manner of people lurked the streets at night, scrounging for food scraps and old clothing. It would only take one of them to alert the soldiers, especially if they thought they could gain something from it. If he and Josan were arrested, it would be over. Thorough questioning would quickly expose their faith.

Josan grimaced. "You're right." He reached out and gripped Timothy's shoulder, gently pressuring him in the direction of the bedroom. "Gather your things and Aaron's. Take the Scrolls with you. The two of you need to get far away from here. I'll stay and do what I can to keep any suspicion from falling on you."

Timothy grabbed his arm and shook his head. "No. I won't leave you here." He'd only ever had three people he loved in this world. He wouldn't lose any more of them if he could help it. "If you stay to face them, I will too. Otherwise, you have to come with us."

Josan let out a sigh. "There's no time."

"Yes, there is." Timothy glanced out the door. No black and gold dotted the path to the cottage yet. "We have maybe ten or fifteen minutes before they get here. More if they keep stopping to question people. Gather whatever you need. We'll find somewhere for you to hide and I'll get Aaron. Then the three of us will get out of Dunlow."

Where they'd go after that, he couldn't say, but something told him they just needed to leave. The soldiers would eventually find what they were after if they stayed.

Josan didn't argue this time. He picked up his other crutch, and Timothy hurried to the bedroom. He grabbed Aaron's hunting pack first and stuffed his brother's clothes and belongings into it. They didn't have much besides their clothing and a few small sentimental items. Once he'd filled his own pack, he rolled up the blankets from their beds and dragged everything into the main room, where Josan worked as fast as he could to pack his things. Timothy caught bits of whispered prayer. His own joined in as he dropped to the floor to retrieve the satchel of scrolls. *This happened so fast, Lord. I don't know if I'm making the right decisions, but please lead us out safely and show us where to go from here.*

They couldn't take everything. Food, clothing, and their very little money took precedence. It wouldn't be nearly enough to start over somewhere else, and the coming winter loomed almost as threateningly as the soldiers. What if they couldn't even find shelter? They would freeze to death here in the mountains. But Timothy had to trust Elôm to provide for what they didn't have.

He helped Josan lift his pack onto his back, and then turned to his things. After securing the satchel's strap across his body, he lifted his pack up over one shoulder and Aaron's over the other, then knelt down to take the blankets under each arm. Grunting at the weight, he pushed to his feet and stepped to the door where he sighed, finding the way still clear.

He nodded to Josan. "Let's go."

The crete stepped out, but Timothy paused in the doorway, looking back over his shoulder into the only home he'd known since shortly after his father's death. Though they'd faced many trials here, it still held memories of all the years he had spent with Aaron and Josan—years he considered precious, despite the hardships. Maybe they were wrong to run like this . . .

But a subtle urging took hold of him again, as if an invisible hand was pulling him away, and he knew it was Elôm's will for them to leave. With this surety, he set his gaze ahead and took the lead, angling for the southern edge of town. He didn't think about the magnitude of what they were doing, not the fact that they'd be leaving behind friends they'd known for years without even saying goodbye, or that he'd never be able to explain to his students why he couldn't teach them anymore. Right now, he had to focus on escape. His life, Aaron's, and Josan's depended on it. *Elôm, help me.*

A few yards from the cottage, he looked back at Josan, who struggled to keep up on his crutches. Timothy slowed and cast an anxious glance toward where the soldiers would surely appear. They had to get out of the open before then. Nothing would condemn them faster than to have the soldiers find them in the midst of escape. If only he could help Josan run.

Slowly and steadily, they made it into the cover of town. Once they were within the shadows of the buildings, Timothy breathed a little more easily, though all his nerves prickled with apprehension. As a boy, he'd once followed his friends into an abandoned mine shaft they'd been forbidden to enter, but the anxiety of that rebellious moment paled alongside the life and death choices he had to make now. If only the consequences of being caught here only meant facing his father's disappointment, as painful as that had been.

In a narrow alley behind a stack of lumber, Timothy stopped and peered both ways before setting the packs down and facing Josan. "Hide here while I get Aaron."

He would have to be quick about it. As soon as those soldiers realized they were gone, a search would surely begin. If the emperor had gone to the trouble of sending soldiers to this remote valley, they wouldn't simply give up once they found Josan missing.

He turned to go, but Josan caught his shoulder. The crete's eyes shown as bright with determination as Timothy had ever seen, and it transferred into the strength of his grip.

"If you run into trouble, do not come back for me. Do you understand? You and Aaron get to safety, no matter what."

Timothy didn't respond for a long moment. How could he ever just leave Josan like that? He'd been like a father to him all these years. However, staring into those serious eyes, he couldn't refuse. He swallowed hard and barely gave a nod. His voice rough, he said, "We'll be here as soon as we can."

Josan squeezed his shoulder and let him go. Timothy forced himself to turn. *Elôm, please don't let this be the last time I see him.* He jogged out of the alley. On the street, he scanned for soldiers, but found the way clear and ran on. All the way across town again, he forced his legs to keep moving. The fresh adrenaline from the escape helped dull the pain.

Fifteen minutes later, he skidded to a halt at the mine work yard. The place teemed with miners. His eyes darted from face to face, and he prayed for one to be Aaron. When he didn't spot his brother, he went farther, avoiding the overseers. They'd throw him out for sure if they caught him trying to take Aaron away from his work. Instead, he stopped one of the miners heading into the mine.

"I'm looking for my brother, Aaron Carliss. It's an emergency. If you see him, please tell him I'm here."

The man nodded and disappeared into the mine. Timothy spun around and gave the same message to every man he could. After repeating it numerous times, he paused for a breath. His heart hadn't stopped racing since he left the warehouse. Lifting his face toward the sky, he closed his eyes and began to pray. *I always knew this might happen, Lord. I don't know if we'll get out, but we need Your guidance and protection. Please lead us past the soldiers to safety and show us what to do next. And if we're caught . . .*

He swallowed.

"Tim?"

His eyes popped open, and he spun toward the mine. The moment Aaron saw his face, he ran to meet him.

"What's going on?" His expression was tense. "One of the men said there was an emergency."

Timothy checked around for anyone who might be listening.

The miners appeared too focused on their work to notice them, but he kept his voice low. "Soldiers questioned me at the warehouse. They're looking for who wrote the letters. They went to question Josan, but I reached him first and we got out." He hesitated. The news would be as shocking and heavy as falling boulders in the mine. "Aaron, we have to get out of Dunlow before they find us."

Aaron's eyes grew wider, and his mouth opened, but he closed it again. He glanced across town, toward home, before nodding.

"Let's go." His voice was husky. After all, their familiar life, as difficult as it was, had just ended, and they faced an unknown future; one they didn't even have time to prepare for.

Timothy took the lead, and they moved quickly through town until they came across a small group of soldiers. The sight of their uniforms just about sent Timothy's heart through his ribs as he and Aaron dashed around a corner. They waited a moment, but the men hadn't spotted the two of them. Moving on, they took the streets more cautiously. When they finally reached the alley opposite Tolman's mine, Timothy breathed out a heavy sigh to see Josan still waiting there.

"Have you seen any soldiers?" Timothy asked.

Josan shook his head.

"Good. Hopefully they're sticking to the north and don't know we're gone yet." Timothy handed Aaron his pack. "I grabbed everything I could."

Aaron slid his arms through the straps and hoisted the pack up onto his back. His face had taken on the hard, determined expression Timothy was so used to when times were tough. It gave him a boost of strength to know he had his brother at his side and they could make decisions together.

"Well, we've always talked about leaving Dunlow," Aaron said in a deceptively light tone. "I just never expected it to be like this." He looked down the alley and immediately fell into the role of leader, quickly and easily assessing the situation. "We'll stick to the side streets for cover and head south. Once we leave the outskirts, we'll try to reach cover before anyone spots us."

He glanced at Josan. No doubt he shared Timothy's thoughts. If only the crete had both legs, they could all get to the high country where no one could find them. But that was impossible. They'd have to find safety elsewhere.

Wasting no more time, they headed out of the alley and turned south. Not five minutes later, the thump of fast-approaching footsteps shot adrenaline through Timothy's limbs. He and Aaron grabbed Josan, and they ducked into an alley to hide in the recess of a large door. Moments later, a group of soldiers hurried past.

Timothy shook his head. "They're looking for us."

Nearby, a voice shouted out orders. It wouldn't be long before the entire city swarmed with soldiers, narrowing their escape routes down to almost none. Timothy leaned his head back. *Elôm, what do we do?*

Aaron pushed away from the door and faced them. The look in his eyes stole Timothy's breath.

"I'll distract them and lead them away from here. Tim, you get Josan out. I'll catch up once you're safely away."

He moved to go, but Timothy grabbed his arm. "No!" Though Aaron tried to pull away, Timothy held firm. He was not a child anymore. Aaron couldn't escape him as easily as he had when he'd first taught Timothy how to wrestle. "We get out together. I won't let you sacrifice yourself."

"Who said anything about sacrifice?" Aaron flashed a grin, but it failed to reach his eyes. "I know this town like the back of my hand. They don't. They won't catch me."

"What if they do?"

"They won't."

Timothy hung his head. As much as he hated it, none of them would make it out of Dunlow without some sort of distraction, and Aaron was the best one to provide it. His brother had an uncanny knack for survival. How many cave-ins had he miraculously survived in the last several years?

"Tim, listen to me." Aaron's voice dropped to a grave degree. "Do not come back. I'll catch up with you, all right? Just don't come back." He stared at him, willing Timothy to voice his understanding. "Promise me, Tim."

Timothy looked away and shook his head. How could he make a promise like that, to just leave his brother to whatever fate befell him? And yet, Elôm would be the One to determine that fate. Timothy had to trust Him to keep his brother safe from the soldiers just as He'd kept him safe in the mines.

"I p . . ." His voice faltered. He cleared his throat. "I promise."

Now Aaron did give him a genuine, almost sad smile. And with that, he tugged himself free of Timothy's grip and ran out into the street.

LIAM COULDN'T STOP the clenching ache in the pit of his stomach as his brother gave out hasty orders to the men. This was one of his first real assignments, and it had unsettled him from the start. Why was it so important they find this man anyway? He was only one person. What harm could he do? According to the information they'd gained from other citizens, he didn't seem like much of a threat. Actually, most people had spoken of him fondly. It hardly seemed worth the time and energy Marcus had them put into this.

But with a sigh, Liam strode down the street to search, just as his brother had ordered. Marcus was so calm and sure about these things. He did his duty with ease and confidence. He never felt sick over it or questioned anything. Liam envied him. If only he could be the soldier they all expected him to be. He tried, but his heart was never in it. Just like today. When they'd found the cottage and discovered signs that the inhabitants had left in a hurry, his first instinct was to hope they wouldn't be found. It would be different if they were actually criminals, but how did simply believing something break the law? It made no sense.

A flash of movement caught his eye. He stopped short at the corner of an alley and looked down it. His already-aggravated stomach gave a violent twist. Two people attempted to flee—

one man missing a leg. One of his crutches slipped, and he would have crashed to the ground if the other man hadn't caught him. They looked back at Liam, their faces taut with grim acceptance. Recognition registered. The younger man was the same one they had questioned at the warehouse. He hadn't seemed like a criminal.

The one-legged crete pushed away from the other and braced himself against the building. "I'm the one you're looking for. Take me and let him go."

"Josan," the young man gasped.

The crete held up his hand to silence him, but his eyes locked with Liam's. "He was only trying to help me. He's of no concern to you."

The moisture fled Liam's mouth. These two stood at his mercy. Conflicting thoughts jumbled in his mind. Marcus had chosen to bring him along. He'd ordered him to search, and trusted he'd do his job. He'd be a hero if he brought them in, not the slow-witted fool most of the garrison believed he was. He could actually do something right for once. But could his conscience take that? With all the stories coming out of Valcré, he knew exactly what would happen to these two if he took them into custody.

He let his shoulders sag. No, better to continue as the fool than to live with the knowledge that he had caused the deaths of two people.

"Go." The word was past his lips before he could give it too much thought.

They stared at him, their eyes wide and unblinking.

"Get out of here," Liam said more firmly, "before someone else sees you."

Breaking loose from the shock, the younger grabbed the elder's fallen crutch and handed it to him.

"Thank you," he said, and they rushed on as fast as they could.

Liam silently urged them to hurry as he watched until they were almost out of the alley. When someone called his name, he jumped and spun around. Marcus strode toward him, and his heart skittered as if caught. He glanced down the alley. The two men had just disappeared. He faced Marcus again, and his brother's brows lowered.

"Did you see anyone?"

Liam shook his head. "No." He winced at the lie.

"Well, come on," Marcus said with no sign of suspicion. The fact that he believed him entirely only fueled Liam's regret. "Parker thought he saw someone fleeing north."

Liam took another quick look down the alley before he hurried after his brother. At least the other men had gone the opposite direction.

Kyrin wrinkled her nose. "What's all the smoke from?"

Even at the southern end of Dunlow, a thick haze hung over the city, coating the inside of her nostrils and leaving a bitter taste in her mouth. The way it settled heavily in her lungs was almost suffocating. How did people survive here?

"Ore smelters," Mick answered. "In a town like this, they run almost constantly."

Kyrin tried to take a deep breath, but coughed. "It's horrible." She shook her head and looked up at Jace. "You shouldn't be here."

His hesitance to reply told her she was right, but he said, "I'll be fine."

She didn't believe that for a moment. If they didn't get any definitive answers quickly, she would leave and he would follow. She wouldn't risk him becoming seriously ill.

She turned her eyes to the buildings ahead. Though the town

was much larger and more populated, it didn't appear any more welcoming than those in Keth. She couldn't spot one establishment that didn't bear a thick coat of grime or stand in need of repairs. Dunlow's citizens must not have believed it was even worth an attempt to present a good front.

"How do people live this way?" she murmured.

"People come to the Valley hoping to strike it rich," Mick explained, "but most end up living as little better than slaves in the mines. Only mine owners like my family are wealthy. Everyone else lives day to day on their wages. Just enough to eat, but not enough for a fresh start."

"So they're trapped here?"

"More or less."

Kyrin understood being trapped by circumstances, though living conditions here starkly contrasted with the luxury she'd known at the palace and even Tarvin Hall. These people would probably drop everything for a chance to live as she had.

When they reached the town, they split into two groups of four to either side of the main road. That way they could stick close together in case trouble arose. They would have to be on their guard for soldiers today.

Shortly, Kyrin, Jace, Kaden, and Trev came upon the first shop along the street—a cobbler, according to the cracked sign out front. Kyrin pushed open the door, and they all stepped inside, though the men held back. As much as she disliked it, she had agreed to do the talking since it had worked to their advantage in Keth.

Kyrin put on a sweet smile and approached the man at the service counter. He looked at her over a pair of spectacles, his tilted head revealing a bald spot. A half-finished shoe rested in his hand.

"Can I help you, miss?"

"I hope so. I'm looking for a man named Josan Silvar. Do you know if he lives around here?"

"Sure, I know Josan."

Kyrin's heart skipped a beat.

"I see Josan once in a while," the cobbler continued. "Not lately though. He doesn't get out much." He peered at her closely. "He a friend of yours?"

"I don't know him personally, but I'm trying to get a message to him from his family." She reclaimed the smile that had slipped in her surprise. The last thing she wanted was to arouse any suspicion.

"I didn't know he had any," the man said in interest. "It'll be good for him to hear from them. Things get kinda bleak around here."

Kyrin could certainly see that. "Could you tell me where he lives?"

"He has a cottage on the east side of town, a little north of here. It's off by itself, so you shouldn't miss it."

Kyrin's smile widened as she thanked him and bid him good day. She turned and exchanged a satisfied look with the men. As long as they avoided the soldiers, they could have Josan and the Scrolls to safety within an hour. Jace opened the door to let her out of the shop. She took a step across the boardwalk. Her gaze immediately caught on a group of men in gold and black, and warning signals fired through her nerves. She froze. Kaden bumped into her, and she spun back toward the shop, grabbing his arm. "Turn around!"

He frowned, but obeyed.

"Do not look back," she whispered. She looked up at Jace. "Do you see those soldiers just up the street?"

He nodded, his eyes alert and fixed on the men.

"Tell me when they're out of sight."

Kaden gave her a look that questioned her odd behavior. "What is it?"

"Marcus."

"What?" He started to turn, but Kyrin squeezed his arm.

"Yes, Marcus, but don't look or he might see you. He must be the one in charge of finding Josan."

Kaden scowled.

"They're heading east," Jace said a moment later.

Kyrin turned cautiously. Josan wouldn't be the only one hunted if Marcus happened to see and recognize them. "That's toward Josan's place. We better get the others and find him before Marcus does."

They stepped into the street, and spotted the others just exiting the shop across from them.

"We know where Josan is," Kyrin announced as they met them, "but I just saw my brother Marcus and his men. We have to get Josan and get out of town before Marcus sees me or Kaden."

Trask nodded, and Kyrin pointed the group east. None of the roads led in a completely straight path, but they traveled quickly while avoiding untimely intercepts with the soldiers. Kyrin's stomach tightened with unease. How could she be afraid of her own brother? Would he actually pursue them if he did spot them? She didn't want to believe so, but . . .

Two figures caught her attention, and she skidded to a halt. Kaden nearly collided with her again, and everyone else slowed to look back at her.

"What's wrong?" Trask asked.

"Two men just disappeared around that corner." She nodded down a street toward the south. "One looked like a crete."

"Are you sure?"

Kyrin replayed the scene in her mind. She'd caught only a glimpse, but it was enough to know one of the men had long hair, much like Captain Darq. "Pretty sure. Do you think it could be Josan? If he knows about the soldiers, he could be trying to escape."

Trask glanced east, but then nodded. "Let's find out."

They changed directions, heading south. When they came around the corner, they caught sight of the two men farther down the narrow street. Now Kyrin was sure of it. One of them was a crete. They hurried to catch up, and Trask called out, "Josan Silvar!"

The two men stopped and looked back, their eyes, especially the crete's, wide and wary.

Trask held up his hands as the group drew closer. "We're friends. We came here with Captain Verus Darq. Your father sent him to find you."

A great sigh released from the crete's lips, and his tense expression relaxed. To the young man beside him, he said, "He's telling the truth. I know the Darq family." Josan's eyes settled on Trask. "There are soldiers searching for us."

"Don't worry. Captain Darq and his men are nearby. We'll help you get to them."

The young man at Josan's side stepped forward. His dark brown hair fell in slight waves almost to his chin, and his handsome, clean-shaven appearance brought out his youth. Yet, Kyrin found that his brown eyes held the greater, deeper experience and wisdom of one more aged. It intrigued her as something beyond the ordinary.

"Please, can you try to find my brother? He left to distract the soldiers so we could get away."

The pained intensity of his plea squeezed Kyrin's heart. She would want the same if it were Kaden.

Trask quickly gave this consideration. "Which way did he go?"

"Last I saw, he headed north."

Trask turned to the group. "Rayad, take Kyrin, Kaden, Jace, and Trev, and get them to safety. Holden, Mick, and I will look for his brother." He faced the young man again. "What is his name and what does he look like?"

"His name is Aaron Carliss. He's only a bit taller than me and has short brown hair and blue eyes. He'll probably have his pack and bow with him, unless he dropped it somewhere."

"We'll try to find him."

"Thank you."

"Now, you'd better go before the soldiers show up," Trask urged.

Kyrin and the others came forward, and Trev offered to take Josan's pack so he could move more quickly. The group split and went off in opposite directions, though the young man sent a yearning look after Trask, Holden, and Mick.

Kyrin paused at his side. "They'll do everything they can to find him."

His eyes, level with her own, switched to her and warmed with gratitude. He nodded and they hurried after the others.

After a few blocks, they slowed to another stop as Josan struggled with the pace. Winded, he said, "You should go without me. You'll need to run once we're in the open."

The young man shook his head, but Rayad beat him to a reply.

"Not happening."

Kaden stepped up. "Here, climb on my back. I can carry you the rest of the way."

Kyrin watched for Josan's reaction. Would the fierce crete pride allow acceptance of such an offer? But Josan clearly wasn't like most cretes. With a brief nod, he handed his crutches to the young man and wrapped his arms around Kaden's neck when he knelt in front of him. Once he had a secure hold, Kaden pushed back to his feet, and they resumed their pace.

Moving much more quickly now, they reached the edge of town in a few minutes. They paused to make sure the way was clear and then ran down the road. With this final sprint, they came around a crooked bend, where they met Darq and the other cretes, and slowed to a stop. Josan slid down from Kaden's back and reclaimed his crutches as the crete captain approached them.

"Josan Silvar?"

He nodded, and Darq extended his hand. "Captain Verus Darq."

"Pleased to meet you, Captain." Josan glanced at his shoulder tattoos. "I remember your father well."

Darq scanned the group before his gaze rested on Rayad. "Where are Trask and the rest of your men?"

"They stayed behind to look for his brother." He nodded at the young man. "He tried to distract the soldiers while they escaped. I may go back once everyone is safely in camp."

Captain Darq nodded and led everyone up toward the new camp the cretes had made closer to the valley floor.

Aaron's mind raced as fast as his pounding feet. He had drawn the soldiers away, but now they were closing in. He'd meant every word to Timothy about avoiding capture. He had no intention of giving them the opportunity to cart him off to Valcré for execution, but one slip, one miscalculation, would land him right in the soldiers' hands.

Weaving through an alleyway congested with junk piles, he slid to a stop at a corner and scanned the area to plot his next move. He had reached the far northeastern corner of town. If he could just get west, he could skirt around the soldiers before they cut him off.

"There!"

His heart crashed against his ribs, and he spun around. A group of soldiers sprinted toward him. He smashed his fist into the wall in frustration and took off running, straight east. Gone was the careful planning. Outrun the soldiers. That was it.

The mountains loomed before him and gave him a surge of hope. If he could reach the slopes, they would never keep pace climbing after him. Not if they didn't want to break their necks risking the treacherous climb. He couldn't be worth that much to them. Pushing for every bit of speed he could manage, he threw off his heavy pack, every muscle straining in the effort.

He hit the slopes at a dead run. His feet slipped in the loose gravel and almost threw him off balance, but he found his footing and charged on. Though pain seared through his legs at the incline, the thought of Timothy drove him forward. He would not leave his brother to face the world and take care of Josan on his own. He looked ahead to a sheer cliff rising up about thirty feet. If he made it to the top, he'd secure his escape.

Footsteps and sliding gravel echoed behind him as he hit the cliff face, only then coming to a stop. He dug his fingers into the highest crevice he could reach and dragged himself upward. The joints in his fingers cramped and burned as he clawed at any hand and foothold he could find. Several times his grip slipped, but he never slowed. The old days of running from the bullies who'd always picked on him for being shorter than the other kids in town were paying off. Before eventually learning how to defend himself, the mountain slopes had been his best escape route. He never would have learned to climb so fast otherwise.

Over two-thirds of the way up the cliff, he reached a narrow ledge. With this solid footing beneath him, he paused to look up. Only another six feet separated him from freedom. But the rock face was smooth and offered no adequate crevices for him to advance any farther.

"No!" He searched frantically with his eyes and fingers. He was too close to fail now.

"Stop! Or we'll shoot!"

Aaron froze and looked down. Eight soldiers stood directly below him. Four had their bows nocked and ready. He breathed hard through his nose and scanned the cliff again. Had he the time, he could work his way up, but if any of those men were even half as good a shot as he was, he'd be dead.

"Come down. I don't want my men to have to shoot you."

Aaron rested his forehead against the cold rock and growled. He never surrendered. Never. Not to bullies, not to circumstances, and definitely not to the emperor's men. He turned and pressed back against the cliff to look down at the soldiers. "What do you want with me?"

"What's your name?" the soldier in a captain's uniform asked.

"Aaron. What's yours?"

"I'm Captain Marcus Altair."

"Well, Captain, I don't know exactly what's going on, but I'd really appreciate you calling off your men." Aaron turned his eyes upward again. There had to be a way out of this.

"Come down, and we can talk," Marcus replied.

"Yeah?" Aaron glanced at him. "Does this talk involve me bound or unbound?"

"That depends on why you're running."

Aaron snorted. "First you and your men question my little brother, and then you come chasing after us. You'll have to excuse me for seeing it as hostility toward my family."

"We're only looking for information," the captain replied in a pacifying voice. "Running would indicate you have something to hide. Do you?"

"You tell me," Aaron grumbled. His eyes snagged on a small, jutting rock about waist-high. He looked up at the cliff's edge. Just maybe, if he jumped, he could grab the edge and use the rock to propel himself up and over. He winced. Risky. He would need more time to think it over. After all, if he missed, he'd fall right into the soldiers' laps, if it didn't kill him first. The latter would probably be preferable. He looked back down at Marcus. "What kind of information are you looking for?"

"We're searching for a man named Taan. He's an enemy of His Majesty, Emperor Daican."

Aaron turned to face the cliff again, but kept talking. He just had to stall them for a bit. "What's he guilty of?"

"Treason. He's been known to spread lies about the myth of Elôm."

Aaron scowled. Did this soldier even think about what he was saying? Or was he just spoon-fed the emperor's lies to spit out at times like this? "So, just because a man chooses to believe in a God other than the emperor's, that constitutes treason?"

"Just come down and we can discuss it."

"No. You answer my question. Why is it treason?"

The gravel beneath Marcus crackled as he shifted. "Because the emperor has forbidden it."

"Oh, so it's right, then, to slaughter people because they have different religious beliefs?"

Marcus answered in a carefully controlled tone. "The penalty for treason is death. That's how it has always been."

Had they been having this conversation face to face, Aaron would have looked at him in disgust. "But what makes belief in Elôm worthy of death? What harm does it do the emperor?"

Now emotion did creep into the captain's voice. "My sister's misguided beliefs led her to attack the emperor after he bestowed on her great a honor. That's the kind of radical action these false beliefs lead to. Now, I'm warning you for the last time. Come down or we'll shoot."

Time had run out. Aaron had to make his choice. Surrender, or make his move and risk being shot or falling? Either way, he faced an almost sure chance of death. Yet, in the end, he'd rather take his chances than willingly give his life into their hands.

He gathered his energy, murmured a prayer, and lunged for the ledge above his head. His heart missed a beat, but his fingertips gripped the rock and held. He scrambled for the foothold, holding his breath in anticipation of an arrowhead slamming into his back. His foot found the rock, and he propelled himself up. But, in the next instant, it gave way beneath him. He slammed against the cliff. The air rushed from his lungs. Taking the full weight of his body, his fingers slipped.

For a gut-wrenching moment, time stood still, and he knew he was falling. He slid down the rough rock surface, the sharp edges ripping into his skin. Piercing pain shot up through his feet and ankles as he hit the ground, and his knees buckled. Rolling, he landed hard on his right shoulder. A jagged rock gashed into the skin. He groaned through his teeth and lay dazed, but his heart still beat and his lungs still drew breath, even though he wasn't sure that was the best thing at the moment.

The soldiers converged on him. They jerked his arms behind his back and hauled him to his feet, where he came face to face with Marcus. He looked the captain in the eyes. They might have caught him, but that didn't mean they would get what they truly wanted. He'd protect Timothy and Josan straight to his grave.

Marcus just stared at him for a moment before ordering his men, "Take him to the cottage. We'll question him there."

JACE CRADLED A warm mug of coffee in his fingers, but his attention focused on the cretes and the others talking around the small fire. From his seat near the edge of camp, he could still listen in on the conversation while having a little space—just how he liked it. Gem sat behind him, and her warm breath drifted across the back of his neck. He glanced at her, and she blinked her inquisitive eyes as if asking him about the two new strangers.

With a shrug, he murmured, "Not much to tell yet." The men hadn't been in camp long enough for him to form an opinion of them. At least Josan seemed friendlier than Falcor and Leetra.

He turned back to the group, and his gaze rested on Kyrin. She poured a cup of coffee and brought it to Timothy, who sat apart from the group as well. They still awaited word of his brother and, ever since arriving in camp, everyone's interest had become so focused on Josan they seemed to forget all about the quiet young man with him.

Timothy smiled at Kyrin as he accepted the cup. "Thank you." He took a sip and shook his head. "I don't remember the last time I had coffee."

"Feel free to help yourself." She offered him a kind smile in return.

She might not be a people person, but she was very good at stepping up to help when someone felt out of place and needed it, as Jace knew firsthand.

Timothy thanked her once again, and Kyrin turned in Jace's direction. She crossed the short distance between them, bringing her comforting presence with her, and took a seat beside him. "How are you?"

He had noticed her concerned looks every time he started coughing since they'd left Dunlow. "I'm fine."

Silence followed as she stared at him, her eyes both probing and skeptical. She didn't believe his standard reply—not that he could blame her.

"Really," he insisted. "I've been much worse."

His lungs did hurt, but no more than after a hard run, and the coughing didn't leave the tang of blood in his mouth like it had last spring. As long as they stayed away from town, the effects would be gone within a day.

Kyrin's face softened in acceptance. If she had intended to say anything more, the conversation at the fire distracted her. Jace shifted his attention to Captain Darq, who addressed Josan.

"This is difficult to ask, but where's your brother, Torin?"

His expression sad, but accepting, Josan answered, "He's gone. Has been for years."

"I'm sorry," Darq murmured, and the others offered their quiet sympathies. "What happened?"

"Mining accident. I'm afraid I've seen many good men perish in tunnel collapses. I nearly did myself. It took my leg, but Elôm spared my life."

Jace winced, his lungs growing heavier at the idea of being buried alive or crushed to death in a mine. Beside him, Kyrin rubbed her arms, and her face looked a little pale. Of course.

Mines were just like caves, and to be buried in one would be the worst fate for someone with claustrophobia.

"Why were you here in the Valley?" Talas asked, drawing them both back to the conversation. At least they'd moved on from the talk of cave-ins.

"This is where we believed Elôm had called us." Josan spoke with a certainty that said he still believed it. "The people here live very bleak lives. They yearn for hope, and we came to offer it. Recently, it became more necessity than choice. You'd be hard-pressed to find businesses anywhere that will hire cretes these days, except for the mines. The owners will hire anyone who's willing to work. Like those families here, it soon became the only way we could survive."

"Your father deeply regrets the way things ended between you," Darq told him. "It'll grieve him to learn of your hardships."

Josan shook his head. "Then I hope to put his mind at rest. Our hardships were not of his making, but the will of Elôm."

His words settled in Jace's mind, and he contemplated his own hardships. If only he could be as confident as the crete. It was hard to be so accepting when he'd known such evil in his life. He still struggled to find Elôm's purpose in it.

"We heard you had a complete collection of the King's Scrolls," Darq said, and Jace pushed his thoughts aside so he could concentrate on the matter at hand. "Do you still have possession of them?"

"I have the copies." Josan motioned across the fire. Timothy rose and pulled the strap of a worn leather satchel from his shoulder, and brought it to the crete. Josan opened the flap to let them all see the scrolls nestled inside. "Unfortunately, they've never been completed. This is less than half of what's contained in the originals."

"What happened to the originals?"

"I hid them." Josan closed the satchel and handed it back to

Timothy, who hung onto it as if it contained a priceless treasure. "A few years ago, when we began to sense things changing and the danger growing, I believed it too great a risk to keep them in our possession where they might be discovered and destroyed. So I made arrangements with a traveling merchant who is an old friend of mine to have them hidden where the emperor would never think to look."

"And where is that?" Darq asked, voicing the question in everyone's curious expressions.

Josan's eyes roamed the group, but he hesitated to speak.

"Do not fear," Darq assured him. "Each person here has been carefully selected. The location will be safe with them."

Jace glanced at Kyrin. Good to know Darq had such high confidence in all of them.

After another moment, Josan nodded. "The Scrolls are hidden in Auréa Palace."

For nearly a full minute, the only sound was the crackling of the logs in the fire.

Echoing everyone's shock, Darq repeated incredulously, "The Scrolls are hidden in Auréa Palace?"

"Right under the emperor's nose." Josan smiled a little at their expressions. "I disguised them as crete family histories. No sane Arcacian would ever look at them."

Darq released a light chuckle. "Clever." However, his mirth faded. "But it does present a problem if we were to try to reclaim them."

More like an impossibility, in Jace's opinion. None of them would be able to enter the palace. Even if the emperor didn't know them, the danger would be far too great. Still, the determination on Darq's face, as well as several others', disagreed.

At the faint clacking of pebbles in the rocks below camp, Jace's attention snapped to Glynn, who stood on watch. The crete looked toward the sound and then turned back to wave an all clear. A few moments later, Trask and the others appeared. Timothy jumped up to meet them, his eyes hopeful, but then his expression fell. His brother wasn't with them.

"You didn't find him?"

Trask grimaced, regret shadowing his eyes. "I'm sorry, but we believe he's been taken prisoner. We saw a group of soldiers leading a man matching his description to a small cottage outside of town. Your cottage, we think."

Timothy hung his head. "Is there any way we can reach him?"

"I don't know. It looks like the whole unit is setting up camp around there. It would be risky to get too close."

Josan came up behind Timothy and grasped his shoulder. He looked at Trask, and then Darq. "There must be something we can do."

Darq's intense eyes shifted to his lieutenant. "Glynn, once it gets dark, take Talas and Falcor to see what it looks like." To Timothy and Josan, he said, "We'll do what we can."

The rope dug painfully into Aaron's wrists as it jerked tighter. He ground his teeth, glaring at the soldiers, who had no concern for his comfort or his injuries. His bruised and strained muscles ached, but the open gash in his shoulder throbbed most fiercely as it oozed and bled down his sleeve. So much for civility and the soldiers simply wanting to talk.

Once the knots were so tight he had no hope of working them loose, the soldiers sat him down hard in a chair they'd pulled away from the table. Despite the futility of it, he tugged against the ropes. Though he, Timothy, and Josan had abandoned the cottage, it was still home, and he longed to throw these men out of it.

The soldiers shoved the table to the side to make room in

front of him. They came to attention when Marcus and another, older, man stepped inside. A third man lingered at the door with a look of hesitation. He briefly caught Aaron's gaze before the captain came forward. Aaron leaned back in his chair to stare up at him.

"You could have made this easier for yourself," Marcus said, his sincerity almost believable.

Aaron smirked. "Somehow I think I would've been sitting here just the same either way."

"We're not your enemies."

"No?"

"No," Marcus replied firmly. "We're trying to gain the truth, that's all. We just want your cooperation. Answer my questions truthfully, and I'll see about your release."

Aaron snorted. He didn't believe that for a second. They'd haul him off to Valcré and that would be it.

"Why were you running?" Marcus asked, maintaining his calm and collected manner.

"I told you, you questioned my brother and were coming to question the man who has taken care of us for years. Your intentions seemed hostile, so we left."

"We're not hostile. We came only to ask questions. Now, just tell us where your brother and the crete went, and we can get this straightened out."

"No."

Marcus sighed, but even Aaron had to admit he was remarkably patient. "Why not?"

"Because, Captain, I don't trust you or your men."

"The only reason you would have to fear us is if you were an enemy of the emperor and Arcacia."

"I'm no enemy of Arcacia," Aaron ground out. Half crete or not, he'd been born here. He was every bit as Arcacian as these soldiers. Despite how his opinion of the country's officials was rapidly sinking, he had nothing against the country itself.

However, Marcus's eyes narrowed at his lack of mentioning the emperor, his diplomatic tone becoming very businesslike. "Do you know Taan?"

"No."

Marcus's jaw shifted as he studied him. Then he asked, "Do you believe in Aertus and Vilai?"

Aaron hesitated, but let a slight smirk grow again. "Sure, I believe the moons exist. They're right there in the sky every night."

Marcus's eyes slid closed as if in exasperation, and he shook his head. "I'm talking about the gods. Do you believe in them?"

Aaron's heart gave a hard thud against his ribcage in the short silence that followed. Still holding the captain's gaze, he answered coolly, "No."

Something flickered in Marcus's eyes. Disappointment, maybe? But his expression hardened again. "So you're a follower of Elôm?"

Aaron sat up straight in his chair and nodded firmly. "I am."

The man beside Marcus let out a menacing grumble and fingered his sword. Had he the chance, he probably would have performed an execution right there.

"Then you're an enemy and traitor to both your emperor and Arcacia," Marcus said, his tone bearing the smallest hint of regret. "And, as we've already established, that's a crime punishable by death."

Aaron did not waver. "So be it."

Marcus gave his head a shake and frowned down at the floor as if in thought. When he did look at Aaron again, his eyes held a plea that proved he wasn't as anxious for blood as the man at his side.

"Perhaps I can find a way to lighten your sentence *if* you tell me where your brother and the crete are."

Aaron released a hard laugh, but he let his voice go ice-cold. "You really think I'd give them up for a chance to save my own life?"

A slow sigh slipped out of Marcus.

"Let me question him, Captain," the other man cut in, his voice edged with a growl. "I can get him to talk."

Marcus's lips tightened in a grim line. Indecision warred in his eyes. Reluctance followed, but he nodded to the man, who wore an ugly sneer on his bearded face. "See what you can find out."

He turned and walked toward the door where the other soldier stopped him.

"Are you sure about this?" He spoke quietly, but not enough to keep Aaron from catching the uncertain waver in his voice.

"We need the information. That's why we're here," Marcus replied, almost as if convincing himself as much as the other man.

Aaron watched the exchange. They were brothers. He could tell.

Marcus put his hand on his brother's shoulder and nodded out the door, but before they could leave, Aaron spoke. "Captain."

Both sets of brown eyes landed on him. He nodded at the other soldier. "Would you give him up if you were in my place?"

A grimace flitted across Marcus's face. He did not speak, but Aaron read the answer in his expression—an unequivocal no.

Liam trailed after his brother as they passed through groups of men, who were in the process of setting up tents around the cottage. He avoided confrontation at all cost, but something burned inside him that he couldn't just ignore this time. He didn't know what to do with it just yet but, as much as it frightened him, much of what their prisoner had said made sense.

"Marcus."

His brother did not check his stride. He tried again, more forcefully this time. Marcus spun around to face him, but his eyes lacked their usual softening toward him. Though he spoke calmly, his stance was rigid, and an underlying air of frustration leaked out.

"What?"

Liam hunched his shoulders. Though taller than his brother, he sure didn't feel like it. His tongue turned to wood in rebellion against the thoughts rolling about in his mind. He could back down—just fade again into the background where he was most comfortable, and let things be—things he had no control over anyway. But he couldn't do it. Not this time. Forcing his back straight and his tongue to work, he pushed forward.

"Is this really necessary? Torturing a man?" Just saying it left him sick. Marcus had never given such an order before. That bothered him more than anything.

Marcus put his fists on his hips. "He's a traitor and has information we need to find the others who are, no doubt, traitors as well. He may say he doesn't know Taan, but I strongly suspect the crete they lived with is the man we were sent here to find. How else do you expect me to find him?"

"Do we really need him?" Liam blurted out before he could second-guess himself. "Why is it so important? What harm could he really cause? If—"

"Liam." The tone was much sharper than Marcus usually used with him, and his stomach bunched. His brother went on in the same firm voice, but concern grew in his eyes. "They're spreading lies. The same lies that nearly got Kyrin and Kaden killed, and still may. We must stop this before it gets out of hand.

One person with a voice people will listen to can cause more damage than you think."

*What if they're not lies?* The question rang loud and clear in Liam's mind, daring to be spoken. But fear of the consequences kept it trapped behind his lips. He swallowed the words and instead said, "I just don't want you doing something you'll regret."

Marcus's jaw clenched, and he stepped closer. His voice dropped to match his deathly serious expression. "My decisions are not open for discussion, nor is it your place to question them."

Liam felt the sting of these words like a slap to the face. Before he could scramble together a reply, Marcus continued, this time with a deep plea in his voice.

"Do not question me in front of the men . . . or I'll have to take disciplinary actions. Please, don't make me do that." He grimaced in obvious distaste over the prospect. His voice lowered even further. "You do not want word of this to get back to the General."

Numbing cold flooded Liam's system. Their grandfather knew precisely how to make his life a living hell. He'd suffered under his demeaning and demoralizing punishments for years as the General tried to transform him into a respectable soldier. Liam couldn't imagine what might be in store for him should this get out. He swallowed against the pressure that had built up in his throat, and lost all will to utter another word.

The hooves of the five horses clacked loudly in the crisp, quiet evening and echoed between the mountains. William Altair looked up at the darkening sky. The stars would soon show. His eyes dropped, and he was glad of the not-too-distant lights in Dunlow. The narrow, rocky road would grow treacherous once full darkness set in. He focused on the campfires casting an orange glow to the northeast, and then urged his horse into a trot. He and the handful of men who had accompanied him had been in the saddle all day, and he was ready to stretch his legs and get some food in his stomach.

Ten minutes later, they rode into camp. The men along the way saluted him with their fists to their hearts, and he nodded to them. He looked ahead for where Marcus had set up his head-quarters and spotted it near a small cottage. He'd nearly reached it when a soldier ducked out of a tent nearby.

"Father!"

He reined his horse to a halt and smiled as Liam approached. However, his smile faded upon seeing the overwhelming relief on his son's face—the same sort of relief he'd seen other times when he intervened in one of the General's unreasonable demands for Liam. William dismounted and turned to dismiss his men to find food and shelter for the night.

"What are you doing here?" Liam asked as soon as he faced him again.

"The General thought my time would be best spent aiding you and Marcus in your search." Actually, William had hinted at it first. He truly hated to sabotage his son's mission, but if the man they sought was influential enough for the emperor to send a company of men after him, then it was important to keep him alive and out of the emperor's hands. "So, what news do you have for me?"

Liam's face fell. "Marcus caught a man trying to escape town today. He believes he acted as a decoy. His brother and a crete man got away." Clear guilt flashed across his face as he gulped, and William suspected there was more behind those last words. Liam glanced at the men nearby and dropped his voice to a low, but desperate, murmur. "You have to do something. They've been questioning him to find out where the other two went."

A knot formed in William's previously-hungry stomach. He took Liam's arm and walked a few yards from the tents to gain a bit more privacy for their conversation. "Who's questioning him?"

"Scerle."

William winced. Scerle had quite a reputation as an interrogator. "How long?"

"Since late this morning. They took a break for lunch, but he's been in there all afternoon." Liam's face contorted in his distress.

William laid his hand on his shoulder to reassure him. Liam had always been averse to cruelty—with good reason. Before he could speak, Marcus called behind them, and they looked toward the cottage. William's oldest son approached and saluted. Though he appeared as surprised as Liam had been, he did not question his father's presence.

"I hear you have a man in custody." William took over the situation.

Marcus nodded and maintained his manner as a soldier. "We believe he's closely associated with Taan. We've been questioning him for information concerning the crete."

William did not speak for a long moment, though it was apparent Marcus waited for confirmation of his actions. Finally, William asked, "Has he said anything?" He had to handle this carefully, lest his sympathies be revealed.

"No."

"May I see him?"

Marcus gave a quick nod and motioned to the cottage. "He's inside."

William strode across the fire- and torch-lit distance and up to the open door, where he stopped to take in the scene. The prisoner sat in a chair in the middle of the room, with his hands bound behind him. His face showed bruising and some swelling, and a ribbon of blood trailed down his chin and neck. The most serious injury appeared to be the bloodied gash in his shoulder. Scerle had no doubt exploited that to the greatest possible extent. Still, the prisoner could have fared worse. Marcus must have given Scerle limitations. William found some small measure of relief in this.

His eyes now switched to the interrogator. Scerle sat in another chair in front of the prisoner. He had a cup of water in his hand and took a long drink, loudly breathing his appreciation. With slow, deliberate movements, he let the remaining water trickle out onto the floor in front of the prisoner.

"You thirsty? Well, you better start talking if you want a drink."

William clenched his fists and fought to keep the uproar of injustice and concern for the prisoner carefully concealed.

The man watched the last of the water dribble away, and then set his eyes on some object across the room. Despite the stubborn set to his jaw, he looked spent. Even if the physical abuse wasn't as great as it could have been, hours of questions had to have worn him down. However, his tired eyes didn't show defeat, but solid, steely determination that stirred William's admiration.

He stepped into the cabin, and Marcus followed.

"Just give him some water. We're not barbarians," William commanded.

Scerle jumped to his feet, quickly remembering to salute, but his expression was anything but respectful. "We can't give him water. I've been working on him all day. I can break him, but not if you give him water and strengthen him."

William didn't see that happening. Water or not, the man wouldn't break—not if he had family to protect. His mind and body might be wearing down, but his will wasn't. Strange that Scerle could not see that after all the interrogations he had conducted. But maybe he was too confident, stubborn, and eager to inflict pain.

The interrogator's cold eyes jumped to Marcus, his commanding officer. William glanced at his son. Marcus hesitated, but then said, "The captain is right; we're not barbarians. Give him a little water."

"With respect, sir, I don't believe that's wise."

Marcus frowned, and his voice echoed his authority. "A little won't make much difference."

The man scowled and muttered a curse under his breath. William made a mental note to warn Marcus to keep a tight rein on him. Though his son made an excellent captain, he was still very young, and the older men like Scerle were bound to test their limits. He waited a moment for the man to follow orders, but he remained stubbornly in place. Losing patience, William snatched the cup from him and drew water from a nearby bucket. He started to fill the cup, but stopped halfway so he wouldn't undermine Marcus's orders.

He turned to the prisoner and put the cup to his lips to let him drink. When the last drop was drained, the man looked up at him, and his deep blue eyes harbored mistrust, but also a guarded, unspoken thank-you. If only William could offer more in the way of compassion, or at least let him know they were of the same faith and that he wasn't alone here.

William set the empty cup on the table and motioned to Marcus as he stepped back outside. Once it was just the two of them, he faced his son. "I don't think you'll get anything from him. He looks pretty set on silence to me."

Marcus sighed and rubbed his neck as weariness crumbled the strong, professional mask he'd been wearing. William could understand the intense pressure he was under to fulfill his first real mission. "I don't think so either. Scerle won't want to give it up, though."

William looked him in the eyes. "It's your call, Marcus."

"I know." He stared out at camp, though his gaze was unfocused as his mind contemplated other things. William watched him, praying. He didn't know what he should pray exactly—only that his son would choose to hold off further interrogation for now.

A moment later, Marcus's expression changed, hardening in the way it did when he believed he was doing the right thing but felt conflicted. "The General would order us to press on. This is what he sent us for. We need to find out where the crete is hiding . . . any way we can."

Set on his decision, Marcus turned into the cottage again, and William's heart sank. How he longed to call his son back, to sit down with him, and explain things and have him understand. But it couldn't be. From the time he was a boy, Marcus's loyalties had been divided. In the end, it was always the General who had the strongest influence on him—holding him to his duties, no matter what the cost may be.

His spirit burdened, William turned and walked away from camp. He needed to pray and, for that, he sought solitude. Leaving the glow of campfires behind him, he walked into the rocky darkness of the Sinnai slopes. With camp far behind him, he stopped and stared up at the night sky now riddled with pinpricks of light.

He drew a deep breath. *Guide me, Lord. Show me how to reach my sons before it's too late. And show me how I might aid this prisoner. I have no doubt he's a child of Yours. If there's anything I can do for him—*

A shadow flashed at the corner of his vision. Before he could react, a strong arm wrapped around him and a razor edge caught against his throat.

KYRIN BIT DOWN hard on a yawn that escaped anyway. The excitement of the last few days had drained her, yet, in a way, she enjoyed being out and about and seeing more of Ilyon. She'd spent too much of her life isolated in Valcré. Still, it didn't distract her from what the group had yet to face, particularly Timothy. To see him sitting and waiting anxiously at the fire stirred up all the fear and heartache stored with her memories of when Sir Richard had held Kaden captive. As she loosed the tie to her bedroll and rolled out the blankets next to Kaden's things, she prayed for Timothy and his brother. There was nothing worse than sitting helpless when a family member was in danger. She picked up the top blanket to shake it out when a stir of commotion sounded behind her.

"Captain!" It was Glynn's voice. "We've captured one of the soldiers!"

Kyrin looked over her shoulder as the three cretes entered camp. Talas and Falcor led a man in a black and gold uniform between them. Her breath caught in her chest, and the blanket dropped right from her hands. "Father!"

She rushed toward him, but Darq snagged her by the arm and cast a suspicious look at their prisoner. Kyrin tugged against his hold, her heart nearly bursting with impatience. "It's all right; he's my father."

But Darq wasn't convinced. "How do we know we can trust him?"

"Because I'm a follower of Elôm," William told him calmly.

The suspicion cleared, and Darq finally released his hold as he ordered Talas, "Cut him loose."

Talas obeyed immediately. As soon as her father's arms were free, Kyrin ran into them. He squeezed her tightly, and then opened one arm to pull Kaden in as he joined them. Holding them both, he breathed near Kyrin's ear, "It's so good to see you two."

"I thought we might never see you again." Thickness constricted Kyrin's throat. Being branded a traitor had destroyed any hope of a reunion with her family before now. *Thank You, Elôm!*

Their father held them a moment more before looking into their smiling faces. "Well, here I am."

"I saw Marcus in town," Kyrin said, "but I didn't know you were here too."

"I actually just rode in about an hour ago. I stepped outside of camp for some time to pray and met your friends." He nodded to Talas.

The crete gave him a contrite smile. "Sorry about the knife."

William waved the apology off. "No harm done. If you hadn't brought me here, I would never have seen these two."

Kyrin took her father's hand. His skin was cold against hers. "Come by the fire. I want to introduce you to everyone."

He followed her and warmed up near the flames as she and Kaden introduced him to their friends. Kyrin was especially pleased to introduce Jace. He hung back in the shadows, but she beckoned him closer. He seemed a bit reluctant—intimidated, possibly—but he accepted her father's greeting and then quietly stepped back again. If only Kyrin had time to tell her father more about their friendship and how much Jace meant to her.

After greeting everyone, William's eyes settled on Josan. "I assume you're the crete my son is searching for."

"Yes, though Taan is just the name of my clan. It kept us safe for a while, but no longer, I'm afraid."

Timothy stepped up beside him, his eyes hungry for information. "You said you just arrived, but did you see my brother? We believe he was taken captive."

"I did," William answered, and Kyrin caught the hesitation in his voice.

Timothy swallowed. As much as he wanted information, it would no doubt be difficult for him to hear. "Is he all right?"

"They have been questioning him concerning your whereabouts." William paused, but continued with the truth, "They've been rough on him, though not as much as they could be. From what I saw, he looks to have a very stubborn streak of determination."

Timothy gave a sad smile. "That he does."

Kyrin looked up at her father as her sympathy for Timothy came on strongly again. "Do you think there's any way to rescue him?"

Before he could answer, Glynn spoke. "That was the reason we took Captain Altair captive. We had thought we could trade him for Aaron."

"Perhaps we still can," Darq said thoughtfully. His eyes rested on William. "If you are willing, of course."

"I'm willing."

"We'll go down with the dragons. That will give us the advantage and help ensure the trade goes smoothly. We have no desire to harm anyone, but they don't know that. We just need to determine the best time to make our move."

"If I were you, I'd move soon," William told them. "When

I left, they were about to start another round of questioning, and I think this time it'll be rougher."

Darq nodded. "Then we'll leave immediately." He paused when his eyes came to Kyrin and Kaden. "Unless you two don't wish for your brother to see you."

"We could go, but keep to the shadows," Kyrin suggested.

"Right then; we'll saddle up."

Most of the group turned toward the dragons, but a quiet voice stopped Kyrin. "I'll saddle Ivoris for you."

She looked up at Jace, and a smile broke out. "Thank you."

He nodded and glanced once at her father, before ducking his head as if embarrassed and walking away to join the others. Trev offered to saddle Exsis, which left Kyrin, her brother, and father alone at the edge of the fire.

Kyrin faced him and drew a deep breath as her chest tightened up. "I wish you could stay longer." Though this short time was more than she could have hoped for, she wasn't ready for goodbye when they had no assurances of when they might meet again.

"So do I," he replied. "Maybe there will be a chance to see you once more before you leave."

Kyrin gave an eager nod. "We'll ask Captain Darq what our plans are once we have Aaron. Then we can figure out where to meet you to say goodbye." Anything to put it off for just a bit longer.

"We'll do that. Now, while we have a little time, why don't you tell me about these last few months. Last I heard concerning the two of you was that you'd escaped. No further details."

In the next several minutes, Kyrin and Kaden took turns briefly recapping the events that had led up to settling in Landale. They told him a little about camp and their goals there, but it wasn't long before the others were finishing.

The cretes hadn't even bothered to saddle their dragons. Instead, they all stood talking with Josan. When Trask's group had finished, they gathered at the fire again, where Darq stepped forward.

"Captain Altair, before we go, there's a matter we wish to discuss with you."

"Yes?"

Darq glanced at Josan, who nodded his approval, and then asked, "Could you get into Auréa Palace?"

Kyrin's heart missed a beat, and an objection rose up inside her, but she bit her lip to keep it contained. She couldn't make her father's decisions for him, as much as she hated where she knew this conversation would go.

He gave a slow nod. "If I had a reason to seek an audience with the emperor or one of his advisors. Why?"

"If you'd be willing to further aid us, we have need of someone to retrieve certain items from the palace library."

"Go on."

"There's a complete collection of the King's Scrolls disguised as crete family histories hidden there."

William's brows rose, mirroring Kyrin's initial reaction to the news, but he let Darq continue.

"We'd like to return the Scrolls to Josan so he can complete his copies. We also believe they would be safer in Dorland, at least for the time being. It's possible they're one of the last complete collections in Arcacia. Obviously, you understand the risk involved in this, so it's entirely your choice."

William folded his arms and considered it. Kyrin waited, gauging his expression. Her thudding pulse gave away her hope that he would decline and stay far away from the emperor. The memories of Daican's deceptive smile and smooth words still gave her chills. Then again, her father's cover of loyalty was intact, and the emperor would have no reason to suspect him. If only it brought her comfort.

"I can try," William decided after another moment.

Kyrin let out a quiet sigh and sent up a prayer for his safety.

Darq was pleased. "We thank you. Your help is much appreciated."

"I understand the importance of protecting the Scrolls, and their ability to encourage and empower the followers of Elôm," William said. "I believe now is the time we're most in need of them. If copies can be made and distributed, it will offer hope as people begin to despair."

"Well said," Josan replied. "People do indeed need hope, as well as guidance, and Elôm's Word is the greatest source of that. It is also a source of strength; not only in difficult times, but in our daily lives."

The others nodded in agreement.

"Any idea how you'll get into the palace?" Darq asked.

"Emperor Daican will want a report on what's happened here," William answered. "I can be the one to bring that information and, while I'm there, find the Scrolls."

"How soon can you leave?"

"Once you have Aaron, there won't be much left for my son and his men to do. I'll offer to ride to Valcré in the morning and explain the situation to the emperor."

"We'll accompany you. Unseen of course. We can discuss any further details once we camp tomorrow night."

With these plans established, they turned to the dragons. Along the way, William said to Kyrin and Kaden, "Looks like we'll see more of each other after all."

Despite her uneasiness concerning the emperor and the danger, Kyrin's smile was quick to surface. She would savor every moment they had together in the next couple of days. Only Elôm knew when they might have the chance again.

At the dragons, Kaden offered to let Timothy ride with him while Kyrin took their father. In moments, everyone but Josan had mounted.

Kyrin looked over her shoulder at her father. "Are you ready for this?"

"Not quite what I'm used to, but this might be the only chance I'll ever get to fly. I always wanted to when I was a boy."

Kyrin chuckled. "So that's where Kaden gets it from. You should've seen his face when we heard we'd be getting dragons."

Just before they took to the sky, Darq told Trask and his group, "Stick with me. Glynn and the others will announce our arrival."

With Trask's nod of understanding, the cretes commanded their dragons into the air and the others followed.

"Hang on," Kyrin told her father right before Ivoris launched herself upward.

The cold night air blasted Kyrin's face and sent a shiver through her body, but it was invigorating and erased all remnants of sleepiness. The sky widened into a sparkling black canopy above them. They rose above the rocky slopes that hid their camp, and lights twinkled ahead of them. Even from here, the fires from Marcus's camp were clearly visible. Following Darq's lead, they flew straight for it.

They approached the area rapidly, and when they drew close, Talas, Glynn, Falcor, and Leetra sped ahead of the others. Right as they reached the camp, all four dragons released an ear-splitting roar. Another shiver tingled through Kyrin. The dragons circled camp, and a frenzy of movement erupted below them. Just before joining the rest of the group, Storm and Glynn's dragon opened their mouths and spewed out steady streams of fire onto the open ground, several yards from the edge of the soldiers' camp.

Kyrin sucked in her breath, and her eyes went wide at the spectacular sight. The fire fell harmlessly, but lit up the approach of the rest of the dragons, glinting on their scales and lighting up their bright eyes.

Darq landed near where the smoke rose from the charred ground. Everyone gathered around him, though Kyrin and Kaden kept behind the others. Ten yards ahead of them, soldiers gathered in a defensive line in front of their camp. Whether they actually believed they could defend it or not, Kyrin couldn't guess. Likely they were only putting up a brave front. She was no soldier, but even she knew a ground force wouldn't stand a chance against a group of dragons.

A moment later, Marcus stepped forward, his sword in hand. He stood tall and projected confidence, but his shadowed expression betrayed his shock and, perhaps, fear. A niggling of regret twisted inside Kyrin for doing this to him. However, they had to save Aaron, and this was the safest way for all of them.

At the head of the group, Darq stepped down from his dragon and took a few steps toward the other captain. His confident stride and bearing surpassed Marcus's attempts. Backed by the dragons and armed as he was, he must have been a truly intimidating sight to those who did not know his intentions.

"I am Captain Verus Darq of the Hawk Clan." His voice rang out, amplified by the terrain. "I have come for the man you have in custody."

Only silence reigned for a moment. Marcus cast a wary glance at the dragons before his focus shifted back to Darq and he found his voice. His obvious sense of duty came with it. "Sir, our prisoner is an enemy and traitor to our country and emperor. I cannot release him to you."

Although Kyrin couldn't see his face, everything about Captain Darq exuded control.

"I don't believe, Captain, that you're in any position to refuse my demands." Darq gestured to the dragons. "I doubt you or your men have ever faced a dragon before, let alone a dozen of them. Now, we do not wish to harm you, but we will not leave here without your prisoner."

Indecision warred on Marcus's face, and Kyrin silently urged him to forget duty and use common sense. Not one of them, individually or together, stood a chance at resisting. She sighed, and longed to call out to him. It would be hard to fly away without some contact.

The men behind Marcus stood stone-still as they eyed both their captain and the dragons. At last, Marcus appeared to make his decision, though it was visibly difficult for him. He looked back at the men. "Go get the prisoner."

An older man gave a reluctant nod and turned. Kyrin let out another long breath. Thank Elôm that Marcus wasn't so dedicated as to attempt something so clearly foolish as resisting.

"A wise choice, Captain," Darq said with no animosity. "And, as a token of our good will, I have something more to offer you."

At this cue, Kyrin's father squeezed her arm and slid down. He gave her a quick smile before he walked to the front of the group. Glynn took him by the arm and led him up next to Darq.

A new wave of shock cleared Marcus's face of expression. "Father?"

"It's all right," William assured him. "I'm not harmed."

Marcus's shoulders sagged as if in relief.

"I consider it a very generous trade," Captain Darq told him. "Your life, your father's, and your men's in exchange for the prisoner's."

Marcus sent him a cool look, but had nothing to say to this.

A minute later, the other soldier returned, leading the man Timothy had described earlier.

"Cut him loose," Marcus commanded.

The soldier grumbled as he pulled out a knife and sliced the ropes from Aaron's wrists.

"You're free to go," Marcus said in a low voice.

Rubbing his wrists, Aaron didn't hesitate. When he'd gone a couple of yards, Glynn released William. He and Aaron met in the middle and glanced at each other, but kept moving.
As soon as he was close enough, Timothy jumped down and rushed to meet his brother.

"Tim?" Aaron breathed. He reached out and hauled his brother into a strong embrace. "Thank Elôm you're safe."

"Me?" Timothy pulled away and led his brother along with him. "You're the one who got captured."

Aaron just laughed quietly, sounding tired, but relieved.

Trask offered Aaron a spot on his dragon, and Timothy reclaimed his on Exsis.

As Darq and Glynn returned to the dragons, Kyrin settled her eyes on her father. Marcus had a hand on his shoulder, and right there with them was Liam. An ache rose up in Kyrin's chest. That moment made the truth clear—her family could never be together again. She squeezed her prickling eyes shut and tried to draw a breath to free her lungs. Dragon wings beat the air around her, and she took one last look at her father and brothers before leaving them behind.

*Thank You, Elôm.* Timothy felt that the words were woefully inadequate, considering, but he hadn't stopped expressing his gratitude since Aaron had stepped safely into the group's protection. When they landed in camp, he dismounted and helped his brother down. They turned to where Josan waited eagerly. A wide smile claimed the crete's face, and he embraced Aaron.

"Praise the King, you're safe," he murmured.

"He sure provided an unforgettable rescue." Aaron looked at Timothy. "You made some interesting friends in one day."

Timothy smiled and glanced at the group of men and women who'd been so quick to offer their assistance. What a marvel for Elôm to have brought them here, right when they were needed most. Had it just been he and Josan, Aaron would be destined for execution in Valcré.

Introductions followed, and they led Aaron nearer to the fire, where Timothy collected a waterskin and food for his brother. Aaron gulped down the water and then started on the food. Meanwhile, Timothy and Josan filled him in on what he'd missed. As Aaron downed the last bite of food, Leetra approached them, holding a leather bag. She looked down at Aaron and spoke matter-of-factly. "I'll tend to your shoulder."

Timothy exchanged a glance with Aaron, who said, "Don't worry about it. Timothy can handle it."

Leetra stood up a little straighter. "I've worked with the finest physician in our city. I know what I'm doing."

"It's hardly more than a scratch," Aaron insisted. "Tim will do just fine."

Her jaw shifted sideways, her lavender eyes smoldering. Without warning, she smacked the bag into Timothy's chest and spun on her heel. He grabbed it before it could fall to the ground and watched her stalk off. Raising his brows, he knelt down next to his brother.

"She's friendly," Aaron muttered under his breath.

Timothy sent a quick glance over at Leetra, where she now stood with the other cretes. Her arms were crossed, and her chin tipped up in blatant disregard for the two of them. He wanted to tell her that Aaron meant no offense, but it was probably better to let it go and avoid questions.

Carefully, he helped Aaron pull his arm free of his bloodied coat and shirtsleeve. The gash was badly inflamed, but nothing Timothy couldn't handle. He opened the pack Leetra had left and found clean cloths, bandages, and ointment. After cleaning the wound thoroughly and applying a salve, he wrapped it.

"Any other injuries I should check?" he asked, tying off the knot.

Aaron shook his head. "A few bumps and scrapes, but nothing I haven't gotten in the mine." He pulled the edge of his shirt down over his arm to shield his exposed skin from the cold air. "Got an extra shirt? My pack's lying out on the outskirts of town, if someone hasn't claimed it already."

Timothy nodded and helped his brother up. Leaving the others at the fire, they walked to the shadows at the edge of camp, where the supplies rested, and Timothy dug a clean shirt out of his pack. Aaron changed into it and tipped his head toward the group. His voice low, he asked, "Do they know?"

Timothy looked at them too. "No. Josan hasn't mentioned anything, so I thought we'd just go on as we are."

Aaron pulled on his coat. "They'll likely soon guess we're half crete anyway. The rest will probably come out after that."

Timothy agreed. He didn't like keeping the truth from them, but Josan had his reasons, and Timothy was used to following his lead.

STILL, ICY DIMNESS filled the valley as dawn broke, but the sun wouldn't climb past the mountain peaks to offer warmth for another couple of hours. William lifted his saddle from the ground to his horse's back and shifted it into place. He'd already settled his plans with Marcus. His son would remain another day or two in Dunlow to gather any useful information, and William would travel to Valcré alone.

As thankful as William was to have Aaron safe, the look of defeat in Marcus's eyes when it sank in that he'd failed his mission left a lingering regret. Marcus hated to fail, but even more, he hated to disappoint the General. This was surely at the forefront of his mind. And the General would not take the news well. His dedication to his gods and the emperor demanded perfection from not only himself, but also those around him, especially those in his own family.

With a sigh, William knotted the cinch strap and let the stirrups down. His horse breathed out a white puff of air, and he patted its neck. When he looked up, he spotted Liam, who approached with a solemn and reluctant expression. Perhaps it had something to do with the look of guilt William had noticed the night before.

Liam paused when he reached him and glanced around. He'd never been good at hiding a guilty conscience. "Can we talk before you go . . . privately?"

"Of course."

They walked several yards away from the horse, and William stopped to face his son. "What's on your mind?"

Liam grimaced, hesitating a long moment before his words formed. "I have to tell you something." He licked his lips, and William waited calmly. He'd learned long ago not to jump to conclusions when it came to Liam.

"Yesterday, while we were searching, I saw the crete man and the brother shortly before Marcus caught the other one. The crete only had one leg. I could've stopped them, but . . ." He seemed to gather his courage before finally spitting it out. "I told them to go. I let them escape, and I lied to Marcus."

William stared at his son. Liam had done an incredibly risky, yet brave, thing in letting them escape. This could be the opening William had waited and prayed for. A chance to see if Liam was open to the truth.

But he quickly reined in his thoughts at the devastation and fear in Liam's eyes. After all, the punishment for such actions would be horrifyingly severe, perhaps even warranting execution. William sobered, and Liam started rambling.

"I know I shouldn't have. I know I'll be punished for it. I just had to tell you. I—"

"You did the right thing."

Liam frowned. "I . . . did?"

William gave him a firm nod and made a quick scan of the area before looking his son in the eyes. "I would've done the same thing."

It took Liam a long moment to absorb this. He shook his head, his brows still bent in confusion, yet something eager sparked in his eyes. "You don't believe we needed to arrest them?"

"No." William let out a breath. Why couldn't he have more time? He spoke carefully, but directly. "Liam, there are things . . . a great many things I don't agree on with the emperor."

Liam's expression opened up in his eagerness, as if a soul-deep hunger were being satisfied. "Like killing people for how they believe?"

"Yes, I believe that's wrong." William had never spoken so openly with either of his eldest sons.

"So do I," Liam murmured.

William's heart gave a small leap. Liam was right on the edge now. He could sense it. All he needed was a little push. The truth begged to come out, but he couldn't overwhelm Liam. Not here and now when he couldn't stay to help him with all the questions, uncertainties, and fears that would follow. It was difficult enough for William to live the life of an Arcacian soldier, serving Daican and being forced to hide his own faith. He couldn't imagine the struggle it would cause his son. Could he even survive it? The General already had him under such intense scrutiny.

Determination solidified inside William. He would get Liam out of the army. He'd tried, unsuccessfully, in the past, but things were different now. Liam was a man and capable of making the decision himself. Between the two of them, they would find a way. But first, he needed to complete his current mission.

He gripped Liam's shoulder. "There are many things I've wanted to tell you. If only we had time now but, as soon as we're back at Fort Rivor, we'll talk, all right?"

Liam nodded enthusiastically.

William caught movement out of the corner of his eye. Marcus had come to stand by his horse and waited there to allow them to finish their conversation.

Liam's face grew troubled again. "Should I tell Marcus what I did? I hated lying to him."

"No," William said quietly. "I don't think Marcus is ready to hear it. He won't understand. But perhaps he will someday. Then you can tell him."

He squeezed Liam's shoulder and prayed for that day to come as they both turned and walked toward Marcus. William's eldest son had questions in his eyes, but he didn't voice them.

"Ready to leave?" he asked.

"Almost." William picked up his saddlebags and bedroll.

"I'll ask around town for information on Josan," Marcus said as William worked. "Maybe he isn't this Taan we're looking for." A dim thread of hope lifted his voice, but doubt overtook it. "If we don't find anything new, we'll return to Fort Rivor."

William faced his son and the disappointment in his eyes that was so hard to bear. "If I arrive there first, I'll inform the General of what happened and tell him that I got captured." Perhaps it would give Marcus some small measure of comfort not to have to deliver the news himself.

His son was silent for a moment before he asked, "What were you doing outside of camp anyway?" No suspicion or accusation lurked in his eyes, only genuine curiosity.

"I was praying."

Marcus's brows lifted a fraction.

"For you and Liam," William continued. "I pray often for you, and your brothers and sister, for the actions and choices you make. It's very important to me."

Marcus seemed unsure of a response at first but, finally, he said, "Thank you," and William heard the appreciation in his voice.

He smiled at his son, and then took his horse's reins to mount. From the saddle, he looked down at Marcus. "Before I go, I wanted to tell you to remember the men you seek are people too, just like you and me. It's not wrong or weak to have a heart and show compassion."

Marcus bowed his head as conflict skimmed across his face. "I know, but . . . sometimes it's difficult when duty comes first."

"You're right; it is," William agreed. He studied his son for a long moment. "You're a good man, Marcus. I just don't want anyone or anything to steal that away from you. Reputations are tricky things. We know that better than most. Once you have one, it's not an easy thing to be rid of, so make sure it's one you won't regret living with."

Marcus nodded, truly appearing to take this to heart.

William's smile returned to encompass both his sons. "I'll see you back at the fort." His eyes settled on Liam. "Then we'll talk."

Both Marcus and Liam gave a nod. William nudged his horse, turned south, and trotted out of camp.

Sunset left deep shadows among the rocks where Kyrin waited with Kaden alongside the road just south of Keth. She tapped her fingers on her arm, anxious for the first glimpse of their father's arrival. But it wasn't the only thing fueling her need to fidget. Shifting, she looked over at Kaden and took advantage of the opportunity to talk privately about the previous night's developments.

"How do you feel about Father being the one to get the Scrolls?"

Kaden glanced at her but, as far as she could tell, he wasn't nearly as nervous as she was. "I guess if he's careful it should be all right."

"I just wish he didn't have to see the emperor," Kyrin murmured, and then fell silent as she considered the danger of the situation—not only in getting the Scrolls, but also in the life their father lived. Life as a believer in Elôm seemed so perilous outside of the support she and Kaden had from those in Landale. Her father was on his own.

"What?"

Kyrin broke from her thoughts and met Kaden's questioning look. That's when she realized how tightly her forehead had scrunched together. She softened her frown and shook her head.

"I was just thinking . . . if not for Mother, we might be able to talk Father into getting Michael and Ronny and joining us." So many things would be different if their mother was different.

"Kyrin." His soft tone both cautioned and encouraged her.

She sighed at the familiar discontentment lurking inside her and picked at a thread on her sleeve. "I know. I shouldn't blame her."

Kaden stared at the road for a long moment and then shrugged. "It's probably best for them to avoid becoming outlaws for as long as they can. At least they get to live a normal life."

Kyrin could see the wisdom in that and forced away her uncharitable feelings. It was selfish of her to want to uproot them from a comfortable home just so she could have them near her. Her eyes prickled, and she blinked hard. The last thing she wanted was to be so melancholy when her father arrived.

"Hey." Kaden's voice drew her gaze to him again, and he smiled encouragingly. "I'd like to have them in camp too."

Kyrin's discomfort faded as he coaxed a smile from her. Trust Kaden to come to her rescue. He, more than anyone else, understood her tendency to blame their mother—how she struggled to feel love toward her. It was never easy to push aside how her mother had given in to the General's insistence that she and Kaden be taken to Tarvin Hall at such a young age, disregarding her husband's wishes to the contrary. And even harder when Kyrin recalled how her mother had treated her father sometimes. Would she ever love her mother the way she did her father?

A few minutes later, a clacking in the rocks up the valley road drew their attention, and their father appeared. All previous thoughts vanished in Kyrin's excitement, and she and Kaden left the cover of the rocks to meet him.

"Good," he said as he dismounted near the side of the road. "I was hoping I was getting close."

"I hope we didn't go too far," Kyrin told him. "Captain Darq thought this would be a good place to camp."

"This is fine. How long have you been here?"

"Since noon."

He looked surprised, and Kaden said, "It's too bad you need your horse. You could've ridden with us."

Their father smiled. "I would've liked that."

After helping him unsaddle and feed his horse, and tie it where the dragons wouldn't spook it, they led him up to their camp in an outcropping of rocks. The others greeted him kindly, and they all scrunched around the fire for a warm meal. While they ate, Kyrin and Kaden shared more about their life in Landale. Kyrin still wished her father could join them. His enthusiasm about the camp was easy to see in the eager way he discussed it with Trask.

Darkness had fallen across the valley by the time they finished their supper. As different members rose to rinse their supper dishes, Jace quietly offered to take Kyrin's plate for her.

"You don't have to do that," she told him.

But he said, "I don't mind."

With heartfelt thanks, she handed him her plate, and he turned to extend the same offer to both her father and Kaden. Warmth bloomed in her chest and blossomed into a smile. Jace had come so far in the few months she'd known him, and she thanked Elôm for such progress. Her eyes lingered on him a moment before her anticipation to speak privately to her father returned.

She shifted her attention to him. "Do you want to go for a walk?"

When he nodded, Kyrin and Kaden led him away from the campfire and followed the crooked path that angled down toward the road again. Aertus had almost completely risen above the mountains, and Vilai wasn't far behind, giving them ample light to pick their way along the rough terrain. Once the voices of camp had died away, and the silence of the night surrounded them, Kyrin stopped. Her heartbeat quickened as she turned to face her father. All evening she'd waited for the right moment to share her news, and she couldn't contain it any longer.

"I have something to tell you. Something I learned from Rayad just after I came to camp."

Her father waited, interest piqued, and Kyrin said, "Your father, Jonavan, wasn't a traitor. At least not by our standards."

Her father's brows drew together. Kyrin hastened to explain everything Rayad had told her about how Jonavan had led men to force a village to worship Aertus and Vilai, only to end up joining the villagers in their opposition. Though he'd been executed and branded a traitor following the struggle, all evidence suggested he'd believed in Elôm before his death.

William stood silent for a long moment. Kyrin had never seen her father cry, but moonlight reflected in the moisture built up in his eyes. Two tears trailed down Kyrin's face in the shared emotion. Her father stared out at the dark valley as the information sank in. He shook his head and cleared his throat, though his voice still came out raw and quiet.

"I had no idea."

Kyrin put her arm around him, and he hugged her close. "He was a hero," she whispered, unable to imagine how she would feel to go her whole life believing her father was a traitor and then find out the truth. She looked up, and watched a slow smile come to his face in a moment of open vulnerability she hadn't witnessed before.

He drew in a deep breath and let it out slowly before smiling down at her and squeezing her shoulder. "Thank you for telling me. Maybe someday others will know the truth too."

"Quite a few know now. The important thing is that you know, and we know."

Her father agreed. He shook his head again, still absorbing the news.

"Maybe one day you can even tell Marcus and Liam," Kyrin said hopefully.

"I'd like that." He reached up to rub the tears out of his eyes. "I want you two to pray for Liam."

Kyrin pulled away slightly to see his face better.

"I think he's ready to believe," he told her and Kaden.

Kyrin's heart skipped.

"He saw Josan and Timothy, while Marcus was searching for them, and let them go. He was also very distraught when Marcus allowed Aaron to be interrogated. I spoke with him this morning. He believes it's wrong that the emperor is killing people because of their beliefs. I told him we'd talk as soon as we return to the fort."

He paused, but Kyrin's thoughts were already jumping back to her conversation with Kaden earlier.

"I was afraid to explain things here because I don't know if he could handle this information on his own. And I don't believe he'll be able to continue serving in the army if he does turn to Elôm. I want to get him out, but I'm not sure what to do after that."

"He can come to Landale." The excitement of the prospect burst through Kyrin. "Trask would be happy to have him, and he'd be safe there. He'd be able to learn and grow and wouldn't be under any of the emperor's or Grandfather's influence."

William nodded slowly, a slight smile on his lips. "He would love that."

Kyrin looked over and traded a grin with Kaden. They might

not get to have their father and younger brothers in camp, but it looked like they would get one of their older brothers. If only they were done with this mission. She could already imagine him in camp with them. But then her thoughts drifted to Marcus, and her excitement faded. It wouldn't seem right without him there as well.

"What about Marcus?"

Her father sighed, and his expression sobered. "He needs your prayers too . . . maybe even more than Liam. I still don't know how to approach him."

Kaden broke in now, frustration edging his tone. "How can he not see what he's doing? How wrong it is?"

"I think he does somewhere deep inside. I can see the conflict in him and how he struggles with his decisions at times. The problem is that he truly believes he's doing the right thing. He's very much the way I was when I was his age. He feels an almost painful need to prove himself. For me, it was to prove I wasn't my father. For him, it's to prove his worthiness to the General and to himself. Your grandfather has very high expectations, but I think Marcus's personal expectations are even higher. He fears failure. That's why he's so dedicated to succeeding, even when it means ignoring the part that wishes things could be different."

Kaden grumbled, but Kyrin could see more similarities between her two brothers than her twin would ever admit. They both had their own stubbornness, and were both dedicated to what they believed. They just happened to be on opposing sides.

She sighed and hung her head. As excited as she was about Liam, she was equally sad about Marcus. She longed to save him, somehow, from the emperor's grip, but how did you save someone who didn't want to be saved?

"Is there nothing you can say to him?" she asked, her voice small.

"I'm afraid veiled words won't penetrate," her father replied, "especially as time goes on and he begins to make a name for himself. The only way may be to tell him the truth outright, but what he'll do with it . . . I don't know."

A cold hand seemed to grip Kyrin's throat, and she had to swallow to loosen it. "You don't think . . . he wouldn't turn you in . . . would he?"

Her father's hesitance put a hard knot in her stomach.

"No . . . I don't think he would, but it would trouble him deeply."

"Will you tell him?"

"Sometime. His eternity is far more important than my life here." He must have sensed Kyrin's rising fear at the risk involved and offered her a reassuring smile. "But we don't know what the future will bring. Right now, the only thing we have is to pray. We'll pray for guidance and the right circumstances. We can only guess what may happen or how Marcus will respond. Elôm is the One working on his heart. He can bring about the perfect events to open it to the truth."

Kyrin gave a quick nod. Her father was right, and she willed hope to take hold.

Hours slipped by, with the moons arcing across the sky above Kyrin, Kaden, and their father. They found a small grouping of rocks to sit on not far from camp, but far enough that they would not disturb everyone's sleep, and talked of all manner of things. Oftentimes, Kyrin just sat with her arms around her knees as she listened to her father and brother talk, enjoying the sound of their strong voices, and smiling at the way Kaden's rose in enthusiasm.

Sometime around midnight, Kaden rose and blew on his

hands. "It's getting cold. I'll get us some coffee."

Kyrin and their father thanked him. They were quiet for a moment as he walked away, but Kyrin picked out a hidden smile crinkling the corners of her father's eyes. She tipped her head questioningly, and he finally asked, "So you and Jace . . . you're just friends?"

Kyrin's eyes widened, but she looked down as her cheeks warmed even in the cold. She'd not been prepared for such a question, though she supposed she'd given her father adequate reason to wonder, the way she'd spoken so highly of Jace in the last hours.

"Yes, just friends." She looked up again to meet his interested look and shrugged, still self-conscious. "Besides, I don't think Jace would ever feel that way. He has too much he struggles with. He's so tortured by his past, and I've seen him so broken. I can't imagine the pain and fear of wondering if you have a soul."

"But you believe he does?"

Kyrin looked him in the eyes, and deep conviction strengthened her voice. "I know he does."

Her father nodded. "Me too."

Kyrin sighed. She didn't know what she would have done if he hadn't agreed.

"Well, whatever happens in the future, and if one of you decides you do want to become more than just friends, just be mindful of and careful with your feelings. You're far too precious to settle for someone who won't treasure you."

Kyrin smiled at his words and nodded firmly. "I will." She laughed lightly. "And don't worry. Any man with interest like that will have to answer to Kaden. He's already made that clear."

Her father joined in her quiet laughter. The sound of it seemed to chase away the chill around them, and Kyrin wished more than anything that he would never have to leave them.

"Good for him," he said.

As if drawn by their mention of him, Kaden returned with three steaming cups of coffee. He passed them around, and Kyrin took her first sip. She breathed out in satisfaction as the hot liquid warmed her insides.

"Talas put more on if we need it," Kaden said.

Kyrin smiled again. They probably would need it. They still had much more to talk about.

WITH A LOUD gulp, Gem swallowed down the hind section of a mountain goat—part of what Talas and Glynn had brought back after a brief hunting excursion at dawn. Though the dragon could easily have consumed more, she gave a contented rumble and dipped her head toward Jace to rest it against his chest. He rubbed her cheek scales and smiled at how quickly she could go from ferocious carnivore to gentle and loving. She purred and whiffled his coat with her warm, meaty breath.

Amidst her little chirps and warbles, Jace's gaze wandered over to the fire and landed on Kyrin. She and Kaden stood near their father, who discussed his plans with Captain Darq. On this second morning of their journey, Valcré stretched out in the distance from their mountain campsite. William had met them in the late afternoon the day before and had chosen to spend the night with the group before riding into the city.

Though Kyrin's face was calm, she kept twisting the cuff of her sleeve between her fingers, and she'd been distracted during breakfast. Not that he could blame her. Valcré didn't hold much good for either of them. Just seeing the city brought up old memories he wished he could erase too. If only they could avoid the city and call the mission a success now that they had Josan. The sooner they could get the Scrolls and leave it behind, the better. They were much too close to Emperor Daican. Jace didn't envy Kyrin's father in having to face him.

Gem gave him a little nudge at his inattention, and he turned back to her, but his gaze stopped on Falcor. The crete eyed the Altairs with an expression like stone, as usual. Jace clenched his jaw and hardened his own face to match. Even after all this time, the crete had not warmed up to them.

Someone stepped into his line of sight and blocked his view of the crete. His eyes refocused, and he found Leetra facing him with hands on her hips and an accusatory glare.

"Do you have a problem with Falcor?" Her voice was as icy as the breeze coming off the mountains.

Jace lifted his brows. The question should be whether or not Falcor had a problem with them. He was the one who regarded them all with a cold indifference, not that Leetra was much better. Before Jace had a chance to decide how to respond, she spoke again.

"He's a good man, a natural leader, fearless warrior, and very highly respected in our community." She raised her chin higher. "And soon he'll be my husband, so if you have a problem, say so."

Jace's muscles went taut, and embers stirred in his chest that he would not let flare to life. A scowl threatened, but he breathed deeply before speaking in a low voice, "Would it hurt to show a little gratitude toward those who have chosen to help you? Some of us are risking a lot." He tipped his head at the Altairs.

She blinked, her face suddenly blank, and her gaze faltered. It was difficult to tell on her brown cheeks, but they might have turned a bit pink. She shifted, but apparently pride didn't allow for an apology. With one quick glance at him, she walked away.

He peered after her as she sat down by Falcor, but from her stiff, unyielding posture, he didn't anticipate a noticeable change of heart—another good reason to complete this mission and return to camp. He huffed out a short breath and fixed his attention back on his dragon.

A short time later, someone spoke his name. He turned to come face to face with William. Self-consciousness kicked in, but the kind way William looked at him was so Kyrin-like it put him more at ease.

"Sir?" he asked.

"Before I leave, I wanted to thank you for the way you've protected Kyrin. She shared some things with me over the last couple of nights, and you have my deepest gratitude."

Jace looked down and shrugged. No fathers he'd ever known had wanted him anywhere near their daughters. "It was nothing," he slowly raised his eyes back to the captain's, "compared to what she's done for me."

He wasn't sure he would have survived before she brought hope and a sense of purpose back to his life. He hadn't even wanted to. An upwelling of emotion rose into his throat and pricked his eyes. He tried to swallow it away, but it didn't quite remove the roughness in his voice. "I'd do anything for her. Anything to protect her."

"It does me good to know that," William said. "I've been unable to be around for her most of her life. It comforts me to know others like you will be."

He offered his hand. Jace took his forearm, and William gripped his firmly. They stood a moment while William sized him up before saying, "I see a man of strong character in you, Jace. Don't believe any lies to the contrary."

Jace's throat constricted again as these words struck a raw chord in his heart. He nodded slowly and had to work the tightness loose before managing a hoarse, "Thank you."

William gave him the warm, compassionate smile Jace was so used to from Kyrin, and actually made him feel he was worth something. After that, William returned to the fire. Jace, however, did not move as he breathed deeply until his emotions fell back behind the wall where he usually tried to keep them contained.

A nauseating ache built in Kyrin's stomach. She'd dreaded this moment all morning. She glanced at Kaden as they stood quietly while their father readied his horse. Though her brother had seemed unconcerned the last time they'd spoken of this, the tautness of his jaw betrayed his misgivings. Kyrin pressed her fingers into her middle. It had been better when Kaden wasn't worried.

When their father finished and took in the sight of their faces, he offered a heartening smile. "Don't worry. Everything will be fine. I'm among the emperor's men every day. This is not much different."

But it was, or at least it felt different. Facing the emperor himself seemed far more dangerous than facing his men, where her father blended in more easily.

"I have a perfectly legitimate reason to visit the palace," he continued. "The emperor will be far too busy with other things to question my motives. I'll have supper with him, if he wishes, get the Scrolls out, and leave in the morning. It'll be over and done in a matter of hours."

Kyrin gave a quick nod and tried to convince herself it was as easy as that. If her father wasn't worried, and she couldn't detect that he was, then she shouldn't be either. However, she looked at him with all seriousness.

"Beware of Davira. Avoid her, if you can. I think she's the one who found me out." Goose bumps crawled down her arms at the memories. Of course, the princess had no supernatural powers, but Kyrin couldn't stop her fear that Davira would suspect her father just by seeing him.

"I'll be wary," William promised.

Kyrin drew in a cold breath that ached in her lungs and throat. She shouldn't allow herself to get so upset, but tears burned her eyes. Her father must have seen them, and his smile gentled as he opened his arms to her. She stepped into them and let the comfort of his embrace wash over her.

"Are you sure about this?" she murmured. She wasn't going to ask, but the question slipped out.

"Yes, I'm sure." The confidence in his voice boosted hers.

Kyrin closed her eyes and prayed silently as she nestled her head against his shoulder. When they parted, he kissed her forehead and kept his hands on her shoulders.

"Remember, Elôm is at work in this. It's no coincidence we met up in Dunlow."

A smile finally claimed Kyrin's face, and she latched onto the forgotten truth. Elôm had surely orchestrated this, and she had to trust Him with the outcome. Her father squeezed her shoulders, and then turned to Kaden. Father and son hugged tightly.

"I wish I could go with you," Kaden said, his voice husky.

"I know. Perhaps someday it will no longer have to be like this."

Kyrin shared that hope. The last two days had given her a glorious taste of how life could be together, and she longed for it to continue.

Her father and brother parted, and Kaden took his place at her side again. Their father looked at the two of them and, this time, his eyes appeared a bit moist. "I love you both so much."

Kyrin fought to keep her own tears from robbing her voice. "I love you too."

Kaden had to clear his throat. "Me too."

Their father smiled at them and turned to his horse. They couldn't prolong the inevitable. After mounting, he looked down at them before his eyes shifted to Darq and Talas, who had approached.

"We'll be waiting at the arch at ten tonight," Talas assured him.

William nodded. "Wait there an hour. If I don't show up, I've been detained and will bring the Scrolls out with me in the morning." His gaze returned to Kyrin and Kaden. "I'll see you tomorrow."

The two of them nodded, and their father guided his horse away from camp. Kyrin stood on the edge as he made his way down the slope, not moving until he disappeared among the trees below.

THE GOLD-HUED SURROUNDING wall of Auréa Palace loomed above William as his horse clopped down the cobblestone street. People passed him, bustling from one location to the next. Some nodded in respect as they hurried on their way. He hadn't visited Valcré since the emperor's public decree against worshipping Elôm, but life seemed to go on as normal. Most probably thought nothing of the executions, though he hoped the city had a strong secret following of those who believed in their King.

Halting his horse, he addressed the guards at the main gate. "Captain William Altair with news for the emperor."

The guards nodded in recognition of him and allowed him to pass. William nudged his horse and rode into the sweeping courtyard. His eyes slowly climbed the towering stories of the palace before dropping back to the entrance. At the base of the wide front steps, he stopped again and dismounted. An attendant took his horse, and he climbed the steps, where the door guards let him inside.

The grand foyer opened up before him to display the full glory of its polished gold and black marble floor, glittering chandeliers, and rich, dark wood, all accented by tapestries and fine art. After taking a moment to adjust to the splendor, he focused on a man who approached—one of Daican's low-level aides.

"Welcome to Auréa, Captain," the tall, thin man greeted him. "Can I help you?"

"I have news for Emperor Daican pertaining to the search in the Graylin Valley."

The aide gave a quick nod. "Please, follow me."

William trailed him into one of the more spacious meeting rooms close to the emperor's office.

"If you will wait here, I will inform His Majesty of your arrival. Please, make yourself comfortable."

William nodded, and the man left him alone. Clasping his hands behind his back, he let his gaze roam the furnishings, but he did not take a seat. He wasn't as concerned about this as his daughter was, but this would be the first time he would see the emperor since the executions had begun, and that in itself was unnerving.

He did not have long to anticipate the meeting. In a short couple of minutes, footsteps echoed in the hall—confident, steady strides. The door opened a moment later, and Daican stepped in, followed by Sir Richard. William briefly made eye contact with the cruel man, but turned his full attention to the emperor and bowed at the waist. "Your Majesty."

"Captain Altair." Daican came to stand before him. "I was not aware you were part of the search in the Valley."

"General Veshiron sent me to aid my son in his mission."

"And what news do you bring?" The emperor's voice had risen in eagerness, no doubt with hopes they had caught the crete.

"Not good news, I'm afraid."

Daican's brows inched down, though his voice and manner remained calm. "Go on."

"When I arrived in Dunlow three days ago, my son had apprehended a man in connection with a crete named Josan Silvar. This man's brother and the crete escaped, but Marcus hoped to learn their whereabouts from the prisoner." William paused and braced himself for the emperor's response. "I regret to inform you that I was taken captive by a group helping the crete. They were well armed and had a large group of dragons. They threatened my son's men and offered me in trade for the prisoner. Marcus had no choice but to accept or the dragons would have killed everyone."

A heavy silence followed. The anger of defeat glittered in the emperor's eyes, but he maintained almost perfect control over his emotions and hid them better than Richard, who wore a dark scowl. William was careful to project just the right amount of penance over his capture to cover his true intentions.

"Do you believe the crete was this Taan we've been after?" Daican questioned, his voice still calm and even.

"He could be, my lord. Marcus stayed behind in Dunlow to see if he could find any more information before returning to Fort Rivor."

"But even if he finds it is the same crete, they're likely long gone by now."

"I would expect so."

The muscles along Daican's bearded jaw twitched as he contemplated the design in the rug. Finally, his deceptively generous eyes rose back to William. "Did you recognize any of the men who held you captive?"

William cringed inwardly. "Half of them were cretes. The others must have been Arcacian rebels." He prayed the vague answer would satisfy the emperor.

Daican's very gaze seemed to probe him for further information. "Did you learn anything of interest from them?"

"They didn't hold me long. They were anxious to rescue the prisoner."

"I see," Daican murmured. He nodded again in apparent acceptance of what was done. "Thank you for delivering the information, Captain. You must be weary from so much travel.

Please accept my invitation to remain as long as you like and join me for supper this evening."

"Thank you, my lord. I would be honored to join you and rest here for the night. Tomorrow, I intend to ride on to Fort Rivor to bring the news to General Veshiron."

"Of course," Daican replied. "Now, I must return to my office. Do you have anything planned for your day?"

"I do, my lord." William hoped not to say more, but Daican's questioning stare prompted him to speak. His insides reacted again. This was one of the most difficult aspects of serving the emperor while hiding his forbidden faith. Everything he did felt like a lie, especially covering for his actions. Was it all wrong? He couldn't say for sure, but the conflict of it weighed on him. "I thought I would look through the library . . . for information we have on the cretes. Perhaps it could be of some use."

Daican stared at him a moment. "Excellent idea."

William silently exhaled.

"Let one of my aides know if you need assistance."

"I will."

Daican motioned to the aide by the door. "See that Captain Altair is shown a room and served lunch." To William, he said, "I'll expect you for supper at seven."

With Richard following, the emperor left the room, and William breathed a little more easily.

Many said Auréa's library was one of the most amazing sights in Arcacia, and William didn't argue that fact. Row upon row of full bookshelves occupied the giant hall, but that was only the ground level. Around the perimeter of the massive space, large balconies rose one above the other, to the vaulted ceiling six stories up. Between the ancient scrolls, books, and parchments, there had to be well over a million separate articles to read. William just stood at the door for a long moment in uncertainty of where to begin. Would one day be adequate time to find the Scrolls? The last thing he wanted was to have to manufacture an excuse to stay longer, and he prayed for success.

"Can I help you, Captain?"

William turned to the old spinster librarian. "Miss Winna." He gave her kind smile. She was a slight, but dignified woman, her long gray hair coiled up around her head. Though a bit stiff, she'd been kind to him on the few occasions he'd had reason to interact with her in previous visits to the palace. "Actually, I'm looking for information on the cretes—family histories and such. Perhaps you can tell me where to start."

One of the woman's thin brows arched. Not many people had interest in the cretes anymore. "I believe," she said slowly, "you should look down here."

She walked to the end of the hall with short, quick steps. William followed. In the far right corner, Winna waved her hand toward multiple bookcases.

"Most of what we have on the cretes would be in this area."

William eyed the shelves. It would still be a daunting search, but at least he had a place to start. He smiled again. "Thank you for your assistance."

She gave a curt nod. "If you need anything else, I'll be around."

Left alone to his mission, William scanned each of the bookshelves. At least he could skip over the books. That narrowed the search by about half. He had seven scrolls to find intotal and, Elôm willing, they would all be together. Most of the scrolls on the first shelf alone matched Josan's description, but only the King's Scrolls would be marked with a tag bearing a small hawk symbol.

William slid a ladder down and meticulously searched every shelf. For each scroll he pulled out, he checked the description tag before sliding it back into place. He came across many crete family histories, but none bearing the symbol he sought. The shelves contained a surprising amount of information on the cretes. Most of it must have been collected years ago, when they still inhabited Arcacia.

The morning passed swiftly, and he had only searched half the bookcases before a servant appeared to guide him to a parlor for his lunch. He followed reluctantly, but returned to the library within the hour.

With afternoon creeping forward, his sense of urgency rose. What if the Scrolls were not here? Being disguised as family histories, the emperor could have had them thrown out. But William didn't believe Elôm would allow that to happen, so he pressed on.

After losing count of how many shelves he'd searched, he leaned against the ladder and sighed. He closed his sore eyes and rubbed them as he prayed for guidance and success. He was quickly running out of time. When he opened them again, he turned to the next bookcase to see how many scrolls it contained, and his gaze snagged on the edge of a tag halfway up. He tipped his head for a better look. A dark spot on the tag resembled part of a bird symbol. His heart rate jumped, and he peered around the library. He wasn't sure where Winna had gone, but the hall was silent.

William moved the ladder into place and climbed up to the scroll in question. Sliding it out, he flipped over the tag and let out a breath that had caught in his lungs. It was just what Josan had described—a family history title with a small black hawk inked beneath it. He reached for the other scrolls and checked each tag. A small smile grew as he pulled the seventh and final scroll free and tucked it under his arm with the others.

He climbed down the ladder and glanced again at the Scrolls, feeling the magnitude of what he had in his possession. *Elôm, we desperately need Your Word right now. Help me get these Scrolls safely to the others where they can be used for the greatest good.*

With a thankful heart, he left the bookcases and strode toward the entrance to the library. He'd almost reached the door when Winna walked in. He paused, keeping his manner calm as he showed her the Scrolls. "Would it be permissable for me to take these back to my room to look through?"

The woman bent and squinted to inspect one of the tags. "Of course." She sniffed. "I don't know why we even keep such histories. They're of no value to any of us."

William just smiled and thanked her, continuing on his way with a silent prayer not to meet anyone else. However, as he neared his room, another man came around the corner. His heart lurched against his ribs, but the moment he recognized the man, he let out a sigh of relief. "Aric."

"William, I just heard you were here." Emperor Daican's head of security glanced at the Scrolls. "The emperor told me of the news in Dunlow and said you were looking for information on the cretes." A hidden question settled in his eyes.

William glanced up and down the hall and motioned for Aric to follow. Inside his room, he closed and locked the door, laying the Scrolls on the table. After scanning the room just to be sure, he faced Aric and barely more than whispered, "These are a complete collection of the King's Scrolls."

The other man's eyes widened. He, too, spoke quietly, though his voice held a reverence that seemed to fill the room. "The King's Scrolls?"

William nodded. "They were disguised as crete family histories and hidden in the library."

Aric stared at the Scrolls, and then shot a look at the door as if someone could be listening. He shook his head. "Right here in the middle of the emperor's palace?" He came closer to the table. "Have you looked at any of them?"

"Not yet."

William reached for one and pulled the leather tie loose. Gingerly, he rolled the scroll open. A couple of feet of the parchment contained a dizzying list of crete names and information that would deter anyone, but it came to an abrupt end and pulled away from the main body of the scroll. Glancing at Aric, William continued to unroll this second section. There, in crisp black ink on the age-old parchment, were verses of Scripture. Both William and Aric bent over to read it. William barely breathed as he took the words in. He'd heard verses and passages passed down from believer friends, but he'd never seen them for himself. If only he could sit and read for hours, but he rolled the scroll up again.

Aric looked at him, his eyes and tone deathly serious. "You have to get them out of here. The emperor must never find out."

"I'll get them out tonight and pass them off to friends who will be waiting." William secured the tie. "I just hope Daican doesn't question my leaving so late."

"Well, he knows you're searching for information. Tell him you're going to the library at Tarvin Hall."

William nodded. It would be nice to see Sam and let him know about the Scrolls. Then it wouldn't be a total lie.

With the Scrolls found, William's next challenge was supper. Thankfully, the emperor was agreeable and engaging, despite the loss of Josan, and Prince Daniel proved to be an enjoyable dining companion. He had a keen interest in the different places William had been and the people he'd met. William sensed a bit of wanderlust from the young man, and his disdain at being kept near home. The tension between him and his father escalated throughout the meal, but a question Daican directed at William near the end brought the most discomfort.

"How is your family dealing with the treason of your son and daughter?"

His tone suggested genuine concern, though William had his doubts. He met the emperor's gaze and held it steadily. "It has been difficult, especially for my eldest sons. They were all close."

"It's a shame the name Altair seems to bear such a curse. Let us hope it does not breed any more traitors among your family." A flash of something cold and cunning crossed Daican's face.

William nodded slowly. "I pray every day that my children will follow the right path."

"As do I," Daican murmured, casting a glance toward his son. He smiled faintly. "After all, our children are our legacy."

"Yes, they are," William agreed, and thanked Elôm when the conversation shifted to a far less dangerous topic.

As the night grew late, restlessness tugged at him, though he took great care to hide it, particularly with Davira at the table. The princess, however, seemed to have little interest in him. Kyrin would be relieved. Close to ten, Daican finally announced that he and his wife would retire for the evening. After trading a few words with Daniel and his father and bidding the queen and princess a polite goodnight, William took his leave.

When he reached his room, he paused for a short prayer and slipped the strap of the satchel over his shoulder before walking out again. He kept his pace steady, but unhurried. The guards at the entrance only nodded to him before letting him out. He descended the steps and crossed the moonlit courtyard. The sound of his footsteps alerted the guardsmen at the gate as he drew near, but they, too, let him pass.

The moment he reached the street, he let out a long sigh and thanked Elôm. The riskiest part was behind him. He followed the street down from the palace, in the direction of Tarvin Hall but, when he reached the shadows, he turned northeast. About a block from the palace loomed a giant archway dedicated to the exploits of past heroes. An elaborate garden surrounded it and, though the plants had died off for the winter, it still offered plenty of cover for his covert meeting with Talas and Falcor. Darq had chosen those two since Talas had visited Valcré before and knew the city, and the two cretes were the stealthiest and quickest of the group. Even if someone happened to spot them, the chances were slim that anyone could catch them in the cover of darkness.

Coming around a corner, the arch rose up ahead of him. Its white marble almost glowed against the dark sky. Bare shrubs cast a strange patchwork of shadows. William scanned the dark areas as he approached the arch. Talas and Falcor stepped into the open when he reached it.

Moonlight lit up Talas's bright, eager eyes. "Do you have them?"

With a smile, William reached for the strap of the satchel. At the same moment, something glinted to Talas's right, and William's heart stalled. "Look out!"

The crete turned right as Falcor's dagger plunged into his midsection. Talas gasped, his eyes rounding as they locked on Falcor's stony expression. "What—"

A groan choked off his words as the other crete pulled his dagger free. The length of it dripped crimson. Talas sank to his knees, gripping his stomach.

William reached for his sword, but a commanding voice echoed through the garden.

"Don't move!"

A sensation like ice slithered down William's back, weighing down his limbs. His heart reacted with a painful thud. Everything up to this moment had gone perfectly . . . too perfectly.

"Take your hands away from your weapons."

William looked around to all the black and gold forms closing in. He squeezed his sword hilt, but resistance would be futile. Slowly, he raised his hands.

Soldiers rushed in. One grabbed his sword and the satchel, while two others wrenched his arms behind his back. Once they'd subdued him, the owner behind the commanding voice stepped into view. William gritted his teeth and stood up as straight as he was able to face Sir Richard. The man strode up to him. A savage light flickered in his cold eyes, and his voice oozed with contempt. "William Altair, you're under arrest, charged with treason against the emperor and the gods."

The charge settled heavily in his ears—a charge he had anticipated for all the years he'd served his King. One all believers now had to fear. He'd just hoped he would've had more time to make a difference.

If Richard waited for a reaction, William didn't give him one. Instead, his gaze shifted past the man and landed on Talas, who still knelt under the arch. Deep pain contorted the crete's face, though it wasn't merely physical. His chest shuddered, his hands covered in his own blood. William met the crete's eyes where a spark of determination flamed to life. Setting his jaw, Talas looked up at Falcor and the soldiers nearby. With one last glance at William, he jumped to his feet and took off in a flash. A soldier grabbed for him, but missed as Talas raced out of the garden.

"Falcor, take some men and get after him!" Richard snapped. "Make sure he doesn't survive the night."

Falcor motioned to a handful of men and ran off in pursuit of Talas. William stared after them and begged Elôm that the crete would escape and find help, if only for himself, before he bled to death.

An iron fist latched onto his coat and jerked his attention back to Richard's pitiless eyes.

"You're coming with me."

*ELÔM, PROTECT MY children and the others.*

Such prayers dominated William's thoughts on their march to the palace. Now that Falcor had betrayed them, he'd probably told Daican everything—exactly where they were camped and who was present. William prayed the dragons would deter an attack. After all, on foot, Daican's men wouldn't stand a chance. But what he feared even more was what Falcor could do in camp before his betrayal came to light. As long as they still trusted him, they would be at his mercy and, as he'd proved with Talas, he had none.

William stumbled and caught his balance as the soldiers shoved him up the palace steps behind Richard. His eyes rested on the man, then shifted down to the satchel containing the Scrolls. No doubt Daican would have them destroyed at the earliest opportunity.

William couldn't understand Elôm's plan behind this, but he held his head high as they marched through the palace. Despite his lack of understanding, he would trust his King, regardless of whether it led to life or death, and he did not fear that. What he did fear was the pain it would cause his family to lose him. *Lord, I pray for rescue; not for my own sake, but theirs. Please spare them from having to bear the loss.*

They passed through the darkened halls to the throne room, where Richard pushed open the heavy doors. Light spilled out. Still gripping his arms, the soldiers guided William inside. At the far end of the spacious hall, the entire royal family had gathered. Daican and Solora sat regally on their thrones, while Daniel and Davira stood behind. The emperor peered at him, his eyes piercing, yet his face was more hard than angry. Thanks to Falcor, Daican must have had a good twenty-four hours to simmer and prepare for this moment. The only time the crete could have brought him such detailed information of their plans was when he'd gone out on patrol the night before. He'd been gone plenty long enough to meet with Daican.

The queen wore little expression at all, while Davira's cold look held enough hatred to rival her father's. Only the prince appeared uncomfortable. He likely had not known about any of this until now. William doubted he could have hidden the knowledge when they had talked so companionably over supper. The young man was much more genuine than his father.

At the foot of the throne, the soldiers forced William to his knees. He kept his eyes down for a moment before looking up at Daican, but did not try to rise. The emperor's attention had shifted to Richard, who handed him the satchel. "Here are the Scrolls, just like Falcor said."

Daican flipped open the flap to glance at them before handing the satchel back. Now his eyes fell on William, exposing the ruthlessness he'd hidden during supper.

"So, another Altair joins the ranks of traitors." He spoke coolly, more in a tone of disgust than outrage, yet it carried a hint of his feelings of betrayal. "And I gave you every opportunity to prove your loyalty."

William winced slightly in memory of his lies and avoidance of the truth in the last few hours—lies Daican had seen right through and met with his own false act of hospitality. While the truth would not have spared William, the deception did not sit well.

"It's little wonder now that your children turned on me," Daican's voice sharpened, "when both their father and grandfather have done so. Tell me, do the rest of your sons merit arrest?"

"No." William's heart stuttered as his thoughts raced to Marcus and Liam. "It's only Kyrin, Kaden, and me. The others are loyal to both you and your gods."

Daican snorted out a laugh. "You openly deny serving Aertus and Vilai?"

William straightened his posture, but did not raise his voice. "I do."

"You must have no desire to live."

"That's not true, my lord, I want very much to live. If I thought you to be a man of mercy, I might even beg for my life." William's next words caught in the back of his throat as the emotion of the situation set in. "The last thing I want is to leave my wife widowed and my children fatherless, but I'm fully aware that's not in my hands."

Daican's eyes narrowed, as if he were trying to read a confusing book. "If you care so much about your life, then why risk throwing it away?"

"Because, my devotion to Elôm is greater than even my life. If He has called me to die here, then I trust He has a purpose. It may not be something you, or even I, can understand."

Daican stared at him for a long moment, and then released a cold laugh. "You're a fool."

William took the insult in silence.

"Have you nothing more to say for yourself?"

"Only, my lord, that it has never been my intention or desire to disrespect your authority." The conviction growing inside William strengthened him. "Though I believe in a different God, we both believe you were placed in this position of power by divine will. I've always sought to serve you well . . . except when it would have forced me to violate my conscience and beliefs. My only crime, my lord, is that I follow my faith as steadfastly as you follow yours."

He prayed the emperor would see his sincerity, and that they were alike in their dedication to what they believed. Perhaps, somehow, it would lead to a change of heart.

However, a flame kindled in Daican's eyes to reveal the anger that did indeed smolder deep inside. He stood from the throne, the raised dais allowing him to glare down on William. His voice rose to a dangerous intensity.

"William Altair, by your actions and your own admission, I find you guilty of treason for consorting with enemies of your emperor and Arcacia, as well as denying your gods. For these crimes, I sentence you to death tomorrow at dawn."

William breathed in sharply. So soon? All the hope he'd held inside sank into his stomach, but he clung to the faith that would see him through to the end, whether it was on an execution platform or not.

Daican's voice lowered and ground out through his clenched teeth. "It's high time another Altair faced the executioner's blade."

He waved his hand, and the soldiers grabbed William's arms and dragged him to his feet.

"Take him away," Daican spat.

William locked eyes with him once more before the men yanked him around and led him back down the length of the hall. Behind him, he caught the sound of Daniel's voice as they passed through the doors.

"Father, he's always been a good soldier. Surely—"

He didn't catch the end of it, nor Daican's response, but he carried no hope that the emperor would change his mind.

Falcor followed his escort, scowling at the man's back. He didn't need to be led around like a child, but security wouldn't allow him anywhere in the palace alone. Not that he couldn't have slipped away, but he knew better than to push his luck, so he forced himself to put up with it.

Still, he despised humans. Because of them, his people inhabited less than half the area they once did, and exercised no power in the affairs of their world. They did little more than hide alongside the giants in Dorland. But he would change that. He would gain back his people's land and prestige, even if it meant aligning himself with Daican for the time being. It was a tenuous alliance, but each had something the other needed—Daican had the resources, while Falcor possessed the knowledge and skills. Though he didn't trust the emperor to hold up his end of the bargain, it wouldn't matter for much longer. Soon he would have a powerful force at his command, and if Daican wanted it to work in his favor, he would have to cooperate. Until then, Falcor followed orders and bided his time.

He erased the scowl, or most of it, as they entered the emperor's office. Daican sat at his desk, while Sir Richard rested against the edge. With narrowed eyes, Daican's right-hand man peered down his nose at Falcor. He always tried to intimidate him, but Falcor wasn't intimidated by anyone. He could take the man down before he even saw it coming. Giving Richard an answering glare, he turned his attention to Daican, who questioned, "Did you find him?"

"No."

The emperor's jaw went taut.

"He has nowhere to go. He won't make it back to camp with that wound. Chances are he's holed up in a dark alley, and someone will come across his body in the morning." No crete should be found dead on the streets of an Arcacian city, but Talas was a necessary sacrifice for the greater good of their people.

"You'd better be right." Daican settled back in his chair, his voice pleasant, yet laced with warning. "I don't want any complications. If there are . . . it's on you."

Falcor boldly held his gaze. Daican couldn't get rid of him—not just yet anyway—and they both knew it. Disgust crept into Daican's eyes over this, and Falcor allowed the barest hint of a smirk. He might follow the man's orders, but he was no lackey.

However, so as not to cause unnecessary friction, Falcor went on to assure him, "The men are still searching. That will limit his movement. Without proper treatment, he won't survive long, if he's not dead already."

"Just as long as he doesn't get word to the others."

"He won't."

The emperor's eyes narrowed. "You should return to camp to make sure."

"Do you have the Scrolls?"

Daican gestured to the satchel on the desk. Stepping forward, Falcor grasped the strap.

"Falcor."

His eyes lifted to Daican.

"You make sure they don't end up with those."

Falcor gave a brief nod. "They won't." He picked up the satchel and slipped it over his shoulder.

"Do you have a good story for why you're returning alone?"

"Yes."

"And the Altair girl will believe you?"

Falcor paused for only a moment. "She has no reason not to."

The emperor stared at him long and hard. "Had you been here to finish training the men as I'd asked, the dragons wouldn't have been a problem, and I could've sent men to eliminate *all* of them."

Falcor dug his fingers into the satchel, imagining it was the emperor's neck instead. He spoke coldly. "Had I been here, you wouldn't have even known the Scrolls were right here in your palace."

Daican shifted his jaw, but finally seemed satisfied, and Falcor turned to go.

"Make sure they remain in camp until dawn," the emperor said behind him, "then finish things and get the Scrolls back here."

Falcor glanced over his shoulder, resisting the mighty urge to scowl. He didn't need to be told twice.

The guards escorted him back out of Auréa, and finally allowed him to go on alone once he passed the gate. When he was out of earshot, he spat out a string of choice words through his teeth. If he didn't need the power of this alliance, he would have cut the emperor's throat by now. Both his and Richard's.

On the return to camp, he moved stealthily, keeping a watchful eye for any sign of Talas. While he truly didn't believe the other crete could ever make it out of the city in his condition, it never hurt to be cautious. Talas had a strong streak of luck.

Half an hour after leaving the palace, he met up with Glynn, who stood watch outside camp. Both of them walked up to the fire where the others were gathered, and all eyes focused on him.

"Were you successful?" Darq asked.

With a nod, Falcor handed him the satchel, and Darq immediately passed it to Josan. The older crete opened it and pulled out a scroll. A wide smile reached his face. "It's them."

He gave the satchel to Timothy, whose eyes lit up like he'd just received the most precious gift in the world.

"Where's Talas?"

Falcor's eyes jumped to Darq, but he maintained a calm outward appearance and carefully moderated his voice. "He chose to stay behind and make sure all seemed well with Captain Altair. He thought it would make them feel better." He nodded to the Altair twins and monitored their reactions out of the corner of his eye. The girl had seemed suspicious of him since the first night, so the look of true relief that washed over her face pleased him. She'd bought his story. And why wouldn't she? It was just the sort of thing Talas would do.

Satisfied, he bent down to pour himself a cup of coffee. All he had to do now was keep up this pretense for a few more hours. That wouldn't be difficult with everyone focused on the Scrolls. He sipped his coffee as they all crowded around Timothy, who opened one of them. A lot of wasted enthusiasm for some old writings. While he didn't entirely dismiss the existence of Elôm, he'd seen no evidence of Him helping the cretes over the years.

His attention shifted from the Scrolls to Timothy and his brother. They were half crete—he was sure of it. He wrinkled his nose. That a crete would ever marry a human repulsed him. Friendship was bad enough. The way Talas had bonded with them was disgusting and left Falcor with little regret over what he'd done to him. As far as he was concerned, humans were only one small step above ryriks.

Speaking of ryriks, he caught Jace watching him intently. The half-blood ryrik regarded him with even more mistrust than the Altair girl. Falcor met his fire-lit eyes for a moment, and then casually turned back to his coffee. Inside, however, he reminded himself to be careful. He wasn't about to be brought down by the lowest life form in camp.

Daniel slouched in one of the chairs in his room, turning a dagger over in his hand, fixated on the reflection of candlelight in the metal. Finally, he paused and listened. Not a sound had come from the other side of his door for a while since he'd walked away from the argument with his father. No matter what he'd said, his father refused to show Captain Altair leniency. Well, he'd see about that.

Snapping his dagger back into the sheath, he pushed to his feet. He eased his door open and peered down the hall to his parents' room. Dim light peeked from under the door, but he heard no voices, which meant his father was probably in his office.

He pulled his door shut silently behind him and crept down the hall to the stairs. On ground level, he gave his father's office a wide berth as he made his way to the far side of the palace, where the inside door to the dungeon stood. His father might have filled in the tunnel Miss Altair had escaped by, but it wasn't the only undetectable exit out of Auréa. All he needed to do was get Captain Altair out of his cell and past the guards. He could then disappear without anyone ever knowing how.

Daniel's pulse kicked up. His father would surely suspect him, which wasn't necessarily a bad thing. Maybe this would finally get him disowned.

He came around a corner and bit back a curse. One of the security guards stood in the hall at the dungeon door that was usually left unguarded. He scrambled for an alternative plan, but the guard had already spotted him. He would have to improvise. Putting on an air of confidence, he approached the blond-haired young man. He was one of the new guards—Collin, if Daniel remembered correctly. He'd come from Tarvin Hall at the same time as Miss Altair.

"Evening," Daniel greeted, hiding his motives behind a smile.

"My lord," Collin responded with aggravating stiffness.

Daniel loathed being treated as pampered royalty but, tonight, he would use it to his advantage. He stared at the guard expectantly. When Collin failed to understand his intentions, he said, "Well? Aren't you going to let me pass?"

"I'm sorry, my lord, but only security and the emperor are permitted in the dungeon."

Daniel raised his brows. His father was really taking precautions. He drew his shoulders back, accentuating the couple of inches he had on Collin. He would come across as the arrogant spoiled brat most people probably believed him to be, but a man's life was at stake. "I'm the prince."

"Again, I apologize, my lord, but those are my orders."

Daniel shifted his jaw. He'd expected a newer recruit to back down more easily. He hated to take it further, but he'd come too far to back out now. "What authority do you have to refuse your prince?"

"*My* authority."

Daniel stiffened at his father's voice, and the curse jumped back to his tongue. The only thing that stopped him from using it was the thought of how his mother would scold him if she were here. She hated foul language. He turned slowly to face his father's narrow-eyed suspicion.

"What do you think you're doing?" His father glanced at the dagger in his belt, and anger hardened his face. "Were you going to give him a weapon?"

*Maybe.* "I just wanted to go down and talk to him."

"No. You will return to your room and stay there until morning."

Daniel snorted. "Seriously? You're confining me to my room like a child?"

"You're lucky I don't have a guard posted there as well. Now, go."

Daniel clenched his fists, refusing to move for a moment. But the standoff wouldn't result in Captain Altair's release, no matter what he tried. Muttering, he stormed past his father and back to his room. Who cared if he woke everyone in the palace with his stomping? He certainly wouldn't sleep tonight.

Talas pressed into a corner as soldiers jogged past. He leaned his head back and breathed hard, squeezing his eyes shut in a grimace. It was bad. He could feel it. Looking down, he found blood had saturated his jerkin and was working its way its way down his pant leg. He needed to stop the bleeding, but didn't have the time or supplies. Staunching the flow as best he could with his hand, he sucked in his breath, dizzied by the searing pain, and pushed on.

Each step sent burning waves pulsating through his nerves. He ground his teeth, his heartbeat pounding in his skull, and willed away the nausea and lightheadedness that threatened to overtake him.

"Elôm," he gasped, bracing himself against another building to look around and get his bearings. Weakness crept through his body, but he only had another couple of blocks to go. With a cross between a groan and growl, he set his jaw and pushed away from the building. He was going to make it. He had to. Forcing away the pain, he jogged at first but, after a short distance, his legs almost buckled, and he had to slow down. His head pounded harder, blurring his vision. The surroundings grew even darker and started to fade, but a flare of panic cleared his senses.

Willpower kept him moving, one step at a time, until he reached a door. He raised his fist, though it suddenly weighed a hundred pounds, and managed a weak knock. *Please let this be the right house.* At this point, he couldn't be sure. He tried to pull his arm up for a second knock, but his strength gave out, and he collapsed against the door. His heart beat sluggishly now. *I failed.*

But the door gave way, and he fell forward, squinting up at the blurry figure before him.

*"Talas!"*

The voice was hollow and far away. A dark-skinned hand grabbed his arm. Talas fought to rally his voice, but he could no longer resist the overwhelming force drawing him into oblivion.

WILLIAM BLEW ON his icy hands and stuck them back under his arms. Had more light reached the cell, he might have seen his breath. The guards hadn't left him with much when they took his coat and uniform. Only the linen shirt he'd worn underneath it, and his woolen pants, shielded him from the cold. At this rate, he'd be hypothermic by morning.

He leaned against the cell bars and glanced down the hall. It wasn't entirely dark. Far off, a torch flickered and illuminated two guards stationed there. They'd brought him straight here without questioning. Either the emperor had learned enough from Falcor, and was content to kill him, or he knew he had no chance of breaking him in the few short hours before dawn.

And those hours seemed to slip away quickly, just like sand in an hourglass. The desperate urge to hold back time lurked inside him, along with the crushing knowledge he was powerless to do so. Alone in this dark cell, his mind cycled through the faces of his beloved family—his wife, Lydia, their sons, and Kyrin. He had no misgivings about dying for his faith, but thinking of their pain was the one thing capable of gnawing at his resolve. The death of his own father had nearly crippled him for over a year. Even after that, it colored everything for a very long time. If only his children didn't have to endure the same experience.

His thoughts also turned to Liam and their conversation back in Dunlow. Unless a miracle happened, they would never talk now, and he questioned his decision to wait. Had he been right, or had he made a huge mistake? Holding his head in his hands, he prayed for peace for both himself and his family.

In the midst of these prayers, footsteps approached. He looked up as Aric reached the cell, and pushed to his feet. The other man placed a torch in the holder on the wall before turning to face him.

"William, I only just heard." Regret etched his face. He glanced at the guards. "The emperor thinks I'm here to ask questions. He thinks you might be more open with me, being that we're friends." He shook his head, his expression one of quiet distress. "What happened?"

"Falcor, one of the cretes, is a traitor. He must have met with Daican and told him everything."

"That would explain why the emperor has been planning for your execution all day."

William frowned. "All day?"

"Yes. Ever since this morning, word has spread through the city that there will be a significant execution at dawn, but I'm afraid he kept me out of this one. Only Richard and his men knew it was you. I'm still one of the few people who know you're down here."

A small spark of hope ignited in William. "Kyrin, Kaden, and the others are camped north of here. If you can get word to them . . ."

He let his voice die as Aric hung his head and shook it. "The emperor has all entrances guarded and has forbidden anyone to leave the palace grounds until tomorrow. Anyone who does will be arrested and charged with treason. After what happened with Kyrin, he's not taking any chances."

William squeezed his hands around the cell bars, the cold metal pressing into them as Aric's words sank in. He gave a short nod of acceptance. His fate would always rest in Elôm's hands alone.

"We won't give up," Aric assured him. "If there's a way, I'll find it."

William looked into his eyes. "No, don't risk it. It's too important for you to remain here and maintain your cover."

"I can't just let him kill you."

"You have to." The words slipped out quietly, but he held to them. "The information you gather can save countless lives. You can't sacrifice that just to save me." Aric grimaced in response, and William witnessed the hesitation in his friend's eyes. "You wouldn't want that, either, if you were in my position. I'm not the only one who will die in this struggle. We must do what we can to save the most people."

Aric said nothing, but William took it as his reluctant agreement.

Drawing a deep breath, he reached up to unclasp the leather cord around his neck. He let it rest in his hand and stared for a long moment at the dusty blue stone hanging from it. Tears gathered in his eyes as he brushed a finger over it and relived the memories of where it had come from. For over ten years he had worn it, close to his heart. He held it out to Aric.

"I need you to make sure this gets to Kyrin." His voice cracked at the end, and he tried to clear the pressure in his throat.

Aric didn't reach for the necklace. "We'll think of something . . . find some way . . ."

"Then you can give it back to me." This time he managed his words with more strength. "But if this ends the way I think it will, then I want to know Kyrin will have it."

His expression still taut, Aric glanced at the guards again, tucking the necklace safely in his pocket.

"Let her know it's so she will always remember me."

William smiled faintly with thoughts of his precious daughter. How he hated having missed so much of her life, but he praised Elôm that, by His grace, she'd grown into the most beautiful young woman—both inside and out. He couldn't be more proud, especially knowing she had so bravely faced this very same situation.

"Also, make sure she and Kaden know I love them, their brothers, and their mother more than anything in this world. They're the greatest blessings and treasure Elôm has given me, and they need to tell their brothers and mother that, if they ever have the chance."

Aric cleared his throat. "I'll make sure of it."

William let out a soft sigh as a small burden inside him lifted. He ached to tell them himself, but at least they would hear it from someone. "And tell them that, even though they might not be able to see Him in this, Elôm is at work. He has a plan, and this isn't happening against His will. It's not the end. We will see each other again and, once we all reach eternity, the wait won't seem long at all."

Though he was usually so strong and composed, tears swam in Aric's eyes. "They'll be told. You have my word."

"Thank you," William breathed.

Aric peered down the hall again. "I wish I could stay, but the emperor might grow suspicious."

"Go," William urged him. He'd taken a great risk already.

With a heavy sigh, Aric turned.

"What time is it?"

Aric glanced back. "A little after eleven."

William remained where he stood until his friend disappeared. He had only a few more hours, and he would not let them go to waste. Dropping to his knees in the middle of the cell, he closed his eyes. He could think of nothing more important than using these last hours to pray for his family.

The echo of footsteps signaled that the time had come. William released a weighty breath as dread clenched his stomach in a savage grip and peace battled it from his heart. For a moment, he did not move, his soul reaching out for all the serenity and strength Elôm had to offer.

"I accept Your will, Lord."

The conflict inside him quieted at these murmured words, and he pushed to his feet with a grimace as his cold limbs straightened after hours of prayer. Confident in his faith and choices, he turned to face the guards. Aric marched with them. Though his face remained expressionless, deep pain and regret filled his eyes. No one should have to assist in the execution of a friend.

Aric unlocked the cell to let the guards in, and they fitted a pair of icy shackles around William's wrists. Gripping his arms, they guided him out of the cell. Aric took the lead of the procession through the dungeon, and William listened to the steady, slowly-climbing rhythm of his own heart that would soon be silenced. A will to fight jolted his nerves, but he kept it at bay.

When they climbed the staircase and stepped out into the courtyard, a frigid gust of air struck his face and bit through his shirt. He squinted, even in the low light. A layer of bright white snow blanketed the area. Large flakes still fell, gathering in his hair and melting against his skin. He glanced up at the dark clouds once before he focused on the group waiting ahead of him.

Wrapped in a thick fur-lined cloak, Daican stood at the head of the group with his family, but William's eyes went to Daniel's rigid posture. The prince shot his father a glare to rival the coldness in the air. His gaze then met William's, softening with remorse. William knew the emperor would never change his mind, even at the request of his own son. If only Daican shared more of his son's good qualities, Arcacia would be so different.

Richard waited to the side with a dozen palace guards. William locked eyes with the emperor as the distance between them shortened—one belief against another, and neither one would give in. One of the guards pulled William to a halt, and the rest surrounded him.

Following Daican and Richard's lead, they passed through the wintery courtyard. Snow swirled about them as they marched through the empty streets. The hard, icy flakes stung William's face, and he started to shiver, but his steps never faltered. He walked as tall and steady as the soldier he'd been most of his life.

At the end of the freezing march, the central square opened up before them to reveal the sea of people waiting. The sight hit William like a physical blow to the chest. Not even Kyrin's retelling of her experience here had prepared him for the sheer numbers so willing to gather to see the termination of a life. Like a wave, an audible murmur swept ahead of them. The people parted as they drew near and let them pass to the center, where the execution platform rose up from their midst. William's eyes settled on it, and he forced down a hard swallow.

One by one, they climbed the stairs, their boots squeaking against the snow. The execution block immediately drew his eyes. How many other children of Elôm had and would die here and add their blood to the stains already present? He pried his gaze away and scanned the crowd, whose voices had grown in volume. But they immediately hushed when Daican stepped forward.

"Citizens of Arcacia." His voice echoed out through the frigid air. "Here stands a man guilty of the most detestable of crimes. Just like his father, his daughter, and his son before him, he has betrayed his emperor and our gods. I give you the traitor, William Altair."

As one, the crowd raised their voices and fists in an uproar of outrage. William closed his eyes and shut out the emperor's following words of condemnation. He knew the truth of why he stood here and was willing to pay the price, as others had before him. Silently, he whispered, "Save these people, Lord. Let true faith return to Ilyon. Don't let our struggles be in vain. Make Yourself known again."

Hands grabbed him, and he opened his eyes. Daican faced him with a hard, twisted expression of anger, hatred, and betrayal. "Have you any defense for yourself?"

"You know what I said last night, and I stand by it."

Scowling, Daican jerked his head at the guards, and they forced William to his knees. His heart hammered the inside of his ribs. He glanced to his right, catching a glimpse of Aric. His friend had a hand on his sword, desperation growing in his eyes, but William gave the slightest shake of his head. He would not let his friend do this. It would only lead to both their deaths.

Again, a hand gripped his shoulder and pushed him forward. He tried to breathe steadily, but struggled as every nerve in his body screamed to fight. *Strengthen me, Lord, and let this bring You glory.* They pressed his neck down against the block, and he closed his eyes. Tears gathered behind his eyelids as he slowly breathed out one of his last breaths. However, from the fear grew anticipation for the new and perfect life he would soon experience. Even so, his heart broke for those he would leave behind to struggle on in their broken world. His duty as a husband and father called for him to be there to protect them, but he had to leave them in Elôm's capable hands.

In a trembling whisper, he prayed, "It will be my heart's greatest joy to see Your face, my King. Please take my last prayer here in this world and carry my family through this."

A DROP OF ice water splattered against Kyrin's neck. She shivered and wiped it away. Parting her eyelids a slit, the gray light of early morning greeted her. Snow still fell, as it had when she'd finally lain down to sleep sometime around midnight. It caked her blanket in a clinging shell. Regardless, she pulled the wool material up to her ear to trap all possible warmth and closed her eyes again.

Floating on the edge of sleep, a sound penetrated her consciousness. Her eyes popped open. What was it? It had been subtle. Had she dreamed it? She pushed back her blanket, shivering as the icy breeze hit her exposed neck, and looked over her shoulder to peer down the line of sleeping bodies next to her.

Her eyes landed on Falcor, who bent over a still form. She frowned and pushed herself up a little farther to see that it was Josan he crouched over. The older crete let out a soft groan as Falcor raised a fist. Beneath it, metal glinted and drops of scarlet fell from the sharp point. A jolt shot through Kyrin's nerves and stalled her heart. She gasped, and Falcor's head turned, his eyes locking with hers in a moment that was no more than an instant, but felt like full minutes.

Then he broke eye contact, and the world spun back into motion. With the dagger still in one hand and the leather satchel containing the Scrolls in the other, he jumped up.

"No!" Kyrin's voice rang in the clearing. "Wake up! Everyone, wake up!"

The men scrambled from their bedrolls as Falcor bolted. Darq, who stood watch, spun around and reached for one of his swords, but Falcor's dagger slashed across his chest before he could fully draw the weapon. The captain doubled over, and Falcor ran past him to the dragons. Glynn pursued him but, for a frozen moment, the rest of them just watched the two dragons and riders disappear into the snowy sky. Kyrin's heart pounded a chaotic beat. What had just happened?

Leetra moved first, rushing to Darq, who clutched his left side, but Timothy's cry captured their attention.

"Josan!"

He and his brother knelt beside the crete, whose labored breaths shuddered through camp. Deep red stained half the man's jerkin. Timothy pressed his hand over the wound, but blood oozed around it at an alarming rate. Kyrin covered her mouth. *Please, Elôm, let him be all right.*

"Help him," Darq ground out through his teeth. He grasped Leetra's shoulder and turned her toward Josan.

Grabbing her medical bag, Leetra dashed across camp and dropped down next to the wounded crete. Timothy moved his hand away as she pulled open Josan's jerkin and used a small knife to cut open his shirt. When she peeled away the saturated material, blood welled on his chest. She quickly covered the source again.

Kyrin couldn't see much of the crete girl's face, but it was enough to understand the look she gave Timothy. Leetra shook her head and opened her mouth, but was slow to speak in a low murmur. "There's nothing I can do."

Timothy just stared at her a moment, his jaw muscles tensing, and moisture gathered at the rims of his eyes. It was as though Kyrin could see right through them into his heart as it broke with grief. Tears rushed to her eyes.

Josan gripped Timothy's arm, and his gaze jerked down.

"Timothy," the crete gasped, putting great effort into his words. "You must . . . listen."

Timothy grasped Josan's hand and leaned forward so the crete wouldn't have to try so hard to speak. Everyone moved back to allow Timothy and Aaron to have their last moments with him. Even so, Kyrin could still hear their quiet words.

"You have to . . . tell them," Josan said as he looked up into Timothy's eyes. "Now that the Scrolls are gone, they need to know. They need hope."

Need to know what? Kyrin exchanged glances with her friends, but not one said a word as Timothy only nodded.

Josan coughed and choked as he fought for another wheezing breath. "I don't know why Elôm chose to spare me over your father, but it's been a privilege . . . to watch over you and see the faithful young man you've become. Be strong, Timothy . . . and steadfast in your faith. Elôm has called you . . . to a powerful ministry. Continue to pursue it diligently. He will guide you and strengthen you to fulfill it."

A tear slipped down Timothy's cheek. He nodded again and spoke hoarsely. "I will."

Josan's eyes shifted to Aaron. "I know you'll continue to watch over your brother."

"Until the day I die," Aaron said in a solemn oath.

"You're a good man. Your father would be very proud," his eyes slid back to Timothy, "of both of you."

Timothy managed a sad, but fleeting, smile. More tears fell. "Thank you for everything. For taking care of us, and for . . . this."

Josan smiled, peaceful and satisfied. "It was an honor."

Letting out a slow, seeping breath, his eyes closed, and his chest did not rise again.

No one moved. Disbelief froze Kyrin like the ground beneath her feet, the cold sinking deep into her bones. Their mission had been to save Josan and the Scrolls. Now both were gone. In one cruel, unexpected instant, they'd failed. Her eyes followed each individual tear that rolled in silence down Timothy's face. Somehow, his still, forlorn expression and quiet tears were far more heartbreaking than if he had cried aloud. Her own tears wavered on the edge of falling.

A dragon's wing flaps tugged her blurry eyes away from Timothy. Glynn landed at the edge of camp and rushed to Darq, gripping his shoulder. "Are you all right?"

The captain gave a short nod. "Where's Falcor?"

"I lost him in the fog."

In that moment, it was as if a thunderclap echoed in Kyrin's head and vibrated all the way down to her feet. She put a hand to her chest as the air rushed from her lungs, and her knees went weak.

"Father!" Her wide eyes flew to the others. "If Falcor is working with the emperor, what if he told him about my father? What about Talas?"

The wave of horror that had just overtaken her swept through the others and cleared their expressions of all but the terrible implications of this betrayal.

"And what about Sam, Tane, and Aric?" Trask asked. "Does he know about them?"

They looked at each other, and then all eyes came to rest on Kyrin. She stood lost for a moment before understanding—she was the only one who could truly remember what information Falcor had been privy to. Her mind choked, still processing both her sorrow and her fear. She closed her eyes and strained to focus.

Images and snatches of conversation flashed in her mind as she tried to pick out any names or sensitive information. She grimaced. Already her head pounded and nausea stirred her stomach.

After a moment, she shook her head. "I don't think so. I don't remember any of us mentioning them by name." A miracle. She looked at Darq. "Have any of you told him about them?"

"He knows we have people in Valcré, but only a select few know who."

Confident these three were safe, Kyrin's concern jumped back to those who weren't. "We have to find out about my father and Talas." A horrible feeling rolled through her middle that Talas's absence wasn't on account of the noble reason Falcor had given.

Kaden moved first and grabbed up his sword. "I'm going down to the city."

"I'm going with you." Kyrin turned to snatch up her weapons. Her heart pounded with pleas to Elôm for her father's safety. Nightmarish images of him in Auréa's dungeon overran her thoughts. She'd known this was a bad idea. She should have begged him not to go!

"Wait."

They both turned to Rayad.

"It could be a trap, and the two of you are too well known. If you're recognized, you might not escape."

"We can't just stay here," Kaden responded, his voice raised.

"I'll go," Rayad said.

Kaden looked ready to argue, but Jace cut him off.

"So will I."

Kyrin looked up into his eyes as he stepped in front of her. He touched her shoulder. His firm, yet gentle grip, along with the earnestness in his expression, instilled in her a small ounce of encouragement.

"We will find out where he is. I won't come back until we do. I promise."

Kyrin believed him, but her heart cried out to search for her father herself. The waiting would be more than she could stand. It was a war of wisdom against emotion. Fighting the emotion, she forced a nod. "All right."

With her acceptance, Kaden surrendered as well.

Jace and Rayad rushed to buckle on their weapons. Holden joined them, since he knew the city better than they did. Just before the three of them left camp, Jace looked at Kyrin again. He said nothing, but his promise rested in his eyes. He then followed Rayad and Holden down the rocky slope away from camp. They disappeared in the fog and snow that swirled around the mountains long before they reached the trees. Kyrin drew a shaky breath. She was supposed to see her father ride up that slope, not watch more loved ones leave. She did not move until she heard Darq's voice.

"Glynn, scout the area. The emperor would be foolish to send men against our dragons, but make sure."

Glynn nodded and hurried to the dragons again. As he flew off, Kyrin prayed Jace, Rayad, and Holden weren't walking right into the hands of Daican's men.

"Leetra."

Darq's voice had taken on a sharper tone. The girl flinched. She hadn't moved from her place a few feet away from Josan's body. Her face was gray and slack, her eyes larger than ever. It was as if she were just now coming back to reality.

Darq stepped toward her, but grimaced and stopped. His tone, however, did not soften. "Did you know about Falcor?"

At the name, her face paled yet another shade. "No, Captain." Her lips trembled, and her eyes turned watery. Kyrin had never seen her so vulnerable.

"You're the one who requested he join us. How do we know we can trust you?"

Kyrin thought Leetra might burst into tears at this question, but she gathered her resolve and held herself up straighter. "You don't, Captain. You'll have to arrest me until you know for sure." Her voice lost a little strength at the end.

"She's telling the truth about Falcor." Darq's eyes swung around to Kyrin, and she reinforced, "She didn't know." The brokenness and betrayal in Leetra's eyes and her voice couldn't be faked.

"You're sure?" Darq questioned.

Kyrin nodded in certainty. Leetra had been just as blindsided as the rest of them.

Accepting her word, Darq gave a nod and then winced again. "Leetra, I need you to take a look at this wound."

She didn't move at first, except to cast an uncertain glance at Josan's body, but then she hurried to where Darq took a seat by the fire. While Leetra helped him take off his jerkin and shirt, Kyrin's gaze shifted to Timothy. He and Aaron still knelt beside Josan. His tears had ceased falling, but they lingered in his eyes.

Then he wiped his bloodied hands in the snow and brushed the backs of them across his face. After covering Josan with the blanket, he pushed to his feet, his sad eyes meeting with Kyrin's. He walked over to her and Kaden, and cleared his throat. "I'd like to pray with you for your father and Talas."

Gratitude and awe for his concern after just witnessing the death of his mentor filled Kyrin's heart. "Thank you."

Timothy bowed his head, and she and Kaden did the same. His quiet, but steady, voice rose with prayers to Elôm, and the snow crunched around them as the others joined in.

A horse's hooves echoed in the fog before they could see who approached. The remainder of their group stood at the edge of camp with weapons ready just in case. Kyrin breathed in and prayed with all her might it would be her father—that he would ride into camp to see them, just as he'd said he would when he left the morning before. She squeezed her fists. "*Please.*"

A few moments later, dark shadows took shape in the cloud of white. She squinted. The first form she recognized was Jace, followed by Rayad and Holden. But her eyes sought the horse. A fourth figure appeared and stood even taller than Jace. He led the horse behind him. Kyrin recognized Tane in the same moment it became clear the horse's rider was too small to be her father. A wave of cold dread washed through her. The rider hunched in the saddle was Talas.

Jace broke away from the others, jogging the rest of the distance to her and Kaden. The moment she looked into his eyes, she knew. Every muscle, every nerve, every thought froze in unwillingness to believe it. Entirely numb, she stared up at him.

Jace's chest rose and fell heavily. Pain invaded every inch of his face, but nowhere more so than his eyes. He opened his mouth, but his voice wavered. "Your father . . ." He faltered, and his eyes glimmered with moisture. His next words were only a ragged whisper. "He was executed."

She was paralyzed—trapped inside her own body with a rising tide of emotion and sorrow. She fought to breathe, but her lungs collapsed. Her thoughts spiraled and tangled into a panicked, desperate attempt to find a way for this to be a mistake. It couldn't be true. This couldn't happen.

Tane appeared at Jace's side and pulled something from his pocket. As soon as her eyes locked onto the blue stone, it hit her, shattering her will and hopeless denials. All over, she began to tremble, barely managing to grasp the necklace in her hands.

Her eyes remained fixed on it, but it blurred behind a flood of tears. Tane's words penetrated the suffocating haze, but were low and distant.

"He wanted to make sure you had that . . . so you would always remember him."

*No!* The frantic scream clawed up her throat and broke free in an anguished sob. "No! *No!*"

Again and again, she choked out the word. She stumbled back blindly as streams of hot tears scalded her cold face.

"No!" She fell to her knees. "Elôm, why? Why?"

She bent over. Sobs ripped through her chest and racked her body. An arm closed around her, and she turned into Kaden's chest. She wrapped her arms around him, grasping a handful of his jacket in one hand and the necklace in the other, holding on as if they might be torn away from her too.

She sobbed into his shoulder until she could barely breathe. Waves of pain tore through her nerves every time the reality hit her. Their father was gone. Never again in their lifetime would they feel his strong embrace, see his loving smile, or hear his kind voice. Kyrin squeezed her eyes closed and clenched her teeth so hard that pain shot through her jaw as her heart still screamed for it to not be so.

Beneath her chin, Kaden's shoulders shook with his own sobs. Tears poured afresh from Kyrin's eyes, and again she asked why. Why their father? Why now? Why like this? He'd placed himself in danger to retrieve the Scrolls, Elôm's Word. Why did he have to die for it? And now the Scrolls were gone. Had he died for nothing? Another deep sob tore from her throat. She couldn't bear it. She couldn't lose him like this. Her father was too good a man. But there was nothing, not a single thing in all the world, that she could do about it. Some way, somehow, she would have to live with it, but she couldn't imagine the future without him.

DANIEL BRUSHED PAST his parents, his boots smacking hard against each snow-covered step up to the palace entrance. The guards barely had time to open the doors for him before he barged through. Inside, he yanked off his cloak and practically flung it at the waiting footman. He didn't usually treat the servants so discourteously, but he was about ready to snap. If the weather hadn't been so cold and miserable, he would have gone straight to the stable for his horse and ridden as far from here as he could. If only he'd succeeded in freeing Captain Altair. He could have gone with him and left this life for good.

He immediately started for the staircase to his room, but his father's commanding voice echoed behind him.

"Daniel."

He froze and curled his fingers. Good thing the large vase on the pedestal to his right was just out of reach. He would have taken great pleasure in smashing it and seeing the painted depictions of Aertus and Vilai in a hundred shattered pieces. Even more pleasure in the look on his father's face if he did.

He looked over his shoulder and forced his voice through clenched teeth. "What?"

"We need to talk," his father said in no uncertain terms and strode down the hall with a clear expectation for Daniel to follow.

Daniel contemplated refusing. He didn't want to talk to his father. Ever. He looked at his mother, who gave a firm nod. Fine. He'd do it for her, but he didn't expect it to accomplish anything.

Trailing his father, Daniel walked into one of the sitting rooms, specifically avoiding any other breakables. He didn't trust himself not to hurl one at the wall . . . or his father. His mother and Davira came in after him, and his mother closed the door. Daniel almost scoffed. As if the servants wouldn't hear them arguing anyway.

He turned to his father, who gave him the infuriating "what's wrong with you?" look he'd used when Daniel was a child. Daniel tightened his fists again and answered it with the most defiant expression he could muster.

His father's eyes narrowed. "I won't have you sulking around like a weakling for the next few days all because of the execution of a traitor."

"He *is* a weakling," Davira muttered as she joined their father.

Daniel glared her. If they had been children, he would be sorely tempted to pull her hair. Hard. She would be his next target if he started throwing things. He switched his glare to his father. "I don't see how I'm weak for not understanding why you would execute a good man like Captain Altair."

"He had a chance to prove his loyalty," his father ground out. "I could've had him arrested the moment he set foot in the city. I gave him a chance to come clean and make things right. Instead, he betrayed my kindness and aided our enemies."

Daniel shook his head as the urge to break something surged within him. "So he took some old scrolls. So what? What did he do to warrant death? What did any of them do?"

"They have turned their backs on their emperor and their gods. In the absence of such loyalty, they are capable of anything, and could tear this empire apart."

"You mean like Miss Altair's fake attack against you?" His father's eyes rounded and sparked with anger. Anyone else might have feared that look, but Daniel didn't. He gave a short, hard laugh. "What, you thought I actually believed that like all the other people you've lied to?"

His father took a step closer, and Daniel stood up taller.

"It does not matter what she did or didn't do to me," his father responded in a low, aggravated tone. "What matters is that she stood before the gods and denied them in front of me and the entire staff. What's to stop her or others from doing the same to me? If they won't respect the gods, they won't respect the authority the gods have placed on Arcacia's throne. And if enough turn their backs on them, why would Aertus and Vilai bless and prosper our empire?"

"Do you really believe these gods of yours are real or that powerful, or would even care about any of this?"

His father's eyes flashed and he snapped, "Of course they do."

"Well, it sure seems they made a huge mistake when they made me your son." Daniel let sarcasm drip from his every word. "Perhaps I was accidentally switched with some other poor fool who would comply with all your demands like a good, obedient heir."

"I should have been the heir," Davira said, shooting him a venomous look.

Daniel gave her a twisted smile. "Maybe you should talk to your so-called gods about that."

"Oh, I will and, maybe, if I'm lucky, they'll strike you dead and then I will be."

"I look forward to their answer. No doubt I'll be waiting forever."

Daican stepped between them. "Enough. I'll not have either of you praying harm on each other."

"You don't have to worry about me." Daniel peered around his father to look into his sister's furious eyes. "I have no need to pray to non-existent gods. And I have no fear of them striking me dead either."

His father whirled on him. "I don't know where you picked up such a blasphemous attitude, but I will not stand for it. You will change it, and you will learn to respect your gods or, so help me, I'll find a way to change you myself."

Daniel almost dared him to try. "You know what the problem is in all this?" He leaned a little closer. "You're a tyrant."

Absolute outrage morphed his father's expression, but Daniel didn't give him a chance to reply. He turned away and walked toward the door, reaching for the knob.

"Where do you think you're going?" his father practically roared.

Daniel looked back. "Oh, I don't know. Maybe I'll go and find out more about this Elôm so many are willing to die for."

"Don't you dare!"

"Or what?"

The only answer he received was his father's threatening glare. After all, the only alternative his father had was to have him executed too. Daniel shook his head. He was done with this conversation. Yanking open the door, he stalked to his room, swearing to himself that he'd die before he'd let his father turn him into the sort of man he was.

Jace stood at the fire, but the warmth wouldn't penetrate the coldness that had settled inside him when they'd met Tane in the city and learned the news. His mind kept going back to that moment and the utter devastation on Kyrin's face. Telling her was one of the hardest things he'd ever had to do.

He looked to where she and Kaden sat alone at the far edge of camp. Though he could not hear her anymore, every so often her body shook with sobs. To see her in such agony tore him up inside. He would never forget the pain of losing Kalli and Aldor—the way it had crushed his will to live, sucking any hope of joy out of him. Had he the power, he would have spared Kyrin such pain at any cost. If only he could take it and bear it himself. He'd gladly suffer in her place.

Weight built in his chest until he found it difficult to breathe, and he turned away to seek a moment of solitude. He walked over to the dragons and pressed his icy hands against Gem's warm scales. The dragon gave a mournful whine. He glanced at her, but hung his head. His eyes burned and filled with moisture. If ever he wanted to cry, it was now, but he didn't know if he was able. Why hadn't he done something? He'd known something wasn't right—he'd felt it. The only reason he'd joined this mission was to protect Kyrin, but he'd failed to protect her from the greatest pain of all.

Heat seeped and twisted its way through his veins from the fire growing inside him. His eyes slid to Gem's saddle. It was too late to make things right, but he could fly down and stop Daican from ever taking another innocent life again. The burn engulfing his chest awakened his fighting instincts. After all, if he succeeded, how many lives would it spare in the future? How much better off would Arcacia be? He wrapped his fingers around his sword.

But a smaller, quieter admonition settled amongst the heat. It would be wrong, and the regret that followed would consume him. He would despise himself. But Kyrin deserved to have her father avenged. He closed his eyes against the conflict.

"Jace."

He flinched and looked up, blinking to focus on Rayad.

"Are you all right?"

Jace's voice remained trapped for several seconds as he struggled with the raging emotion inside of him. Finally, he shook his head and whispered a ragged, "No."

Rayad came to stand at his side—a presence of comfort, strength, and integrity that Jace envied. Jace turned to face him, opening himself up in complete honesty.

"I want to kill the emperor." He swallowed the bitterness the confession left behind. "I want to stop him. I want to make him pay for what he's done."

He looked away. He'd tried so hard to change in the last couple of years—to reject the violence that ran in his blood—especially since meeting Kyrin, but had he gained any victory over it at all? How could he have when every impulse urged him to take action against the emperor?

Rayad's voice held no condemnation. "I don't think there's a person in this camp who doesn't feel the same way."

Jace met his gaze again. Could he really believe they felt it with the same passion he did?

Rayad went on, "You're not the only one who wants to see Daican answer for what he's done. Knowing how Kyrin and Kaden feel, and judging by the look on Captain Darq's face, I'm sure you're not the only one who would like to see to it personally. That's understandable."

He sighed, and his eyes expressed the depth of his own sadness. "It's hard to see right now in the midst of such sorrow, but Daican will not go unpunished. Sooner or later, he'll answer to Elôm, and His judgment is far more thorough and fitting than ours."

Jace dragged a hard breath into his lungs. He wanted to believe that, but it led him right to the heart of the hardest part in all this. His voice raw, he asked, "But why did He allow it to happen in the first place?"

"I don't know, Jace," Rayad responded, quietly and honestly. "It doesn't seem right or to serve any purpose at all. However, if there's one thing I've learned in my life, it's that, even when nothing makes any sense to us, there's still a purpose. And as hard as it is at times, we have to believe that and let it carry us through."

"I just don't see any good reason Captain Altair had to die. We don't even have the Scrolls to stand as something he died for." The words choked through the back of Jace's throat. He'd seen too many good, innocent people die. People who'd treated him with kindness and helped him believe he was more than the ryrik blood beating in his heart. Why were they always the ones to die?

"I know," Rayad murmured. "I don't either, but I know I must trust, even when it's the most difficult thing to do."

Jace's shoulders sagged as the heat inside him died away and he grew cold again. He looked past Rayad, settling his eyes on Kyrin. "I wish I could do something for her."

"Just be there. That's all any of us can do for them."

Aric entered the palace, shivering, though the cold was only half of it. He'd passed William's last message along to Tane, and then wandered from one street to the next as if he could outpace the sorrow. Every part of him rebelled at returning to Auréa but, if he didn't turn up soon, Daican would suspect him. The very thought of the man made his fists clench. He'd had no choice but to close his mind off to the events of the morning, yet now he felt himself coming undone. He shook his head, fighting it, but suddenly he couldn't go on. He reached out and braced himself against the wall. He breathed shallowly as the reality he'd tried to avoid finally took hold. Before he could stop them, tears trickled down his cheeks.

He'd been forced to witness executions before, but this was personal. William had been one of his closest friends, but now he was gone. The emperor had taken his life with no more thought than breathing. Aric gritted his teeth. How badly he'd desired to take the emperor down, right there on that platform in front of everyone. How badly he *still* desired to. *Elôm, help me.* The struggle almost overwhelmed him.

"Aric."

He stiffened at the emperor's voice, and for just that moment saw everything slipping away—his cover, his position, his life. But he hardened his expression and resolve and turned slowly. Daican would see the tears, but let him see. If he didn't have some understanding, then he was an even crueler man than Aric thought.

"Your Majesty?" His deep voice came thick.

The emperor studied him with eyes that lacked the slightest regret over taking a life. Aric stared straight back, waiting.

"You mourn over Captain Altair?" Daican's cool tone hid his feelings on the matter.

"Forgive me, my lord, but yes. He was a longtime friend." Aric felt the cord around his emotions fray, coming dangerously close to snapping. He cleared his throat, his heart hollow as he spoke. "But do not take my regret as condoning his actions."

What bitter, loathsome words. How he hated this charade, now more than ever in his life. Hated that he hadn't acted on the platform. He would forever regret it, but what could he have done? The only thing it would have changed was that his body would have fallen next to his friend's. William hadn't wanted that. For this reason, he must go on with this hateful pretense.

With slow, calculated movements, Daican nodded. "Of course, you must mourn for a friend, especially when their death comes from such misguided ideals."

"Thank you, my lord, for your understanding," he murmured and hoped his present hatred for this man remained hidden inside him. "Is there anything you want me to see to?"

Daican regarded him a moment before shaking his head. "No, as long as security is handled, take the day."

It was a rare moment of genuineness, and Aric again murmured a hollow thanks before walking off. He needed the time to gain better control over his emotions and seek Elôm's strength.

Leetra tied off the thread that stitched together Talas's wound and wiped away the blood that had seeped out. She'd been able to do more for him than Tane's family had but, even with her skills, she had no way of knowing just how much damage the blade had done. He would either survive . . . or he wouldn't. She could only wait now.

She glanced at his face. A crete's skin shouldn't be so pale. The last crete she'd seen in such perilous condition had been Gem's previous rider when he'd fallen from the dragon he was training and been impaled on a tree limb. Even their best physician hadn't been able to save him. If only their physician were here now. Maybe he'd give Talas a greater chance.

A hard, aching lump climbed into Leetra's throat. Falcor had done this—her fiancé, the man who would have soon been her husband. How could he? How *dare* he? To betray his people and commit murder—to betray her? She squeezed the cloth in her hand, the heaviness in her chest mounting as she imagined him standing in front of her and what she would say to him if she had the chance. If Talas died . . .

"You're looking mighty fierce there, Lee."

Her gaze jerked to her cousin's face as he let out a weak laugh, but then he scrunched his eyes closed in a grimace.

Leetra didn't soften her expression. This was absolutely no time for laughter. But trust Talas to try to lighten the mood, even if he was the one lying there, quite possibly dying.

"Don't talk."

He opened his eyes again and blinked a few times to focus on her. Any previous mirth in his look had disappeared. "It's not your fault, you know. None of us would have suspected Falcor was capable of this."

Leetra bit down so hard her teeth threatened to shatter. How could it not be her fault? She knew Falcor better than any of them. At least, she had thought she did. *She* had invited him to come. Why? Just so she would have someone who shared her feelings—one who agreed that they didn't need to involve any Arcacians in their affairs. Elôm should strike her dead for her arrogance and what it had cost them.

She swallowed against the tightness in her throat, barely forcing out a rough reply. "I said, don't talk."

But Talas was persistent. "You can't blame yourself."

A hot tear burned down Leetra's cheek before she could stop it. She scowled and rubbed it against her shoulder before giving her cousin a hard look. "Do you want to die?"

"I'd certainly prefer not to."

"Then why aren't you listening to the physician who's trying to save your life?"

Talas closed his eyes, as if in surrender, and said no more.

By noon, the wind picked up, gusting down from the mountains and swirling the snow that fell in thick flakes. Jace glanced up at the heavy clouds and then over at the dragons, where Leetra was doing everything she could for Talas. Captain Darq was there with her, while Glynn kept watch in case the emperor had grown bold enough to attack them in spite of the dragons.

But then Jace fixed his eyes on Kyrin and Kaden. They hadn't moved in hours—not even to warm up by the fire. By now they must be freezing. Jace walked over to the supplies and collected two dry blankets. Neither Kyrin nor her brother noticed him until Jace handed one to Kaden. The younger man looked up at him, his eyes red and dull—the opposite of their usual spirit.

"Thanks," he murmured, though Jace could barely hear him.

He nodded. If only he could do more. He turned to Kyrin. Unfolding the blanket, he wrapped it around her shoulders and felt her trembling under his hands. He wasn't sure if it was from the cold or trauma, but he suspected a bit of both. She clutched the blanket to her throat and looked at him with an expression so full of loss he couldn't breathe for a moment. Losing Kalli and Aldor had destroyed him. Only Kyrin had been able to pull him from that dark state. Would he be able to help her the same way? What if he couldn't?

Her mouth opened a little, though she couldn't seem to find the voice to thank him. But he didn't need it. He sat beside her, struggling for a way to help. He had so little knowledge in such areas beyond his own pain, but Rayad's words echoed in his head. *Just be there*. Swallowing to loosen his throat, he said, "I'm sorry."

It sounded so inadequate, but he didn't know what else to say. She gave a weak nod. Though snow-encrusted strands of hair hid most of her face, a solitary tear rolled down her damp cheek. He looked down to where she was staring. Her right hand rested in her lap, her red fingers grasping the necklace Tane had given her. The simple gray-blue stone wouldn't strike anyone as valuable, but it clearly meant a great deal to her. She glanced at him. Her voice barely rose above the growing howl of the wind, and was small, broken, and childlike.

"The blacksmith back home helped me make it when I was a girl. I gave it to my father when Kaden and I left for Tarvin Hall. I—" A choked sob cut her short. "I told him it . . . it was so he would always remember me."

She hunched over and cried mournfully. Jace's heart constricted with shared pain. He put his arm around her shoulders and pulled her close, wishing he could somehow shield her from the sorrow. She felt so small and fragile—nothing like the strong young woman he'd come to know. Would she ever be the same again? She curled herself into a ball and nestled against him as she continued to cry. Jace looked over at Kaden, who could only stare sadly at his sister. Rubbing Kyrin's arm, Jace rested his cheek on the top of her head, praying as he never had before. The icy snow stung his skin, but he didn't pull away. She needed all the comfort and warmth he could give her.

A few moments later, she spoke again, though Jace didn't quite catch her muffled words. He raised his head. "What?"

"It's my fault," she barely managed through trembling lips.

Jace shook his head. How could she think such a thing? "No."

"Yes, it is," she insisted. "I knew something was wrong with Falcor. I should've said something . . . done something. If I had, this wouldn't have happened."

Jace grimaced. These were feelings he should carry, not her; not on top of her grief. After all, he'd had just as much call to confront Falcor, but hadn't. He remembered how his guilt had nearly consumed him after Kalli and Aldor died. He couldn't let Kyrin feel the same.

"No. You can't blame yourself." He hesitated. What would Rayad say? But instead, his mind latched onto something she had once told him when he was at his lowest. "This is all in the hands of Elôm. It's not your fault."

A small cry broke out, but Kyrin said no more. Jace could

only hope she believed what he said as he struggled to believe it himself and give up his own burden of guilt.

Despite how the hours passed, Jace did not leave Kyrin's side. Her tears eventually subsided, but she remained huddled against him, staring off into the gloom. The cold had long ago numbed the feeling in her face, but the rest of her body ached fiercely—a deep, throbbing, feverish ache.

She wanted to move, to get up and be stronger than this, but she couldn't seem to summon the motivation. Her heart kept crying, *Elôm, why?* She still struggled to comprehend and accept the reality of it. She didn't want to face the future, which now felt unbearably empty without her father. It hurt too much. She longed to escape the pain—to run as fast and as far away from it as she could—but she was trapped right in the very center of it. If only she could fall asleep until it passed, but that still wouldn't bring him back.

Her frozen cheeks burned before she even knew the tears fell again. The warmth brought awareness of just how cold she was, even with Jace so near. A tremor passed through her body, followed by another, until she shivered all over. Jace held her a little tighter, and she buried her face against his coat. The air seemed colder all of a sudden and bit deep down into her bones. She peeked through her hair and it hit her how dark the sky was. Twilight had descended. Had they really sat here for that long?

When her teeth started to chatter, Jace moved for the first time in a while. "You need to get by the fire."

Did she even have the strength to move? Did she want to? She just had no will. Jace rose first and reached down to lift her to her feet. He didn't let go until he was sure she could stand on her own. Her legs wobbled at first, but gained strength as blood circulated more freely. After arranging the fallen blanket around her shoulders, he turned and offered a hand to Kaden. He pulled him up and guided both of them to the large fire burning in the center of camp, where their friends quickly made room for them.

The warmth of the fire was welcome, but stung Kyrin's face and cracked lips as they thawed out. She stared into the flames with dry, gritty eyes. Pressure throbbed in her head. No doubt, in a few hours she would have a splitting headache. Her tears welled just imagining it.

"Are you hungry?"

She blinked and looked at Jace. "No," she managed hoarsely. Right now, she felt like she wanted to throw up.

Fighting the threat from her stomach, she gathered her fuzzy thoughts and forced them onto someone beside herself, like Timothy and Aaron, who had also suffered a terrible loss. "How is Talas? What happened to him?"

Captain Darq's intense eyes met hers across the fire. "Falcor stabbed him. He's resting now with Storm."

Kyrin swallowed hard, but her throat only ached more. "Will he be all right?"

Darq gave a helpless shrug. "We can't say for sure. If he weren't crete, he wouldn't have survived this long. It may save him yet. We'll just have to wait and see."

A bleak pall of quiet settled over the group. The others passed around supper, though they didn't have much of an appetite either. The despair only seemed to grow stronger until, at last, Darq spoke again. "What did Josan mean?"

For the first time all day, Kyrin remembered the mysterious words spoken by the dying crete. She slowly raised her eyes to Timothy. Fatigue weighed his drawn expression as he looked at the captain. He cleared his throat, his voice hoarse. "He wasn't really Josan Silvar. He was Torin Silvar."

Kyrin frowned as she forced her muddled brain to process, but she wasn't the only one with a confused look for Timothy.

He took a deep breath. "The man who died in the mine accident, our father, was Josan. The man you knew as Josan was Torin, our uncle."

Captain Darq's eyes grew. "You're Silvars?"

Timothy nodded in confirmation.

"But why would Torin call himself Josan?"

Timothy didn't answer immediately but, when he did, his voice cut out, forcing him to try again. "To protect me." He hung his head and shook it. When he looked up, his eyes glistened. "I'm the one the emperor is after. I'm the one who writes the letters."

Kyrin sat dumbfounded with the others as this information sank in.

"You're Taan?" Darq finally found his voice.

"For the last few years, yes," Timothy answered. "I assumed the name for my father, after he died."

Again, they just stared at him. Timothy was only a couple of years older than Kyrin, yet he'd built such a reputation as a teacher of Elôm that Daican wanted him dead. She couldn't help but look at him with some awe.

Darq shook his head. "I still don't understand the secrecy of the names."

"When we lived north of Dunlow, before my father was killed, many of the townspeople suspected him of being the author of the letters. Then, when we moved to Dunlow shortly after my father died, Josan . . . Torin insisted that Aaron and I use our mother's name and call him Josan, in case anything like this ever happened. He wanted to make sure any suspicions would fall on him and not us. Had he not . . . I would be the one dead right now."

His head bowed again, and he rubbed his eyes with his fingers. Aaron put his hand on his shoulder, his own eyes moist.

After a moment of silence, Darq said, "You're half crete then?"

Timothy looked up and nodded. "Our mother was human. She died just after I was born." He cleared his throat of the roughness. "I know this is a lot to take in, and it wouldn't be wise of you to just take our word for it, but we do have proof of our lineage."

He pulled his right arm out of his coat and shirtsleeve to expose his shoulder. Tattooed on it was an intricate brown design like the ones Kyrin had seen on the other cretes. Darq rose to get a closer look. After inspecting it, he nodded. "These are accurate Silvar family markings. Only Josan or Torin could have replicated them."

He gave Timothy a grave look. "We must get you to safety." To everyone else, he said, "We'll leave here first thing in the morning, just as soon as we tend to . . ." he paused, voice lowering, ". . . Torin's body. It'll be difficult for Talas to travel, but we have no choice."

MUFFLED VOICES DRIFTED in from outside. Dawn must have arrived, though it was hard to tell under the dim shelter of Exsis's wing. Kyrin only knew it was the longest night she'd ever lived. Even her first night alone in Tarvin Hall, or in the emperor's dungeon, couldn't compare to the sorrow that ate away at her heart. She shifted her head against Kaden's shoulder. Jace had convinced her to try to sleep, but she couldn't bear the thought of being alone, so she'd sought shelter with her brother and his dragon. It had been about midnight then and, by that time, the falling snow and wind had intensified into a blizzard. However the howling had died away sometime in the dark, miserable hours.

She sighed and squeezed her eyes shut. Her body ached even worse than before and an agonizing headache hammered the inside of her skull, as if trying to crack it open. All night, she'd drifted in and out of sleep for only minutes at a time before awakening to her heart and mind screaming, *No!* It was a wonder she hadn't screamed it aloud.

A fresh wave of sorrow crashed over her, as it had many times in the night. Tears rolled down her face. She raised her head just a little to wipe them away from her stinging cheeks and lips. She sniffed, but could only breathe through her mouth. Her tongue felt like a dried out sponge, while her throat was raw and swollen. No amount of swallowing brought relief.

Beside her, Kaden breathed heavily. She glanced at him. Even in the dark, his cheeks glinted with wetness, and it broke Kyrin's heart. The last time she'd seen him cry was the day they'd left for Tarvin Hall. He never cried after that—at least not in front of her. Not until yesterday. She laid her head back on his shoulder and gripped his arm tightly.

Neither of them moved for several minutes, until the voices outside grew louder. Clearing his throat, Kaden brushed his sleeve across his face, and his husky voice cracked when he spoke. "It'll be time to leave soon."

Kyrin gave a little nod, though moving seemed an insurmountable task, and Kaden pushed away from Exsis. The dragon lifted his wing. Kaden ducked out first and turned to offer his hand to Kyrin. She gripped it, and he pulled her to her feet.

Outside the snug cocoon, the surrounding snow—pristine white and lit up by the sun just peeking over the horizon—seared her eyes and speared into her brain. She closed her eyes with a soft groan, putting her free hand to her head. It was as if all the blood rushed in at once and threatened to explode. She gripped Kaden as she swayed dizzily, her legs almost buckling.

"Are you all right?"

She squinted up at him and attempted a nod, but it only made her head pound worse. Keeping hold of her hand, he led her to the fire where the rest of their group gathered. Slowly, she grew accustomed to the brightness and could look around without crippling pain. The night's blizzard had left the world covered in over a foot of snow, creating a dazzling view; breathtaking, if not for the sorrow.

Jace stepped around the fire to offer both her and Kaden a cup of coffee.

"Thank you," she whispered as she brought the cup to her lips.

She let out a sigh after the first sip of the strong, steaming liquid. Finally, something to relieve and soothe her aching throat. It even helped the headache after a while. Rayad came next with a small bowl of porridge. Kyrin eyed the mushy substance with an intensifying churning in her stomach, but the fatigue and weakness in her limbs called for nourishment. She accepted the bowl and brought a spoonful to her mouth. It went down hard, sticking at the back of her cramped throat on the way down. She managed to eat most of it before giving the rest to Kaden, but even he wasn't very hungry.

For several long moments, she stared into the flames as she searched for the shattered remains of her fortitude. At some point, she would need to get over this, to move on, but it was so hard. She didn't want to move on, yet life couldn't be lived forever in grief. *Help me,* she cried quietly inside. Blinking away the tears that ever waited to spring up, she looked around the fire at her companions.

"Talas. Is he . . . all right?"

"He's conscious, which is good," Darq answered. "He's still with Storm. He'd like to speak to you two."

Kyrin glanced at Kaden, and they followed the captain to the dragons while the rest of the men packed up camp. Leetra was there with her cousin. Underneath Storm's wing, she helped him sit up and rest against the dragon's side. Talas sucked in his breath before letting out a groan, his eyes shut and teeth clenched. Kyrin winced and prayed for his full recovery. They'd suffered too much loss already.

Once settled, he sat for a moment and caught his breath. Kyrin and Kaden knelt down so he could see them better. When he focused on them, pain and regret stole away any brightness in his eyes and roughened his voice. "I was there when your father was arrested."

The air caught in Kyrin's lungs as emotion wrapped around her chest. Was she ready to hear this? The wounds to her heart were so raw, but she read in Talas's eyes his need to speak.

"It was an ambush. The emperor had men hidden around the arch. Falcor stabbed me before your father and I realized what was happening. I was able to break away. I tried to get word to Tane . . . but I couldn't stay conscious long enough to give him any information." Talas's eyes closed again, and he groaned, but it didn't come from physical pain this time. "If I had, he could've brought word to you, and you could've stopped it. I'm so sorry."

Tears flowed hot and fast down Kyrin's cheeks and off her chin. Her lips trembled, and she swallowed down the sob rising in her throat. If only they'd known. It would have been so simple to rescue him with the dragons. But she shook her head. She'd thought about what Jace told her yesterday—what she herself had said in the past—and had come to the hard, but true conclusion—her father had been meant to die. They'd had so many ways they might have saved him, but he'd died anyway. For a reason unknown to her, it was Elôm's will, and both she and Kaden had to accept it. *Help us trust You!*

"There was nothing you could do," she murmured. "You tried . . . thank you."

Timothy sat quietly next to Josan's blanket-wrapped body. A week ago, he, Josan, and Aaron had sat in their tiny cottage, never imagining that their life would change in such a series of drastic instants. Just like when his father had died, it had happened before he even knew it. Now the only family he had left was Aaron.

*No*. That was no longer true. Now he had family in Dorland—a grandfather. How would it affect the man to know that the two sons he'd wanted so much to reconcile with were both dead? Moisture burned Timothy's eyes. He would have to tell his grandfather that his father and uncle would have reconciled in a heartbeat—that they never held any bitterness over the past. But how would his grandfather and other extended family receive him and Aaron? Would it be with open arms, or with suspicion for two half-blooded cretes they'd never known existed? If only Josan were there to take them to Dorland and introduce them. It was a dream he'd rarely spoken of, but had always longed for.

"It's in Your hands, Elôm," Timothy murmured. "All of it. Even things I don't understand."

He had to smile through his tears. All the pain and hardship Josan had faced in this life was gone now. He would never have to endure it again. And for that, Timothy was thankful.

Footsteps crunched in the snow. Timothy wiped his face and looked up at his brother, whose eyes reflected his sorrow.

"The grave is finished."

Sighing, Timothy pushed to his feet and helped his brother lift Josan's body. The weight and lifelessness of it sent a rush of emotion that nearly choked him. He forced himself to dwell on the truth that, just because Josan's body remained here, it did not mean he didn't live in eternity, and the time until they would see each other again was only temporary.

They carried Josan up the mountainside to a small plateau just above camp, where the other men had cleared the snow and one of the dragons had dug a grave in the frozen ground. After laying him in it, they stood for a moment of quiet remembrance.

Timothy lifted his eyes to the surroundings—the sparkling white snow, the frosted dark green pines below them that were the first trees he'd ever seen, the breathtaking view of the shimmering Sidian Ocean to the west, the clean, pure air.

Timothy cleared his throat, though he still spoke hoarsely. "It's good he's buried up here, on the mountain. He spent too long in the Valley. I know how he missed the Dorland trees and being in the mountains."

"It is a good place," Darq agreed. "Much like where we bury our loved ones back home."

Timothy offered him a faint smile. Josan deserved a proper crete burial.

For the next half hour, he and most of the men gathered stones from the mountainside to cover the grave. When they finished, everyone gathered around for a final farewell. Silence surrounded them at first, while Timothy battled the intense ache in his chest and gathered the proper words.

"None of you had a chance to get to know my uncle well." He forced his voice to come out steadily. "But he was one of the strongest and most caring man I've ever known; he and my father. They sacrificed so much to help others." He paused for a breath, but tears were already clogging his airway again. "Josan hadn't even fully healed before he moved Aaron and me to Dunlow because he hoped it might offer more opportunities. He spent every penny he'd saved on the cottage for us. Every time things grew tougher, he was the one who sacrificed so that we could live better. I don't know where we'd be without him."

Following the short funeral, the group slowly turned to make their way back toward camp but, for a moment, Jace couldn't move as he stared at the stone-covered grave. He couldn't restrain the images of Kalli and Aldor's graves back at the farm. The memories and the sorrow surrounding everyone cut him deeply.

He'd barely spoken to Josan, but he respected his selflessness and humility. He blinked hard at the cold breeze that made his eyes water, yet it was more than that. Why did two such honorable men like Josan and William die when men like Daican and Falcor lived on to cause pain and ruin? It made no sense. And why was death such a huge part of his life? A tempting thought entered his mind, to wonder if it was some sort of curse that followed him, but Kyrin had already confronted him once about such thoughts. For her sake, he wouldn't let them take hold again, though fear of it lingered.

Rayad gripped his shoulder and stood with him, much as they had at the farm.

"Let's go," he murmured after a moment.

Jace finally tore his eyes from the grave, and they trailed the others back to camp. As they neared, Kaden's angry voice snapped Jace from his dreary thoughts.

"They can't just get away with what they've done."

His eyes jerked up and latched onto Kaden, who was grabbing up his supplies in swift, irate movements. Kyrin stood before him and spoke imploringly. "Kaden, please."

He stalked past her, straight for the dragons. Dread washed through Jace.

"Kaden, stop," Kyrin tried to no avail.

She followed him, but Jace intercepted her. He knew exactly what was going through Kaden's mind. "I'll talk to him."

Her pleading eyes met his. "Please stop him. He's going to get himself killed."

Jace nodded and hurried after her brother. "Kaden." He didn't look up from tightening Exsis's saddle, but Jace pressed on. "I know what you are doing, but you can't."

Kaden's gaze did rise now. His eyes were red and moist, but

also hard with the driving need to take action, to avenge—feelings Jace knew too well.

"They killed my father," Kaden said, his voice stretched taut and almost breaking. "They killed Josan and took the Scrolls. They're destroying everything! Someone has to do something."

He went back to work on his saddle.

Jace tried desperately to think of the best thing to say. Didn't the same thoughts still lurk at the back of his mind and whisper for action? Even after his talk with Rayad, they still tempted him. But whatever those thoughts demanded, he had to get through to Kaden, and he was quickly losing time. He glanced at Kyrin, who watched from a distance with fearful eyes. She could lose her brother today too. Jace wouldn't let that happen. He'd resort to force if necessary, but that was the last thing he wanted. He had to make Kaden understand.

"Listen, if I thought this was the way to do it, I'd be on Gem right now joining you, but it isn't." He paused to let the words sink into his own mind. "We can't do this. They'd just kill us, too, and what would that accomplish? We both know if you go down there, you won't come back."

Kaden glanced at him, but didn't stop. He didn't care. Not right now, anyway. Jace struggled. He'd never been good with words. But another look at Kyrin centered in his mind the most important thing in all of this.

"If nothing else, think of Kyrin. Do you really think she could bear to lose you too? Is your revenge worth your life when it won't change what's already happened? I know it isn't to her. She needs you, now more than ever."

Jace could not bear to see how it would devastate her to lose both her father and brother in the space of a day. She would never recover.

At last, Kaden stilled. A brutal battle raged on his face, and a tear dripped from his eye. He swiped it away and looked up again. Surrender settled in his eyes. He gave a slow nod, and Jace let out a long breath. *Thank You, Elôm.*

Once each of the dragons was saddled, Captain Darq recruited Jace and Kaden, the tallest and strongest of the group, to help Talas onto the captain's dragon. It wouldn't be a pleasant trip for the wounded crete, but he would have to endure.

As they prepared to leave, Rayad approached Kyrin and Kaden with a compassionate look. "I wanted to give you something before we leave. Tane left it for you yesterday. Aric wrote down things your father wanted you to know."

He handed a folded parchment to Kyrin. Her breath caught as she took it with shaking fingers. Part of her desired to open it immediately, desperate for her father's words, while another part of her wasn't sure she could do it. She needed time to allow the words to sink in, and to cry over them. Time she didn't have now. Working to keep tears from overflowing, she looked up at Kaden. Praise Elôm he was still here, thanks to Jace.

"We'll read it when we get home?"

He nodded, his teary eyes meeting hers.

Carefully, Kyrin tucked the parchment into the inside of her coat.

"Aric tried to find a way to get him out," Rayad told them quietly. "But the emperor took no chances, and your father didn't want Aric to risk himself."

Kyrin stared at her feet, using every thread of willpower to keep from crying. As horribly painful as it was, she was so proud of what her father had done. He was a hero, just like his father, and she would make sure people remembered him that way.

"Thank you," her voice broke, "for telling us."

Rayad nodded and squeezed her shoulder, then Kaden's. As he walked away, Kyrin stood for a moment to recover. She touched her coat where the letter rested close to her father's necklace. Kaden put his arm around her shoulders. She sighed, regaining her composure, and looked up at him. "Can I ride with you? I don't want to be alone."

He nodded, and they walked toward the dragons.

There, Jace met them. He glanced at Kaden, but his focus rested on Kyrin. The gentle remorse and sympathy in his eyes nearly overwhelmed her. How could anyone believe someone who cared so deeply could ever be a monster?

"It'll be cold flying today. Why don't you wear this over your coat?"

He gave her one of his wool shirts. She sank her fingers into it and pulled it over her head, pushing her arms through the sleeves. It added a comfortable layer of warmth, not only to her body, but also to her battered heart.

She looked up at him, achieving the smallest hint of a smile. "Thank you."

He gave a nod, and his eyes lingered in a moment of shared sadness before the three of them turned to their dragons. Kaden offered Kyrin a hand and pulled her up behind him on Exsis. Settling in, she looked over at her dragon. "Ivy, *réma*."

The dragon perked up, ready to follow. Kyrin pulled on her gloves and wrapped her arms around Kaden.

From his dragon, Darq commanded, "Glynn, Leetra, take the rear and follow at a distance. I want to make sure Falcor doesn't try to follow us."

The two cretes nodded, and Darq's dragon took to the air. The rest followed.

Once they reached their desired altitude and turned east toward Landale, Kyrin looked back at Valcré. From this height, she could see the entire city, and her gaze stopped where the central square lay. Her stomach nearly turned itself inside out. She closed her eyes tightly and rested her forehead against Kaden's back until the city was well out of sight.

The snow-covered forest of Landale drew a deep sigh from Kyrin. After all day in flight, she longed to get down, get inside, and get warm. Even with Jace's shirt, the cold seeped in and sank into her core. Her whole body ached, as if it had taken a terrible beating. The still-throbbing pain in her head was the worst. She had spent much of the flight with her eyes scrunched closed against the sunlight.

When they set down in camp, Kaden slid off first and turned to help her down. She gripped his strong arms until her legs felt steady, and then she let go.

"I'll be back in a minute," he murmured, and turned to help the other men with Talas.

Kyrin wrapped her arms around herself, looking toward the cabin, but didn't move. Others from camp had begun to gather to meet them. Kyrin ducked her head, afraid to face them and answer their questions. Speaking of what had happened would destroy her weak resolve.

When the men had everything handled, Kaden returned to Kyrin and, together, they walked toward Lenae's cabin. The thud of Kyrin's pulse echoed painfully in her head. As they drew near, the cabin door opened and Lenae stepped into the doorway. A warm smile lit her face, but it died the moment she witnessed their expressions. She put her hand to her throat and came out to meet them.

"What's wrong? What happened?"

Kyrin attempted to rally herself, but the emotion flooded in too quickly. She managed an unintelligible syllable, but the rest of her voice halted, snatched away by the crushing sorrow. She couldn't say it, but it didn't matter. Kaden said it for her.

"The emperor executed our father."

There was no hope for stopping the tears now. They spilled down Kyrin's cheeks. Lenae had to let this sink in a moment, but then gathered Kyrin into her arms. Kyrin laid her head on her shoulder and cried softly as the woman rubbed her back. After a few moments, Lenae pulled away gently, slipping one arm around Kyrin's shoulders and the other around Kaden.

"Come inside and get warm. Both of you."

She guided them toward the open door. Inside, she helped Kyrin slip out of Jace's shirt and then set two chairs near the fireplace, while Kyrin and Kaden removed their coats. When they sat down, Lenae bent next to Kyrin and, with the tender care of a mother, she felt Kyrin's cheek and forehead.

"You're a little warm. Are you hurt anywhere?"

"My head," Kyrin whispered weakly. Right now, it was so painful and heavy it felt ready to fall right off her shoulders.

"I'll make you some tea." Lenae rose for a kettle and herbs to help the pain.

Kyrin stared into the fireplace, losing herself in the flames. She let her mind numb and tried not to think of anything. Not the pain. Not the loss. She flinched when Lenae placed a warm mug in her hands. Kyrin glanced at her and took a sip that she swallowed down hard. Her throat ached with the tightness of a new wave of grief.

A few minutes later, someone knocked lightly on the door, and Lenae let Jace in. His eyes immediately sought Kyrin. "I brought your things."

She noted the roughness of his voice and watched him set her supplies on the table. He'd been so kind and helpful. Kyrin appreciated it immensely. If only she were more capable of expressing it beyond a murmured "thank you."

He glanced at Kaden. "We brought your things to the shelter, and both Exsis and Ivy have been taken care of."

Kaden echoed Kyrin's thanks. Jace shifted his eyes back to Kyrin's, where they held, his concern and sorrow for her completely unguarded. She wanted to assure him that she would be all right, but would she?

TIMOTHY RESTED HIS forehead on his fingertips, staring down at the words he'd just finished writing. He willed more words to come, but he was mentally spent. Leaning back in his chair, he laid the quill pen aside and closed his eyes in a fight against the despair that threatened to rise up. He refused to let it consume him.

It was difficult, though. Josan's death left behind a painful, gaping void inside him. His uncle had been such a powerful spiritual influence in his life. Timothy would sorely miss his prayers, as well as his comforting and nurturing strength and wisdom. Tears clogged his throat. He rejoiced that Josan was now eternally free from burdens and pain, but a more selfish part of him still wanted his uncle here to help him with all that lay ahead.

When the cabin door opened, Timothy blinked. Aaron stepped in. His brother closed the door quietly with a glance at Talas, who rested on a bed in the corner—the bed Trask had given up for him. Rayad and Warin had offered their beds to Timothy and Aaron, but they declined and laid out bedding on the floor instead. Still, their kindness touched Timothy. He hadn't known many people who would do what the men and women of this camp had done for them.

Aaron pulled out a chair next to Timothy and sat down. "How's it coming?"

Timothy glanced back down at the pages of parchment and despair lurked again. For many hours the night before, he'd written down all the Scripture he could remember. He hadn't known what else to do. Amidst the sorrow surrounding them, he felt lost without the Scrolls. They'd been available to him all his life, but now he had nothing. Not even his own letters, which had been with the copies of the Scrolls that Falcor had also taken.

He sighed again. "I think I've done all I can remember."

Aaron picked up the stack of parchment near him, about fifty pages' worth, and flipped through them. "This is a lot."

His tone held encouragement, but Timothy shook his head. "It's nothing compared to what we had."

Aaron looked him in the eyes. "But it *is* something."

Letting his brother's words have their effect, Timothy nodded. "You're right."

Aaron gave him a small smile. Though it didn't hide the weariness and sadness his brother also felt at the loss they'd suffered, the gesture gave him the boost of hope he needed.

"Come on." Aaron pushed up from the table. "You need to get out."

Timothy didn't dispute that. With quiet steps, the two of them crossed the cabin, and Timothy grabbed his coat as they headed outdoors. He breathed deeply as he pulled it on, the crisp air refreshing his fatigued mind. He scanned the campsite. It hadn't snowed as heavily here, and the temperature was warmer. If it held, the few inches of snow would disappear in a day or two with how warmly the sun shone down.

They stepped away from the cabin, angling toward the edge of camp, and Timothy glanced back at the cabin Kyrin and Lenae shared. His heart hurt deeply over what had happened to

Captain Altair. He prayed for Kyrin, Kaden, and the rest of their family—for their healing and comfort through the sorrow that never faded completely.

At the camp's perimeter, Aaron stopped and stared into the forest. Timothy paused beside him.

"All my life, I've never seen trees until the last couple of days," Aaron said.

Timothy shook his head, taking in the sight of one dark tree trunk after another as far as he could see. He tried to imagine what their bare limbs and the forest floor would look like covered in greenery. It was surprisingly difficult without a single memory to aid him. Spring would be a wondrous time.

Pondering this, he looked at his brother. "What do you think we'll do now?"

Aaron stuck his hands in his pockets and shrugged. "Captain Darq mentioned something about taking us to Dorland to meet our grandfather. I suppose they won't make any plans until Talas has recovered."

Timothy considered this in silence. He wanted to meet their grandfather. Since their mother had been an orphan, he'd never had family outside of his brother, father, and uncle. Still, something inside him hesitated at leaving. Maybe it was the unknown of entering into the cretes' dramatically-different lifestyle. What would they expect of him and Aaron? He shrugged these questions off for the time he would actually face them. If he had learned anything from the last week, it was that it only took one small event for everything to change.

He glanced over his shoulder for another look around the camp that could possibly be their new home, and his eyes caught near the dragons. One lone person stood among them. Leetra. Her small size gave her away. She rested against her dragon with her head bowed. Though her back was to him, the jerking of her shoulders told him one thing—she was crying. Odd. She seemed so strong and stoic yet, with the loss of two good men and the Scrolls, it was easy to forget that the one who'd caused it all had been Leetra's betrothed. The pain of his betrayal must be excruciating.

Knowing what little he did of her, she probably wouldn't welcome an intrusion, but his heart urged him to help her. Maybe it was the crete way to suffer silently and alone, but he didn't believe it was necessary.

"Excuse me a minute," he told Aaron, and walked toward her.

Her soft cries drifted toward him as he drew near. Suddenly, she spun around. Her eyes shimmered lavender and spilled tears down her cheeks. For that split-second, all her walls were gone, leaving her deepest vulnerability laid bare. But the moment she registered his face, her own hardened. She swiped her fingers across her cheeks as if the tears were toxic and glared at him.

Timothy held up his hands. "I'm sorry, I didn't mean to disturb you . . . I just came to see if there was any way I could help."

"There isn't," she snapped and turned away from him.

Timothy stood lost for a second or two, but he wouldn't give up that easily. "There's no shame in tears. You have every right to cry." His voice dropped a little. "I can't imagine how difficult it must be for you to have been betrayed by Falcor."

Her whole body tensed, and she turned back to him. This time her eyes flashed in anger, but not for him, he realized. She took a step forward, her voice low and cold.

"He's responsible for the murder of two men, he nearly killed my cousin, and he would have killed you had he known who you are. Given half a chance, he probably would have killed Captain Darq too. And I . . ." She placed her hand on her chest before curling it into a tight fist. "*I* was going to marry him."

Her jaw clenched, and she shook her head as she spoke

bitterly. "I should've been able to see, but no. I was just stupid enough to fall for his act and his lies." Tears glimmered once more in her eyes.

Her pain and anger only intensified Timothy's desire to help her. He wanted to reach out with a comforting hand, but he held back and merely spoke instead. "He hid his intentions well, from all of us. It's not your fault."

For just an instant, as she looked into his eyes, her defenses dropped again to reveal a desperate longing, but it was just a flash. She looked away, muttering through her teeth, "Easy for you to say," and strode past him.

Timothy's gaze followed her, but he could no more make her accept his words than he could change the past. One thing was certain, though—he didn't think he'd ever forget the sight of her lavender eyes when she'd first turned to him. He'd never seen such eyes.

Kyrin buried her head under the blankets to capture every bit of warmth from the covers and block out the light. She didn't know what time it was, but she had slept most of the night. How could she not when her body needed it so? Her muscles still felt stiff and achy, but at least the headache had subsided to a dull throb between her eyes. Another cup of tea or coffee would probably take it away completely.

For several minutes, she lay still and searched for the will to get up. It was easier to lie there and try to block everything out. To rise and face the day would require composure and an acceptance of change. *I don't want change.* She focused on Lenae's quiet footsteps below her instead of the tightening in her chest. A moment later, someone knocked on the door and Lenae opened it.

"I came to see if Kyrin was up yet."

Kyrin rolled onto her stomach and pushed herself up on her elbows, brushing hair out of her eyes. Reaching out, she parted the curtain of the loft. "Kaden?"

He looked up at her. His eyes were clearer today. Determined.

"I'll be down in a minute," she told him.

Letting the curtain fall back into place, she pushed back the covers and slid out of bed with a sigh. Below, Lenae asked Kaden if he had eaten lunch yet. When he said no, she invited him to sit down while she made something for him and Kyrin before taking food over to Trask's cabin for their guests.

Kyrin rubbed the grittiness out of her eyes and grabbed her clothes—a pair of woolen leggings, a wool shirt, and sleeveless suede overdress that fell just past her knees. She reached inside her collar to tug on the cord around her neck and bring the stone into reach. Squeezing it against her palm, her eyes settled on the folded parchment resting on top of her dresser. She and Kaden had been too weak and exhausted to read it the night before. Slowly, she picked it up and left the loft.

Downstairs, she washed her face and sat down across from Kaden. She laid the parchment on the table between them. Kaden glanced at it, but said nothing. A couple of minutes later, Lenae set a bowl of soup before each of them. Kyrin stared at the food, and then glanced hesitantly at Kaden. Their eyes met in understanding. Gathering her resolve, Kyrin closed her eyes, bowing her head as they each said a silent prayer. It was difficult, at first, to form any words. *I know I have so much to be thankful for, but it's hard to see when things seem so bleak. Help us to see and make it through this.* She peeked at her brother. *Thank You so much that I still have Kaden and all my friends.*

She picked up her spoon and stirred it through the soup as she tried to find an appetite. Kaden didn't dive in either. Finally, she forced herself to take a bite. Despite her lack of appetite, her stomach accepted the food hungrily, and she managed to finish the entire bowl right after Kaden finished his.

Now they sat for a moment in silence. Lenae had gone to the other cabin, so it was just the two of them. Kyrin looked from the parchment to Kaden, and back again. At last, she reached for it, gingerly unfolding the message and placing it where she and Kaden could both read it. She swallowed hard and scanned the words.

By the end, she could barely see the parchment. She pressed her palms to her eyes, though the tears leaked through anyway. She fought to keep the grief and longing for her father at bay, but it wore her down.

"Are you all right?"

At Kaden's husky voice, she pulled her hands away from her face, looking into his teary eyes. "I don't know." She choked a little and fought not to break down into sobs. Wiping her cheeks, she asked, "Are you?"

His answer wasn't immediate. Quietly, he said, "I will be . . . eventually."

Kyrin nodded. *Eventually*.

Kaden looked down, battling his own tears. "He would want us to keep going; to keep fighting."

She nodded again, more firmly this time. That was just what their father would want. Using her sleeves, she wiped away the remaining tears and drew deep breaths to calm herself. Once in control of her emotions, she looked determinedly at Kaden.

"I know one thing we must do. We have to get to Liam, somehow. Now, especially. He needs us."

THEY COULDN'T REACH the fort fast enough for Liam. Traveling through the snow had been difficult, but since it had nearly melted, it turned the road to a bed of ankle-deep mud that sucked at his boots and drained his energy. On top of it, a cold drizzle fell from the gloomy sky. By now, his cloak was nearly soaked through. Thankfully, they had only another two miles to go. Then he and the rest of the foot soldiers could seek warm shelter and change out of their wet, mud-spattered uniforms.

He glanced toward the head of the column, where Marcus led the way on horseback with his lieutenant, Parker. They hadn't spoken much on their return journey—even less so when they drew near to the fort. He didn't have to be a genius to guess that his brother's somber mood was on account of having to report their failure in Dunlow to the General. Liam hung his head. The discomfort Marcus suffered was his fault. He could have turned the crete in. Yet he still believed he'd done the right thing in letting him escape. Even so, he hoped his father had arrived ahead of them to offer more reassurance. He'd been questioning everything since they left Dunlow, particularly concerning the things his father wanted to tell him.

At last, Fort Rivor appeared. However, its daunting gray walls situated on a bare hilltop put a knot in Liam's gut. He'd spent most of his life there, but it certainly didn't give the feeling of coming home. More like entering a prison yard, but at least it offered shelter. He shifted his attention to the thousands of off-white tents and other shelters that surrounded it. Smoke from sputtering fires rose all across camp. Even in the dreary weather, the place buzzed with activity. No amount of rain or mud would halt drills and training. Some soldiers who struggled might be forced to march until hypothermia set in but, even then, they wouldn't be dismissed immediately. He shivered, pulling his cloak closer at the memories of his own miserable experiences.

They climbed the gradual slope that cut through the center of camp and halted at the wall of the fort. Marcus dismounted and turned to dismiss the men. Gladly, they moved off to find shelter, but Liam lingered. He'd caused his brother enough trouble. Leaving now felt like abandoning him. "Do you want me to go with you?"

Marcus handed his horse off to a waiting attendant before turning to him, his eyes solemn. "No, that's all right." He put his hand on Liam's shoulder. "Go get changed and warm."

Liam didn't try to hide his gratitude. The thought of facing their grandfather with bad news left him colder than the weather.

Just before he turned away, a soldier came from the fort. "Captain Altair."

Marcus faced him.

"General Veshiron wants to see you and your brother in his office."

The knot in Liam's stomach yanked tighter. There went his escape. Marcus cast him an apologetic look and led the way into the fort. Inside the headquarters, they followed the dim halls to the General's office. Marcus straightened at the door and drew a deep breath before knocking.

"Enter," the General's commanding voice resonated from within.

Marcus opened the door, and Liam followed him into the office, forcing himself to stand at his brother's side instead of behind him. A chill hung in the room, though perhaps Liam only felt that way. It was not a friendly space—filled with dark furniture, showcased weapons, and an abundance of black and gold trimming. A massive desk sat in the center and, behind it, a wide cabinet displaying countless medals and awards.

The General stood behind his desk and almost made the piece look small. After a quick glance at his stern face, Liam stared down at his boots. If only he could make himself invisible. Marcus, however, stood up straight and tall, ready to accept whatever the man had to say. Liam could only wish for such courage.

Clearly wanting to get it out and over with, Marcus said, "General, I regret that I bring disappointing news from Dunlow—"

"I know about Dunlow," the General cut in.

Liam glanced at Marcus. Their father must have arrived already with the news, but apparently hadn't been able to spare them from facing the General themselves. Marcus opened his mouth to speak, likely a well-rehearsed apology, and to take responsibility for his failure, but the General continued.

"It's been taken care of."

Now Liam did look at their grandfather. How could it be taken care of? The crete and those with him had escaped . . . hadn't they?

"I have news for you two," the General said, his tone and eyes as hard as ever. "Five days ago, your father was arrested and executed for treason."

Liam's heart stopped. His lungs collapsed, expelling all their oxygen. He hadn't heard right. He couldn't have. It was impossible. A sickening sensation buzzed in his head and pulsated all the way down to his feet. The room sat frozen and airless until Marcus gasped, "What?"

"He was caught aiding the very men you were after, and he admitted before the emperor that he had no belief in the gods." The General scowled in contempt. "He was another one of those Elôm followers. A traitor, just like his father."

Shock and grief hit Liam so hard he barely had the strength to contain it. *No*. It couldn't be. He tried to breathe, but his lungs wouldn't comply. He had to get out—out of this room, away from this man who had always disparaged their father. How could he look at them now with such a lack of compassion?

"May I be dismissed?" he choked out the words, ashamed of how weak he sounded.

His grandfather just let him stand there for a cruel, agonizing moment before waving his hand. It was a pitiless gesture, but Liam took it and turned for the door. Fumbling with the knob, he yanked the door open and rushed out. He strode down the hall, but his weak pretense of strength crumbled faster than he could move. His vision blurred behind sheets of moisture, and his head spun. Shoving open the front door, he stumbled out past the wall. There, in the middle of the mud, rain, and cold, he couldn't go any farther. He bent over and braced his hands against his legs, but the last of his strength gave way, and he dropped to his knees. Bile rose up in his throat.

He dug his fingernails into his palms and dragged in a ragged breath, fighting to come to terms with the news, but the truth of it broke open the grief building inside and drowned him. As the first tears fell, he brushed them away, but they came too quickly. He gasped, and a painful, desperate cry came with it. What would he do without his father? He needed him. There were things his father needed to tell him.

Liam bent over and put his head in his hands, his chest heaving with silent cries. His father was a good man—the kindest and most compassionate man he'd ever known—yet the emperor had killed him—killed him merely over a difference in beliefs, just like Aaron had said in Dunlow. It was all wrong. If this marked the difference between followers of Elôm and followers of Aertus and Vilai, then how could the emperor be right? How could murder ever be right? That's what it was. His father had been murdered.

Liam's fists shook as a burning demand for justice engulfed him. But what could he do? He was nothing more than a pathetic excuse for a foot soldier. Powerless. The anger drained as quickly as it had flared, leaving behind a dark, overwhelming emptiness that yearned for comfort.

The agony of it consumed him until soggy footsteps came up behind him. Trying to blink his vision clear of tears, he looked over his shoulder. Marcus stood there—a ghostly pale version of his usual strong self. His eyes mirrored the mix of confusion, denial, and grief that slowly destroyed Liam inside. He appeared to want to say something, but was incapable of it. Lacking his own voice, Liam pushed to his feet, and the two of them embraced.

Kyrin glanced out the window as she chopped onions for the stew Lenae prepared for supper. The sunshine that had at least taken the gloom from the cabin was gone, replaced by dark clouds and cold rain. It did nothing to help her attempts to let life fall back into a normal routine over the last two days.

Blaming the sudden stinging in her eyes on the onions, she resolutely turned her focus back to her task, mentally listing the other things she could do to help. Work was a good way to stay occupied. Idleness invited too much time to think and for emotion to take hold. She scraped the onions into a bowl and had just reached for another when the door opened. Kaden stepped in, rain droplets beading on his coat.

"Tane is here. He wants to see us."

Though he did not speak with urgency, ice flowed through Kyrin's limbs and solidified in her chest. It would be a while before any news from Valcré didn't immediately make her fear the worst. She stood a moment to calm herself and set her knife aside. At the door, she grabbed her cloak and put it around her shoulders as she followed her brother outside. They hurried through the chilly mist to Trask's cabin.

Inside, many of their friends had gathered. Kyrin glanced at Talas as Kaden shut the door. He was propped up in bed, his eyes alert and color good. The crete had healed surprisingly fast, which Kyrin learned was normal for his race, thank Elôm.

Now her eyes shifted to Tane, who sat at the table. He gave her a gentle, understanding smile. She managed one in return, and they exchanged quiet greetings as Trask invited her and Kaden to join them.

Kyrin faced Tane. "What brings you from Valcré? Do you have any news about the Scrolls?" No doubt the emperor had destroyed them, yet she clung to a dim hope that Elôm hadn't allowed such a thing.

Tane shook his head. "Aric is looking into it, but he's hesitant to question the emperor directly. Daican has been very suspicious the last few days." He paused, resting his clasped hands on the table, and spoke carefully. "But that isn't the reason I came. I know this is difficult to discuss, but I thought you two should know . . . your father has been buried at home. From what I know, it took place yesterday."

Kyrin struggled to draw in air against the phantom cords constricting around her lungs. She hadn't let herself even contemplate what would happen to her father's body. To know he actually had a grave and that it was at home both tore her heart and relieved it.

"How?" Her voice trembled. "Why would the emperor give him a grave?"

"Aric arranged it. He knew you would want a proper burial. He was able to convince the emperor it would serve as a constant reminder to your family of the consequences of treason."

So grateful for his thoughtfulness, Kyrin nodded, but as her mind processed thoughts of her family and the effect her father's death would have on them, it suddenly occurred to her. *Liam!* And, for the first time in days, a clear purpose rose up out of the ashes.

"We have to go."

Kaden frowned at her sudden determination. "It could be a trap. Even if Aric was the one to suggest it, the emperor could be using it to his advantage. He has to know we would want to go there."

"But if we leave right away, Daican will have no reason to suspect word of the burial has reached us already. Kaden—*Liam*," she stressed. "What if Liam is there, at home, now? We have to try to see him. This is our best chance."

Needing no further prompting, Kaden rose from the table. "If we leave now, we could almost reach Mernin by nightfall."

Kyrin was ready to pack immediately, but Tane stopped them. "Are you sure that's wise? Mernin is right near Fort Rivor. You could easily run into soldiers. If they catch a glimpse of your dragons, they'll know something's up."

"We can leave the dragons in the forest once we're near Mernin and travel the rest of the way on foot," Kaden replied. "If it's just Kyrin and me, no one will suspect a couple of travelers on the road."

Kyrin agreed. Even if it was dangerous, even if they were

unable to see Liam, this was something she needed to do. When their father had ridden away that morning outside of Valcré, it had been with the full expectation of returning. Their goodbye wasn't meant to be permanent and didn't feel adequate. She had to say that final goodbye and honor the sacrifice he had made. She wouldn't feel a sense of closure until she did.

The men exchanged hesitant looks. Not one of them appeared entirely onboard with this plan, yet none of them had the heart to speak in protest.

"Are you sure you should go alone?" Rayad asked.

"Fewer people will draw less attention," Kaden answered.

"I'll go along." They all looked at Jace. "One more person won't add suspicion, but will still be added protection." He appealed to Kyrin with his eyes.

He was right, and she would like him to be there. She looked at Kaden, who nodded.

"All right. We'll leave right after lunch."

Kyrin packed her supplies onto Ivoris to leave camp for a second time in just over a week. Had it really been so short a time since they'd set out on their mission? And here they were setting out again, but for far different reasons. She swallowed the lump it brought to her throat. Until they reached Mernin, she wouldn't let herself think about how hard it would be to stand at her father's grave. She only knew she needed the closure, so she focused on that.

Their friends gathered around them for a few final words and goodbyes.

"Be careful," Rayad cautioned. "Avoid everyone you can."

The three of them nodded.

"You're sure things will go well with your mother?" Tane asked.

They had little hope of visiting the grave without the rest of the family knowing. To face her mother after all these years, especially now, riddled Kyrin with doubts and perhaps even a bit of fear, but she couldn't escape it.

"From what my father told me, she knew of his faith, but never turned him in. I don't believe she would do that to us." It wasn't a guarantee, but they had to go with it. "And she might be the perfect way to contact Liam." She prayed some good would come of this.

Rayad spoke again, his concern evident. "Remember, if you're not back in three days, we're coming to look for you."

Why couldn't they just be left to their grief? Could their grandfather not even allow them one day to mourn? Liam ground his teeth as these questions tumbled through his mind while he trailed after Marcus. They'd had just over an hour to come to terms with their father's death before being summoned again. And, as always, Marcus followed orders. It was cruel. Unmercifully cruel. But then, their grandfather was a cruel man. He always had been.

Liam struggled to keep his emotions hidden behind a fragile mask of composure that felt ready to shatter. There was no telling what the General wanted now, but Liam had little strength to face anything more.

All the men from Marcus's unit filed into the fort, where the General awaited them.

"This way," the man ordered sharply and marched off.

The men followed him around the back of the fort. There

Liam saw them—the new additions. Two life-sized figures of Aertus and Vilai had been erected in the large courtyard, protected by an elaborate awning. The men halted as the General turned to face them.

"With the increase of traitors being discovered, including in our army, the emperor has decreed that all soldiers are required to report and show their devotion to the gods at least once every week. Attendance and participation is mandatory. Anyone who refuses to show up or bow will be arrested and executed. There have already been eleven arrests here in Fort Rivor. If you don't want your name added to the list, bow before your gods."

Almost as one, the men around Liam dropped to their knees, including Marcus. However, Liam's muscles seized and his joints locked up. He had to work hard to lower himself to the ground beside his brother.

Shallow breaths shuddered in his lungs. He'd bowed before Aertus and Vilai before, many times, but there'd never been any emotion involved. After a lifetime of unfulfilled dreams and unanswered prayers, he'd followed the expected worship practices with little thought. Yet here, in this moment, a deep, pulling conviction pounded in his heart. This was wrong. He didn't know why exactly, but he felt it. Maybe because he knew if his father were here with them, he would still be standing right now. One man among a hundred, choosing to die rather than submit to what he did not believe in. His father had made that choice, and as hard as it was to bear, Liam believed he was right. He refused to accept that his father had died for nothing. His eyes rose to the idols. In one week, he'd be here again, but he wasn't sure if next time he would bow.

"THE CROSSROADS MUST be close," Kaden said. "It's only another two miles from there, right?" He glanced at Kyrin.

She nodded and adjusted her cloak. Mud clung to the hem, making it heavy and cumbersome. She'd rather cast it off, but the air was too chilly. For over two hours, she, Kaden, and Jace had trudged along the edge of the wet road where the path wasn't quite so rutted and sloppy. Not knowing who might be around, they'd left the dragons deep in the forest where they'd camped for the night. In her weariness, Kyrin longed for one to ride, but they pushed on. They didn't have much farther to go now.

She glanced at the sky. At least it hadn't rained since the previous afternoon. Even so, the clouds hung low and thick with the threat of rain, and the air was misty.

"I wonder what Michael and Ronny look like," Kaden said, drawing her attention away from the weather.

Such thoughts had been on Kyrin's mind all morning. They were so close to meeting the family they hadn't seen in over ten years. It was tragically fitting that this would bring them together and back to their home. Their two younger brothers had only been babies when they'd left. A longing had grown inside of her to finally see them again, yet a more fearful part of her secretly hoped they would be able to visit their father's grave and contact Liam without anyone else ever knowing they'd been there.

Kyrin looked at Kaden, that fear rising to the surface. "How do you think Mother will react to us?" Though she believed what she'd told Tane, that their mother was not a threat to their safety, she did feel a threat to her emotional well-being.

Kaden shrugged. If only Kyrin could be so unconcerned. "I don't know. I think—"

Jace held up a hand for them to stop.

Kyrin halted. "What?" she whispered.

"I heard something."

They all listened and, as Kyrin scanned the area, a long-ago memory formed. "It's the crossroads."

Movement flickered behind a thick stand of evergreens and underbrush ahead and to their right, but before they could even hope to respond, a group of five soldiers on horseback appeared less than thirty yards away, coming along the west road from Fort Rivor.

It was clear they'd been spotted. The three of them tensed, and Kyrin tried to keep her heart from racing. They must remain calm and not draw suspicion. It was their best chance of the soldiers riding on without paying them any attention. Kyrin drew in a deep, steadying breath, but it seized the moment the lead soldier locked eyes with her.

"Kyrin?"

Marcus's voice barely reached her, but it sent her heart plunging toward her feet. For a millisecond, everything stood still as a wave of dread crashed down on her. "Run!"

She, Kaden, and Jace tore off into the trees without looking back. *Please don't let them come after us!* Doom spread throughout her entire body with the rush of adrenaline. Of all people for them to come across, why had it been her brother? She pumped her legs as hard as she could to match stride with Kaden and Jace.

Something pounded like hooves, but she wasn't sure if it was horses or the blood in her head.

"Please!" she gasped out.

The wet ground slipped and oozed beneath her. In a breath-snatching moment, she lost her balance and stumbled, but managed to keep running. Still, it slowed her pace, and that pounding grew louder. She didn't dare look back, but the sense of something near sent a crawling sensation up her back. Begging for speed and endurance, she pushed her body harder.

The ties of her cloak yanked against her throat. She screamed, but the ties closed off her windpipe. Jerking to a halt, she fell back against the hard muscles of a horse's shoulder. Her fingers flew to her throat and clawed at the ties to loosen them. A strong arm wrapped around her, and then another. Her throat opened up, and she cried out as she fought to tear herself away from her captor. Just ahead, Kaden and Jace skidded to a halt and yanked out their swords as they spun around. Kyrin squirmed with all her might as the two of them rushed to her aid, but they stopped when sharp metal pressed against the underside of Kyrin's chin. She froze.

"Everyone, stop!" Marcus's voice rang out from somewhere behind Kyrin. Her captor turned just enough for Kyrin to see her brother.

"Marcus, please," she cried. "Please, let us go."

The blade pressed harder to her throat. She sucked in her breath.

"Easy, Scerle," Marcus told the man.

"They need to drop their weapons." Scerle's voice was gravelly and unpleasant, and his bad breath reached Kyrin's nose even facing away from him. She gritted her teeth.

"Release her, Marcus." Kaden sent their brother a demanding glare.

A fighting light had also begun to grow in Jace's eyes as he stared at Kyrin's captor, as if calculating just what it would take to get her away from him. If only the man knew what he would be up against if Jace did find a way to reach him without endangering Kyrin.

Marcus raised his hands in a calming gesture. "Just lower your weapons and we'll talk."

But Kaden wouldn't have any of it. "Not until you tell your man to let my sister go."

A slight wince crossed Marcus's face, perhaps at Kaden's use of 'my sister' instead of 'our'. He gave his men a hesitant glance. That's when Kyrin noticed Liam. He, too, had dismounted and come up behind Marcus.

Kyrin said his name in desperation.

He seemed to share her dismay and stepped up quickly to face their brother. "Marcus, she's our sister."

"We're not here to cause trouble. We came to visit Father's grave." Kyrin's voice cracked at the end, and tears momentarily blurred her eyes, but not so much that she missed the pain that flooded Marcus's.

"Captain," Scerle snapped. "Family or not, they're traitors to the emperor. They must be brought in. To release them would be treason."

Marcus's jaw went taut, his face etched in turmoil.

Kaden took an angry step forward. "We'll be killed if you bring us in. Executed, just like Father. Is that what you want?"

All eyes locked on Marcus. The war on his face was almost painful to witness as he stood in indecision. *Please*, Kyrin both prayed and mentally urged him. *Don't do this*.

Scerle must have detected the struggle and decided they'd waited long enough. "Drop your weapons!" His knife pressed harder into Kyrin's throat, cutting through the first layers of skin.

Panic flared. She grasped at the man's wrist and hardly dared to breathe.

"Marcus!" Kaden shouted. "You tell him to let her go!"

Scerle matched his volume. "Put down your weapons!"

"Let her go!"

Kyrin squeezed her eyes shut as a warm drop of blood oozed down her neck and the men shouted back and forth. *Oh, Elôm, please help!* Any moment she could be dead. The pressure of the blade grew.

"Drop your weapons!"

Marcus's voice rose above the others, and Kyrin's eyes popped open. Her eldest brother stared at Kaden. The indecision had faded, replaced by a tortured, yet steely resolve.

"Both of you, put them down," he forced out every word, "if you want her to live."

Kaden looked ready to fight him on the spot, while Liam gaped in open horror. How could their brother do this to them?

"Do it," Scerle snapped, "or she dies right now."

Kaden's sword lowered a couple of inches, though his tight grip on the hilt whitened his knuckles. No, this couldn't happen. Kyrin's heart battered her ribs. All three of them would die if Kaden and Jace surrendered. Fear ripped through her every nerve, but she knew what she had to do.

"Don't do it!" she cried out. "Run! Save yourselves! Please!"

The knife went deeper, and she could not hold back a whimper. *Elôm, save me!*

"Three seconds and she dies," Scerle growled, and Kyrin believed it. If she wanted Kaden and Jace to live, she had only a brief few moments before she would join her father in Elôm's presence.

She locked eyes with Kaden, begging him to run, while she mentally ticked off the seconds. She had just about counted to three and tensed for the moment the blade would cut her throat, when Kaden threw down his sword. Jace's hit the ground at the same time. A huge breath trapped in Kyrin's lungs rushed out, but relief was fleeting. They'd only postponed her death and added theirs to it.

The other soldiers rushed in to collect Kaden and Jace's weapons. Only when the two of them were tightly bound did Scerle take the dagger from Kyrin's throat. They seized her weapons too, and a soldier approached with a length of rope, but Marcus took it from him. He walked up to Kyrin without meeting her eyes.

"Give me your hands."

Choking back tears, Kyrin raised her wrists, and he tied the rope around them snuggly, but not cruelly tight. All the while, he avoided her gaze.

"Marcus," she murmured.

Finally, he did look up, and she read the deep regret and uncertainty in his eyes. This tore him apart inside and gave her the hope to try one more time.

"Please, don't do this." Her tears pooled in a desperate, heart-aching plea.

He almost broke, yet the dedication which bound him so completely to his duties took over. Tying off the knot, he turned to give orders, though his voice was rough. "Mount up. We're heading back to the fort."

He tugged lightly on the rope, and Kyrin trailed after him on the way to his horse. They passed Liam who stood dumbly. Kyrin looked up at him, and they traded a helpless look. He was as much a prisoner of the circumstances as they were.

Kyrin looked back to find Kaden and Jace. The soldiers had tied the two of them behind their horses. Kaden was sizing up his guard, as if contemplating taking him out right there. Kyrin swallowed and prayed he wouldn't do anything foolish that would get him killed before they even reached the fort. He glanced at her, and she sent him another pleading look.

When they came to Marcus's horse, he mounted and reached down to pull her up with him. But she backed away as a deep hurt settled in her chest and she began to share some of Kaden's anger. Marcus was their older brother. He should have been looking out for them, not delivering them to certain death.

"I'll walk."

Marcus sighed and took up the reins. He still held Kyrin's rope in his hand, but did not tie it to his saddle like the others. Without a word, he nudged his horse and led the way back to the road. Kyrin walked with him.

She hung her head. Why was everything going wrong? What more could possibly happen? First their father was killed, and now they faced the same fate. *I don't understand.* All she'd wanted was a chance to rescue her brother and have one last goodbye with her father. Had it been too much to ask for? A tear rolled down her cheek, but she brushed it against her shoulder. *Help me be strong, Lord, whatever happens.*

The journey west to the fort stretched out in silence. After the first couple of miles, Kyrin's legs burned. It wasn't easy keeping pace with the horse, but Marcus helped by avoiding the worst mud and allowing slack in the rope. Kaden and Jace, however, weren't so fortunate. The other soldiers cared little where they led their captives.

There came a grunt, followed by a splash, and Kyrin looked back. Kaden had fallen to his knees in the middle of a puddle, and the soldier didn't show any sign of slowing. Kyrin jerked her rope to get to him before the soldier could drag him along like an old carcass, but Marcus immediately called the group to a halt.

"Let him up," he ordered.

Still, Kaden glared at him as he moved to rise. Liam came alongside him, leaning down to hook his hand under his brother's arm and pull him up. Once Kaden was on his feet again, they moved on. Liam remained at his side.

Stumbling after Marcus, Kyrin looked back once more. This time her eyes met Jace's. In them rested the same grim determination she'd seen when they'd faced the ryriks. His one thought would be to find some way to get her out of this, and that shot fear straight into her core. He wouldn't hesitate to sacrifice himself to accomplish it.

*Elôm, please, save us. All of us.* She continued to pray until she looked up some time later, and her eyes caught on the hill in the distance. Her throat swelled and sucked the moisture from her mouth. The might and military power of Fort Rivor loomed ahead.

KYRIN TOOK IN the sight of the hundreds, thousands of tents and soldiers with a shudder. How could they hope to escape this? Even if their friends came looking for them, and somehow discovered they had been captured, not even the dragons could change these circumstances. And would they even survive for three days?

At the entrance to the fort, the men dismounted, and Marcus guided Kyrin to stand with Kaden and Jace. Again, he would not look her in the eyes.

"Guard them," he ordered his men and strode inside.

The group stood in silence with the sounds of camp as a backdrop. Even so, Kyrin could hear each hard breath Kaden took. She glanced up at him. His jaw muscles ticked as he ground his teeth together and glared furiously at the door Marcus had entered. Kyrin hung her head, more hurt than angry now. They should be helping one another, encouraging each other, while sharing the pain of losing their father. It shouldn't be like this.

She looked up again and this time focused on Liam. His eyes were cast down, but she noticed how red they were. He must have sensed her watching and looked up. She tried to give him a smile, but it fell short. The pain was too great. Regrets and remorse passed between them. If only she could speak to him privately. There was so much he needed to know.

Approaching footsteps pulled Kyrin's attention back to the entrance of the fort. Their grandfather appeared, and a sick knot coiled in her stomach. Beside her, Kaden drew himself up taller and straighter in a stance of defiance she hadn't seen in some time. Kyrin swallowed hard. Even under the best circumstances, interaction with their grandfather never ended well.

He marched toward them with the purposeful, intimidating strides of a warrior prepared to destroy any enemy in his path—whether that enemy was stranger or family. No love or compassion softened his face. Kyrin's insides shrank, but she stood firm beside Kaden.

Marcus walked with the General, his expression set, but it didn't completely mask the heartsickness in his eyes. However, it was too late for him to reconsider now.

Their grandfather's cold gaze swept each of them. "Well, now, isn't this fortunate?"

Kyrin peeked over at Kaden and Jace. None of them said a word, though it was a wonder Kaden held his tongue.

The General's attention focused on his grandchildren. "I hear you two have been busy furthering your treason."

Kaden snorted. "More like saving people from the emperor's tyranny."

The General looked imperiously at him. "Is that so?"

Kyrin shivered at his cool, calm composure. It was even worse than his anger. It meant he was in control.

His eyes shifted, and he stepped down to Jace, his rigid stance accentuating the two inches he had on him. It was probably one of the first times in his adult life that Jace had to look up at anyone. Kyrin's nerves prickled with unease. She and Kaden were used to their grandfather's ways, and it was because of them that they were here in the first place. Jace had nothing to do with it, and she wanted her grandfather to stay away from him. But, despite the situation, Jace held the General's critical gaze without wavering.

"So this must be one of the rebels you've thrown in with. Are you so desperate for numbers you'll even tolerate the company of ryrik animals?"

Kyrin's fingers fisted, and her voice trembled in the effort to control the rising disgust for this man who was her grandfather. "He's *not* a ryrik."

"No?" The General's tone dripped with sarcasm and condescension. "You may think me many things, Kyrin, but I'm not blind."

Something in the way he said her name—as if she were some silly child—infuriated her even more, and she glared at him. "He's only half ryrik."

"What's the difference?"

Kyrin strained against the ropes that dug into her wrists. How dare he? However, Jace surprised her again by showing no reaction to the hateful words.

The General's attention returned to him. "Tell me, *half*-ryrik, are you a follower of the Elôm myth as well?"

Calm and sure, Jace answered, "I believe in Elôm, the *true* God of Ilyon."

The General smirked. "It's just as well you believe the lies when you have no soul for it to matter."

*Heartless!* Tears stung Kyrin's eyes at the cruel words, but Jace just shrugged.

"Perhaps I don't, but it doesn't make Elôm any less real."

For the first time, anger crept into the General's eyes. "And it doesn't make you any less guilty of treason." He spun on his heel to face Marcus. "Lock them up."

Kyrin rested against the cold stone wall of their dim cell, her elbows propped on her knees and head bowed. All was quiet. After launching into a tirade about their grandfather and Marcus, Kaden had finally exhausted himself, and none of them had spoken since.

But Kyrin had not ceased praying for a miracle and for strength. She was struggling. Fear, doubt, and despair crowded her mind. Her thoughts wandered back to her imprisonment in Valcré. It had been terrifying, but she'd been confident in her faith, and Elôm had filled her with strength far beyond herself. She longed for that strength now but, for some reason, things seemed different. She felt weaker, more uncertain. The loss of her father had shaken her and taken a heavy toll. She couldn't lose anyone else.

Her throat hurting with held back tears, she looked at Kaden and Jace—the two people in this world she was closest to. It wasn't only her life hanging in the balance this time, but theirs, too, and that was the most frightening of all. The very thought of losing even one of them left her resolve in shreds. *I can't do it, Elôm. I just can't.* She pressed her palms to her eyes to hold back the tears.

However, her fear couldn't change the circumstances. Whatever happened to them would occur without her consent. The only choice left was to accept it as Elôm's will and trust Him to provide her the ability to endure it.

This made itself painfully clear by the echo of footsteps. The three of them rose to wait for the soldiers to enter the cellblock. Kyrin cried out to Elôm, her breaths choppy and shallow. Kaden rested his hand on her shoulder, and she looked at him.

"It'll be all right," he told her.

It was more a foolish hope than solid belief, but it did encourage her.

Marcus led the group that arrived at the cell. He unlocked the door and swung it open. Now that he'd had time to shore up his resolve, he almost seemed a stranger. Kyrin hated to see him this way. This wasn't the kind, familiar Marcus—this was the controlled Marcus, manipulated by the General, and the emperor, and his own misguided beliefs.

The soldiers entered and secured heavy shackles to their wrists. Kyrin shivered when the cold metal pressed into her skin. It left such a helpless feeling. She tried to look at Marcus as they brought her out, but he avoided her eyes and moved to the head of the group, where he led them through the fort. Once outside, they turned to walk deeper into the surrounding camp. The soldiers eyed them as they passed—some with looks of disgust and others with no more than a passing interest. Kyrin looked around for an answer as to why they'd left the fort. Did their grandfather intend to execute them right away? Her knees trembled. Surely it wouldn't happen so quickly.

They didn't have to go far before they came to a muddy, open area with a tall post at the center. The General waited there with a large gathering of soldiers. Kyrin gulped, a horrible sensation twisting her insides.

Trudging through the mud, they came to stand in front of him. A moment of tense silence followed, but the General's booming voice shattered it.

"Treason is one of the most detestable of crimes. It shall never be tolerated in any form. Not here, not anywhere. The fitting punishment for such crimes is death."

He motioned, and one of the soldiers shoved Jace forward. Kyrin's heart almost died in her chest. *No!* She stepped forward, but Marcus grabbed her arm and held her back. She tugged against him, her eyes still riveted to Jace. *Elôm, please!* Her heart pounded back into motion with solid, heavy thumps.

Jace squared his shoulders as he faced the General, who peered at him as if he were nothing more than scum.

"You have openly flaunted your treasonous beliefs against the emperor and the gods. For such an offense, you shall be transported to Valcré for execution, but first, I intend to make you an example so that no man here doubts the gravity of these charges."

The General turned and accepted something from one of his men. Cold flushed through Kyrin's system.

Fingering the cruel-looking whip, the General faced Jace again. "You will receive forty lashes. You're deserving of far more, but I'll let the emperor make that call."

The soldier who'd brought Jace forward unclamped one side of his shackles and proceeded to pull off Jace's coat, jerkin, and shirt. Kyrin couldn't take it. She struggled against Marcus, who took hold of both her arms to keep her still. But he couldn't restrain her voice.

"Grandfather, I beg you, please, don't do this!"

The man didn't even look at her.

"Please," she cried out again, but it was Jace who responded with quiet acceptance.

"It's all right, Kyrin."

She shook her head. Tears clogged her throat and strangled her voice. "No. No, it isn't." He shouldn't be here. He shouldn't have to endure this. *Oh, Elôm, why?*

Her pain had no effect on her grandfather. He was too devoted to the belief system he'd followed so unwaveringly all his life. Apparently, not even family could turn him from following through with his dedication to what it demanded of him. No wonder Marcus hadn't swayed having lived under such influence.

The soldiers led Jace to the post, chaining his arms up over his head. He rested his forehead against the post and closed his eyes. Though he outwardly portrayed acceptance, the muscles in his shoulders and already-scarred back tensed. Kyrin could barely hold back the burn of tears. This was so wrong. She begged for intervention. She couldn't bear to see him harmed like this. Hadn't he endured enough undeserved ill-treatment?

The two soldiers backed away, and the General just stood for a long moment, during which Kyrin's stomach churned and threatened to come up.

"Liam!"

Kyrin flinched at the force in her grandfather's voice.

Nearby, Liam snapped to attention. "Sir?"

The General thrust the whip toward him. Liam looked from it to his grandfather's face, his brows bent in confusion.

The General scowled. "You will administer the punishment to the traitor."

Kyrin's heart stalled again as Liam's face went white. His eyes widened, and he stammered, "Sir . . . I-I'm just a foot soldier."

"And you've been given an order; now obey it!"

Kyrin and Liam both flinched this time. Marcus's grip around Kyrin's arms loosened, and she fought to pull away from him. Maybe he could just stand there and watch, but she couldn't. She had to do *something*—for Jace and for Liam. But Marcus caught her arms again. Beside her, Kaden, too, struggled to break free.

"There's nothing you can do," Marcus whispered sharply in her ear, though a tremor distorted his voice.

Kyrin still strained against him as she watched Liam. His shoulders sagged under the weight of the situation. He cast a hesitant glance at Jace and then at Kyrin. Holding her gaze a moment, he drew his shoulders back. His eyes returned to the General. "I'm sorry, sir, I can't."

Shocked murmurs passed through the soldiers, though they instantly fell silent. Anger ignited in the General's eyes. The leering tower of a man seemed to grow several inches as he straightened and fully faced his grandson. Even Liam couldn't match his height.

"Are you refusing to carry out a direct order from your general?" His voice was like ice about to break.

Despite the rage building in the man, Liam was no longer pale, and strength filled his eyes—strength that Kyrin had never seen before. He knew exactly what he was doing and had full confidence in his decision. "Yes, sir, I am."

Pride burst through Kyrin's chest, but fear drowned it just as fast, and she trembled over what would happen next.

The General's face flushed a dangerous shade of crimson. "Parker!"

The lieutenant hurried forward. "Sir?"

His voice very even, but edged in a murderous tone, the General ordered, "Disarm this man and bind him. For his insubordination, he will share in the traitor's punishment."

A blast of cold struck Kyrin's core. She pulled against Marcus. "You have to do something! You have to stop this!" She looked over her shoulder and caught a glimpse of his eyes. His resolve was shaken and revealed his uncertainty, but he shook his head.

"He's the general. I have no power in this."

Hot tears pooled in Kyrin's eyes and coursed down her cheeks. He could at least try. Their brother and her best friend were about to be cruelly and unjustly punished. How could he not even try voicing his doubts and reasoning with their grandfather?

Helpless, she watched Parker strip her brother of his weapons and uniform, finally attaching shackles to his wrists. Liam stood unresisting and in full acceptance of his fate. Kyrin then looked at their grandfather, who stood so cold and unfeeling. Deep, painful anger burned away the coldness inside her. Had he no heart? Instead of any remorse, he only muttered callously, "Finally shows some guts and it's wasted on rebellion."

The soldiers secured Liam to the same post, just opposite Jace. Parker glanced uncertainly between Liam and the General and cleared his throat. He spoke, but it took a few words before his voice gained strength. "Liam Altair, soldier of His Majesty's army, you have been found guilty of insubordination to your commanding officer. The punishment for such is twenty lashes—"

"Forty," the General cut in. "Forty lashes."

Parker hesitated and glanced at Marcus.

"He directly defied his general in front of every man here," the General said, in response to his hesitance. "It will be forty."

"No!" Kyrin cried out. Every time she thought she had witnessed the height of his cruelty, he surpassed it. "You can't do this to them!"

The General turned, his gaze landing with solid force on Marcus. "Captain, you keep her silent. I don't care how."

Marcus squeezed her arm to gain her attention. "Kyrin, do not make me have to gag you." His voice lacked its usual strength.

Kyrin's face contorted helplessly, but Kaden took up her protest.

"You accuse Jace of being an animal, without even knowing him, and then you turn and engage in *this* kind of cruelty?" He wrestled against the soldiers as he locked eyes with his grandfather. "You're the monster."

"Silence!" the General bellowed. "Unless you wish to join them."

"No!" Kyrin cried again in desperation. She couldn't bear that. Not Kaden too.

"Then both of you had better hold your tongues!"

He watched for any sign of disobedience, seeming almost hopeful Kaden would cross the line. Kyrin held her breath, biting back the outcry to echo Kaden's assessment of their grandfather. She glanced over at her twin. He had his jaw clenched, but his fiery glare never left the man.

Satisfied, the General turned back to Parker. "Carry on."

Parker cast one more glance at Marcus, but his captain remained silent, so he continued with Liam's sentencing. "You will receive . . . forty lashes. Do you understand the charge and the sentence?"

Looking right at his grandfather, Liam answered, "I understand."

With this, the General passed the whip to Parker. The lieutenant was hesitant to take it, but he didn't dare refuse. He walked around the post and stopped behind Jace, who reached up to grip the chain of his shackles. When Parker let the whip uncoil, Kyrin had to choke down her stomach as it lurched toward her throat. The first lash cracked, and Jace jerked. Kyrin pressed her hands over her mouth to stifle the sob that ripped through her chest. After the second lash, she shut her eyes tightly and bowed her head, her shoulders shaking. She could not force herself to watch. Hearing was painful enough. She covered her ears with her hands, but couldn't shut them tightly enough to block the crack of the whip or the cries it finally tore from Jace, despite how strong he was.

It seemed to stretch on for a miserable eternity—first for Jace and then for Liam. Tears ran through Kyrin's closed eyelids to feed the steady drip from her chin. She didn't know if she could take any more when everything finally fell silent except for her own choking breaths.

She opened her eyes. The sight of blood and torn flesh blurred in and out with her tears, and her stomach wrenched violently. She squeezed her eyes shut again, faintness washing over her. Marcus's grip tightened on her arms as she swayed. Unconsciousness would have been a relief, but it passed. She cowered at the General's close voice and opened her eyes. He stood before her and Marcus now, blocking her view of Jace and Liam.

"Take them inside. I'll be there shortly."

He moved away as Marcus guided Kyrin around toward the fort. She caught one more glimpse of Jace and Liam's wounds as they turned—a sight that would haunt her always.

Ragged, halting breaths were all Jace could manage as the pulsating pain of a thousand exposed nerves radiated across his back. His throat ached from every cry that had been ripped from him, in spite of his fight to restrain them. He'd been determined not to show such weakness, but the pain had torn away his strength, mirroring the agony he'd once endured as a teen and had wished to die from. Even here, his mind had begged for unconsciousness to take him. But even worse was that Kyrin had to witness it.

The cold breeze bit into his blood- and sweat-dampened skin and sent tremors through his muscles. The spasms only intensified the pain, and he clenched his teeth against the unbidden cry rising in his throat. On the other side of the post, the soldiers released Liam, who groaned softly as his arms lowered. The lieutenant, Parker, took one of his arms to support him and guided him toward the fort. At the sight of the long, inflamed welts and raw wounds crisscrossing Liam's back, Jace's stomach turned.

The other soldiers dispersed among the tents. Would they just leave him here in misery? Then the squish of footsteps approached, and a soldier unchained both of his wrists. He let his arms down slowly, barely stifling a groan. When he turned, he found the General still standing there with a group of six soldiers.

They each gripped the hilts of their swords and watched him as if prepared for a wild animal attack.

The General flung his shirt at him. He caught it out of reflex, but this time couldn't hold back the groan at the pain it ignited.

"Dress," the General ordered. "Either that or you can freeze to death. It makes little difference to me."

Jace held his stone-cold gaze for a moment and then looked down at his shirt. To get it on would be torture itself. Steeling himself, he stuck his arms into the sleeves and raised it up. He bit his lip, almost to the point of drawing blood, to keep from crying out, and his eyes watered, but he got it over his head and pulled the hem down over his exposed skin. Immediately, he felt the blood on his back soaking into the fabric. The General tossed over his jerkin next, and then his coat. He managed to get them on, but the soldiers jeered and mocked every show of pain he let slip. By the time he finished, the effort and the pain left him dizzied.

"This way." The General marched off through the camp.

When Jace didn't move right away, one of the soldiers prodded him forward. Blinking hard to keep his vision from wavering, he followed the General. But they didn't head in the direction of the fort. Jace glanced back at it. "What are you going to do with Kyrin?" His raw voice lacked the strength he intended.

"My granddaughter is none of your concern," the General practically growled back at him without pausing.

Jace looked back again. She was his only concern.

They did not stop until they reached the edge of camp. Here, several sets of stocks were set up—all empty and waiting. The soldiers brought Jace to a halt as the General finally turned to face him. It was hard to stand up completely straight, but Jace managed, gritting his teeth and trying to keep his breaths from shuddering.

The General's eyes bored into him. "I don't know how much influence you've had in the choices my grandchildren have made, but I aim to see that you suffer for it, as will any others who are responsible."

A fist smashed into Jace's ribs from the right. His breath left his lungs in a gasp, and the sudden tensing of his muscles shot fire through his wounds. Before he could recover, a second soldier punched him hard in the jaw, and he fell to his knees. Heat flared in his chest, but not hot or fast enough as the soldiers struck him again and again, with the General looking on.

THE SOUND OF the whip and anguished cries still echoed in Kyrin's ears. How many more pieces could her heart break into before she couldn't bear it any longer? Hysteria threatened, willing her to scream and cry until the pain was spent, but she fought it back. She couldn't lose it here. Somehow she had to be stronger than that.

"Jace." Her voice came out so clogged it barely rose above a whisper. She tried again and forced her words through her tight throat. "I want to be with Jace."

But Marcus did not slow or respond.

Kyrin tried to look back at him, but stumbled as he kept her moving forward. "Where is he?" Would their grandfather just throw him back into a cold cell, wounded and bleeding?

Still, Marcus would not answer. Inside the fort, he and his men led her and Kaden into a bleak meeting hall, where two heavy chairs sat apart from the others. He motioned to one of them. "Sit down."

Kyrin sank weakly into the chair without resistance. For Kaden, however, the soldiers had to wrestle him down into it. Once they were both seated, the soldiers chained their wrists to the arms of the chairs. Having completed his task, Marcus stepped back and faced them. His mouth opened as if he meant to speak, but he hesitated, and Kaden beat him to it.

"Are you satisfied?" He was too angry, and would never cry in front of his brother or grandfather, but his voice echoed unshed tears.

Marcus grimaced. For the first time, anger glinted in his eyes as emotion finally broke through. "I didn't choose this for you. You did by your own actions."

"You brought us here!"

"I had no choice." Marcus's voice rose. "*You* betrayed the emperor, not me."

Shaking his head, he turned and strode from the room, leaving the other soldiers to guard them.

Kyrin let her head fall back against the chair as small, hitching sobs caught in her throat. *Oh, Elôm, why is this happening?* Why couldn't Marcus see?

Beside her, Kaden gave an angry cry and yanked his wrists against the chains, but they held fast . . . thankfully. Kyrin shuddered at what their grandfather might do if he actually managed to break free.

They waited for several minutes before heavy footsteps echoed in the hall. Kyrin fought to compose herself. Tears had already proven worthless with her grandfather. Anger coiled inside her chest instead. After all, he was the reason Marcus so blindly followed his duties. Their grandfather had pressured him since childhood. And their grandfather had caused the pain and division in their family. A small voice admonished her that anger was the wrong reaction, but she'd rather be angry than sniveling.

Their grandfather strode in a moment later. "Leave us," he commanded the soldiers.

They nodded and walked out. The door closed with a deep thud, and the General faced Kyrin and Kaden, his fists on his hips.

"We have much to discuss and very little time for you to

make the right choice." Always he spoke as a commander, never a grandfather. "Tomorrow morning, a prisoner transport is leaving for Valcré. I'd rather not put you on it. With my influence, I believe I can get you a pardon if you convince me and the emperor of your repentance. You'll start by reestablishing your devotion to the gods. Then I'll take you before the emperor, where you'll also assure him of your devotion and cooperation."

A ringing silence followed, broken by Kaden's disgusted tone. "You really expect our devotion and loyalties to be swayed so easily?"

The General's eyes narrowed to dark slits. "I expect you to use some common sense. Your lives are on the line, and I won't see you throw them away for nothing."

"It's my life to lose. I won't have it dictated by you."

The General scowled. "You're a child. You don't have the wisdom or experience to see the foolishness in your actions."

Kaden shoved himself up, his chains rattling as they pulled tight. "I'm not a child. My childhood was stolen a long time ago when Kyrin and I were forced into Tarvin Hall, something you probably had a lot to do with."

Kyrin shrank into her seat as the General stepped closer to face Kaden. His bulk and height were especially daunting as he glared down at him, but Kaden was by no means intimidated, and stood his ground.

"Apparently, it did little good if we're even having this conversation. I clearly should've paid far more attention to your training."

"So you could control me the way you control Marcus and Liam and the rest of the family?"

"Kaden," Kyrin cut in. She was angry, too, but not so much that she couldn't see her brother was taking it too far. Her fear for him quickly outgrew her anger, but he didn't seem to hear her. *Please protect him, Elôm!*

The General stepped closer yet, so their faces were now only inches apart. "You should've learned duty and respect."

"I respect those who deserve it."

Kyrin gulped at the way their grandfather's fist tightened. Would he hit Kaden? He looked to be considering it but, instead, he shouted out, "Guards!" To Kaden, he snapped, "You need time to cool off and get some sense back into your head."

The doors opened and the soldiers marched in.

"We'll take him to the stocks," the General told them.

Kyrin straightened. *Don't leave me alone!* They unchained Kaden from the chair and shackled his arms behind his back. As they guided him to the door, he looked back at her with remorse in his eyes, but it was too late now.

Kaden yanked against the soldiers as they led him through camp, and he glared at the General's back. How could the man even be family? How could he order the merciless beating of two innocent men, one of them his own grandson, and then just expect to order Kaden and Kyrin to deny their faith? He strained against his shackles. Every muscle in his body was wound up to fight. He hated being powerless, especially when others were suffering.

"Why don't you just give me a sword and you and I can be done with this." It was a stupid challenge, but everything inside him screamed for action.

The General spun around, and the soldiers jerked Kaden to a halt. His grandfather let out a harsh bark of laughter. "You would fight me?"

Even now, Kaden refused to back down. "Yes."

His grandfather just laughed in his face, but his voice vibrated with dangerous intensity. "I've had a sword in my hand longer than you've been alive. You may have excelled in your training, but it takes more than skill to beat a man with experience."

He spun around and marched on. The soldiers shoved Kaden after him. He breathed hard through his nose, refusing to acknowledge that his grandfather was right.

At the edge of camp, they arrived at the stocks. Here, Kaden's eyes latched onto the only person to occupy one of them. His lungs and throat locked up.

"Jace," he gasped as concern doused his anger.

Jace glanced up. Dark blood was caked around his right brow and swollen eye, dripping down to join more blood at his chin. This was not the condition they'd left him in at the whipping post.

The anger exploded back into Kaden's heart. His eyes flew to his grandfather. "What did you do to him?"

The General raised his chin. "Exactly what he deserved."

The fight inside Kaden erupted. He wrenched against the soldiers. They tried to restrain him, but he rammed his shoulder into one and sent the man to the ground. The soldier scrambled to regain his feet to help his partner, but the General reached them first. The force of a sledgehammer plowed into Kaden's gut. His lungs emptying, he fell to his knees, gasping for air. His grandfather's hard fist locked onto his collar and yanked him to face him.

"You're quickly spending my patience," he said through his teeth. "You'd better think long and hard about your future and have a satisfactory answer for me when I return."

Kaden was still trying to catch his breath as the soldiers dragged him over to the stocks and sat him down in the mud, where they unchained him just long enough to lock the boards around his ankles, and then his neck and wrists. He twisted and squirmed as his grandfather strode away, but the uncomfortable restraints were solid.

Kyrin tensed at the sound of her grandfather's returning footsteps. "Elôm, help me."

She had worked her tears under control, determined to be strong, though she still ached for the confidence of having Kaden at her side. Her grandfather scared her more than she wanted to admit, but she had faced the emperor alone. This was no different.

The General walked in a moment later and shoved the door behind him, though it stood open a couple of inches. Kyrin watched him cross the room to stand in front of her and resisted the urge to cower. Anger still shadowed his eyes. There was no telling what Kaden might have said on the way out. Kyrin almost cringed considering it. However, she did detect the slightest trace of softening when her grandfather peered down at her. She dared not hope she had any advantage with him, but she tucked it away in her mind.

"Now, perhaps, we can actually talk," he said.

Enough ire still smoldered inside Kyrin to form a retort Kaden might use, but antagonizing him wasn't the answer. She bit her tongue and swallowed down the words.

When she did not speak, the General did. "You're in very serious trouble, Kyrin." This time he almost seemed to care when he said her name. "You'll be dead within a week if you don't accept my offer. Think about it. I'm giving you a chance to start over, to stop running, and live the life you were meant to live."

The allure of the words tugged at the place in her heart that desired a normal life, but she could never go back to the way things were—never wanted to. Especially now that her father was dead and she had witnessed the lengths her grandfather was willing to go to force his will and beliefs on others. Right now, her own life didn't concern her.

"How can you do this? To Jace and to Liam? How could you be so cruel?" She choked on the tears she fought to keep down.

"Rebellion and treason are never to be treated lightly."

Kyrin squeezed her fists and shook her head. They weren't rebels or traitors, but if that's how her grandfather chose to see them, then she was just as guilty as Jace and Kaden. "If that's the case, why don't you have me punished and put in the stocks as well?"

The General frowned deeply. "You're a girl."

"The emperor didn't have any qualms about that when he threw me into a cold cell, wearing only a shift, and then dragged me in front of a mob throwing rocks and screaming for my execution."

"You brought that on yourself by throwing his generosity in his face and threatening his life."

Now Kyrin pushed up from her seat, leaning forward. "I never did any such thing. I served him and did my job up until the moment I was arrested. The only thing I did was refuse to bow in the temple. It never even crossed my mind to attack him."

The briefest flicker of confusion appeared on the General's face before hardening. "Are you calling the emperor a liar?"

Kyrin nodded firmly. "Yes."

The General narrowed his eyes. "How dare you!"

"How dare I what? Speak the truth?" Kyrin almost shouted. "The first time I even knew I'd been accused of attacking him was on the execution platform as he listed my crimes. Do you honestly believe I'd be stupid enough to attack him in his own palace surrounded by guards? Will you really choose to believe him over your own granddaughter?"

If he swayed at all, she couldn't tell. With an expression bordering on a scowl, he said, "You've hardly proven yourself trustworthy."

At his mistrust, an unexpected stab of pain passed through Kyrin's chest, and she sank back into the chair. Suddenly, the fight had gone out of her. Family was supposed to stick together.

"Why can't you believe me?" She looked up at him, unable to keep her eyes from pooling. "Do you even love us?"

The General folded his arms and cleared his throat. "Of course I do."

"Then why do you treat us like this?" She ended with a hitching sob, and lost the battle against her tears.

"I'm trying to help you reach your full potential and acquire positions of influence and honor." It was one of the only times she had ever heard her grandfather speak in a quiet voice. "Don't you want that?"

"I want to be myself," Kyrin cried. "I want to live in peace with my family and my friends. I want you to accept us, all of us, for who we are—our strengths as well as our weaknesses." She swallowed. "Do you have any idea how much it hurts to see how you treat Liam? How cruel you are to him?"

The General bristled. "Liam is a soldier. It's high time he took it seriously."

"But he's not meant to be a soldier." Kyrin's voice rose again. "He never was, but that doesn't make him stupid, or slow, or incompetent, or any of the other horrible things you've chosen to believe of him. He's just different. We can't all be you. Stop trying to make us!"

"Enough," the General snapped. His jaw shifted, and Kyrin believed he was actually uncomfortable. Re-gathering his composure, he said, "This argument is pointless. We're here to discuss your fate. If I were you, I'd focus on that."

Determination hardened inside Kyrin. She sat up straight again. "I will never deny my God or turn from my faith."

The General threw his arms out in exasperation. "Then you'll be executed."

"I've faced it before. I'll do it again."

Her grandfather bent down to look her in the eyes. "You have all the power in this, Kyrin. Kaden will listen to you. If you both want to live, you'd better rethink this and talk to him."

Kyrin stared into his steely gaze. "Kaden can make his own decisions. I've already made mine."

Marcus knew better than to eavesdrop, but couldn't help himself. What to do with what he had heard spoken between the General and his sister was the question. Had the emperor truly lied? If so, what else could he have lied about? He shook his head as he walked down the hall. These were dangerous questions to ask and, truth be told, he didn't want to ask them. But they remained like burning coals at the back of his mind.

Trying to refocus his thoughts, he pushed open the door to the infirmary and stepped inside. The surgeon was just tying off the wrapping of bandages that covered his brother's back and shoulders. Liam glanced at him with pained eyes and then stared back down into his lap. But that one hurt look flooded Marcus with guilt. He'd seen men beaten before, but never his brother. Liam was the last man in this fort who deserved such punishment.

Marcus walked closer to the table. "Give us a minute," he told the surgeon.

The man nodded and left the room. As the door closed, Liam slid off the table, his breath catching, and reached for his shirt. He moved slowly and struggled to reach up and pull it over his head. Marcus stepped in to help, but Liam offered no acknowledgement. Gathering his jerkin, he brushed past him and turned for the door.

"Liam," Marcus said in surprise.

His brother just stood a moment before facing him. He swayed a little and reached for the table to steady himself. He should sit down. When Marcus looked into his eyes, he found something unfamiliar. Mixed with the abundant hurt was anger. He stood speechless while Liam just looked at him.

Marcus put his hands out. "What is it?"

Liam shook his head in disbelief. Marcus wasn't used to him acting like this. He was always so mild-mannered, but the heated emotion in his voice when he finally spoke was very real. "How could you let this happen?"

The question knifed right into Marcus's chest. Kaden had used the same accusing tone. "What? I didn't do anything." But the words caught in his throat on the way out, burdened by the growing sting of guilt.

"No, you didn't. You just let our brother and sister be taken captive. You just let the General beat a man Kyrin clearly cares for." Liam's voice dropped to a wounded tone. "You just let him beat me."

"There was nothing I could do," Marcus tried to tell him, his heart rate rising. Yet, even as the words left his mouth, he had no conviction in their truth. "If I had let them go, it would've been treason, and I had no power to stop the General."

"You could have tried! What would he have done? Lecture you?" Liam took a step closer. "When has he ever punished you? When has he ever made you trudge through the elements until you collapsed, and then ridiculed you in front of everyone just because you didn't understand an order fast enough? When has he ever made you the laughingstock of the whole fort?"

Marcus swallowed hard, each true word driving a new blade into his heart. "I've always tried to make things easier for you . . ."

"Making things easier and standing up for someone are two different things. Father stood up for me. He *always* tried to stop the General, no matter the consequences. He even took some of my punishments for me. Did you know that?"

Marcus stared blankly at his brother as he absorbed this information. No, he hadn't known. He shook his head as his voice abandoned him.

"Don't you see how much he hated our father? Or how much he hates me? And still you follow him without question, even to the point of handing over Kyrin and Kaden to their deaths."

The wounds in Marcus's heart opened even deeper, but Liam wasn't finished, his own wounds finally coming to light.

"I've never been as smart as you or Kyrin, but I know enough to see something is wrong here. What are we fighting for?"

"We fight for the emperor and Arcacia." The words had been drilled into Marcus so many times through his life that they rolled off his tongue without thought. He'd always believed them, but suddenly, they left a vile taste in his mouth.

"But what about the people of Arcacia? Why are we fighting them? The emperor has already killed our father, and now Kyrin and Kaden will be next. How is that right?"

Marcus grimaced. He was a soldier. He obeyed—he served. He didn't question authority, especially not the General's or the emperor's. But could he shut his mind to what his brother was asking? What choice did he have?

"They've chosen their fates." The words scratched against his throat, bitter and revolting.

Again, Liam gaped at him. "You truly accept that?" His voice rose. "The emperor killed our father over a difference of beliefs! Do you really believe he died for nothing? Are Kyrin and Kaden going to die for nothing? Have you ever stopped to consider what it is they believe? Don't you think it's something we should consider if they're willing to take it that far? We both know how smart Kyrin is. If these were just myths and lies, do you honestly think she would fall for them? Would die for them?"

Marcus's mind spun. Thoughts rushed in that he had never allowed before, and now that they had taken hold, they could never be easily removed. As much as he hated to admit it, Liam was right. Could he go down that road? Once he did, there would be no going back. Yet, in a way, he'd already reached that point. Even if he did choose to ignore it, the questions would always remain to haunt him, robbing him of any peace. He shook his head, not knowing what to say, and stared at the floor.

"I'm done, Marcus."

His eyes jumped back up to Liam as icy cold locked up his system. He'd never seen this kind of calm resolution in his brother's demeanor.

"I quit," Liam declared. "I won't fight for what I don't believe in."

"Liam, you can't," Marcus choked. "You'd be deserting, and the General will charge you with treason, just like Kyrin and Kaden."

Liam shrugged. "Then I guess he'll have to send me to Valcré with them."

The ice solidified in Marcus's veins. Not only had he lost his father, but he would soon lose three of his siblings.

"What's more important to you?" Liam snapped him from his daze. "Your family, or an emperor who's willing to kill off any one of us for daring to disagree with him?"

With these final words, Liam left Marcus standing alone in deafening silence. He'd never been so confused in all his life. He never thought he'd have to choose. He'd always believed serving his family and serving the emperor were one and the same, but it was becoming painfully clear that was not so.

KYRIN SAT ON her cot and leaned back against the wall of the small room where she had spent the rest of the afternoon and evening. Her grandfather had placed her here for time to reconsider, but all her thoughts centered on the future that awaited her. Silent tears ran down her cheeks. Come dawn, she, Kaden, and Jace would be put on the prisoner transport and, in two days, would face the emperor. Their execution would probably come quickly after that. She didn't want to think of the three of them standing on that platform, dying one by one, but the vivid memories of standing there once before made it too easy. She wiped the back of her hand across her face. The shackles still around her wrists clanked in the darkness.

A click echoed at the door, and it swung open. Dim light from the hall silhouetted a dark figure that slipped inside. Kyrin's heart collided with her ribs. She scrambled up and backed against the wall. What now?

"It's all right. It's me."

Kyrin breathed out slowly. "Marcus?"

He took her by the arm and guided her near the door, where the light fell on their faces. The desperation and gravity in his expression stunned her. In a low whisper, he said, "Kyrin, I need you to look me in the eyes and tell me . . . is Elôm real?"

Kyrin stared at him. It wasn't a skeptical or casual question, but one burdened with a deep thirst for the truth. With a solemn, sure tone, she answered, "Yes, Marcus, He is."

Her brother's shoulders sagged as he hung his head, and she barely caught his quiet murmur. "Then I truly am on the wrong side."

Kyrin's heart went out to him, sympathetic to the sheer weight of what he must feel. It had taken her days to understand the extent of the truth Sam first shared with her, and she'd already held strong disillusions toward the emperor. She touched his arm. "You don't have to be."

His eyes climbed to hers again, and for a silent moment, they just looked at each other as his lifelong beliefs clashed with her words. Would he heed them, or would duty once again win the conflict? She held her breath and listened to each hopeful beat of her heart as it offered up pleas to Elôm. Her brother needed Him.

At last, Marcus cast a quick glance out the door and, despite the lingering uncertainty in his eyes, he reached into the pocket of his coat. With his other hand, he took hold of Kyrin's chains. "We need to get out of here."

Kyrin sucked in a quick breath, but her thoughts raced beyond herself. "What about Kaden and Jace, and Liam?"

"Liam is waiting outside. If we're careful, we can avoid the sentries and get Kaden and Jace on the way out. I assume, once we reach the crossroads, you three can lead us to safety."

"Yes."

Marcus tossed the shackles onto the cot. "Good. Come on."

Her pulse drumming, Kyrin followed him through the fort. The quietness of the stone hall amplified their footsteps, but no one seemed to be around. When they reached a service door, Marcus unlocked it and peered out as he eased it open. It was pitch black outside. He motioned to Kyrin, and they both slipped out into the walled courtyard. Kyrin shivered in the chill air and glanced at the sky. A couple faint stars twinkled, but most were hidden by clouds. Her attention dropped back to Marcus as they crossed the open space.

"What time is it?" she barely whispered.

"A little after one, so we don't have a lot of time."

As Kyrin's eyes adjusted, they caught on two towering figures. Goose bumps that had nothing to do with the cold rippled up her arms. The two idols brought her mind back to Auréa's temple. She swallowed to moisten her dry throat, fixing her eyes straight ahead in an attempt to ignore the ominous atmosphere hanging in the darkness.

At the back gate, she and Marcus passed through the wall. Liam waited on the other side. He sighed in relief when they joined him. Kyrin wanted to ask him if he was all right since the confrontation with their grandfather, but she was afraid to speak aloud. She couldn't see much of his face in the dark, but the shade of his skin seemed pale.

"See anyone?" Marcus whispered.

Liam shook his head, and Marcus took two objects from the bundle he had in his arms. Turning to Kyrin, he handed over her quiver and staff. She strapped them on and followed her brothers toward the edge of camp.

They kept low, passing stealthily between darkened tents. Kyrin thanked Elôm that the grass was wet and wouldn't crunch with their footsteps and awaken any sleeping soldiers. Most fires had burned out by now, providing them plenty of cover. Still, her whole body drew tense in high alert. If even one person spotted them, it would be disastrous.

They took the long way around near the perimeter of camp and carefully avoided sentries. The nearness to which they had to pass one set Kyrin's heart to drumming, but she finally spotted the stocks in the darkness and Jace and Kaden's still forms. Her grandfather had made Jace sit out here with his wounds?

Marcus reached them first and was greeted by Kaden's sharp whisper. "What are you doing here?"

"Getting you out."

Kyrin came up behind Marcus and her eyes fell on Jace. The dark, battered look of his face drew a gasp from her chest, and she rushed to his side. "Are you all right?" She lightly touched the side of his face. Sticky blood met her fingertips.

"Yeah," he ground out.

He struggled to draw a full breath. Clearly, he wasn't all right. The fact that he hadn't simply told her he was fine spoke volumes about his condition. Her fingers trembling, she pulled out the pegs that secured the stocks. As soon as Kaden was free, he joined her, stumbling as his stiff limbs received circulation again.

"What happened?" Tears clogged her voice as he helped her free the final pegs.

"Grandfather's men beat him up," Kaden ground out.

Kyrin's stomach reacted. How cruel did a man have to be to have someone whipped and then beaten again? Moisture gushed into her eyes, but she blinked it away. Now wasn't the time to dissolve into tears. They had to get away—had to help Jace. She and Kaden removed the planks, and Kaden grasped one of Jace's arms.

"We'll help you up," he said, "as soon as you're ready."

Kyrin took his other arm. Jace bent his knees up and prepared to get to his feet. Already breathing hard, he set his jaw and nodded. Both Kyrin and Kaden pulled up as Jace struggled to get his feet underneath himself but, once standing, he bent over and wrapped his arm around his chest. He hissed out a breath and groaned. Kyrin tightened her grip as he swayed and was frightened by what she saw. She'd never seen Jace in so much pain.

"Is anything broken?" Kaden asked.

"I don't know," Jace said between each labored breath.

Panic threatened to claw its way into Kyrin's mind. Could Jace even move in this condition? How would they get away? What if his ribs were severely broken and punctured his lungs? He'd die. *Elôm, no.* She glanced at Marcus. The shock in his eyes told her he hadn't known about this, thankfully, or she didn't know what she would have said to him. He cast an uncertain look at the fort before asking Jace the one question they all needed to know.

"Can you walk?"

Jace looked at him, forcing himself up straight. "I don't have a choice." His voice was painfully raw.

"We'll help you," Kaden told him.

Jace nodded again. "Let's go."

He sounded determined, but Kyrin felt the tremors passing through the taut muscles in his arm. How could he ever fight the pain long enough to reach the dragons? His eyes caught hers, and immediately he shuttered the uncertainty she glimpsed in their pained glint. A nearly suffocating dread descended on her at what the next hours would bring, yet they had no choice but to press forward.

Her feet and legs aching, Kyrin stumbled to a halt where the road branched north and south—the point where this had all begun. But instead of rejoicing over the escape, and that both Liam and Marcus had seen the truth, it had turned into a nightmare to be added to the list of most miserable nights she had ever experienced—a list that had grown awfully long in the last few months.

Beside her, Jace sagged to the ground, his arms wrapped around his chest as he struggled for more than short, wheezing breaths. His eyes shut tightly; his face contorted in pain. Kyrin's vision wavered, and she covered her mouth with her hands. She couldn't bear to see him in such agony. He'd given it his all, fighting through the pain of the last hours, but he still hadn't been able to maintain a steady pace for more than a few yards at a time before having to stop just to try to breathe. He couldn't go on.

Kyrin turned her head away as a couple of tears rolled down her cheeks. *Elôm, what do we do? Please help us, please.*

"How much farther?" Marcus asked. Even in excellent shape, the trek had him slightly winded. Though he never said anything, Kyrin had seen Liam, too, struggle with the pain of his wounds. It was a miracle Jace had made it this far.

"At least another seven or eight miles." Despair lurked in Kaden's voice.

Now that someone had said it, reality settled in. Marcus winced and glanced at the sky. Kyrin prayed it was just her imagination, but the deep darkness of night had brightened. Dawn was near.

"You won't make it." They all focused on Jace. He had that look in his eyes that scared Kyrin so much. "Not with me."

"There must be something we can do." Kyrin refused to consider the alternative.

Jace shook his head and ground out his words. "You have to go . . . now. I won't let you be taken prisoner again because of me."

"And I won't just let you give yourself up."

Jace's gaze warred with hers, both of them determined. He hadn't walked away from her when facing the ryriks, and under no circumstances would she ever walk away and leave him here. She'd rather face her grandfather again.

His gaze shifted to the right of her. "Kaden, you take her and go."

"No!" Panic shot through Kyrin. "I'm not leaving you."

Jace gritted his teeth, fighting for breath. A fierce light lit up his eyes as he seemed to gather strength. "Kaden, do it now before you lose any more time."

Kaden looked from him to Marcus and Liam. They all bore the same grim look. Then, Kaden turned to Kyrin and took her by the arm.

"No!" She tried to pull away. To leave Jace behind would be like ripping her heart out. Already it tore apart within her. Kaden's hold didn't loosen. She turned to face him and grabbed the front of his coat. "Kaden, please, please, we can't do this. There has to be another way. We have to think of something. Please."

"There's no time," Jace urged them. "Go, now."

Kaden stared down at Kyrin, a deep sadness in his eyes. Underneath his resolution, he didn't want to do this anymore than she did. His jaw twitched. Finally, his gaze shifted to Marcus. "Home is only another two miles, right?"

Marcus nodded.

Kaden looked back at Kyrin, who hardly breathed. Did she dare hope he was thinking what she was? Still looking at her, he said, "Marcus, take them home and get Jace taken care of. I'll continue on and leave a trail for Grandfather to follow. Home is probably the last place he'll expect you to go. I'll get the dragons and come for you as quickly as I can."

Kyrin let out a huge sigh, and her knees wobbled. *Thank You, Elôm.*

Kaden looked down at Jace. "Can you make it another two miles?"

Despite the struggle it was sure to be, Jace nodded.

Kaden looked back toward the fort and then up the road before focusing on Marcus. The two stared at each other a moment before Kaden spoke. "Take care of them."

"I will."

"Go then. I'll cover your trail."

Wasting no time, Marcus walked over to Jace and helped him up. Supporting him as best he could without causing more pain, he guided him south in the direction of Mernin, keeping to the edge of the road where they wouldn't leave as many tracks. Kyrin and Liam followed, but after a few steps, Kyrin looked back and locked eyes with Kaden.

"Be careful and . . . don't get caught."

"I won't," he promised.

THE PALE LIGHT of the cold morning grew steadily to illuminate the frozen gray world. A few snowflakes floated down from the clouds, but little sparkles of sunlight shone low in the trees. Kyrin shivered and pulled her collar tighter to her throat, but kept her other hand around Jace's arm. It was more emotional support than physical. Marcus was the one who kept him moving—one painful step at a time.

Consumed by prayers for his recovery and relief from the pain, she didn't pay much attention to the surroundings, but when her eyes lifted from the path, her feet halted. Her breath hitched as memories and familiarity rushed in.

Tucked in a clearing just off the main road leading to the nearest town of Mernin, a large house sat against a backdrop of bare trees. Nine white-framed windows stared out from the two-story, gray brick dwelling, and snow dusted the dark shingles. Smoke curled from each of the two chimneys. Most of the windows were dark except for a faint glow on the lower level. Kyrin's heart thumped. *Home.*

"Kyrin?"

She started and looked at Marcus, not realizing they had stopped too. They moved on, but Kyrin's legs trembled as they took the cobbled walkway to the front door. She hadn't walked this path in ten years. Nausea bubbled up inside. Her mother lived inside this house. In just moments, they would come face to face, but instead of filling her with joy and anticipation, the urge to run away gripped her. Kaden should be here. He was her support in situations like this. He knew her uncertainties and the struggles she harbored concerning their mother. She needed him as the buffer between them—as an ally. But he wasn't here. She would have to face it herself.

Kyrin pulled in a hard breath of cold air that stung her lungs as they came to the door, and Marcus took a key from his pocket. Beside her, Jace let out a soft groan that immediately corralled her wandering thoughts. She wasn't here to see her mother—she was here to help Jace. He was her number one concern above all else, including her mother.

The door opened to a darkened entry. Marcus helped Jace inside, and Kyrin and Liam walked in behind them. Another wash of memories overwhelmed Kyrin and transported her back to the days when she and her brothers had raced into this room to meet their father every time he came home from the fort. She closed her eyes, recalling it so vividly—hearing their delighted shouts and giggles, seeing their father's smile, and feeling the warmth of his hug. Tears built up to sting her nose, and she tried to rub it away. She risked losing the battle until a surprised but familiar voice came from down the hall.

"Marcus?"

Kyrin's eyes snapped open and flitted to the woman in the nearby doorway—her mother, Lydia. Questions and concern filled the woman's brown eyes as they took in her son and an injured Jace, but then they fell on Kyrin, and her entire countenance changed. Her eyes widened as her expression morphed into open shock and disbelief.

"Kyrin?"

Kyrin couldn't breathe. The emotions rushed back, but so

convoluted, she couldn't respond. Part of her ached to rush into her mother's arms for the first time in a decade, but all the many hurts that had built up in her heart restrained her. More than she'd even realized until this moment. Just like the memories of her father, memories of her mother replayed with stunning clarity—the criticisms toward her father's way of doing things, the way her mother just stood by or even agreed with the General's harsh criticisms, the way she had not tried to keep Kyrin and Kaden . . . They fought and clambered their way to the forefront to warn her of all the future hurts that could come if she left her heart open.

Her mother took a step toward her, and Kyrin stuffed the emotions back down, deep into the recesses of her heart, and raised a protective barrier around it. Keeping her face straight and expressionless, she said, "My friend is badly injured. He needs help."

Lydia stared at her as if not comprehending, but then nodded slowly. Her gaze lingered, and Kyrin caught a glimmer of moisture before her eyes shifted to Marcus in uncertainty. "Bring him into the dining room. I'll tell Ethel to heat some water."

With one final look at Kyrin, she pulled her eyes away. Marcus moved off with Jace, but Kyrin stood paralyzed and shaken. She hadn't known what to expect, but the ache intensified in her chest—a mix of both longing and regret. Then Liam touched her shoulder, and she snapped out of her daze. *Jace*. She fixed her thoughts firmly on him and hurried after Marcus.

"Kyrin, grab that stool." Her brother motioned to a low, backless stool in the corner when she entered the dining room. "He can't lie on his ribs, so he'll have to sit."

Kyrin set the stool at the table and helped Marcus ease Jace down. Once sitting, Jace leaned against the table, struggling for full breaths. *Please don't let him die*. It was the first time Kyrin let the thought fully form. What if he was even more seriously injured than they thought? *No*. She wouldn't let herself think it. *Keep fighting, Jace.*

"Liam, we need light." Marcus cast his coat aside and rolled up his sleeves. He looked at Kyrin. "We'll need to get his coat and shirt off to assess the damage."

He spoke calmly, but what they would find underneath sent waves of dread rolling through Kyrin. Even so, she pulled off her coat and moved closer to help him. While Liam gathered and lit all the candles and lamps, Kyrin and Marcus helped Jace slip his arms out of his coat. When they pulled away his jerkin, it revealed Jace's blood-soaked shirt.

Moisture bit Kyrin's eyes, but she needed to stay strong and focused. She cleared her throat. *Steady me, Lord.*

Lydia entered the room then with a bowl of steaming water. She paused at the table and stared at Jace in the light. Hesitation and suspicion grew in her eyes. "He's a . . ."

She didn't finish, but Kyrin knew what she'd intended to say. Indignation flushed through her. If her mother's first thoughts upon seeing Jace sitting there so terribly wounded were that he was some kind of monster, then perhaps Kyrin's earlier longings were ill-founded. She walked around the table to take the bowl.

"No, he's not." Her voice came out harsh and stung her conscience as she turned away.

An elderly woman entered the dining room after Lydia with an armful of clean cloths. She and Kyrin exchanged glances. Ethel had been the housekeeper since before Kyrin was born, but she was too stiff and proper for Kyrin to have any fond memories of her. She set the cloths on the table near the basin and backed away as she regarded Jace with a pinched expression.

Marcus picked up two cloths and wet them in the basin as he looked at their mother. "We'll need more water and bandages. Also a pair of shears and some wine."

She nodded and turned for the kitchen. Kyrin hesitated, but then stopped her. "Do you have anything for the pain?" She couldn't stand to continue seeing Jace suffer so.

Lydia looked back and nodded again. "I'll make something up."

Kyrin swallowed as words stuck in her mouth, feeling difficult and awkward, but she forced them out. "Thank you."

Her attention returned to Marcus, who handed Jace one of the folded cloths.

"You'll probably want to bite down on this while we clean your back. We'll have to clean away most of the blood with water first and then wine." He paused with a wince. "It won't be pleasant."

Jace took the cloth and squeezed it in his fist as he gave a short nod. Kyrin couldn't imagine the pain he had yet to endure once they started. Would it ever end? She was truly thankful when her mother returned with a small cup. A strong herbal scent lingered in the air as she brought it to Jace.

"This tastes very bitter, but it's potent and will dull the pain quickly. It'll last a few hours."

"What is it?" Kyrin wanted to know.

"Willow, nettlewood, and fassar root," her mother answered. "It's slightly toxic, so it shouldn't be taken regularly or the toxins will build up, but it's good for emergencies."

As soon as she finished this explanation, Jace downed the cup. Kyrin prayed it would indeed take effect quickly, especially as she and Marcus tended his wounds. Her mother also set a pair of sharp shears and a full bottle of wine on the table.

Marcus reached for the shears and used it to cut open the back of Jace's shirt. Kyrin then helped him slowly peel the saturated fabric away from Jace's skin. Jace groaned deep in his throat, and Kyrin gritted her teeth as her stomach threatened to empty at the sight of the wounds. About half the lashes had broken skin. To see them up close destroyed her resolve.

"I don't know if I can do this," she gasped, putting the back of her hand to her mouth. She'd assisted Lenae with minor injuries at camp, but nothing like this. This was serious. This was Jace. Her vision wavered, and her head grew airy.

"Yes, you can."

She met Marcus's eyes, and the quiet, yet firm, tone of his voice stilled her panic. She pulled in a deep breath to clear her head and nodded. Her stomach still convulsed, but she held it down and took a wet cloth from the basin. Working to keep her hands from shaking, she joined Marcus in cleaning away as much of the blood from the numerous lacerations as they could. She didn't want to cause Jace more pain, but this was impossible. He bit down on the cloth, but couldn't hold back the deep groans that broke free.

When at last they had cleaned away most of the blood, besides that which was fresh and still oozed from the wounds, Marcus rinsed his hands in the basin and reached for the bottle of wine. He hesitated and looked down at Jace. "I'm sorry, but we have to use this to fight any infection."

Jace pulled the cloth from his mouth and took several deep breaths. "Do it." He put the cloth back and gripped the edges of the table, resting his forehead against the surface.

Marcus traded a look with Kyrin, and she pressed her hand to her middle. This would be the worst of all. With a fortifying breath, Marcus poured the wine onto Jace's back and used a fresh cloth to disperse it among the wounds. Jace's muscles jerked taut. He groaned, but it became a hoarse cry that made its way around the cloth between his teeth. Kyrin's tears came hard and fast. She put her hand on his head, not knowing what else to do, but wanting him to know she was there. She had to bite her lip to keep from telling Marcus to stop.

Just as he was finishing, Jace went limp and almost fell off the stool, but she and Marcus held him steady. He didn't completely lose consciousness, because he reached up suddenly and gripped Kyrin's arm. She rested her hand over his and squeezed it.

"We're almost done, Jace." Her voice trembled.

Kyrin wiped her eyes and glanced across the table to where her mother stood watching. She accepted a look of sympathy, grateful for any comfort at the moment.

Marcus mopped up the excess wine, and then let Jace rest for a bit. After a few minutes, he seemed to start breathing a little easier, and Kyrin prayed it was her mother's painkiller taking effect. Marcus then went over the rest of Jace's injuries, most notably the deep purple bruises around his ribs.

"Well, if the ribs aren't broken, they're badly bruised," he said. "Either way, there's not much we can do. We'll wrap them and that might help the pain once the herbs wear off."

Kyrin helped him with the bandages, wrapping them snugly around Jace's ribs, but not so tightly that it would restrict his breathing or cause further pain to his back. When Marcus reached for another roll, he looked at Liam, who sat in a chair at the side of the table.

"You should have Mother clean your wounds and change the bandages before we have to leave." He slid the half-empty bottle of wine across the table with an apologetic look.

Lydia's eyes went straight to her son. "You're injured?" She came around the table. "Let me see."

Liam carefully pulled off his shirt. When Lydia began removing the bandages, she gasped at the first sight of the whip wounds that matched Jace's. Her horrified eyes jumped to Marcus. "Who did this to them?"

Marcus spoke in a low voice and cast his eyes down as if out of guilt. "Parker . . . under the General's orders."

"My father ordered this?" Lydia gestured at Liam.

Marcus nodded.

Lydia stared open-mouthed, though Kyrin didn't know why she was so surprised. Her mother looked at each of them as uncertainty took over her expression. "What's going on? Why are you here?" She paused, fear in her eyes. "Why is Kyrin here?"

Marcus released a hard sigh and explained, in brief, the events of the past twenty-four hours. The dismay on their mother's face grew and reached its peak when Marcus recounted their escape.

She touched her chest. "You deserted?"

Marcus closed his eyes in a grimace, his tone a bit hard. "Yes, I deserted."

Panic rushed into Lydia's voice. "Marcus, you must go back, you and Liam. You—"

"I can't." Marcus shook his head as he straightened to face her. "I won't."

"Why not?"

"Because I'm starting to see things I always tried to ignore, but I can't anymore." He swallowed, though his voice was rough. "If serving the emperor means accepting that my father died a traitor and letting my siblings meet the same fate, then I won't do it. I thought I could, but I was wrong. I should never have brought Kyrin, Kaden, and Jace in. This is the consequence of that." He gestured to Jace and Liam. "And I'm going to do anything I can to see there aren't further consequences."

"But you'll be hunted, fugitives and, if you're caught, you'll be executed." Lydia's eyes pooled. "I can't lose any more of you."

Marcus sighed again, but spoke gently. "Kyrin and Kaden are already living as fugitives. If I hadn't done this, you would have lost them forever. And Liam too."

Kyrin looked questioningly at her brother. She didn't know anything about this.

"Surely your grandfather would have prevented their executions," Lydia pressed.

Kyrin exhaled in frustration. Did her mother never see the cruelty of her own father? Was she that far removed from what took place at the fort and how horribly he'd treated Liam all these years?

Marcus shook his head. "A prisoner transport was leaving for Valcré this morning. He would have put them on it, unless Kyrin and Kaden accepted his conditions, which they weren't going to do." Kyrin exchanged a glance with her mother while Marcus continued, "Liam already decided he was done and was prepared to join them. I did what I should've done from the beginning . . . protected them."

Lydia's chest trembled, as if she were trying not to cry. Kyrin watched her, and it was perhaps the first time she truly looked at her since arriving. Her mother wasn't young anymore, yet still so pretty. Her long, honey-brown hair was gathered up in a loose bun with shorter lengths falling around her smooth, ivory face. She'd matured, yet not really aged from Kyrin's memories of her.

But behind her beauty, Kyrin noticed other things—her fragile expression, the redness of her eyes telling of more than the emotion of the moment, and the soul-deep weariness in them. It struck Kyrin then that if they'd buried her father only two days ago, it must have been the first her mother knew of his death. She'd only been mourning for a couple of days. A chip broke off the wall around Kyrin's heart.

"I know this is difficult to understand," Marcus spoke more gently. "Even I don't fully understand it. I hope Kyrin and Kaden can explain, but I truly think what they believe, and . . . what

Father believed, is true. If that's the case, then the emperor is wrong, and I can't continue to serve him knowing that."

A couple of tears dripped down Lydia's cheeks, and she started shaking her head before he finished. But, in a moment, she wiped the wetness away, her face blank, and set about tending Liam. Marcus breathed out a long breath and helped Kyrin finish with Jace's bandages.

Now that they'd cared for all of Jace's most serious injuries, Marcus let Kyrin take over to clean the bloodied cuts on his face. Gently, she pushed some of his hair back and dabbed the cloth around the gash near his brow. He glanced up at her, and she met his eyes. Pain still resided in them, but not as great as before. She hoped he knew the depth of her relief that they had not left him behind. Though she'd only known him for a few months, she couldn't imagine not having him in her life.

Behind Kyrin, Marcus said, "He'll need fresh clothes."

"I can get some of mine," Liam offered as their mother finished with his bandages. He rose, and she helped him pull his shirt back on before he left the room.

A brief moment of silence followed as Lydia started gathering up the scattered medical supplies. Finally, she asked in a tired voice, "What will you do now?"

"Kaden will meet us here any time," Marcus said. "After that, they'll show us where to go."

"Your grandfather will be looking for you."

"That's why we split up. Jace wouldn't have made it farther than this."

The conversation died when someone else stepped into the room—an elderly, but sturdy-looking man. Kyrin's heart reacted in warm familiarity.

"What's going on here?" His bright blue eyes landed on her and rounded. "Kyrin?"

Unlike his wife, Ethel, Carl was a friendly, easy-going sort of man who had always fascinated Kyrin and her brothers with his fanciful stories. He'd been much more like a grandfather than the General. It helped that he'd had a soft spot for Kyrin. A smile came to her face for the first time in what must have been days. Without hesitation, she went to hug him.

"My goodness, is it really you?" he said looking her over. "Where's the wide-eyed little girl I used to sneak candy to?"

"All grown up, sadly," Kyrin responded with a half-smile.

"But lovelier than ever; just like your mother."

Kyrin ducked her head. "Thank you."

When she raised her eyes again, they shared a look that went beyond words. Despite Carl's bright eyes, the sorrow Kyrin wasn't sure would ever fade settled in his expression. He and her father had always been good friends.

Carl cleared his throat and looked from her to Jace and then to Marcus. "Trouble at the fort?"

"You could say that." Suddenly looking as weary as their mother, Marcus sat down and went into another explanation. Carl didn't say too much, but Kyrin sensed from his manner that he condoned Marcus's actions. After all, he'd never thought too much of the General, from what Kyrin remembered.

When Liam returned with a stack of fresh clothing for Jace, Kyrin and her mother stepped out of the room while Marcus and Carl helped him change. In the hall just outside the doorway, Kyrin leaned back against the wall and closed her eyes. The emotions of the last twenty-four hours had left her exhausted, but she took the quiet few moments to thank Elôm both for their escape and for sparing Jace. She also prayed for Kaden's safety. *Please don't let him have been caught.*

Marcus called her back into the room a couple of minutes later. To see Jace cleaned up did Kyrin's heart good. With the herbs in full effect, he seemed more like himself. He even offered a hint of a smile as she approached him.

"Feel better?" she asked.

"Yes."

She knew it would take weeks before the pain of his injuries, especially his bruised ribs, would subside, but at least they'd made him as comfortable as possible. She'd just reached out to help straighten his collar that was a little crooked, when an unfamiliar voice came from behind her.

"Mother, what's going on?"

Kyrin's breath snagged. Her heart gave a deep thud, and she turned around. Two boys stood in the doorway—one thirteen and the other ten. Both had brown hair a little darker than Lydia's, but the same brown eyes. The older one stood a bit tall for his age. They looked at her in curiosity, but something more lit the eyes of the eldest.

"Boys," Lydia said after a moment that seemed to stand still. "This is your sister, Kyrin."

Their eyes went wide. Kyrin stepped around the table to stand before them. Tears rose and thickened her throat, but she smiled as she focused on the older boy. "Hello, Michael."

Hearing her speak seemed to confirm the realness of her presence. Michael said her name and stepped into her arms. The tears spilled over as she hugged her brother tightly. She'd imagined this moment innumerable times over the years. It was nothing like she'd dreamed, but so much more, filling her heart up to bursting with how much she'd missed them. She then turned to her youngest brother. "Hello, Ronny."

His smile came slowly, but full of wonder. They too hugged, and then Kyrin looked at them both.

"It's so good to see you. I know you don't remember me, but I remember you." She shook her head at the memories she had of them—Michael toddling around when he'd first learned to walk and tiny Ronny cradled in her arms. "You were just babies."

"What are you doing here?" Michael asked.

Kyrin hesitated, not sure how to explain, but their mother stepped in. "Her friend was injured and needed help, so they came here."

"Will you be here long?" Michael wanted to know.

Kyrin sighed. If only they could. How could she finally meet her little brothers and then just leave? "I'm afraid we can't."

Her two brothers shared her disappointment.

Michael scanned the room before his gaze returned to her. "Is Kaden here too?"

"No, but he should meet us here soon." Kyrin prayed this was so. He should be there any time. If it grew much later, she would truly worry.

The prospect of meeting Kaden brought a sparkle of excitement back to her brothers' eyes. But, as with their mother, Kyrin saw more—the sorrow just under the surface. Both had shadows beneath their eyes, and Ronny seemed pale for an energetic young boy of his age. The heartache that stabbed Kyrin's chest in that moment snatched her breath. She was only one of six struggling with the loss of their father, and Michael and Ronny were so young. Not only that, but they wouldn't truly know why their father had died like she did. All they would know were the lies.

Kyrin was glad when her mother spoke again, because her voice was gone.

"Do you want breakfast?" she asked, looking between Kyrin and Marcus. "Ethel and I can make something quick."

Marcus glanced at Kyrin and nodded. "Yes, thank you."

Appearing relieved to have that to do, Lydia picked up the basin from the table to take to the kitchen. Kyrin stared at the remaining supplies. It didn't seem right to leave them until her mother or Ethel came back for them. Fighting reluctance, she picked them up and followed her mother.

In one corner of the house across the hall, she came into the warm kitchen. The fire burned brightly, and she could almost smell the gingerbread cookies she and Kaden used to love. A tiny smile tugged at her lips at the memories of how Ethel used to shoo Kaden out, scolding him for sneaking cookies from the cooling racks. Just like sneaking into the kitchen at Tarvin Hall. Some things never changed.

The memories evaporated when her mother turned to her. Feeling uncomfortable now, alone with only her and Ethel, Kyrin avoided eye contact and walked over to the counter to set the supplies down. There, her eyes were drawn out the window to the backyard. Out across the frosted, wilting grass lay a mound of fresh dirt and a bleak, gray stone. Everything inside Kyrin went still. It took a long moment before she noticed her mother at her side. She gasped a little, her lungs depleted of air, and looked into her mother's eyes. Moisture pooled at the rims, and Kyrin's welled too. Her voice scratchy and halting, she said, "That's why we came." She nodded out the window. "That's why Marcus found us on the road."

Lydia gave a short nod as she looked away from Kyrin, blinking her own tears away.

Kyrin glanced out the window again and then returned to the dining room. Now that she'd seen it, the grave drew her despite her growing fear to face it. She picked up her coat and pulled it on. Glancing at each of her brothers and Jace, she said, "I'll be back in a few minutes."

No one replied. She walked into the hall and let herself out the back door. It was still cold, but warming up, and the sky was clearing. Kyrin forced herself to breathe steadily and keep moving, but her feet slowed as she drew near. That was the moment it truly sank in; shattering the walls and barriers she had built to protect herself from the sorrow. Her steps slow and shaky, she went the final couple of yards and struggled to read the gravestone through her tears. Only three words. *William Altair. Traitor.*

Teardrops rolled down her cheeks, and she dropped her eyes to the fresh mound of earth. Small sobs hitched in her chest. A week ago, her father had been with her—had embraced her and spoken with her. How could this grave be all that was left of him? The tears flowed heavier, and the cries deeper, shaking her shoulders as she hugged her arms around herself in loss.

"Father," she cried, desperate for his voice. Choking, she looked up at the sky. "Why? Why did he have to die?"

Her chin dropped back to her chest as the grief crushed down, but a memory—as clear and vivid as if she were reliving it—entered her mind. She was in Auréa Palace with her father just after her promotion.

*"The trouble with Marcus is his devotion to his duty as a soldier. To believe in the King, he would have to realize that his loyalty and dedication to the emperor and his gods are for naught. I'm afraid it would take a miracle."*

He was right, and she'd known it.

*"Maybe Elôm will give us a miracle."*

She could see the small smile come to her father's face and hear the hope in his voice.

*"We will pray so."*

Right there, Kyrin understood that Elôm had given her an answer. This was why. Her father's death had been the one thing powerful enough to open Marcus's eyes—to get him to question and to see. This was their miracle.

She covered her face and wept into her hands.

"It worked," she whispered, her lips trembling. Though her father couldn't hear her, she had to say it, if only for herself. "Marcus is beginning to see and believe. I know you would tell me it was all worth it, and I believe it, but it's *so* hard. I wish you were here. I miss you . . . and I love you so much. I can't wait to see you again. It's so hard to go on without you."

She wiped her sleeves across her cheeks, though a few more tears fell in spite of it. For a minute or two, she stood quietly—praying and remembering. When she sensed someone near, she looked over her shoulder. Her mother stood a few feet away, her eyes glimmering and her reddened cheeks tracked with moisture. Kyrin slowly turned to face her.

Lydia licked her lips. "I know there's a lot to work through between us . . ." She winced. "But I want you to know, despite the way it may have appeared at times, I loved your father. I've not always done the right thing, but I did love him. And I know how much you loved him. I'm *so* very sorry you've lost him. If I could do something . . . I would."

Kyrin squeezed her eyes shut to hold back another flood of emotion. The struggle raged between hurts and forgiveness—love and pain. She'd felt betrayed, abandoned even, by her mother, and was afraid to trust her again. They were both hurting and needed each other, yet the past was so hard to let go.

Her heart pounded—steady, thudding beats that echoed inside her head with the rolling thoughts. Then her eyes popped open. It wasn't her heart—not entirely.

*Horses!*

THE RUMBLE OF galloping horses approached hard and fast. Kyrin and her mother looked toward the house and then at each other in shared fear. The back door burst open a second later, and Marcus, Liam, and Jace rushed out.

"It's the General!" Marcus called.

Kyrin gasped. *No!*

Lydia ran to the house. "Stay inside," she told Michael and Ronny. The two boys stood in the doorway, their eyes wide.

Kyrin raced to meet her brothers and Jace.

Marcus handed over her quiver and weapons. "We need to get out of here now."

Kyrin pulled her bow free and slung her quiver over her shoulder as they ran toward the trees. Where was Kaden? What if they had him? She couldn't hesitate. They just needed to run. The pounding hooves grew louder. In the next moment, the General's voice thundered out.

"Stop right there!"

It was hopeless. They couldn't outrun the riders any more than they had been able to outrun Marcus's men. Skidding to a stop at the edge of the forest, they turned to face the General. He and his twenty men reined to a halt, with a few yards separating them. Kyrin reached back for an arrow. She would not be taken easily this time. Before anyone could make a move, Marcus stepped to the front with his sword drawn.

The General glared at him. "I never would've believed it had I not seen it with my own eyes. What have you done?"

Marcus drew a breath, but his grandfather didn't give him a chance to speak.

"I'd expect such foolishness from Liam, but never from you. Have you gone mad? You're on the verge of throwing away everything. Years of training wasted, opportunities thrown to the wind . . ."

Marcus shook his head. "Stop."

The General didn't even hear him, continuing the list, but Marcus's voice rose up with force and authority. "Stop!"

The General fell silent and gaped at his grandson.

Marcus breathed harder, but kept his voice even and controlled. "No amount of training, or opportunities, or prestige is worth losing another member of my family."

"Your father was a fool, and it got him killed. If Kyrin and Kaden insist on following him, then they can reap the consequences, but I'll be dead before I see you throw your life away. Now, stand aside. Liam, too, if he knows what's good for him. Kyrin and the ryrik are traitors, and they'll answer for it."

Marcus remained firmly rooted where he was and took his sword in both hands. "If you want them, you'll have to come through me."

"This-this is madness!" the General sputtered. "I raised you better than this. What's wrong with you? What are you thinking?"

"I'm protecting my family. Now that my father is gone, I realize that job has fallen to me."

The General gave a disgusted snort. "Protecting them from what? The consequences of their own actions?"

"Protecting them from you," Marcus declared, "and the emperor."

The General scowled. "Don't you see what's happening? You're letting their situation and your own emotions blind you."

Marcus shook his head. "No, I was blind before, but now I'm starting to see things very clearly. It took me until now to realize . . . you are wrong. You have always been wrong. And my greatest regret is that I realized it too late to protect my brother from your cruelty. Too late to stop you from allowing your men to brutally beat an unarmed and already-injured man . . ." His voice wavered. "Too late to tell my father how sorry I am for not honoring him with the amount of respect he deserved. Respect I so foolishly gave you instead."

To hear such words almost broke Kyrin's heart. Under different circumstances, she would have hugged her brother. The General stared at him dumbfounded. Kyrin could only imagine what ran through his mind after grooming Marcus for his position since childhood. She hadn't missed the way he'd said he raised him. It infuriated her.

Re-gathering his wits, the General spoke icily. "This is your last chance, Marcus. If you stick with them, you'll be treated as a traitor and face the same consequences. You'll be shown no mercy. But if you come back with me, I'll overlook this indiscretion as a foolish act of emotion."

The ensuing silence was almost deafening, but Marcus broke it with his one, firm word. "No."

Their grandfather went rigid in the saddle. "You're making a terrible mistake."

"Maybe . . . but it feels right to me. The first truly right thing I've done in a long time."

"So be it." The General motioned, and his men drew their swords. In a commanding voice, he ordered Kyrin and the others, "Drop your weapons or you'll die here."

No one moved until Kyrin drew back her bow and had it aimed in a heartbeat. She held it steady, willing her nerves to calm.

"I don't want to shoot you, Grandfather, but I will if any of your men try to take us."

He locked eyes with her, but there wasn't a spark of warmth to be found. "You may do that, Kyrin, but it won't stop all of us."

He raised his hand. As soon as he gave the signal, the men would charge. Then Kyrin would have to choose. Would she shoot him? Could she? Her gaze jerked to Marcus, and then to Jace and Liam. They didn't look ready to surrender. What was the right choice? Did they fight and die here, or surrender and die later?

The General's hand began to drop, and Kyrin sucked in her breath. Her bowstring slipped on her fingers, but before it fully released, a shattering roar rocked the air above them. In a burst of light and heat, a wall of fire appeared between them and the soldiers as a dragon swooped over their heads. The trees rattled with wind gusts as, one by one, dragons landed beside them—Kaden and Exsis first, followed by Ivoris, Gem, and Rayad and his dragon. The horses shrieked, rearing and fighting against their riders, who struggled to keep them from bolting.

By now, the fire had died to small flames and a wide swath of sizzling, charred grass. With a swoosh of wings, a final dragon landed near them, bearing Leetra. Kyrin had never been so relieved to see her.

The crete's dragon blew out a stream of smoke and growled at the soldiers. Her eyes deep purple with intensity, Leetra glared at them. "I suggest you put those swords away and ride back to wherever you came from."

Every eye focused on the General. Strangling his horse's reins, he nodded to the soldiers. With the hiss of metal, they shoved their swords back into their scabbards. The General's fiery eyes swept Kyrin and the others and landed on Marcus. "Last chance. Are you with me or with them?"

Marcus barely paused. "Them."

At this, the General's face changed, growing stone cold as he severed ties with his grandson. Marcus was now the enemy and, as the General had said, there would be no mercy should they meet again.

This reflected in his voice as he ordered, "Back to the fort."

With one last death glare, he turned his horse. He glanced toward the house, where Lydia stood in the door with the boys, and then rode out with his men.

"All the way to the fort," Leetra called after them in warning.

Everyone remained still until the echo of hooves faded down the road, and Kyrin's heart had a chance to calm. She let her arms fall to her sides as the remnants of adrenaline drained from her body. She looked down at her bow, but didn't want to think about what would have happened had the dragons not shown up when they did.

The riders dismounted. Kyrin put her weapons down and rushed to Kaden. "I was so worried you'd been caught."

"No, I made it just fine, but Grandfather must have figured out our ploy."

Kyrin's attention then shifted to Rayad, who approached Jace with a look of grim concern. He reached for Jace's shoulder, but held back as if unsure it would cause him pain. "Are you all right?"

Jace nodded. "I will be."

He held his ribs, but didn't seem to be in nearly as much pain as before. Still, Kyrin wanted to get him to sit down and rest again. It couldn't be comfortable or easy for him to stand there and to have had to get up and move so quickly. How did he even have the strength?

"Good," Rayad breathed. He took in the sight of Jace's battered face and winced. "Kaden mentioned what happened."

From her dragon, Leetra spoke up. "I'm going to make sure those soldiers don't double back and surprise us. I'll check in with you later."

Once she had flown off, Kyrin asked Rayad, "What are you two doing here anyway?"

"I had a feeling we shouldn't have let you come alone and just couldn't help myself."

Kyrin smiled at his concern. "Thank Elôm for that. How did you convince Leetra to come?"

"I didn't. I think she's feeling guilty because of her relationship with Falcor. She offered to join me in case there was trouble."

Leetra had never seemed to be the type to put herself out for others, beyond those of her own race, but Kyrin was truly grateful she'd come to make sure they were all right.

Movement from the house drew their attention. Michael and Ronny stepped outside, followed more tentatively by their mother. Her face was very pale, though Kyrin couldn't know if it was due to shock from the sight of the dragons or over what had just occurred with the General. However, her expression lifted when she and Kaden saw each other. Kaden glanced briefly at Kyrin, and then started forward to meet his mother and younger brothers with none of Kyrin's reservations. Kyrin stood with a mix of happiness for him, but sadness for herself.

The others followed slowly behind Kaden, but Marcus didn't move. Kyrin turned to find him staring off toward the road where the General and his men had gone, a sick look on his face. He'd lost everything—everything he had worked for his entire life; his position, his influence and, perhaps most painful of all, his relationship with his grandfather. He had idolized him since childhood and dreamed of following in his footsteps. Now that future was nothing more than ashes. Kyrin could hardly imagine having worked so hard to achieve something, only to have it destroyed in one devastating blow. She walked to his side and wrapped her hand around his arm. He blinked and looked at her.

"You still have us, and we love you," she murmured earnestly. "I hope that's enough."

"It is," he said, his voice quiet. He cleared his throat and repeated more firmly, "It is."

Kyrin gave him a small, understanding smile and stayed at his side as they walked toward the gathering at the house. They were just in time to see Kaden hugging their mother tightly. Regret pinched Kyrin's heart. This reunion was much different from hers.

When their mother stepped back, tears streaked her cheeks, but it was the first time she smiled since they'd arrived. She cupped Kaden's face in her hands and remarked on how he'd grown. He grinned at her, completely free of any unpleasant memories to come between them. Kyrin sighed. If only she had been able to forget.

The boys greeted Kaden next with great enthusiasm after their brother's dramatic entrance with his dragon. This managed to draw out Kyrin's smile. It was almost as if the boys had known Kaden their whole lives, the way they chattered excitedly.

"Are the dragons dangerous?" Michael asked, followed immediately by Ronny's hopeful, "Can you take us flying?"

Kaden grinned at them. "They're only dangerous when we need them to be. As for flying . . ." he glanced at Lydia, ". . . you'll have to ask Mother."

The two boys spun to face her with pleading looks.

"Please, Mother, can we?" Ronny begged.

"We'll see," Lydia told him. "First let's see to breakfast."

The boys sighed in disappointment, but not Kaden.

"I'm starving," he said.

Lydia smiled and motioned to the group. "Come inside. Everyone."

"They rode straight to the fort and didn't send anyone out while I was watching," Leetra reported a few hours later as everyone was finishing their second meal of the day. "They probably think we've gone by now, or know better than to approach."

Kyrin didn't hold back a sigh of relief. Though they had the dragons, it was good to know her grandfather hadn't gone so far as to gather an army to come after them. She wouldn't have put it past him, considering the mood he'd been in when he left.

Quiet lingered in the dining room for a moment before Rayad looked at her and Kaden from across the table. "We should probably be going."

Lydia spoke up, reluctance in her expression, but her tone genuine. "If you need lodging for the night, we have room."

Kyrin never would have expected her to make such an offer, but her mother truly seemed to be trying to make amends.

Rayad smiled kindly. "Thank you, but I'm not sure it would be wise for you to offer us such hospitality. The last thing we want is to cause you further trouble."

"He's right," Kyrin said, though it hurt her to have to leave so soon. "We've probably stayed longer than we should have already."

"Do you have to go?" Ronny asked sadly.

Kyrin gave him a remorseful look. "I'm afraid so."

Her little brother let out a heavy sigh. Kyrin felt the same. The longer she stayed, the more she wished they didn't have to leave. A part of her heart had remained here when she'd left for Tarvin Hall, and it would still be here when she left again. One morning wasn't enough to satisfy the longing she'd carried with her all these years. Her eyes traveled around the table, committing the sight to memory. Today had been the first time she and all five of her brothers had sat at this table—the first time in many years their family had been nearly complete. But it wouldn't ever be truly complete again.

Kyrin fought to force those thoughts away. She was grateful for the distraction when Marcus rose and said, "I'm going to gather some of my things."

Liam followed him. A moment later, Kaden, too, pushed back his chair.

"I'm going to step out for a few minutes," he murmured.

Kyrin looked up at him. All morning he'd been full of joy—interacting with his brothers, smiling, laughing. It had done Kyrin good to see it after the week they'd faced, but seriousness had returned to his eyes now. The grief they both still struggled with could only be temporarily laid aside. It was time to face it once more.

She watched him leave, and rested back in her chair as she stared at her lap and prayed for both him and herself. She wanted to go out with him, but he needed time like she'd had—time to mourn and say whatever things he might want to say.

"Are you a crete?"

Michael's voice brought Kyrin's attention once more to those around her. Both her younger brothers stared at Leetra, who stood near the door, curiosity sparkling in their eyes. This was much better than their sadness. They were clearly enamored with the girl. Kyrin had grown used to cretes, but she hadn't forgotten how foreign they looked at first. And Leetra, with her dark hair and lavender eyes, was particularly striking now that Kyrin thought about it, especially to two young boys.

"I am," Leetra answered in her usual direct way, though Kyrin sensed a subtle change—a softening—about her.

"We've never seen a crete before," Michael said.

Leetra gave a shrug. "My people don't have many dealings with Arcacia anymore."

The boys went on to ask her all kinds of questions about

the cretes and where they lived. Leetra was surprisingly patient with them, and Kyrin's respect for her grew a little.

Kyrin listened for several minutes before leaving the table and slipping from the room. In the hall, she pulled on her coat and let herself outside, where she leaned against the door for a moment and stared at Kaden, who stood at the grave. An invisible cord wrapped tightly around her chest. She wanted to be strong for him, the way he always was for her, and gathered her fortitude. With a prayer for strength, she crossed the yard. When he heard her coming, he glanced over his shoulder. His cheeks were wet, and he wiped them with his sleeve. They stood side by side in silence for a minute until Kaden found the voice to speak.

"There were so many things I wanted to tell him. So many things I wanted to ask him . . . about being a man."

"I know."

His jaw clamped, and his throat worked, but he didn't say anything again for a few moments. "You're lucky, you know. You'll always have the memories."

The words stunned Kyrin at first. She was so used to her abilities that she hadn't considered Kaden's memories of their father fading with time. The thought pierced her heart with deep sadness. Her eyes filled, and she reached out to squeeze his arm.

"I'll help you remember."

Goodbye came quickly. After preparing the dragons, and saying farewell to Carl, Kyrin and Kaden gathered with their mother and brothers near the house. The awkwardness between Kyrin and her mother lingered as they faced each other.

Fiddling with her cuff, Kyrin struggled to look her in the eye. "Thank you for letting us stay this morning . . . and especially for helping with Jace." She cleared her throat. "I appreciate it."

"You're welcome," Lydia responded quietly.

They held each other's gaze for a moment of silence, and Kyrin saw all the unsaid things her mother held inside—same as she did. Neither one seemed to know how to say them.

Her mother held a small pouch out to her. "More herbs for Jace. He can take some tonight so he can sleep, and then once a day for a couple of days if he needs the relief. After that, they should only be taken occasionally."

Kyrin squeezed the pouch in her fingers. That her mother would do this for Jace weakened her grip on her emotions. She tucked the pouch into her pocket. "Thank you."

Another silence followed before Kyrin worked her tongue loose. "Goodbye, Mother."

Lydia's eyes turned a little misty. "Goodbye, Kyrin." The longing in her gaze was evident. She slowly reached out, and Kyrin accepted a hug.

Her nose stung, and she blinked hard as her mother's arms wrapped around her. She wanted her mother's love so much—she truly did—but fear of being hurt again still clung to her. Though she'd lowered her defenses a little, it wasn't complete. Not yet.

Clearing her throat again, she stepped away and turned to her brothers, but then stopped. She turned back to her mother. "If you ever need us, go to Landale. Follow the main road heading north from the village. A mile into the forest is an old oak tree bigger than any other trees around it. In one of the branches over the road is a red rope. Wait there. Someone will find you."

Her mother's brows lifted, yet gratitude filled her eyes. "I will."

Kyrin then moved on to her younger brothers, and her emotions slipped even more.

"I wish you could stay," Ronny said. Michael was putting on a brave face, but the youngest boy had tears in his eyes.

"So do I," Kyrin replied, "but it's not safe for us to stay here. Not for us or for you."

"You shouldn't have to go." Michael huffed and frowned deeply. "This is your home. You're our family. I don't care what anyone says about what you believe."

Kyrin couldn't help her smile. His indignation reminded her very much of Kaden. The two seemed a lot alike. Then her expression grew serious, and she put a hand on each of her brothers' shoulders. "There's something I want you both to know before I leave."

Their serious faces matched hers as they listened intently.

"No matter what anyone says or tries to tell you, Father was *not* a traitor. He was a hero. People will try to make you ashamed of him and what he did, but there's nothing to be ashamed of." Her voice quivered. "He was one of the bravest men I've ever known, and he did the right thing. No matter what, you have to remember that, do you understand?"

Both boys nodded solemnly.

Kyrin took a breath. "Good."

Then came goodbye. She hugged each of her brothers tightly, unable to hold back a few tears. With reluctance and final farewells, Kyrin, Kaden, and their older brothers turned toward the dragons. They hadn't made it halfway across the yard when Michael shouted, "Take us with you!"

He and Ronny rushed after them with pleading looks.

"Please, we want to go with you," Michael said more urgently.

Kyrin stood torn. How she would love to take them to camp. The last thing she wanted was to leave them here under the influence of their grandfather and the emperor. She wanted them to know and believe the truth. All that prevented her from granting their request was the fear in her mother's eyes. She'd just lost her husband, and two more of her children were leaving her to become fugitives. How could they deprive her of the only two she had left?

Kyrin hesitated, terribly conflicted, but it was Kaden who stepped forward and spoke to their brothers.

"I wish we could, but it's important that you stay here and take care of Mother. It's all up to the two of you. You're the men of the Altair house now, all right? Mother needs you to look after things. Can you do that for us?"

Ronny looked a little scared, but Michael's face set in determination.

"We can do that," he said.

Bolstered by his brother's acceptance of the responsibility, Ronny nodded.

Kaden smiled at them. "Don't worry, we'll come visit and make sure everything's all right. It's not far with the dragons."

Their mother gave Kaden a grateful look, and the group turned once more.

At the dragons, they all mounted—Marcus riding with Kyrin, and Liam with Kaden. Amidst calls of goodbye, they took to the air. Kyrin looked down as the house shrank away, and waved at the three family members standing in the yard. Her chest constricted at leaving them and home behind, but she set her sights on the horizon to the northeast, toward her second family and home.

KYRIN FINISHED SETTING the table and poured herself a cup of coffee to sip while she waited for her brothers. Letting the mug warm her hands, she stepped to the window. Feathery snowflakes floated down through the trees. After two days back in camp, life finally seemed to be settling down for the winter. Though she still missed her younger brothers and thought of them often, she welcomed the quiet. She had half her family with her now, and Marcus and Liam fit in well. Trask and the other members had welcomed them readily, as she knew they would. Timothy had been especially helpful in talking to them about spiritual matters. Liam, who had all but believed already, accepted everything with only minimal explanation. Marcus needed more, and had even stayed up late talking with Timothy the night before. It was more than she could have hoped for, and she praised Elôm.

"See them?"

Kyrin looked back at Lenae as the woman set a plate of sausages on the table. "Not yet, and if they were up any later than I was, I'm not surprised."

Lenae smiled. "You must be thrilled to see your brothers so open to the knowledge of Elôm."

"I am, especially for Marcus. He's almost a different person already. He asks questions, but doesn't doubt the answers. Before now, he wouldn't have even considered it." Her mind drifted back over the last few days. He never would have considered it if not for all that had happened. Such experiences couldn't leave a person unchanged. As horrible as it had been, Elôm clearly had a plan in it. "I'm just thankful Timothy is here. His knowledge amazes me. I never could have explained things like he has."

"He's a very gifted young man. We're blessed to have him here."

Kyrin agreed. "I can't help but envy him sometimes, the way he's dealt with things. He's much stronger than I am." An uncomfortable twinge passed through her, and she let a sigh escape. Ever since leaving home, she couldn't seem to shake a nagging feeling of guilt.

"It's good to have people like him to learn from and emulate."

"And you," Kyrin said.

Lenae gave her a warm smile.

When Kyrin looked out the window again, her three brothers were on their way to the cabin. "Here they come."

She met the men at the door and exchanged morning greetings as they hung up their coats. Their tired eyes suggested that they'd been up well past when she'd gone to bed. She could hardly blame them. She'd hated to leave the conversation, but the exhaustion of the past days had been too much for her.

At the table, they voiced their appreciation for the food Lenae was about to serve. Now that it was too cold for outdoor community meals, the men, with the exception of Lenae's son Jeremy, saw to feeding themselves, but Kyrin's brothers had a special invitation. They took their seats, and Kaden offered a prayer before they filled their plates. Kyrin didn't say much during the meal, but she loved listening to her brothers talk. It was so foreign, but wonderful. And Kaden and Marcus were getting along. She could tell Marcus was making an effort, and Kaden, too, did his part. Everything was just about perfect.

Near the end of the meal, Trask entered the cabin along with a few wayward snowflakes. He smiled as Lenae closed the door against the chill air. "Mind if I join you? I have something I'd like to discuss with Captain Altair."

"Please," Lenae invited.

As Trask took a seat at the table with them, Kyrin's oldest brother said, "Just 'Marcus' is fine. I'm not a captain anymore." His face displayed a struggle that Kyrin attributed to the actions he'd taken as an Arcacian officer and what it had cost. More than once, he'd expressed his distress over it. Elôm's unconditional forgiveness was something he would have to grow accustomed to. From what Kyrin knew, there'd been no such forgiveness under the General's command.

"Actually, I have a proposition that would enable you to keep that title," Trask told him.

Everyone around the table sat intrigued.

"How is that?" Marcus asked.

"I've been discussing this with Warin and Rayad, and we all agree. Part of our goal here has always been to form a militia to aid our allies, should any fighting break out. There are well-trained men here, but none who've been in military leadership like you. We would like you to train our militia, as well as lead them."

Marcus's expression lifted in surprise. "Me?"

Trask nodded.

"Are you certain you want me for the job? I've only been here for a couple of days."

"You're exactly the one we want and need to create this militia, and the men will respect my decision."

Marcus didn't have to think about it long. With an eager light in his eyes, he said, "I'd be honored."

Trask smiled. "Good." He rose and offered his hand. "Congratulations, Captain Altair. You're officially the first commander of the Landale Militia."

Jace tried lying on his less-bruised right side, but it still shot stabbing pains through his chest and pulled at his wounded back. He'd never sleep at night if not for the herbs Kyrin's mother had sent with them. But both Kyrin and Rayad were serious about making sure he didn't get too much, so he went without it during the day, relying on safer, yet less potent painkillers. It didn't help that the wounds needed to be cleaned so regularly. Enduring the fresh pain always sapped his already-depleted strength.

Desperate to regain that strength, he fought to push aside his discomfort and rest, but soon it grew too difficult to breathe properly. With a groan that was as much frustration as pain, he pushed himself up and sat on the edge of Rayad's bed. So much for that. Tyra sat up from her place on the floor, resting her chin on his knee. He rubbed between her ears as she stared up at him. She seemed to sense his pain and had been subdued ever since he'd returned, rarely leaving his side.

Rayad looked at him from near the fireplace. "Do you want me to get you more tea?"

Jace waved off the suggestion. No amount of herbal tea would reduce the pain enough for him to sleep. He would have to wait until nighttime. Gritting his teeth, he reached for his boots and pulled them on.

Rayad rose from his chair and stood at the end of the bed. "What are you going to do?"

"I'm going outside." Frustration leaked out of his tone, and he tried to soften it, though the fiery sting engulfing his back made it difficult. "I'm tired of trying to rest. I need fresh air."

Rayad said nothing, but went to the door for Jace's coat and helped him slip it on.

Jace fastened the buttons, and then looked up. "Thank you." As hard as it was for him to be laid up, he knew it was even more difficult for Rayad and Kyrin to see him like this.

With a look of understanding, Rayad nodded. "Just be careful you don't do anything to aggravate the wounds."

"I will." The last thing Jace wanted was to remain like this any longer than necessary.

He stepped outside after Tyra and drew in the deepest breath he could manage. Both the pain of his screaming ribs and the cold, frosty air made his eyes water, but he blinked it away to look around. Not too far away, Marcus worked with his new company of men. Jace had heard Rayad, Trask, and Warin discussing the idea of the militia and making Kyrin's brother captain of it.

About thirty-some men had volunteered to join so far—fewer than half the men Marcus used to command, but he appeared to take it just as seriously. Already, the group looked well organized.

But the men did not hold Jace's attention. Instead, it landed on the figure standing off to the side observing them. Kyrin. He walked toward her. Tyra trotted ahead of him, her tail wagging. Kyrin smiled when the wolf reached her and bent down to pet her. Then her gaze rose to Jace and ran along his bruised face before meeting his eyes. Her expression held a question. No doubt she thought he should be resting too. However, she didn't say anything when he joined her in watching Marcus.

"Your brother is a good leader." He didn't hold any animosity toward Marcus for not stepping in to stop his grandfather. He'd made enough of his own mistakes.

Kyrin smiled faintly. "Leading has always come naturally to him. Even as children, we all followed him, including Kaden. It's incredible to see him here doing this. He lost so much when we left Fort Rivor yet, in only a couple of days, Elôm has already allowed him to continue doing what he loves."

Jace nodded in agreement, but watched the smile completely fade from her face. She seemed to lose herself in thought, not even seeing her brother and his men anymore. Jace waited for a minute or two. Finally, he asked, "Are you all right?"

She snapped out of her thoughts and looked up at him. "I'm fine."

The words lingered between them. It was odd to hear them from her lips instead of his. Of course, she had every reason to be distracted, after what had happened to her father, but something else seemed to be weighing on her.

She sighed and hung her head. "No, not really. I just haven't responded well to anything that has happened recently. Not about my father, or to my grandfather . . . and especially not to my mother."

She grimaced, scraping the toe of her boot through the light layer of snow. "I treated her poorly, and I was wrong. I was angry and hurt, and I didn't want to let it go . . . I didn't want to forgive." She winced again, but Jace understood her feelings perfectly. He'd found it difficult, at first, to forgive Holden when he'd asked. "I was too afraid of being hurt again, but now I feel horrible, and I wish I could fix it."

"You will," Jace encouraged her, "as soon as you see her again."

"I hope so. Do you think she'll forgive me?"

"Of course." He hardly knew Kyrin's mother but, from what little he'd seen, she'd seemed to have a desire for things to be right between them.

A slow smile crept back to Kyrin's face, restoring the light in her eyes that had been so painfully absent lately. If only she didn't have reason to hurt so much. "Thank you."

Jace frowned. "For what?"

"You've done so much for me during this time. It really means a lot."

Jace ducked his head and gave small shrug. "I wish there was more I could've done . . . more I could do." It seemed inadequate, in light of what had happened.

Kyrin touched his arm, her hand warming his skin even through his sleeve, and spoke earnestly. "You have, for both me and Kaden. I haven't coped well. I wanted to be stronger, but I couldn't. You helped take care of me when I couldn't take care of myself. And you kept Kaden from getting himself killed. So again, thank you."

Jace's eyes stung with moisture, though he couldn't blame the cold this time. He nodded. "You're welcome."

A fuller smile reached Kyrin's lips. "However, you did scare me to death when you told us to leave you behind at the crossroads. Please, don't do that to me again."

Jace's expression remained serious. "I told your father I'd do anything to protect you. I meant it."

Kyrin stared at him. "You did?"

He nodded again. "And it's a promise I intend to keep."

Wrapping a shawl around her shoulders, Lydia stepped into the dining room and stopped in the doorway. Michael and Ronny had their books open in front of them, but they both just stared into space.

"Boys." Their eyes jumped to her. "Shouldn't you be studying?"

"Yes, Mother," Michael responded with a quiet sigh, and Ronny echoed him.

They went back to their work, and Lydia released a sigh of her own. How could she fault their lack of attention? Though she'd tried to get things back to normal, they all knew normal was just a memory. It was just the three of them now. That reality still sent chill waves of fear rolling through her, robbing her of breath and forcing tears to her eyes. An hour didn't pass when she didn't want to buckle under the sorrow, but she had to be strong for her sons. What more could they do but press on?

A banging knock sounded at the door, and she jumped. She rapidly blinked the moisture from her eyes, but couldn't halt the dread that descended. Only one person knocked with such force. The boys looked up, and Lydia grimaced. Her father was the last person she wanted to see. She didn't know how she would come to terms with the fact that he'd been prepared to kill her older children right in front of her. The fear lurking in the boys' wide eyes only added to her feelings.

"Just keep working," she told them, and turned as a second knock echoed through the house. She met Ethel on the way to the entry. "I'll get it."

At the door, she drew a fortifying breath before pulling it open. She had to step back quickly as her father strode in and brushed past her, his eyes intense and searching.

"Where are Michael and Ronan?"

It took Lydia a moment to recover from his abrupt entrance. "They're in the dining room, studying."

Relief flickered in his eyes right before he marched off deeper into the house and peered into each room. Her mouth open, Lydia hurried after him. "What are you doing here?"

"I came to make sure the traitors were gone from this house."

Indignation flared inside Lydia. "If by traitors you mean my oldest children, then yes, they're gone. They have been for three days."

Her father didn't check his stride until they reached the dining room. The boys still sat at the table and looked from him to their mother in question.

"Go upstairs and pack your things," the General ordered.

Lydia's heart stuttered, and she spun around to face him. "What's going on?"

"I'm taking them to Tarvin Hall."

"No!" Lydia would not stand for this. Not this time—not with her sons' desperate eyes on her. Her father's gaze flashed to her, and she said even more firmly, "You're not taking them anywhere."

The General gawked at her. It may well have been the first time since she was a child that she'd openly defied him. His jaw set in the fierce stubbornness he was so famous for. "I will not leave them here to be tainted by the rebellion they witnessed."

"Does it look like they've been tainted?" Lydia asked sharply. She breathed in slowly and tempered her voice. "Just calm down so we can discuss this."

"There's nothing to discuss," her father snapped, and his gaze switched back to the boys. "Go upstairs and pack."

Panic engulfed Lydia at the growing sense that she was about to lose her boys. Then their family would be completely split apart, and she would be alone.

Her two sons looked at each other, and then Michael rose, standing up straight. "I'm not going."

The General's eyes went wide. "You see? Rebellion!"

Michael's gaze wavered between his mother and grandfather. "I'm the man of the house now, and I'm staying to take care of Mother. Ronny too."

"I'll take care of her. Now, go pack." The General pointed forcefully at the door.

Michael swallowed, but shook his head. "No."

Lydia touched her chest. Not many had the courage to stand up to her father, let alone a thirteen-year-old boy.

"You will do as I say!" The General's voice rang through the room.

The boys flinched, but neither moved. Their grandfather took a step closer, but Lydia intercepted. She couldn't trust her father with any of her children. How could she after what he'd done to Liam and how he'd threatened the others? What a terrible thing to fear one's own father. And all these years she'd ignorantly looked the other way.

"Boys, go upstairs." She tried to speak calmly, but her voice wobbled. They looked wide-eyed at her, crushing her heart with their fear and desperation. "I'm going to speak with your grandfather."

With sagging shoulders, her two sons left the room, their faces bleak. They knew as well as she did the unlikelihood of changing the General's mind. But Lydia would not give up without a fight. She was her father's daughter, after all.

"We're leaving in half an hour," he called after them. "Make sure you have what you need."

With each step they took, Lydia's fury grew hotter. When the sound died away, she finally erupted.

"How dare you come here like this, into *my* home and order around *my* children as if they were your own." Her father's brows shot up, but she pressed on. "First you threatened to kill my children right outside their own home, and now you're trying to take away the only two I have left here. Do you want to drive me away?"

His surprise at her outburst faded quickly as his eyes darkened. "I'm making sure they don't become traitors too."

"You don't trust me to raise them?"

"This situation is beyond you. One day you'll be glad of this."

Lydia shook her head. "I'm not glad Kyrin and Kaden went. Not anymore. I'm not glad of the time it took away from us or the distance it created. And, in case you haven't noticed, my children who have, according to you, turned traitor are those

I've had the least amount of influence on. Seems to me you should examine yourself and the men you serve for why that is."

"This is ridiculous," her father growled.

"Is it?" A rush of tears pooled in Lydia's eyes. "The emperor has already stolen my husband—I will not let you steal my sons on his behalf."

Her father stiffened, a dangerous glint in his eyes. "You're emotional and distraught, so I'll overlook your words, but do not speak of the emperor in such a way again."

"Or what? You'll have me arrested for treason?" It was absurd, but then Lydia caught the pitiless hardening in his expression. "You would," she gasped. She stepped back with a hand to her throat, but her anger returned. "It's no wonder Marcus and Liam ran from you."

"This is exactly why I'm taking Michael and Ronan. They're in grave danger of following after their siblings, and you're in no frame of mind to prevent it."

The conversation ended as her father spun on his heel and stormed out of the room. Lydia sagged against the table. Tears rolled down her face, and her shoulders shuddered. In desperation, words gasped past her lips that she never imagined speaking.

"Elôm, help us."

Within half an hour, Michael and Ronny's belongings were packed onto two extra horses that waited with the General's men. Lydia stood with an aching heart as her sons said goodbye to Ethel and Carl. Michael kept a blank face, hardened by his anger, but poor Ronny couldn't hold back tears, especially when it came time to say goodbye to his mother. She gathered him into her arms and rocked gently as he buried his face in her shoulder. Her eyes burned, and she bit her lip at his quiet cries. She stroked his hair.

"It'll be all right," she forced through her clogged throat. "You'll be all right."

She held him for a long moment before parting and cupping his face in her hands. "Be strong. I love you." She kissed his forehead, and then turned to her older son. Now tears glimmered in his eyes. She grasped his shoulders. "Take care of your brother, all right?"

Michael nodded.

"I want you both to take care of each other." She pulled him into her arms, and they embraced tightly. No mother should have her children forcibly taken from her. She sent her father a hard look and then whispered in her son's ear, "I won't forget you two. I'll do everything in my power to get you back."

As they parted, Michael looked at her with wide, but hopeful, eyes. She nodded, cementing her promise. This wasn't over. She hadn't surrendered yet.

When it came time to leave, she helped them mount, and then turned to her father, her voice and heart cold. "All my life I've loved you, followed you, and chosen to ignore all the countless questionable things you've done, but this?" She shook her head. "After what you did to Liam, and how you've driven away four of my children only to come and steal away my last two . . . I don't think I can forgive you for this."

If he felt any remorse at all, he hid it behind his stubbornness. "I'm more concerned with Michael and Ronan's futures than your forgiveness."

With that, he mounted his horse, and the company moved out. Michael and Ronny looked back at her with longing that tore her apart, but strengthened her resolve. She'd overlooked her father's actions for the last time.

*"FOR MY THOUGHTS are not your thoughts, Nor are your ways My ways," declares the Lord. "For as the heavens are higher than earth, So are My ways higher than your ways and My thoughts higher than your thoughts."*

Kyrin sat back to contemplate these words. Never were they more true than in the situations they'd faced just recently. She glanced at Timothy, who sat across from her working on a new letter he planned to share with everyone. With Trask's cabin usually full, Timothy had asked to take advantage of the quietness of Lenae's cabin occasionally to study. He'd gladly accepted Kyrin's request to join him and read the verses he'd copied from the Scrolls, something that benefited all of them. With her abilities, she would have all the words permanently committed to memory, even if they somehow lost the copies.

He must have noticed she'd ceased reading and looked up. "Did you find something?"

"I was just considering these verses here." She slid the parchment around and pointed them out.

Timothy nodded as he scanned the words. "They're some of my favorites, especially when my father died."

"I was thinking about my father too." The ache she couldn't yet quell when she spoke of him overtook her chest and throat.

"I really believe now that it was, at least partly, for Marcus, but when I first received the news, I couldn't imagine why it had happened. There are still many other things I just don't understand."

"Neither do I," Timothy said, which offered Kyrin a surprising amount of comfort. "But some things I don't think we're meant to. Not here anyway. That's where trust comes in."

Kyrin shook her head. "How do you do it? How can you be so dedicated and faithful?"

Timothy ducked his chin self-consciously. "I'm not always." Kyrin had a hard time believing that, but didn't cut in. "But I try. It's how my father taught me. I don't remember a time when he didn't read to me from the Scrolls every night. I'm sure he started well before I was even old enough to understand it. He always used to tell Aaron and me that, as long as we have faith and Elôm's love, we're richer than any king. It didn't matter what else we had or didn't have. I've never forgotten that."

Kyrin gave him a sad smile in a shared sense of loss. "He sounds like he was a very wise man and good father."

"He was."

They both fell silent a moment, claimed by thoughts and memories. Kyrin understood how important Marcus's soul was, but she couldn't help but wonder why Elôm hadn't chosen a different way. And why had a righteous man like Timothy's father died in such a tragic, seemingly meaningless way as a mine accident? As Timothy said, these were probably questions they would never know the answer to until they joined their lost loved ones in Elôm's presence.

A knock startled them. Kyrin looked over her shoulder as Lenae opened the door. Kaden appeared first with his arm around another person. Kyrin's mouth fell open. "Mother!"

She jumped up from her seat as her mother and Kaden entered, followed by Marcus and Liam. "What happened?" She looked to the door Marcus had just closed. "Where are Michael and Ronny?"

Her mother grimaced and answered in a surprisingly bitter tone, "Your grandfather came and took them away to Tarvin Hall."

Kyrin stiffened. Memories rushed, unwelcome, into her mind of when the emperor's officials had come for her and Kaden—of the night they'd spent on the road on the way to Valcré. Kyrin had cried herself to sleep. Kaden had tried to tell her it would be all right, but she still saw the tears he shed when he thought she wasn't looking.

She pulled in a hard breath against the heaviness in her chest. "When?"

"Three days ago. I tried to stop him, but you know how impossible that is." Lydia's shoulders sagged, and she closed her eyes as she touched her forehead. Her face was white, except for her flushed cheeks and nose and the dark shadows under her eyes. She must have ridden all the way from Mernin on her own.

Kyrin took her gently by the arm. "You need to sit down."

She helped her mother slip out of her coat and then guided her to the table, where Lenae set a cup of coffee in front of her. Lydia wrapped her reddened fingers around it and took a long drink.

"Thank you," she breathed.

As Kyrin and her brothers crowded around the table, Marcus asked, "Why did the General take them?"

"He was afraid they'd follow after you four. He didn't trust me to prevent that." Lydia shook her head, her delicate face lined with remorse. "I should've let them come with you."

Kyrin raised her brows at the admission. She had never seen her mother like this. "Why did you come to us?"

Lydia lifted her tired, but determined eyes. "I want them back. You're the only ones who can help me."

Kyrin exchanged looks with her brothers. What their mother

was asking was tantamount to treason. Kyrin and her brothers had nothing more to lose, but their mother had everything. Yet, she was apparently willing to risk it all to get Michael and Ronny back. She'd changed. Kyrin didn't know how or when it had happened, but her mother was not the same woman she'd known as a child.

Kyrin looked at Kaden. "Go get Trask, Rayad, and Warin."

He nodded and hurried out of the cabin.

Once more, Kyrin focused on her mother. "If we get them out, Michael and Ronny won't be able to go back home."

"I know," Lydia said.

Kyrin watched her closely. She needed to make sure that, even in her distress, her mother truly understood what was at stake. "And Grandfather will, no doubt, suspect you came to us, especially if he knows you left Mernin . . . and you won't be able to go back, either."

With a slow nod and quiet voice, her mother repeated, "I know."

They stared at each other for a long moment. It was difficult for Kyrin to reconcile her memories with her mother's current actions. "So you're willing to stay here with us . . . as fugitives?"

"If it means getting Michael and Ronny back, and having you all safe and together, then yes."

Kyrin searched her eyes, but found no uncertainty. Regret that it had to be this way, yes, but not doubt. A love she hadn't felt in a long time rekindled in Kyrin's heart, demolishing the last traces of the walls she'd built, and the words she'd just discussed with Timothy echoed in her mind. Her eyes prickled, but she blinked it away as Kaden returned with their camp leaders. They all gathered at the table, where Kyrin and her brothers explained the situation.

"Can you help us get them out?" Kyrin asked Trask. For her, it wasn't a matter of *if* she and her brothers would do this, but a matter of whether or not they would have help. She wouldn't let Michael and Ronny be trapped at Tarvin Hall like she and Kaden had been.

"We'll do what we can," Trask replied willingly. "We'll have to contact Tane and Sam. Sam is the only one who can actually get them out. I'll send a rider to Valcré right away."

With memories of Tarvin Hall spinning around in Kyrin's mind, a new thought dropped in as if placed there. She latched onto it with a growing warmth and hope in her heart. "There's also a little girl at Tarvin Hall named Meredith. The emperor had her parents killed for worshiping Elôm. I'd like to try to get her out too."

"I'll include that in the message," Trask said.

Kyrin thanked him, and he left with Rayad and Warin.

In the following silence, Marcus shook his head. "So he just came and took them?"

Their mother nodded. "I tried everything. I begged him, I argued, I even threatened to never forgive him . . . he just wouldn't listen."

Marcus sighed and rubbed his forehead. "How was I so blind for so long?"

Kyrin touched his arm sympathetically, but it was their mother who said, "You weren't the only one."

When Lenae brought a plate of food to the table for Lydia, Kyrin welcomed the distraction. All this talk of her grandfather fed the ire building inside her, and if *she* was angry, Kaden was doubly so, but it wouldn't help them right now.

Leaving her brothers to talk with their mother, Kyrin rose and joined Lenae near the fireplace. So much was changing in her life that it made her head spin and threaten to bring on a headache. "After this, my mother will have to stay in camp, permanently. We'll need to provide her with someplace to stay. Lodging is getting a little cramped . . ."

"She'll stay here, of course," Lenae cut in.

"You don't mind?"

"Not at all. Besides, it hardly seems fair for you and me to have the whole cabin to ourselves when everyone else is sharing."

Kyrin agreed. "Good, I'll tell her."

She turned back to the table, but hesitated. Though Lenae was more than happy to welcome her mother into their home, for Kyrin, it held more complications. While she'd forgiven her mother, and deeply regretted her own feelings and behavior, the awkwardness between them would still take time to heal. Living in such close quarters might be a challenge for a while. After all, for the last few months, Lenae had been more of a mother to her than Lydia had ever been. Who would she turn to now for parental advice? Lenae was her first choice for her spiritual wisdom alone, but would that cause friction between the three of them? Kyrin grew tired just thinking of it. *Lord, please guide me and work this out.*

As she resumed her seat beside Kaden, her mother surprised her with a question. "How is Jace?"

"He's still in a lot of pain, though most wouldn't notice. But he is healing." After a week since the confrontation with the General, Jace's wounds were well on their way to closing up, thanks in part to his strong ryrik blood, but the pain in his ribs would still take more time to fade. Kyrin offered a grateful smile for her mother's concern. "Thank you for asking."

"You can sleep up here with me until we make better arrangements." Kyrin led her mother up to her small loft bedroom, setting her pack next to the dresser. "Maybe we can make a quick trip back home soon for more of your things."

She turned. It was a couple of hours after supper, and she'd sent her brothers off to their own quarters so their mother could get some rest. She'd slept very little on her cold journey from Mernin. Kyrin could still hardly believe she'd done it alone.

"You can have my bed." A pang passed through her middle at the modest offering, and she smoothed her fingers along her dress. Her mother had always lived in luxury, never wanting for anything. The General had seen to that. Their primitive camp living was nothing compared to it. After all, Lenae's entire cabin wasn't much larger than the dining room back home.

"Where will you sleep?" Her mother's question broke Kyrin from her misgivings.

"I'll just lay out some blankets on the floor."

Her mother's forehead scrunched. "No, I couldn't make you do that."

"Please," Kyrin insisted gently. "I really don't mind."

She pulled out her dresser drawers and rearranged her things to make room. "You can put what you can in here. Trask can probably get another dresser from the village."

"Thank you." Her mother gave her a timid smile as they switched places. They'd traded these types of smiles all evening—genuine, yet reserved. A barrier still existed between them. Kyrin wanted to do her part to eliminate it, but uncertainty held her back. She just couldn't find the right words.

In silence, she watched her mother unpack. She hadn't fit much into the one bag she'd brought with her. When she neared the bottom, her mother pulled out a shirt and stopped. Kyrin took in the faded blue material, and a chokehold gripped her throat.

"Is that Father's?"

Her mother looked at her. The candlelight shimmered in her moist eyes, and she nodded. "It was one of his favorites."

She held it out, and Kyrin took it, sinking her fingers into the worn linen. It was warm from sitting near the fireplace—almost as if he'd just taken it off. *Don't cry.* But to hold back was impossibly difficult. Images of her father flashed through her mind, and all her emotions boiled to the surface. Her eyes filled to the brim as she looked at her mother, and her lips trembled.

"I'm sorry. I'm sorry for how I treated you. I was wrong." Tears rolled down her cheeks. "I was scared and angry, but I'm so sorry. Forgive me?"

"Oh, Kyrin." Her mother's tears flowed freely as she reached out and embraced her. Still clutching the shirt, Kyrin wrapped her arms tightly around her mother. "Of course I do, but I'm the one who really needs forgiveness. I haven't been the mother I should have been. Can you forgive me?"

Kyrin nodded against her shoulder, her heart aching, yet lighter, freed from the burden she'd carried for so many years.

"Yes . . . I forgive you."

Times of waiting were some of Kyrin's greatest enemies. She couldn't stand the thought of her little brothers in Tarvin Hall. How were they coping? The terror of her first days there, especially when they'd tried to keep her and Kaden apart, lurked among her thoughts. And then there were the bullies. Were her brothers being ridiculed, as she and Kaden had been? Poor little Ronny would be a prime target, and with their father's death so recent, the tormenting could be agonizing. If only they could get them out, but fewer than twenty-four hours had passed since Trask's messenger had left.

To occupy her mind, Kyrin spent the morning helping her mother and Lenae rearrange the cabin. The men had already supplied an extra bed, which they placed in a corner opposite Lenae's. They also hung up a couple of long curtains for privacy. It wouldn't be what her mother was used to, but she seemed happy with the result.

After lunch, Jace and Liam came to the cabin for their daily checkup with Lenae. Kyrin helped by gathering her medical supplies and standing by, ready to hand her things. Lenae carefully removed the light layer of bandages to reveal their wounds, which had begun to scab over. Only a couple of the deepest ones looked to be in any danger of festering. Jace's bruising had yet to fade, however. If anything, the sickly purple and yellow bruises around his ribs looked even worse, but Lenae assured her they were mending.

Jace stayed for a short time to share a cup of coffee with her before leaving again. Suddenly lacking things to do, Kyrin grabbed her coat and stepped outside for some fresh air. Voices came from the far edge of camp, where Marcus had busied himself with training the new militia, and Kyrin wandered over that way. She hadn't been out long when Kaden joined her, obviously looking for something to occupy himself as well.

They stood in silence for a few moments until Kyrin asked, "Will you join the militia?"

"Probably not."

Kyrin looked up at him. "You don't want to be under Marcus's command?"

"It's not that, exactly." He shrugged. "You know me. I'm a fighter, but not a soldier. Besides, if it comes to it, I'd rather fight with Exsis and provide support for Marcus's men from the air."

Kyrin smiled. "You really were born to fly, weren't you?"

A confirming grin reached his lips.

She let out her breath in a slow, white puff. Quiet words followed. "Father always wanted to fly too."

"He did?"

She nodded. "He told me right before we rescued Aaron."

Now Kaden released a heavy breath. It would be a long while before talking of their father didn't hurt, but Kaden looked pleased to share this in common with him. At least parts of their father lived on through them.

Out of the corner of her eye, Kyrin caught movement. Surprise skipped through her. Two riders had just entered camp—the messenger Trask had sent to Valcré, as well as Tane. Word of their arrival traveled swiftly. In moments, Trask and the others left their cabin to meet them. Kyrin and Kaden glanced at each other, and hurried to join the group. Obviously, their messenger must have met the talcrin on the road, since he'd not had time to reach Valcré.

"Tane, what brings you here?" Trask asked as the two riders dismounted.

"There have been some developments in Valcré." Looking around at the group, Tane announced, "The Scrolls are still in Auréa."

Kyrin could almost feel the reaction that swept through them. Her own heart gave a longing flutter. They'd given so much to try to get the Scrolls. Could they possibly still have a chance?

"Daican hasn't destroyed them?" Trask asked incredulously.

"Not yet, which we can only attribute to Elôm's intervention."

"Is there any way we can get them?"

It seemed to be the one question on everyone's mind.

"That's the reason I'm here," Tane replied. "Sam can get to them, but he wants your help. After this, the emperor will know where his loyalties truly lie. Valcré won't be safe for either of us once he acts."

"What's the plan and how can we help?"

"As soon as Aric realized the Scrolls were still in the palace, he and Sam came up with a plan to get Daican to ask Sam to study the Scrolls for any weakness in our faith. They weren't sure he would fall for such a scheme, but he has. So Sam has access to the Scrolls. The tricky part is getting them out. He's not even sure if he can, but he's willing to try. If he's successful, he wants help protecting them and getting them out of the city."

It sounded like a dangerous and desperate plan. What if Sam was caught? Kyrin almost choked on the fear of losing someone else. But if Elôm had preserved the Scrolls, how could they not try to get them out of Daican's hands?

"How soon do we need to be there?" Trask wanted to know.

"As soon as possible. Sam can only keep up this pretense for so long before the emperor grows suspicious."

Trask nodded and glanced over the group. "Looks like we're headed back to Valcré."

"I NEVER THOUGHT I'd enter this city as a fugitive."

Kyrin glanced at Marcus before setting her gaze on the surrounding wall of Valcré. She'd never expected to enter the city again at all. When she left the first time, she'd rather that it would have been for good, but their missions were too important to shy away from it. Even so, her heart beat heavily as every instinct cried to flee the center of the emperor's sphere of influence.

At the last trees before reaching the wall, they stopped. Everyone from their original group, minus Falcor, had come together again to see this mission through. Even Talas insisted on coming, despite Darq's protests, but he assured them all he was perfectly fine and fully recovered. Kyrin wouldn't have gone so far as to say that. Even for a crete, two weeks seemed a bit short for full recovery, but Leetra had grudgingly given him the go-ahead to join them. While the cretes and Timothy had stayed on the mountain, the remainder of the group prepared to enter the city. Trask turned to face them, his gaze touching each person. "This is it. We'd better split up here. Elôm willing, we'll meet back up at camp tonight."

Kyrin tried to fight off the nausea churning in her stomach. If only they could stick together; however, their missions had to be tackled separately.

"All right then, best not linger."

Trask took the lead toward the city, and everyone but Kyrin, her brothers, and Jace followed. Rayad paused to look back. He spoke to Jace, though he included all of them. "Be careful."

"You too," Jace told him.

Rayad gave a quick nod and turned to catch up with the others.

Jace released a sigh, and Kyrin shared the anxiety in his expression. If anything went wrong, this could be the last time they saw their friends. The prayer of protection Timothy had prayed for them just before leaving camp echoed in her mind. She latched onto the words, repeating them in her heart.

Once Trask's group disappeared through a distant gate, Kyrin gathered up her resolve and turned to Jace and her brothers.

"Ready?"

They each nodded. Rescuing Michael, Ronny, and Meredith might not be quite as important as retrieving the Scrolls, but it mattered to her and her brothers. Kyrin's palms grew damp inside her gloves as she looked at the four of them. They'd always had someone like Trask or Rayad around to take charge, but this they had to do on their own, and Kyrin could only pray it would go as they had planned it. Tane had set up everything beforehand with Sam, but she was well aware that things didn't always go according to plan.

Some of her uncertainty faded when Marcus stepped up and took the lead. After all, he was used to being in charge in tense situations. It bolstered her confidence.

They turned east—the opposite direction of the others, so as not to use the same gate. Kyrin prayed that neither group would draw suspicion. Her group was the least likely to be noticed, since Marcus, Liam, and Kaden had all borrowed soldiers' uniforms from the supply stash back at camp. People weren't likely to question the emperor's soldiers.

She shivered against the wind. The bitter cold signaled the full onset of winter, extinguishing any hope of more warm days. She would be glad if they made it back to their campsite by nightfall. Even with the sun shining, the icy breeze snatched away any warmth.

When they reached one of the smaller gates and passed through, a tingle of both apprehension and interest crawled up Kyrin's arms and along her back. She glanced toward the palace overlooking the city. If Daican only knew she'd returned . . . She shivered again.

Marcus led them confidently through the busy streets that climbed gradually toward Tarvin Hall. Merchants, businessmen, and travelers crossed their path as they saw to their last errands of the day. Nothing had changed in the few months Kyrin had been away. She tried to keep her head down and avoid eye contact with anyone. In a city of over half a million inhabitants, it wasn't likely someone would recognize her or Kaden, but she didn't want to risk it.

A few blocks from Tarvin Hall, she stumbled to a halt when she caught a glimpse of the central square. Her heart gave a sluggish beat. It was the last place her father had been alive. Memories of her own experiences there rushed in—of the crowd chanting for her death. Had the same crowd watched her father die? She remembered standing in the crowd at the base of the execution platform, but instead of a ryrik standing at the block, her imagination put her father there. Tears choked off her airway, like the suffocating press of bodies all around her. But then a very real hand touched her back.

"Are you all right?"

She jerked her eyes away and looked up at Jace, her heart now beating frantically. The disturbing combination of memories and imaginings faded. She worked her throat but, in the end, only nodded. Pulling in an icy breath, she moved forward, and they hurried to catch up with her brothers, who hadn't noticed her distraction. But the heaviness of the moment still clung to her like a nightmare. She focused her eyes on the path ahead—the same path she, Kaden, Meredith, and Elise had taken that day shortly before everything in her life changed. Before she knew of Landale or the resistance. Before believers were publically executed for their faith.

In another few minutes, the five of them reached a corner just down the street from Tarvin Hall. To see it dredged up a wide range of emotions. She and Kaden had spent most of their lives there. Yes, there were some good memories, but not enough to outweigh the bad. After their initial look at it, she and Kaden kept out of sight around the corner, letting Marcus keep watch.

Kyrin looked up at the sky, but the sun had sunk too far to the west for her to see it. They shouldn't have to wait long. According to Tane, Sam had instructed the boys and Meredith to leave one hour before the evening meal. Kyrin closed her eyes and murmured a prayer for them. No doubt they were scared, especially poor little Meredith. Kyrin had been terrified when she and Kaden first discussed escaping. Would they be able to act in spite of it? *Michael will take care of them.* She felt confident of this. He had Kaden's fighting spirit. He would get them out.

Behind her, Jace took a deep breath. She looked over her shoulder to catch him holding his ribs, and then met his eyes.

"I'm all right," he said without her needing to ask.

As usual, she didn't quite know if she believed him. It was insane for him to be out in this condition. Liam shouldn't even be here. Oh, she and Rayad had tried every which way they could think of to get them to stay at camp, but Liam wouldn't hear of it, and Jace was even more immovable in his determination. He would be here, even if he hadn't had over a week to rest and recover. That was just Jace. She suspected part of it had to do with the promise he'd made to her father. There was no telling what he would do to keep it. He had already proven that at the crossroads. But if he ended up ripping open his wounds and getting an infection, she didn't know what she would do.

With another thing to pray about, she rested against the wall to speak to Elôm during the wait.

The minutes crept by, as if each one were ten times longer than normal. It was hard to keep track, and her stomach churned again. Had it been too long? Would they even make it out of Tarvin Hall? What if Master Zocar grew suspicious? Nothing seemed to escape him. Finally, Marcus made the announcement they all waited for.

"I see them."

Kyrin sucked in her breath. She wanted to see for herself, but waited for what more Marcus would say. Her heartbeats marked the seconds. She couldn't hold her breath any longer. "Are they coming?"

Marcus was slow to answer. "I'm not sure . . ."

Kyrin exchanged a worried look with Kaden. His fingers flexed near the hilt of his sword, a readiness for action growing in his eyes.

Though Kyrin couldn't see Marcus's face, tension wrung his voice. "I don't think the guard will let them out." He spun around. "Liam, come with me. The rest of you stay out of sight unless there's trouble."

He didn't leave an opening for discussion as he and Liam left the corner. Kaden made a move to follow them, but Kyrin reached out to stop him. Now was no time to question their brother's leadership. She stepped to the corner to peek around it, with Kaden right behind her. Just as Marcus had said, the guard at the entrance to Tarvin Hall appeared to have detained their younger brothers and Meredith. Marcus strode toward them, as if he knew exactly what he was doing, but did he actually have a plan? *Please let this work.*

When Marcus and Liam reached the guard, their voices drifted back to the corner, though they were indistinguishable. Kyrin prayed harder. A suspicious frown appeared on the guard's face. Whatever Marcus was saying, the man wasn't buying it.

"It's not going to work."

Her voice barely left her mouth before the guard reached for his sword. A warning jumped to her lips, but Marcus acted first with a solid punch that set the man staggering.

"Run!"

Michael, Ronny, and Meredith bolted into the street. With secrecy now blown, Kyrin jumped away from the corner. "Over here!"

They raced toward her, Marcus and Liam just behind. Distant voices shouted. Kyrin took her eyes from her brothers long enough to see the one guard in pursuit, but it wouldn't be long until every guard at Tarvin Hall was after them. And how much longer before word reached the emperor?

The moment they reached them, Kaden scooped up Meredith, whose huge eyes held the same terror that was trying to gain a foothold inside Kyrin.

"Go!" Marcus urged.

They all turned and ran down the street. Their footsteps pounded against the cold cobblestone, echoing on the buildings rising up on either side. People stopped and stared at them, no doubt quick to point the guards in the right direction.

At an intersection a couple of blocks from Tarvin Hall, Marcus called them to a halt. The guard who had followed was nowhere to be seen. They stood a moment to catch their breath, and Marcus nodded at Kyrin. "We need to get out of the city. You and Kaden know Valcré best. Lead the way."

Kyrin gave a quick nod, and they set off again. She didn't dare hope the guards had simply given up on them, but she did pray so. They turned left toward the mountains, and Kyrin fought to quiet the thundering of her pulse in her head to work out the best route to take. All they had to do was get out. Once they reached the forest at the base of the mountains, they would have the advantage. Thanks to Jace, she and Kaden were far better in the woods than the emperor's men, who were more used to city life.

A flash of gold scattered her thoughts. They all skidded to a halt as a group of soldiers poured into their path fifty yards ahead, shouting orders to catch them.

Kyrin spun around. "Go back!"

Racing back the way they had come, she led them into a narrow, winding alley with several offshoots. She took the second one to their right. The soldiers weren't far behind, but at least they'd lost sight of them. Using this confusing section of the city to their advantage, Kyrin guided them around in a large circle, managing to lose the soldiers.

Just when she thought she could breathe again, the sound of hooves rang out nearby. She froze. Jace grabbed her arm, and they all ducked behind two produce carts just before a mounted patrol clattered past. Tremors passed through Kyrin at the close call. They stayed down and looked at each other.

"Those patrols will be everywhere before long." Marcus's eyes fell on Kyrin. "Any ideas?"

She grimaced. "We can't keep running like this, especially not against horses." Her legs already burned. Even if they had a clear shot to the gate, they'd never make it all the way at a dead run with mounted soldiers behind them. She breathed a long breath, and the cold air stung her already-aching lungs. How did Jace even breathe? "What if we hide out somewhere until nightfall? We have a much better chance of sneaking out after dark."

Marcus agreed. "Do you know where we can hide?"

Kyrin looked over at Kaden. "What about the bell tower?"

He nodded. "We can keep a lookout there, and with all the other abandoned structures in the area, hopefully it wouldn't be the first place they look."

"Where is it?" Marcus asked.

Kaden gestured in the same direction the soldiers had gone. "Southwest of here, in the old section of the city."

"We'd better get moving before they cut us off."

Marcus peeked over the carts to make sure the way was clear, and then told Ronny on to climb on his back. With Kyrin and Kaden in the lead once more, they set out for the bell tower.

With much prayer and careful navigation, they reached their destination without any more narrow escapes. Checking behind them, they walked into the dim, musty interior of the old bell tower and looked around. Memories swelled inside Kyrin. This was where she and Kaden had made their decision to escape Valcré. Of course, everything had gone wrong after that, but things had worked out in the end.

"We should head up a ways, where no one can see us," Kaden suggested, "and set watch at the top."

They climbed the stone staircase that spiraled up the perimeter of the tower. It grew too dark to see just before they reached the top, until Kaden pushed open the heavy trapdoor to where the bell had once hung, and the evening sunlight filtered in.

"I'll stand watch," Marcus offered, and climbed through the door.

The others took seats on the stairs, still panting.

"Well, we managed one thing," Kaden said between breaths. "We created the perfect diversion for the others."

Kyrin shook her head. "Let's hope their mission, at least, goes according to plan." Racing around the city, pursued by soldiers, was not what she had anticipated when they'd left their campsite.

Her eyes shifted to Jace, who still stood with his shoulder braced against the wall as he held his left side. He couldn't conceal his pain this time. All the running must have been excruciating, but she said nothing. What point would there be now? If only they had some sort of painkiller with them. She still had some of her mother's, but she'd left it with her supplies. He would just have to endure until they made it out of the city. Hopefully, it wouldn't require any more running.

A light sniffle drew Kyrin's attention to the little girl huddled near her. She smiled widely when the girl's deep blue eyes met hers. "It's so good to see you again, Meredith. I missed you."

A little smile blossomed on the girl's face. "I missed you too. And Kaden. Nobody was very nice when you left." The smile faded and she stuck out her lower lip. "They all said you were traitors and should die."

Kyrin looked at her sadly. "I'm sorry they were mean to you."

The little girl nodded and balled her fists in her cloak.

"Are you cold?"

She nodded again.

"Here, come sit on my lap. We can keep each other warm."

Meredith settled in Kyrin's lap, nestling into her chest as Kyrin wrapped her cloak around her. The girl trembled, and Kyrin hugged her tightly. "Don't worry. You're safe now."

After a moment of quiet, Michael said, "Thanks for coming for us."

Kyrin smiled at him. "You can thank Mother. She's the one who came and told us what happened. She's waiting anxiously for us to get you back to Landale."

Ronny's eyes brightened. "So does this mean we get to stay with you?"

Kyrin grinned over his enthusiasm. "Yes, it does."

For a while, they talked of camp, and the evening passed slowly. Though the tower blocked the wind, the stones offered little in the way of warmth. The exertion and adrenaline kept them warm at first, but then the chill crept in. It started in Kyrin's toes and fingers, working its way deeper. Resting her chin on Meredith's head, she looked at the others. Marcus still stood watch, but her other four brothers huddled together for warmth. Jace, however, remained by himself. When he noticed her watching him, he reached up to untie his cloak and brought it over to her.

She shook her head in protest. "Jace, no. You need it."

"I'll be fine for a while." He draped it over her shoulders.

She peered at him, but couldn't tell if he was being gallant or if his half-ryrik blood did keep him warmer than the rest of them. "You tell me if you need it." Empty words. He never would. She would have to watch him closely.

However, the added layer did help, and she settled in to wait again for the sun to set.

Jace looked out across the city's rooftops, which were lit up in the golden orange glow of the sinking sun. Marcus stood opposite him, but neither one spoke. Jace's gaze strayed to the southwest and locked on the circular walls of the old arena. The back of his throat squeezed painfully. He'd killed a man there . . . in a fight to the death. He could still feel the grit of sand in his wounds and eyes and hear his opponent's last breath. Grimacing, he tore his eyes away, only to catch sight of the new arena under construction near the palace. It rose more than twice as high as the old one. A cold lump formed in his stomach as he imagined fighting there in front of so many thousands of spectators chanting for one fighter or another. He shook his head, forcing the images down deep into the area of his heart that held all his deepest fears.

A stiff breeze bit through his clothing, right into his bones, and he shivered. He was colder than he would ever admit, but he gave up on his fight against the elements and stepped back down inside the tower. Dusk was not far off now. Just a little while longer.

"See anything?" Kaden asked as he joined them.

Jace shook his head. "Nothing." Their part of the city was quiet.

He rested his shoulder against the wall and flexed his cold-numbed fingers. He could barely feel them anymore, and stuck his hands under his arms to warm them. If any soldiers did show up, he needed to be able to hold his sword.

"Jace."

Kyrin's stern voice startled him and drew his eyes to her deep frown.

"You're freezing." She reached up to pull his cloak from her shoulders, holding it out to him, but he didn't take it.

"I'll warm up as soon as we're moving again. It won't be long now."

"Long enough." A stubborn look settled on her face, like the day she'd so forcefully insisted he wasn't cursed. "There's no way I'll let you stand there and freeze while I'm sitting comfortably. Now, if you won't take it, at least come sit down so we can share it."

As much as he'd rather suffer and keep her comfortable, he wasn't able to refuse her. He breathed out a sigh and came to sit on the step beside her, moving carefully to protect his ribs. While he settled in, Kyrin looked down at Meredith.

"Can you sit with Jace for a while to help him warm up?"

Even in the dim light, the girl's stormy eyes glittered as they locked on him in interest, but not fear. She nodded slowly. Jace had never interacted with children since his own early childhood and didn't know how to respond to this. Before he could object, the girl rose from Kyrin's lap.

"Be very careful, though," Kyrin told her. "He hurt his ribs not too long ago."

The little girl moved slowly and gently to take a place on Jace's lap, cuddling against him. He sent an uncertain glance at Kyrin, who gave a smile of encouragement. She then stood to wrap one corner of his cloak around his shoulders before sitting and pulling the other around herself.

Settling in beside him, her shoulder pressed against his. His heart gave an irregular thump. It wasn't as if she hadn't touched him before, but her nearness had an odd effect on him. For the first time, he was acutely aware of how gentle and feminine she was. Well, maybe that wasn't quite true. Even in his pain, he had noticed it when she'd tended his wounds back in Mernin—her careful touch and tender ministrations. He could still feel her soft fingertips on his face, but he cleared his throat and banished the memory. Now was not the time to be thinking about such things.

He did suddenly feel much warmer, though it didn't seem to have anything to do with Meredith or the cloak. He glanced again at Kyrin. Bits of hair had fallen out of her cap and framed her reddened cheeks. Why did he only now realize how pretty she was? He pulled his eyes away. What was he doing? This was ridiculous. But . . . was it, really?

Darkness had begun to engulf the inside of the tower when Marcus joined them. Kyrin shifted to look at him over her shoulder.

"I think it's just about time to move," he said. "I'll go have a look around to make sure there's no one nearby."

Kaden pushed to his feet. "I'll go with you."

But Marcus stopped him. "One person is better. Not as suspicious, and easier to slip away if there's trouble."

Though Kaden frowned, he resisted arguing.

Marcus checked his weapons. "I'll be back in a few minutes."

"Careful," Kyrin told him.

Marcus nodded and descended the stairs. When his footsteps died away, Kaden walked up to the trapdoor. "I'm going to keep watch."

As he disappeared, Kyrin looked around at the others. "Let's make sure we're all ready to leave as soon as Marcus gets back."

They stood and stretched their legs. It was good to get the circulation moving through their cold limbs again. Kyrin returned Jace's cloak and made sure Meredith's was secure. Then they waited. Kyrin mentally ticked off the seconds. Soon it turned into minutes. A heavy silence built around them. When she estimated fifteen minutes had passed, she traded an anxious look with Jace.

Finally, Liam spoke. "He should've been back by now."

Kyrin hugged Meredith a little closer to her side. She had to believe Marcus was fine, but what would they do if he didn't come back? Before she had an answer to that, Kaden appeared at the door, his voice sharp in warning.

"Soldiers!"

SAM'S GAZE STRAYED to the door of the small palace study. No sound had come from the other side since the guard had changed about an hour ago. With no windows, it was difficult to tell how late it was, but he guessed the time drew near for their plan to take place. He breathed steadily. He must remain calm and ready for action. And drastic action it was. Though he had expected someday to have to leave Valcré, this was a bit more dramatic than he'd envisioned.

His gaze dropped back to the Scrolls spread out before him. Never in all his years had he been so blessed to read so much of Elôm's Word. And to find verses he'd never heard before! What an indescribable joy. If only Daican knew that, instead of weaknesses he could exploit, the Scrolls were filled with knowledge that would only empower the believers of Elôm. Sam clasped his hands in front of his face.

"Lord, help me get these words to them. Whatever happens to me, preserve Your Word to give strength to Your people."

The doorknob turned. His eyes popped open as Aric stepped in. It was time. Sam rose, and Aric crossed the room to meet him.

"Everything is in place." Aric glanced at the closed door. "Once you take care of the guard, your way should be clear until you reach the gate. If you get past them, I pray Trask and the others can get you and the Scrolls out of the city."

"You're sure you won't be suspected in this?"

"I highly doubt it if I'm unconscious during your escape." Aric pulled a cloth and small vial out of his pocket and handed them over to Sam. "Are you ready for this?"

"As ready as I can be." Sam quickly rolled up the Scrolls, placing each one in his satchel. He then pulled the cork from the vial. An acrid scent wafted into the air, and he avoided breathing too deeply as he soaked the cloth with the liquid. "My father has been trying for years to get me to return to Arda and run for senate, but here I'm about to drug Emperor Daican's head of security and make off with the King's Scrolls. Somehow I doubt that's the sort of thing my people would look for in a government representative."

Aric chuckled wryly.

Sam met his eyes. "So what about you? Are you ready?"

Aric gave a nod. "May I wake to find the emperor livid over your successful escape."

They grinned at each other, before becoming serious once more. If things went wrong, Sam would be in the dungeon awaiting execution when Aric came to. With this understanding passing between them, Sam placed the cloth over Aric's nose and mouth. A moment later, he grabbed the man under the arms as he went limp and eased him to the floor. There would be no going back now. Murmuring a prayer, Sam grabbed his satchel and tipped over a chair so it clattered loudly against the tile floor. He then dashed across the room and pressed himself against the wall beside the door. It opened.

"Sir?"

The guard stepped into the room. Sam moved toward him. The blond-haired man spun around, and Sam recognized Collin. With a dumbfounded, but determined, look, Collin reached for his sword. But Sam was faster and much stronger. He grabbed him and wrapped one arm around him while pressing the cloth to his face. Collin put up an admirable struggle, but quickly succumbed to the drug.

Now it was time to get out before anyone discovered the two unconscious men. Sam closed the door and strode through the dim halls as fast as he dared, keeping a watchful eye. He had a dagger hidden in his jerkin and, while very proficient with it, thanks to his brother, he wouldn't stand a chance against a group of armed guards.

The entrance drew nearer. *Let me not meet with any trouble, Lord.*

"Sam."

He froze at the voice that echoed from the hall to his right. His eyes fell on Prince Daniel, who jogged to catch up to him, and his stomach sank.

The prince slowed as he neared. "I was just coming to see if you wanted to join us for supper. I'd sure prefer your company to my father's or my sister's at the moment." He made a face.

Sam hesitated, seeking the best excuse. "I apologize, my lord, but I have an important meeting with some friends of mine."

He glanced up and down the hall. So far, it was still clear.

Daniel's shoulders sagged. "I see. Perhaps tomorrow then?"

"Perhaps." Regret pulsed in Sam's heart. He'd always sensed an opening with the prince, but had never found the opportunity to pursue it.

Daniel's brow creased as he stared at him. "Are you all right?" His gaze snagged on Sam's satchel. At first, it meant nothing, but slowly an understanding dawned in his expression. His amber eyes widened and rose again to meet Sam's. "That's not what I think it is, is it?"

Sam licked his lips and tried to swallow through his parched throat. "I can't lie to you, my lord."

Daniel's gaze darted around the area before settling on Sam with great intensity. "Go, quickly, before anyone knows."

Sam let out the breath that had remained trapped in his lungs. "Thank you, my lord."

"Just don't get caught," Daniel said in a sharp whisper.

Sam gave a single nod and hurried on his way. A murmured prayer rose to his lips. "Elôm, somehow make Yourself known to him. He's searching and needs You."

By the time Sam let himself out of the palace, his heart pumped hard. He was so close now, but the courtyard seemed to stretch for miles. Maintaining a steady pace, he approached the gate. In the last few yards, he hardly dared to breathe. When he saw the guards, he gave a nod of acknowledgement and kept walking. In that moment came the echo of the palace doors being flung open.

"Stop him!" a voice rang out.

Sam drew a sharp breath. Someone must have found Aric and Collin already—much sooner than he'd hoped.

The guards immediately jumped into action, but Sam dashed past them and through the gates, where he searched the dusky streets.

"Sam, here!"

His gaze fell on Tane, and he sprinted toward the waiting group. The commotion behind him grew—a signal that it wouldn't be long before Auréa's full security force was in pursuit.

Kyrin's heart leapt into her throat as Kaden rushed down and pulled out his sword.

"Where are they?" she asked.

"Heading this way." Kaden turned to her and motioned with his free hand. "Get up by the door. Make sure you stay quiet."

Kyrin gathered Meredith and her younger brothers, and they huddled up by the trapdoor while Kaden, Jace, and Liam faced the stairs with their weapons ready. For a long moment, Kyrin's pounding heartbeat drowned her ability to hear anything, but then the thud of footsteps drew near. Muffled voices drifted into the tower.

Meredith whimpered. "I'm scared."

"Shh," Kyrin whispered gently, and hugged her close. *Please don't let them come in here.*

They waited another minute or two. A glow of light came from just around the curve in the stairs, and Kyrin gasped. Someone was inside. No one moved, but her younger brothers' eyes rounded. Meredith buried her face in Kyrin's shoulder. *Elôm!*

The light increased and boots scraped against the steps. Any moment they would be found and it would be over. A shout echoed outside, and whoever was on the stairs paused. Kyrin held her breath. A long second later, he turned away and left without checking the rest of the tower.

The air gushed from Kyrin's lungs, and the men's tense forms relaxed. *Thank You, Elôm!* Outside, the soldiers moved off, and silence fell again. Kyrin rested her cheek against Meredith and focused on moderating her racing pulse. Tremors passed through her limbs. She hated this city.

The scrape of a second set of footsteps made her go rigid, and her heart almost stalled this time. Meredith released a squeak of fear, but it was Marcus who appeared around the corner. He breathed out loudly.

"Is everyone all right?"

"Yeah," Liam answered, sounding winded as he lowered his sword.

Marcus's eyes shifted back to Kyrin and their younger brothers as if to be sure. "I saw the soldiers leaving, but couldn't tell if they had anyone."

Kyrin worked to speak around her own gasping breaths. "What kept you?"

She couldn't see Marcus's face very well, but his expression sobered.

"The General is still here in the city."

A lightning-like streak of fear shot into Kyrin's core, sending a cold wave through her body. "You saw him?"

Marcus nodded.

"Did he see you?"

"He did, but I led him and his men to the north before doubling back."

"You're sure you lost him?" Kaden asked, his voice slightly raised.

"I'm sure. But we need to go. If they don't find any sign of me, they may return."

Kyrin pushed to her feet, ready to leave immediately. Her grandfather's doggedness terrified her. If anyone could find them, it would be him. She could just imagine him surrounded by a force of torch-bearing soldiers, ready to hunt them down and drag them to the emperor.

"There's a lot of activity northeast of here, toward the palace," Marcus said, "but it's pretty quiet to the south. Is there a gate near here going that way?"

Kyrin nodded. "We're pretty close to one."

"Then I say we get to it and get out. We can use the forest for cover to get back to camp."

Readily agreeing to this plan, Kyrin handed Meredith to Kaden. Cautiously, they left the tower, taking full advantage of the darkness to make their way stealthily toward the city wall. When they arrived at the small gate, they stopped in the shadows of the alley. The area appeared deserted, but torches bobbed up the street, still at a distance, but approaching fast.

"Go!" Marcus urged them, and they all ran through the gate, not slowing until they'd crossed the road and ditch to reach the trees on the other side. Only then did they stop to catch their breath, hunkering down in the underbrush to watch the gate. No shouts or pursuing footsteps broke the cold stillness of the night.

A couple of minutes later, the torches appeared at the gate and illuminated a handful of soldiers. The shriek and clank of metal pierced the night air as the heavy portcullis lowered to the ground, closing off the gate. Once it was secure, the soldiers moved on. Kyrin looked at her brothers. They'd made it out just in time.

Kyrin trudged up the mountain slope toward the beckoning glow of firelight. Her feet hurt, and the rest of her body felt weighted. Once she stopped moving, it wouldn't take long for the biting wind that froze her cheeks to suck the rest of the warmth from her body. Pressing on for the last few yards, she and the others entered the ring of firelight. The cretes and Timothy jumped up to meet them.

"You made it," Darq said.

"Barely." Kaden set Meredith down and stretched his arms.

The little girl immediately attached herself to Kyrin's skirt. Kyrin touched her shoulder and was about to tell her not to be scared, but it was the same moment she realized the other half of their group was missing. Her already aching muscles flushed with dread. "The others haven't returned yet?"

Darq shook his head. "You didn't see any sign of them?"

"No."

The crete glanced into the darkness beyond camp. "Maybe they're not far behind you."

Kaden turned to look the way they'd come as if contemplating going back. "If they didn't get out of the city yet, they'll be trapped."

Darq frowned. "What do you mean?"

"Soldiers were closing all the gates," Marcus said. "We just made it out. All the ones we passed on the way here were closed already."

"They're closing *all* the gates?"

"Looked that way."

"Even for you, it seems unlikely they'd go to the trouble of sealing off the city," Darq said. "It must be on account of the others. That's both good news and bad news. It means they initially made their escape but, like you said, now they're likely trapped inside."

Kyrin shivered hard. Everything was falling apart again. "What can we do?"

"We'll take the dragons and see if we can spot them and pick them up."

"We should hurry before they get caught." Kaden set off for Exsis, but Darq stopped him. Kaden's brows sunk low as he looked down on the captain. After all, it was the third time someone had stopped him from taking action today, and Kyrin thought for sure he'd argue, but the captain spoke first.

"You aren't going anywhere. For one, you won't be able to see in the dark, so you'll be of no help to anyone, and you also look like you need rest."

Kaden's jaw clenched, but he kept quiet and nodded. As the cretes saddled their dragons, Kyrin guided Meredith and her younger brothers to the fire. Just before they left, Kyrin hurried to Darq. "Captain, if they've been captured, the emperor could try to execute them right away at dawn. We can't let that happen." She swallowed. "Not again."

"We won't," Darq assured her solemnly.

A SUBTLE GOLDEN glow spread in the east with the breaking of dawn. Kyrin buckled Ivoris's saddle, and then blew on her icy fingers before tugging her gloves back on. A yawn tried to push its way to her lips. Sleeplessness weighed on her. All night she'd lain awake, staring at the stars or sitting near the fire as the cretes had come and gone from their searching with no success. It was as if their friends had disappeared. Either they'd found a place to hide from the searching soldiers or they were locked up in the emperor's dungeon. It was impossible to say. Soldiers still searched the city, but they could be after her and her brothers. She couldn't see her grandfather giving up the search for them after only a few hours.

Kyrin clung to the hope that their friends were safe, yet even if they had hidden somewhere, the night had been perilously cold. Frost coated the surrounding trees and stiffened the grass. This alone made it imperative that they find them. Now that it would soon be light, they could mount a full-scale search. Every dragon and rider would go out, while Marcus and Liam stayed behind to watch over the boys, Timothy, and Meredith.

As soon as Darq gave the word, they all flew out and glided soundlessly toward the city. Leetra and her dragon immediately headed toward the square. Darq had put her in charge of monitoring any activity there. The rest of them spread out to canvass the city. Darq and Glynn kept the riderless dragons following and ready for their riders to reclaim them.

Kyrin couldn't see much of the dark streets below, so she remained near Jace. He would spot something long before she would. Still, she strained her eyes for any sight of them as they skimmed the tops of the buildings.

"We don't know where they are, Lord, or what's happened to them," she murmured into the wind. "Please guide us to them."

She glanced ahead to where Leetra circled the square and then to the east. The first sliver of sun was just rising above the distant horizon. In another couple of minutes, it would spill its rays across the city and aid their search.

It did so in a dazzling display of gold and orange that glittered on the dragons. They couldn't be overlooked now. Soon the whole city would discover their presence, but it didn't matter. For once, Kyrin felt they were in control. The emperor couldn't stop them if he couldn't catch them.

She brought Ivoris in a small circle over the northeastern portion of the city and leaned over the dragon's shoulders to get a view of the streets that had not yet filled up with morning travelers. *Where are you?* Though a few people stood in the streets, looking up and pointing, none were their missing group members.

Reaching the wall, Kyrin straightened and turned to locate the others. Her eyes picked out movement on a nearby building. *Aaron!* He ran along the roof, waving his arms. How he'd gotten up there she could only guess, but joy burst through her. Elôm willing, the others were alive as well and Aaron would know where they were. Darq steered his dragon down to land on the same building, and Aaron scrambled up behind him. Before taking off again, Darq's dragon gave a loud call, and the captain beckoned everyone to follow.

They turned south. In only moments, Kyrin caught a glimpse of the sight she'd prayed for—all their friends gathered on the street below. A thrill raced through her, but just as swiftly turned into a knot in her stomach. Dozens of soldiers poured into the street from both sides to cut off any escape.

Leetra and Glynn's dragons each gave a shattering roar and dove straight down toward the men. Kyrin's mouth fell open. Would they even fit in such a narrow space? But both dragons and their riders were experts at treacherous navigation. Folding their wings just enough to fit, yet stay airborne, they glided over the street. The soldiers' orderly ranks dissolved into disarray as they scrambled to escape the dragons, which spewed out fire just behind them.

Two at a time, the riderless dragons dove down to pick up their riders. Kyrin's heart gave a leap as each one of her friends made it into the air, including Sam. They'd done it! They were safe.

The shattering echo of a war horn and thunderclap mixed into one blasted these thoughts right out of her head. Something with the force of a boulder slammed into her. Her vision flashed and darkened for an instant. But a jolt of panic cleared her head. She was in the air. Falling. Her saddle and Ivoris were gone with nothing between her and the ground. She didn't have time to think or even scream. She only knew for that brief moment that she was going to die.

The cobbled street raced up to meet her, and she squeezed her eyes shut. *Elôm!* Something latched around her midsection and jerked her upward. The bruising force drove the air from her lungs. A sharp point scraped into her skin. But instead of rushing closer, the ground shrank away. Kyrin struggled to expand her throbbing ribs and wrapped her hands around scales and claws. Coughing, she forced her head up and caught sight of the underside of Ivoris's neck.

Until that moment, all sounds had seemed muted, but horrific roars and shrieks broke in around her. She twisted to look over her shoulder. What little breath she'd managed died in her chest. Trailing right after her and her dragon was one of the most terrifying beasts she'd ever encountered. Pitch black and monstrous, its dark wings outspanned Ivoris's by almost double. Thick, ribbed horns curved down around its head toward its wide snout, and its beady eyes glinted as black as its scales.

The beast's mouth hung open, and heat shimmered around its powerful jaws and pointed teeth. It opened wider to reveal the glow of fire. A scream clawed up Kyrin's throat, and she covered her head as a heatwave blasted her. Ivoris shrieked, piercing Kyrin's ears with the volume. Kyrin's stomach jumped toward her throat as they lost altitude under a cascade of flames. *Please, Elôm, I don't want to die!* The buildings drew nearer as Ivoris flapped frantically.

Another deeper, guttural roar rang out as the fire behind them finally faded. They rose higher in the sky, and Kyrin looked back. One of the other dragons dove at the massive beast and sunk its teeth and claws into its scales. The other beast had a crete rider. But not only that, the attacking dragon was Exsis. Standing in his stirrups, Kaden dragged out his sword and leaned over to drive the blade into the black dragon's side. The animal gave a horrifying shriek. As Ivoris circled around, Kyrin caught sight of a second dragon speeding toward them. Falcor.

"Kaden!" she screamed as the crete dove straight toward him, but it was too late. She lost sight of her brother behind a fountain of fire.

"No!" Her heart almost died in anguish. She couldn't lose him!

She struggled to remember how to direct Ivoris and reach him, but the terror rushing through her body destroyed her ability to recall even the simplest command.

A moment later, Talas and Storm swooped in. As Falcor lifted higher into the air to take on his foe, Exsis broke away from the wounded black dragon. Kyrin let out a small cry. Kaden was still in the saddle. Part of his sleeve looked burnt away, but he was alive. *Thank You!*

Kyrin twisted in Ivoris's grip again in an attempt to locate the others. Five black dragons dotted the sky, including the one Kaden had wounded, and all bore crete riders. Then there was Falcor. He and Talas were locked in battle, their dragons diving, rolling, clawing, biting, and spewing fire. The very sight of it left Kyrin breathless. Her fear for Kaden shifted to Talas. Was he really up to such a challenge? The maneuvering it took for such combat looked like it should have thrown them both right out of their saddles. What if Talas wasn't as recovered as he claimed to be? It would give Falcor a huge advantage.

An enraged roar echoed from nearby. Leetra and her dragon streaked across the sky. She came across the top of Falcor and shredded part of his dragon's wing. The dragon faltered, struggling for stability. This was the turning point. With a blast of fire for distraction, Falcor dove past his attackers and retreated in the direction of Auréa Palace. Though Leetra pursued, she fell back when the black dragons followed Falcor's lead.

What had just happened? Kyrin's head swirled in an attempt to process the overload of emotions, and dangling from the claws of a dragon didn't help. The streets and buildings below her started to spin, and shadows narrowed her vision. She scrunched her eyes together and fought not to succumb to the tug of unconsciousness or her stomach's threat to heave.

When Ivoris started to descend, Kyrin forced her eyes open. The sight of camp sent a cool wash of relief through her tensed-up muscles, and Ivoris set her gently down on the edge. The moment her feet hit solid ground, she fell to her knees and dragged in one breath after another. Her arms shook as she swept her wind-whipped hair out of her face. Amidst a flurry of dragon wings and pounding feet, came the cries of, "Are you all right?"

She looked up. Marcus had reached her first, but more faces crowded into view—all tense with worry. Her brother helped her to her feet, and she caught her breath enough to say, "Yes, I'm all right."

Her ribs throbbed, and a fierce ache engulfed her shoulder but, as far as she could tell, she would live, which was better than she'd thought a few minutes ago. She sought Kaden in the crowd. The skin on his right arm was raw and blistered, but he appeared to be the only one with visible injury.

For a long moment, the whole group just stood staring at each other. Despite the pain and memories it had left her with, the last few minutes almost felt like a horrible dream to Kyrin. No matter how vividly flashes of the fight flitted through her mind, the shock of it left her wondering how it could possibly be real.

The others seemed to share her disbelief but, finally, Darq stepped up to take charge. "We need to gather our supplies and leave immediately."

They all jumped to action, spurred on by one thought: What if those black dragons regrouped and attacked again? Ice crystalized along Kyrin's spine. She rushed to her pack and stuffed her supplies into it. Grabbing it up with her bedroll, she carried it over to Ivoris. She paused at the sight of burnt scales along her dragon's back. Ivoris had taken the brunt of the black dragon's attack, saving Kyrin from severe, possibly life-threatening, burns. Twice her dragon had saved her life today. She set her supplies down and patted Ivoris on the shoulder. "Good girl. Thank you." *And thank You, Elôm.*

She lifted her pack again and attached it to her saddle, wincing at the pain that shot down her arm.

"You're sure you're all right?"

Jace's voice drew Kyrin around. The same half-sick look of concern as before strained his expression.

"You're bleeding," he said with a nod.

Kyrin frowned and looked down. Red tinged the edges of a rip in her coat. She pushed it aside. A little more stained her overdress. "I must have gotten scratched when Ivy caught me." She looked up. "I don't think it's that deep. I'll be all right."

His eyes held hers, a deep disturbance glowing in them as if he were reliving something. He must have seen what happened—seen her fall, and thought, as she did, that she would die.

"Really, Jace." She reached out and gave his arm a squeeze in assurance. "Don't worry."

He glanced down at her hand, and his chest rose as he drew in a deep breath and nodded. Kyrin managed an encouraging smile just for him, and he turned toward Gem. Her smile lingered, and his concern for her comforted and soothed her overwrought nerves. But the commotion of camp reminded her of their haste and the still-present danger.

Scanning the group, her eyes caught on Meredith. The little girl stood petrified. In all the rush, Kyrin hadn't considered how terrifying this must be for her. From camp, they would have had a clear view of what took place over Valcré. Kyrin hurried over and knelt in front of her. Keeping her voice light in spite of the way her heart still pattered, she asked, "Are you ready to go to your new home?"

Meredith shook her head and whimpered. "I don't want to fly."

Kyrin cupped her small, trembling shoulders. "Oh? Why is that?"

"What if the monsters get us?"

"Don't worry," Kyrin soothed, "they won't catch us. That's why we're leaving, so we're gone before they come back. Flying is fun. I promise. Come on, you get to ride with me."

She rose and offered Meredith her hand. The little girl stared at it for a long moment before slipping her own into it. Kyrin led her over to Ivoris.

"This is Ivy. She's really nice. She'll take good care of us while we're flying. First though, we have to get you bundled up. Flying can be cold."

She took a blanket from her bedroll and wrapped it snuggly around Meredith. She then paused to look her in the eyes. "I'm going to look after you, just like I did in Tarvin Hall, remember? I never let anything bad happen to you, did I?"

Meredith shook her head.

"Well, I won't now either."

Kyrin helped her climb up onto Ivoris and settled into the saddle with her, tucking the blanket in so Meredith would stay wrapped and warm. The rest of the group mounted. Following Darq's lead, they took to the sky, anxious to put miles between them and the disturbing creatures that now, apparently, inhabited Valcré.

Kyrin sagged with relief when they set down in a meadow that opened up in the forest around midday. By now, the mountains lay well behind them, along with the danger of a second attack. Her whole body ached, and burning pain radiated from her shoulder and ribs. She'd gone over the attack several times, but everything had happened so fast that, even for her, it was a blur. She was quite sure the black dragon had rammed her and Ivoris and thrown her from the saddle. Her right shoulder must have been the point of impact, which would explain the sharp pain.

A groan pressed up her throat as she swung her leg over the saddle.

"Are you all right?"

She gave Meredith a weary smile. "Yes, just a little sore."

In fact, despite her aches and pains, she was quite all right. Maybe now it was safe to believe they'd succeeded in their missions, though she didn't think she'd fully relax until they set down in camp. She wouldn't make the mistake of letting her guard down again.

But her smile widened. "Didn't I tell you flying was fun?"

A grin sparkled on Meredith's face, and Kyrin helped her down.

As the men worked to start a fire, so they could warm up while they ate their lunch, Leetra held up her medical bag. "Who's first?"

Kaden motioned to Kyrin, and Leetra turned to her. "We can work behind Ivoris."

They walked around the dragon to use her as a screen for privacy while Leetra examined Kyrin's injuries. A long cut across her ribs had bled a fair amount but, like she'd told Jace, it wasn't that deep. At least it wouldn't need stitches. Still, it stung like fire when Leetra applied a clear ointment, and she sucked in her breath through her teeth. Though the force of Ivoris catching her had not broken any ribs, she had an even deeper sympathy for Jace now, as it did hurt some to breathe.

After wrapping a bandage around the cut and concluding the examination, Leetra reported, "You have some bruising around your ribs, and your shoulder will soon turn black and blue, but that seems to be the extent of it. Aside from hurting for a few days and being pretty stiff tomorrow, you should heal quickly."

"Thanks," Kyrin said through clenched teeth. By now, they were nearly chattering in the cold.

She tugged on her clothes as Leetra gathered her supplies and hurried back to the fire, where her younger brothers talked animatedly about the fight as if it were something from an adventure story. If only it was, but she was just thankful they'd all survived it. Those beasts could have easily killed any of them.

Her thoughts drew her gaze to Kaden as Leetra cleaned his burned arm. He groaned when she applied the same stinging ointment she'd used on Kyrin. Leetra raised a brow at him, and he sent her a peevish look.

Hoping to distract him from the pain, Kyrin said, "Thank you for rescuing me from that black dragon." Had he not intervened, Ivoris might have been burned so badly that they both would have fallen from the sky.

Kaden shrugged. "What else could I do? He was about to roast you two. I wasn't going to let that happen."

Kyrin eyed him seriously. "You nearly got yourself roasted."

He just shrugged again.

"That was some pretty impressive maneuvering you did, considering you were never trained in combat flight," Talas told him. "You're sure you're not part crete?"

Kaden chuckled. "I'd be the tallest crete to ever live, so I doubt it."

Laughter bubbled around the fire, and Kyrin soaked it in. When was the last time they had all laughed?

"Seriously, though," Talas continued. "You have the flight instincts of a crete. It's impressive."

"Just doing what I had to do."

Kyrin smiled at her brother. That summed him up perfectly.

The moment Leetra finished bandaging his shoulder, he pulled his charred coat back on, as if to avoid any more of her painful medical assistance and looked at Sam. "What happened to you guys last night?"

"Well, everything was going according to plan. I left Aric and Collin unconscious in the study and didn't expect them to be found for a while, but one of the servants must have come across them. I was barely to the gate when one of the guards sounded the alarm." He shook his head. "They were right behind us for a good while. When we finally lost them and reached the gate, we found it closed."

"We made it out just before they started closing them," Kyrin said. "We were worried, especially when it started getting so cold."

"It was cold all right," Rayad replied, moving a little closer to the fire.

"What did you do?"

"We found shelter in an empty shed behind someone's house. It wasn't pleasant, but we managed," Sam told them. "We knew you'd be looking for us so, once dawn broke, we tried to get somewhere you'd see us. That's when the soldiers found us. Aaron climbed up one of the buildings to get your attention." He looked over at the half-crete. "I've never seen anything like that."

Aaron smiled and shrugged. "I've had a good bit of practice."

They sat quiet for a moment, thinking back, until Trask asked, "So what were those dragon things?"

All eyes went to Darq. The crete captain straightened. "I don't know."

A chill crept up Kyrin's arms, despite the fire. The unknown just made the creatures all that much more disturbing.

"They weren't dragons; that's for sure," Talas said, and Leetra added, "Or cave drakes. They can't fly that well or breathe fire."

Darq nodded thoughtfully. "They looked like a cross between the two."

Talas shook his head. "But that's not possible . . . is it?"

"You wouldn't think so, but if there's a way, you can bet the emperor's found it."

Rayad cast a glance in the direction of Valcré. "I wonder how many he has?"

"It could just be those few." Darq grimaced. "Or he could have a lot more somewhere else."

They fell silent again. If Daican possessed such a powerful force, how could they stand against him? And what if he used the beasts to find their camp? Kyrin rubbed her arms and looked at Trask, but no doubt he had already thought of this. She thought back to the attack and remembered something equally disturbing.

"I don't know if anyone else noticed, but these other dragons had crete riders."

Very slowly, Darq nodded, his expression grim. "I noticed. More traitors like Falcor. We'll have to look into this once we return to Dorland. There could be spies there right now and we'd never know it."

The cretes all grew very solemn at this prospect.

But then, Sam rose, and all eyes lifted. "There's much we have to figure out in the coming days, but let's not forget it's also a time for us to rejoice."

He pulled a satchel from his shoulder, and everyone's faces lit up.

"In this bag are all seven of the King's Scrolls."

Grins broke out, erasing, for a time, the somber mood that had fallen.

Sam turned to the young man near him. "You must be Timothy."

He rose with a wide smile. "I am."

"I'm very pleased to meet you, and even more pleased to give you these." Sam placed the satchel into Timothy's waiting hands, and a fulfilling satisfaction came to rest in Kyrin's chest at the completion of the mission they'd endured and sacrificed so much to accomplish.

A LIGHT JOSTLING nudged Kyrin from her slumber. Her eyes squinted open. The loft was well lit from the windows below, where her mother and Lenae talked quietly. The sound lulled her, and she closed her eyes until the jostling came again. A small warm body snuggled against her back. Kyrin's lips parted in a smile. She would never have a little sister, but Meredith was close enough. With a deep sigh, she let a light sleep reclaim her.

Not too much later she woke again, this time to a sudden commotion and enthusiastic male voices as they came tromping into the cabin.

"Shh!" It was her mother quickly rushing to quiet them. "Kyrin and Meredith are still asleep."

A moment of awkward silence followed, and Kyrin giggled to herself. Typical boys. But it was too late. Meredith wiggled around beside her and sat up. Kyrin rolled over to see her long, tousled tresses and blinking eyes.

"Good morning, sleepyhead."

Meredith grinned at her, but it was different from the smiles she used to give in Tarvin Hall. Behind those was a sad, scared little girl who had seen too much and deeply missed her parents and home. This grin was nothing but sparkling happiness, and it fueled Kyrin's own joy.

Reaching out, she parted the curtains enough to look down at her brothers, who were trying, not so successfully, to quietly find seats at the table. With a chuckle in her voice, she told them, "It's all right. We're up."

She was sure they all sighed in relief and immediately resumed chatting, as when they'd walked in. Shaking her head and laughing, she crawled out of bed, though her sore and stiff muscles slowed her down.

"Are you hungry?" she asked Meredith.

The little girl gave a hearty nod.

"Which dress do you want to wear today?"

They had managed to borrow a couple of outfits from the other girls in camp, and Meredith chose a warm purple dress.

"Good choice." It would look much lovelier on her than the stark gold and black uniform of Tarvin Hall. Kyrin already had new ideas for dresses she could practice her sewing on. A girl like Meredith deserved to feel pretty.

As soon as they were dressed, they joined the boys at the table. It really wasn't big enough for all of them, but they made room. Lydia helped Lenae set food before them, and then joined her children. It had been quite a while since the cabin had been so full of excited chatter. Between eating and tale-telling, Michael and Ronny barely paused for a breath. They'd already informed their mother of most of the events in Valcré, but they hadn't gone into great detail the evening before. Not like they could now. Most amusing to Kyrin was that her older brothers were nearly as animated as the younger.

Their poor mother. The boys took great pleasure in recounting their harrowing escape from the city, completely missing her pursed lips and blanched expression. But she let them tell their story and revel in the adventure of it. After all, it was probably the most thrilling thing Michael and Ronny had ever experienced.

Catching her mother's eye, Kyrin gave her an understanding smile. What mattered now was that they were safe.

Near the end of the meal, Kyrin left the table and walked over to Lenae, who worked on the dishes. Kyrin picked up a towel and a plate to dry. "There's something I wanted to talk to you about."

Lenae looked over, her eyes inviting the discussion.

"I was thinking about when we first met. You said you'd always wanted a daughter." Kyrin glanced over at the table. "I was wondering, since Meredith is an orphan, if you might consider adopting her."

Lenae's hands stilled in the wash water, and Kyrin was quite sure her eyes glittered with moisture. "Truly?"

"Yes. You've taken such good care of me and taught me so much. You're a wonderful mother. I think you'd be perfect for her. She's been through a lot."

"Oh, Kyrin," Lenae breathed, wiping her hands on her apron. "It would be a blessing beyond words to raise her as my daughter. My heart just melted at the first sight of her."

Kyrin smiled widely. "Seems meant to be."

"I wonder what this meeting is about."

Kyrin nodded in agreement with Kaden on their way to Trask's cabin. Jace had come to get the two of them, saying Trask wanted to see the group, but he didn't have any more information than they did.

Almost four weeks ago, Kyrin had sat in Trask's cabin and volunteered to join the rescue group heading for the Graylin Valley. She never could have imagined what would take place in those short weeks, and she wasn't the same person walking into

Trask's cabin now. Too much had happened not to leave permanent scars, on everyone, but with it came growth as well.

Inside the cabin, they found the rest of the group already gathered. She smiled at them. After what they'd faced together, she would always be connected to them, more so than others. They'd been there when part of her life had been ripped away—had seen her at her lowest.

She, Kaden, and Jace took the seats saved for them at the table, and all fell quiet as Darq stood to speak.

"I asked Trask to gather you here because I want to thank you for all you've done. Nothing turned out as any of us expected, and we couldn't have succeeded without your aid. The reason I'm telling you this now is because I've talked to Glynn, and to Timothy and Aaron. We'll be leaving for Dorland in the morning. We have much information to take back with us, and I want to look into the situation with the crete traitors as soon as possible. Talas and Leetra, however, have requested to remain here, if you have no objections."

Kyrin wasn't the only one in the room to look at the cretes, particularly Leetra, in surprise. Had Kyrin been asked, she would have guessed Leetra would be anxious to return to her people as soon as possible.

"After what happened with Falcor and the others, we feel it's only right to stay and help you with whatever comes of it," Talas explained.

"If that's what you wish, you're more than welcome here," Trask told him, and others nodded their agreement.

Leetra might be difficult to get along with at times, but Kyrin looked forward to having Talas, with his upbeat presence, remain in camp. Kaden looked especially pleased by this. Kyrin could see a fast friendship forming between the two of them.

"They can also help you train more dragon riders," Darq said. "I plan to see about having more dragons delivered to you. Now that the emperor has Falcor and his drakes, you'll need a larger airborne force to combat them, should they come looking for you."

"That's very generous," Trask replied. "It would certainly help us feel more secure."

"I have no doubt my people will supply them, once I've explained the situation. And, should you ever need to come to Dorland for any reason, I want you each to have one of these." Darq pulled a leather pouch from his jerkin and emptied the contents on the table. Small, carved pendants of a hawk spilled out, each attached to a braided cord Kyrin couldn't even guess how one might duplicate. They passed them around the table.

"These pendants identify you as trusted friends of the Hawk Clan and, therefore, friends of all cretes. We rarely give them away. They afford you trust that is not easily gained. Guard them well."

Each person nodded solemnly. Kyrin ran her fingers over the smooth hawk figure, and then slipped the cord over her neck, nestling it down next to her father's necklace.

The group gathered once more, early the next morning, this time to say goodbye. Kyrin would be very sad to see them go, especially Timothy and Aaron. She would've liked to have more time to get to know them and learn more from Timothy. She would miss the couple of times they had been able to study together.

He came to her specifically, just after packing his things on Darq's dragon. "I wanted to give you these before we left."

Kyrin looked down to see the parchments covered with the verses he'd written down, and her heart skipped.

"I added as much as I could to them last night. I thought you'd like to finish reading through them and share them with everyone else, especially your family."

Kyrin took the precious copies and held them to her chest. "Thank you so much." She gave him a small smile. "I do wish you were staying so you could teach us."

He smiled in return. "Aaron and I will be back, probably before spring."

"Really?"

He nodded. "We want to get to know our grandfather and the crete culture, but we both feel this is where we're supposed to be and where we're needed."

"Well, I'm glad to hear it. I think you bring a lot to camp." She'd never met anyone who so deeply inspired her faith, and she had a feeling they would all need such influence in the future.

Timothy looked down shyly before raising his eyes again. "I was thinking on what we said about you having those verses memorized when you read them. Maybe, when I return, you might want to help me with copying the Scrolls. It would be incredible for you to memorize them all."

Her heart reacted again at the thought of knowing every word in the Scrolls—what an incredible blessing it would be. "I would be honored to help."

"Good. I'm sure there will be much work to do when I get back." Slowly, the smile on his face faded to a more serious and thoughtful look. "Also, I wanted to say what your father did to help us won't be forgotten. He may not have succeeded in getting the Scrolls himself, but it's because of him that we have them now. I'll always be grateful for what he was willing to do."

Moisture welled in Kyrin's eyes from the ache building in her chest. She swallowed the hard lump in her throat and nodded. "Thank you. It's good to know he'll be remembered as a hero, despite the emperor's claims."

"No one can take that away from him."

Kyrin smiled, despite the sting of tears. It was true. No one could ever take away what he'd done. Not while she, her brothers, and her friends lived to tell the truth.

In another few minutes, they concluded their goodbyes as Darq, Glynn, Timothy, and Aaron mounted their dragons.

"Elôm willing, we'll see you soon," Darq said. "Goodbye, my friends. May the King protect you."

With waves and called farewells, those on the ground watched the dragons take off. Once they were out of sight, Kyrin turned and took in the view. Her mother and brothers stood in a group, looking more content than she had ever seen them. A little to the side, Lenae stood, holding Meredith's hand. The little girl had bonded immediately with the woman the moment she learned Lenae would be her adoptive mother. Kyrin was right. They would be perfect together.

Her gaze sought the rest of her friends and met Jace's where they held for a moment. A smile reached his face. Not a wide one, but something about it—she wasn't sure what—sent a warm happiness deep into her heart. She smiled back, the warmth spreading through her. Everyone she loved was right here. As if to signify the blessed moment, beautiful, feathery snowflakes began falling around them to create a scene that almost took her breath away.

Walking into the midst of her waiting family, Kyrin's eyes settled on her mother. "Well, what do you think of your new home?"

She looked around, taking in the sight Kyrin had just witnessed. Then, putting her arm around her daughter, she said, "I think it's perfect."

# Characters and Information

# Returning Characters

**Aertus** (AYR - tuhs)—Arcacia's male moon god.
**Altair** (AL - tayr)—Kyrin's family name.
**Anne**—The daughter of Sir John Wyland.
**Aric** (AHR - ick)—Emperor Daican's head of security.
**Collin**—A young security guard at Auréa Palace who used to have an interest in Kyrin.
**Daican** (DYE - can)—The emperor of Arcacia.
**Daniel**—Daican's son, the prince of Arcacia.
**Davira** (Duh - VEER - uh)—Daican's daughter, the princess of Arcacia.
**Elôm** (EE - lohm)—The one true God of Ilyon.
**Goler**—An Arcacian army captain and bitter rival of Trask.
**Grey**—The baron of Landale.
**Holden** (HOHL - den)—A former informant for Daican but now part of the resistance.
**Jace**—A half-ryrik former slave and gladiator.
**John Wyland**—A retired knight.
**Kaden** (KAY - den)—Kyrin's twin brother.
**Kyrin** (KYE - rin)—A young Arcacian woman with the ability to remember everything.
**Lenae** (LEH - nay)—A widowed Landale woman.
**Liam**—Kyrin's older brother and an Arcacian soldier.
**Marcus Altair**—Kyrin's eldest brother and an Arcacian army captain.
**Marcus Veshiron** (Veh - SHEER - on)—Kyrin's grandfather and an Arcacian general.

**Meredith**—A young girl from Tarvin Hall. Like a little sister to Kyrin.
**Mick**—A resistance member from a wealthy mining family.
**Rayad** (RAY - ad)—One of Jace's close friends and mentor.
**Richard Blaine**—A knight and old family friend of Daican.
**Sam "Endathlorsam"**—A talcrin man and Tarvin Hall's wisest scholar.
**Solora** (Soh - LOHR - uh)—Daican's wife, the queen of Arcacia.
**Tane "Imhonriltane"**—Sam's nephew.
**Trask**—Resistance leader and son of Baron Grey.
**Trev**—A former member of Daican's security force. Now part of the resistance.
**Tyra**—Jace's black wolf.
**Vilai** (VI - lye)—Arcacia's female moon god.
**Warin** (WOHR - in)—An Arcacian man active in the resistance against the emperor. Lifelong friend of Rayad.
**William**—Kyrin's father and an Arcacian army captain.
**Zocar** (ZOH - cahr)—The head master of Tarvin Hall.

# NEW CHARACTERS

**Aaron**—A half-crete miner from Dunlow. Timothy's older brother.
**Carl**—The Altair's groundskeeper. Ethel's husband.
**Ethel**—The Altair's housekeeper. Carl's wife.
**Falcor Tarn**—A crete from Dorland. Leetra's fiancé.
**Glynn** (GLIN)—A crete from Dorland. Captain Darq's lieutenant.
**Harold**—Timothy's employer.
**Josan Silvar** (JOH - san SIL - vahr)—A crete from Dorland who left to learn more about Elôm.
**Leetra Almere** (LEE - truh AL - meer)—A female crete from Dorland. Falcor's fiancée and Talas's cousin.
**Lydia**—Kyrin's mother and the General's daughter.
**Michael**—Kyrin's younger brother.
**Parker**—Marcus's lieutenant.
**Ronan "Ronny"**—Kyrin's youngest brother.
**Scerle** (SCERL)—An Arcacian soldier and interrogator under Marcus's command.
**Talas Folkan** (TAL - as FAHL - kan)—A friendly crete from Dorland. Leetra's cousin.
**Timothy**—A half-crete young man from Dunlow. Aaron's younger brother.
**Verus Darq** (VAYR - uhs DARK)—A crete captain from Dorland.

# Dragons

**Brayle** (BRAYL)—Holden's dragon.
**Exsis** (EX - sis)—Kaden's dragon.
**Gem**—Jace's dragon.
**Ivoris "Ivy"** (EYE - vohr - is)—Kyrin's dragon.
**Shalmar** (SHAL - mahr)—Warin's dragon.
**Storm**—Talas's dragon.

# LOCATIONS

**Arcacia** (Ahr - CAY - shee - uh)—The largest country of the Ilyon mainland.
**Arda**—An island country off the coast of Arcacia. Inhabited by talcrins.
**Ardaluin Bay** (Ahr - DUH - luin)—The large bay off of Arcacia's western shore.
**Auréa** (Awr - RAY - uh)—Daican's palace in Valcré.
**Dorland**—Ilyon's easternmost country. Inhabited by cretes and giants.
**Dunlow**—A large mining town in the southern end of the Graylin Valley.
**Fort Rivor** (RYE - vohr)—Arcacia's largest military fort located southeast of Valcré.
**Graylin Valley**—A vast valley north of Valcré filled with mining towns.
**Ilyon** (IL - yahn)—The known world.
**Keth**—A tiny mining settlement in the southern end of the Graylin Valley.
**Landale**—A prosperous province in Arcacia ruled over by Baron Grey.
**Mernin**—A town just east of Fort Rivor. Kyrin's birthplace.
**Sidian Ocean** (SYE - dee - an)—The body of water surrounding Ilyon.
**Tarvin Hall**—An academy set up to train children for the emperor's service.
**Valcré** (VAL - cray)—Arcacia's capital city.

# Race Profiles

# Ryriks

**Homeland:** Wildmor

**Physical Appearance:** Ryriks tend to be large-bodied, muscular, and very athletic. They average between six, to six and a half feet tall. They have thick black hair that is usually worn long. All have aqua-blue colored eyes that appear almost luminescent, especially during intense or emotional situations. Their ears are pointed, which makes them very distinct from the other races. They have strong, striking features, though they can pass as humans by letting their hair hide their ears and avoiding eye contact. Ryriks typically dress in rough, sturdy clothing—whatever they find by stealing.

**Physical Characteristics:** Ryriks are a very hardy race and incredibly resistant to physical abuse and sickness; however, they have one great weakness. Their lungs are highly sensitive to harsh air conditions, pollutants, and respiratory illness. Under these conditions, their lungs bleed. Short exposure causes great discomfort, but is not life-threatening. More severe, prolonged exposure, however, could cause their lungs to fill with blood and suffocate them. It is said to be a curse from choosing to follow the path of evil. Ryriks' eyes are very sensitive, able to pick out the slightest movement, and they can see well in the dark. Both their sense of hearing and smell are very keen—much higher than that of humans. In times of great distress or anger, ryriks can react with devastating bursts of speed and strength.

**Race Characteristics:** Ryriks are the center of fireside tales all across Ilyon. They are seen as a savage people, very fierce and cunning. To other races, they seem to have almost animal-like instincts; therefore, it is commonly believed they don't have souls. They are a hot-blooded people and quick to action, especially when roused. They have quick tempers and are easily driven to blind rage. They prefer decisive action over conversation. Most have a barbaric thirst for bloodshed and inflicting pain. They view fear and pain as weaknesses and like to see them in others. They are typically forest dwellers and feel most comfortable in cover they can use to their advantage.

**SKILLS:** Ryriks are highly skilled in the woods and living off the land. They are excellent hunters and especially proficient in setting ambushes. They're experts in taming and raising almost any type of animal. They make the fiercest of any warriors. A ryrik's favorite weapons are a heavy broadsword and a large dagger. Ryriks aren't masters of any type of craft or art. Most of their possessions come from stealing. What they can't gain by thieving, they make for themselves, but not anything of quality. They think art, music, or any such thing to be frivolous. Most ryriks can't read or write and have no desire to.

**SOCIAL:** Ryriks are not a very social race. Settlements are scattered and usually small. They have no major cities. Families often live on small farms in the forest and consist of no more than four to six people. Children are typically on their own by the time they are sixteen or seventeen—even younger for some males. Ryriks have a poor view of women. They see them as a necessity and more of a possession than a partner. Once claimed, a ryrik woman almost never leaves her home. She is required to care for the farm while the men are away. Most ryrik men group together in raiding parties, pillaging and destroying unprotected villages and preying on unsuspecting travelers. Ryriks have an intense hatred of other races, particularly humans.

**GOVERNMENT:** Ryriks have no acting government. Raiding parties and settlements are dictated by the strongest or fiercest ryrik, so the position can be challenged by anyone and changes often.

**PREFERRED OCCUPATIONS:** The vast majority of ryriks are thieves. A few hold positions as blacksmiths and other necessary professions.

**FAITH:** Ryriks disdain religion of any kind. They were the first to rebel against King Elôm and led others to do so as well.

# TALCRINS

**HOMELAND:** Arda

**PHYSICAL APPEARANCE:** Talcrins are a tall, powerful people. Talcrin men are seldom less than six feet tall. They have rich, dark skin and black hair of various lengths and styles. Their most unique feature besides their dark skin is their metallic-looking eyes. They have a very regal, graceful appearance. Men often dress in long, expertly crafted jerkins, while women wear simple but elegant flowing gowns of rich colors, particularly deep purple.

**RACE CHARACTERISTICS:** Talcrins are considered the wisest of all Ilyon's peoples. Some of their greatest pleasures are learning and teaching. Reading is one of their favorite pastimes. They have excellent memories and intellects. Talcrins are a calm people, adept at hiding and controlling strong emotion. They are peace-loving and prefer to solve problems with diplomacy, but if all else fails, they can fight fiercely. They have a deep sense of morality, justice, loyalty, and above all, honesty. They are an astute people and don't miss much, particularly when it comes to others. Besides learning, they are also fond of art and music. Most talcrins are city dwellers, preferring large cities where libraries and universities can be found. Of all the races, they live the longest and reach ages of one hundred fifty, though many live even longer. Because of this, they age slower than the other races. Talcrin names are known to be very long, though they use shortened versions outside of Arda.

**SKILLS:** Talcrins excel in everything pertaining to books, languages, legal matters, and history, and are excellent at passing on their wisdom. They are often sought as advisors for their ability to easily think through situations and assess different outcomes. They are master storytellers and delight in entertaining people in this way. Though they strive for peace, most talcrin men train as warriors when they are young. They make incredible fighters who are highly skilled with long swords, high-power longbows, and spears. When not reading, many talcrin women enjoy painting and weaving. Their tapestries are among the most sought after. Both men and women enjoy music and dancing. They are expert harpists. Beautiful two-person dances are very popular in talcrin culture and are considered an art form. Metal-working is another skill in which talcrins are considered experts. Their gold and silver jewelry and armor are some of the finest in Ilyon.

**SOCIAL:** Talcrins are a family-oriented people and fiercely loyal to both family and friends alike. Families are average in size, with between three to seven children. Men are very protective of their families and believe their well-being is of utmost importance. Their island country of Arda is almost exclusively populated with talcrins. Scholars from the Ilyon mainland often come to visit their famous libraries, but other races rarely settle there. Many talcrins inhabit the mainland as well, but are widely scattered. The highest population is found in Valcré, the capital of Arcacia. They get along well with all races, except for ryriks. Though generally kindhearted, they can hold themselves at a distance and consider others ignorant.

**GOVERNMENT:** The governing lord in Arda is voted into authority by the talcrin people and serves for a period of two years at a time, but may be elected an unlimited number of times. His word is seen as final, but he is surrounded by a large number of advisors, who are also chosen by the people, and is expected to include them in all decisions. Those living on the mainland are under the authority of the king or lord of whichever country they inhabit.

**PREFERRED OCCUPATIONS:** Scholars, lawyers, and positions in government are the talcrins' choice occupations, as well as positions in artistry.

**FAITH:** Talcrins are the most faithful of all races in following King Elôm. The majority of those living in Arda are firm believers, but this has become less so among those living on the mainland.

# CRETES

**HOMELAND:** Arcacia and Dorland

**PHYSICAL APPEARANCE:** Cretes are a slim people, yet very agile and strong. They are the shortest of Ilyon's races, and stand between five foot and five foot ten inches tall. It is rare for one to reach six feet. They are brown-skinned and have straight, dark hair. Black is most common. It is never lighter than dark brown unless they are of mixed blood. Both men and women let it grow long. They like to decorate their hair with braids, beads, leather, and feathers. Crete men do not grow facial hair. A crete's eyes are a bit larger than a human's, and very bright and colorful. A full-blood crete will never have brown eyes. They dress in earthy colors and lots of leather. All cretes have intricate brown tattoos depicting family symbols and genealogy.

**PHYSICAL CHARACTERISTICS:** The crete's body is far more resilient to the elements and sickness than other races. They are very tolerant of the cold and other harsh conditions. Their larger eyes give them excellent vision and enable them to see well in the dark. They don't need as much sleep as other races and sleep only for a couple of hours before dawn. Their bodies heal and recuperate quickly.

**RACE CHARACTERISTICS:** Cretes are tree dwellers and never build on the ground except when absolutely necessary. They love heights and flying and have a superb sense of balance. They are very daring and enjoy a thrilling adventure. They mature a bit more quickly than other races. A crete is considered nearly an adult by fifteen or sixteen and a mature adult by eighteen. They are a high-energy race and prone to taking quick action. Cretes are straightforward and blunt, coming across as rather abrupt at times. They are not the most patient, nor understanding, and they have high expectations for themselves and others. They are a stubborn, proud, and independent people, and don't like to conform to the laws and standards of other races.

**SKILLS**: Cretes are excellent climbers, even from a very young age, able to race up trees effortlessly and scale the most impassible cliffs and obstacles. Because of this fearlessness and love for heights, they are renowned dragon trainers. They are masters at blending in with their surroundings and moving silently, which makes them excellent hunters. All crete males, as well as many females, are trained as skilled warriors. Their choice weapons are bows and throwing knives, though they can be equally skilled with lightweight swords. Cretes are also a musical race, their favorite instruments being small flutes and hand drums.

**SOCIAL**: Cretes live in close communities and often have very large families, maintaining close connections with extended family. They are very proud of their family line and make sure each generation is well-educated in their particular traditions and histories. They consider it a tragedy when a family line is broken. Still, all children are cherished, both sons and daughters. Every crete is part of one of twelve clans named after various animals. Men are always part of whichever clan they are born into. When a woman marries, she becomes part of her husband's clan. Though cretes are proud of their clans, they show no discrimination, and their cities always have a mixed-clan population. Cretes are hospitable to their own people and well-known acquaintances, but suspicious and aloof when it comes to strangers. It takes time to earn one's trust, and even longer to earn their respect.

**GOVERNMENT:** The highest governing official is the crete lord. He is essentially a king, but directly below him are twelve men who serve as representatives of each of the twelve clans. The lord is unable to make any drastic decisions without the cooperation of the majority of the twelve clan leaders. Each crete city has a governing official who answers to the twelve representatives. Directly below him is a council of men consisting of the elders of each major family in the city. In the past, the cretes ultimately fell under the authority of the king of Arcacia, but with the deterioration of the Arcacian government, they've pulled away from its rule.

**PREFERRED OCCUPATIONS:** Hunters, dragon trainers, and warriors are the favored occupations of the cretes. But leather-working is another desirable occupation. This is typically done by the women of a household.

**FAITH:** Most cretes have remained faithful to King Elôm, or at least are aware of Him.

# GIANTS

(Also known as **Dorlanders**)

HOMELAND: Dorland

PHYSICAL APPEARANCE: Giants are the largest race in Ilyon. Standing between seven to nine feet tall, they tower above most other peoples. They are heavily built and powerful, but can be surprisingly quick and agile when the occasion calls for it. They are fair-skinned, and their hair and eye color varies greatly like humans. They dress simply and practically in sturdy, homespun clothing.

RACE CHARACTERISTICS: Despite their great size and power, giants are a very quiet and gentle people. They dislike confrontation and will avoid it at all cost. They are naturally good-natured and honest, and enjoy simple lives and hard work. To those who don't take the time to get to know them, they can seem slow and ignorant, but they are very methodical thinkers, thinking things over carefully and thoroughly. While not quick-witted, they are very knowledgeable in their fields of interest. They are generally a humble race and easy to get along with. They tend to see the best in everyone. Their biggest failing is that, in their methodical manner, it often takes too long for them to decide to take action when it is needed.

SKILLS: Giants are very skilled in anything to do with the land. Much of the gold, silver, and jewels in Ilyon come from the giants' mines in the mountains of northern Dorland. They are also excellent builders. While lacking in style or decoration, the architecture of their structures is strong and durable, built to last for centuries. They have often been hired to build fortifications and strongholds. Unlike other races, it is not common for giants to train as warriors. Only the king's men are required to be able to fight. While not a musical or artistic race, giants do love a good story, and they've been said to have, beautiful, powerful singing voices.

**SOCIAL:** Giants typically live in tight farming or mining communities. Family and friends are important. Families usually consist of two to three children who remain in the household for as long as they wish. Many children remain on their parents' farm after they are married, and the farm expands. Giants are known throughout Ilyon for their hospitality. They'll invite almost anyone into their homes. Some people even find them too hospitable and generous. They are very averse to cruelty, dishonesty, and seeing their own hurt. Despite moving slowly in most other areas, justice is swift and decisive.

**GOVERNMENT:** Giants are ruled over by a king who comes to power through succession. However, most communities more or less govern themselves. The only time the king's rule is evident is when large numbers of giants are required to gather for a certain purpose.

**PREFERRED OCCUPATIONS:** The majority of giants are farmers, miners, or builders.

**FAITH:** Almost all giants agree King Elôm is real, but in their simplistic and practical mindset, fewer giants have actually come to a true trusting faith.

## CONTINUE THE ADVENTURE...

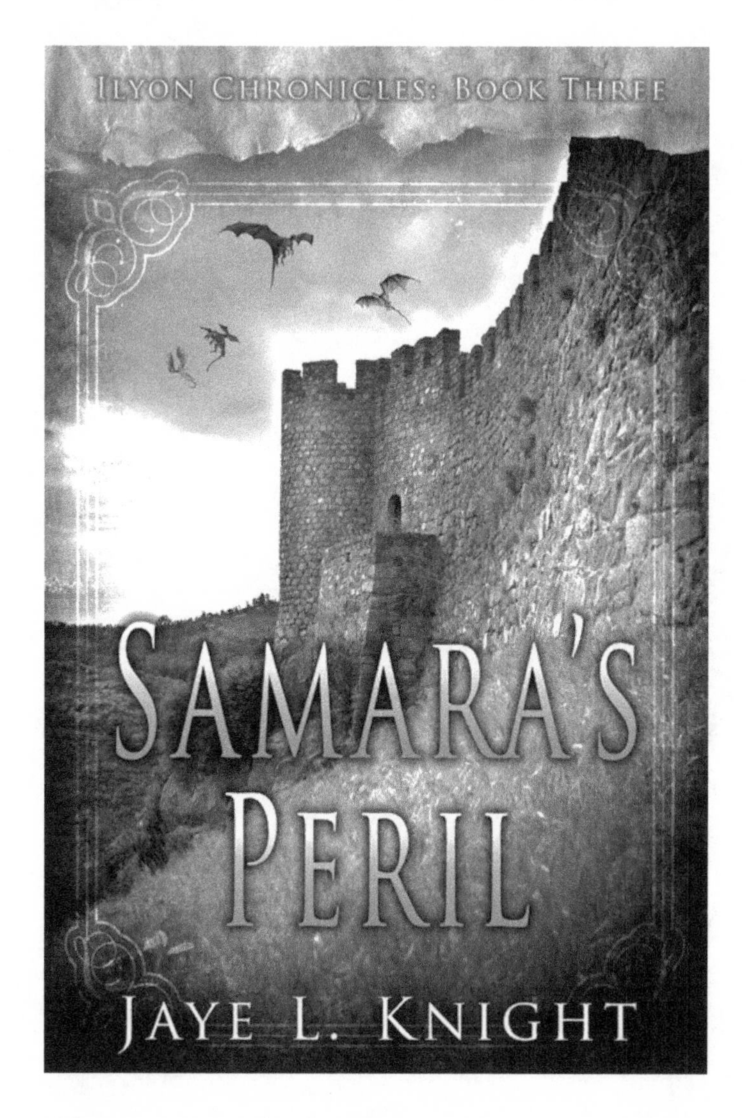


When an imminent threat rises against the country of Samara, those in Landale must face two desperate struggles—one on the walls of Samara's mighty stronghold and the other on the battlefield of Jace's heart, where victory might only be achievable through great sacrifice.

For more "behind the scenes" information on Ilyon Chronicles, visit: **www.ilyonchronicles.com**

To see Jaye's inspiration boards and character "casting" visit: **www.pinterest.com/jayelknight**

# ACKNOWLEDGEMENTS

As always, a huge amount of thanks goes to my mom for how much work she does on my books. Not only do you help make the story shine, but you're a great encouragement to me through all the ups and downs of being an author.

I also give a huge thank you to my beta readers—Jordyn, Kara, Morgan, Rebekah, Addyson, Faith, Erika, Katie, Marion, Shantelle, Sarah, Hannah, and Jen. The book wouldn't be what it is without you.

Thank you to everyone who has joined Jaye's Resistance! When I first started writing years ago, I never dreamed of having such dedicated readers. You're all awesome!

And a special thank you to the members of the Ilyon Chronicles Goodreads group for never failing to make me laugh, especially with your Ilyon versions of Disney songs.

And a very big thank you to my proofreader, Kim, for taking on my project last minute and working so quickly to help me perfect this story.

# About the Author

Jaye L. Knight is a homeschool graduated indie author with a passion for writing Christian fantasy and clean new adult fiction. Armed with an active imagination and love for adventure, Jaye weaves stories of truth, faith, and courage with the message that even in the deepest darkness, God's love shines as a light to offer hope. She has been penning stories since the age of eight and resides in the Northwoods of Wisconsin.

To learn more about Jaye and her work, visit:
www.jayelknight.com

Printed in the USA
CPSIA information can be obtained
at www.ICGtesting.com
LVHW052233091123
763335LV00025B/43

9 780983 774051